CHRISTMAS CHILD

A spellbinding Victorian saga

CAROL RIVERS

JOFFE BOOKS

Revised Edition 2022
Joffe Books, London
www.joffebooks.com

First published in Great Britain in 2019

This paperback edition was first published
in Great Britain in 2022

Cover art by Jarmila Takač

ISBN: 978-1-80405-545-8

PROLOGUE

Poplar, East London
Christmas Day, 1880

Snow fell in silent showers, settling peacefully on the cobbles of the lane as Colleen O'Reilly dragged herself over the carpet of white. Behind her, drops of blood, as red as summer cherries, melted into the snow.

Colleen didn't care that she was bleeding. Nor that her boots barely had soles, or that the ragged shawl around her thin shoulders provided little warmth. She was beyond caring. All that mattered was her baby. Miraculously the infant had survived her premature birth. Cutting her own cord with the rusting shears Colleen had found in the brewery's backyard, had left her weak. Colleen knew her life's blood was seeping away.

Once again, she gazed lovingly at her child. The baby's lips were blue with cold. 'Live my darlin' girl,' she pleaded. 'Live for your mother's sake.'

The tiny eyes flickered. Her baby was still breathing. But Colleen knew her own time was short in the world. To preserve this new life, she had torn up her petticoats and wrapped them around the tiny body. But what use were rags in such weather? The distance between the brewery, where she had sheltered to give birth, and the convent walls, was but a stone's throw. Yet, with little milk in her breasts, her baby would surely die if not from the cold, then from hunger.

Pain clawed at Colleen's stomach. An internal agony raked her insides. 'Don't take me yet, sweet Jesus. Give me strength to deliver this innocent into the safety of the nuns' hands.'

Colleen plodded on as the ice-cold snow froze her feet. Now there was only one place she could go, for Colleen O'Reilly knew she was clinging to life for the sake of her child.

If only she had been a regular churchgoer! But in the months of her belly swelling she had been ashamed. The nuns would surely ask about her condition. And how could she tell them the truth? About her long journey as a girl from Ireland to the shores of England. From the famine of her own country to a richer one — or so she had thought.

'London's streets are paved with gold,' she had heard promised.

Now she knew better. She dared not think of, much less voice, the degradation she had fallen into. The first man said he loved her but sold her into slavery. She had been used for men's gratification, until a new life had formed in her belly. It was then she had found the courage to escape. She would never let her child suffer in the same way.

'Not long now, my sweet,' she coaxed, her rheumy eyes fixed on the way ahead. With every last ounce of her strength, she trudged on through the snow.

The grey walls surrounding the Sisters of Clemency Convent were tall and forbidding. But this morning, as the congestive fluid filled Colleen's lungs, she remembered the secret entrance beyond the closed gates. And it was here she would enter her little girl into God's house. Before it was too late, she would throw herself on the mercy of her faith.

Colleen stumbled to the place that she had discovered a week ago. Hidden behind holly bushes, the brick was crumbling. Late at night she had gone to loosen more of the stones and artfully replace them. Instinct told her to hurry.

Though she'd heard that the orphanage was already full, the nuns could not ignore the cries of a baby. They would not guess that such a shining treasure was the offspring of a whore, a destitute. So, it was through the hole in the wall she would go.

Please God love her just one more time. Until she had found safety for her darlin' child.

PART ONE: EXILED

CHAPTER ONE

November 1894

Thirteen-year-old Henrietta O'Reilly pushed aside a lock of curling copper-coloured hair from her eyes and shivered. The icy water in the big China basin where she toiled was freezing; her fingers were numb to the bone. Yet, after a hard morning's laundering, there was still so much to do.

'A labour of love,' so Sister Patrick regularly assured her. 'You'll be fitting those curling tresses of yours into a halo before long.'

The thought of a halo appealed to Ettie, as she was known by the nuns. All the saints looked radiant in the pictures hanging on the convent walls. Their holy images with auras of gold inspired her. But it was hard to conjure a smile in the ancient orphanage laundry. Draughts as strong as storms rushed in from the broken windows. The mucky steam dampened her clothes. The air smelled strongly of soap and starch, and made her eyes sting.

Not that she minded, for having spent all her life in the care of the Sisters of Clemency, Ettie considered the orphanage her home. Hidden away in the hamlet of Poplar, East

London, it was rare that she ever ventured beyond the high stone walls of the convent.

Sister Patrick was her favourite nun and though she had lived many years in England, she still spoke with her native Irish accent. It was Sister Patrick who, on her way to chapel on Christmas Day fourteen years ago had discovered the dying Colleen O'Reilly.

'Sure, t'was a heartbreaking sight,' Sister Patrick had related many times. 'The ice was hanging sharp as knives from the eaves of the laundry. The snow was banked knee-high. I couldn't believe me eyes when I saw a tiny figure, fallen against the laundry wall. And there you were, safe in the wee girl's arms, a tiny speck of life. With the last of her strength, your mother was keeping you warm against her breast. Wrapped only in filthy rags, she was in no fit state to help herself — let alone her baby.'

'Where is she now?' Ettie had asked when she was small.

'The good Lord called her to be his angel.'

'Is she an angel now?'

'She's a Dublin angel for sure,' Sister Patrick assured her. 'Colleen O'Reilly, Jesus rest her soul, was from the land of shamrocks just like me. She was born in a road I know well meself called Henrietta Street and she named you after it. Though saints preserve us, we all got lazy and know you as our darlin' Ettie.'

Ettie never tired of listening to Sister Patrick's explanations of her heritage. It gave her great comfort to know that Sister Patrick and her mother were so closely connected and that Dublin was the city of her mother's birth. 'What did she look like, Sister Patrick? Was she pretty?'

'Ah, as pretty as a picture she was, just like yourself. A replica. Rich brown hair and eyes the very same shade as God's own soil. And her countenance, well, it might have lit up the whole convent if she'd lived.'

'Did she really love me?'

At this, Sister Patrick would look astonished. 'Jesus, Mary and Joseph, child, why wouldn't she? You were her very own miracle.'

'Will I ever see her again?' Ettie persisted, having studied her catechism sufficiently to believe in miracles.

'Without a doubt,' Sister Patrick would reply. 'Don't we all rest in the arms of our Blessed Saviour and his angels?'

This answer rarely varied. Ettie never felt lonely because she knew her mother was with her. Sometimes she even thought she could see her holy aura lighting up a dark corner. As time went on, this knowledge was sufficient for Ettie to recover from any sadness she might have felt at being orphaned.

Ettie considered the nuns her family. Like a young duckling, wherever the sisters went, Ettie followed too. At a very early age, she would wait outside the chapel door while they said their office. She understood that praying hard for the orphans was the most important duty of their day.

Later, Ettie's little figure could be seen trotting after the line of black habits into the kitchen where she would be ordered from pillar to post, carrying and fetching. Any help was welcomed by the nuns; who somehow managed to run a convent, an orphanage and a schoolroom at the same time.

Every day, at early morning Mass, Ettie knelt on the polished pews of the chapel. Here, she thanked God for giving her such a happy life. Best of all she liked helping the waifs, strays and foundlings who turned up at the doors of the convent orphanage. Just as she had.

A wistful smile came to Ettie's sweet face as she thought of the many children who had passed through the ranks. The nuns made sure that their charges learned the alphabet and their numbers. Some rebelled at first. But not for long. It gradually dawned on them that life in the orphanage was much happier than on the streets. Even if they had to learn the catechism, it was worth their efforts.

As Ettie undid the cords of the wooden ceiling rack, she reflected on her hopes for the future. She wanted to become like Sister Patrick and all the nuns and dedicate her life to children. Her ambition was like a rosy glow inside her; she woke up with it each morning and went to sleep with it at night. Sister Patrick always encouraged her. 'For sure, you are a fine scholar, so you are. Sister Bernadette has taught you a little French, and you've learned your numbers from Sister Catherine. If I didn't know better, I'd say meself you were an old soul.'

'What's an old soul, Sister Patrick?'

'Someone who's walked this earth before,' answered the nun mysteriously. 'But no more questions now. Me tired brain can only stretch so far.'

Lowering the clothes pulley, Ettie began to fold the wet wimples and caps over the long wooden struts. With great care she made certain each one was flat. The ironing afterwards, so Ettie had discovered, was easier if the white headdresses were prepared properly. She knew this was another labour of love and would be rewarded by God.

A gentle voice broke into Ettie's reflections. A raffia basket overflowing with dirty clothes landed on the table. The smiling, unlined face above it belonged to Sister Patrick.

'Ettie, we still have the children's smocks to wash. Mother Superior will inspect us soon.' The nun removed her small, round wire pince-nez, which were fogged up due to the moist heat of the room and squinted at the newly rinsed articles. 'Ah, so the wee girl is ahead of me!'

Ettie beamed, for she loved to please. Her training over the years had made her a conscientious worker. After a full day's housekeeping, she went to the schoolroom to help the children most in need. Whenever a pupil struggled in lessons, they were sent to Ettie. She would spend many hours with them, teaching in her own childlike way all the lessons that the nuns had taught *her*.

Although Ettie was given Sunday afternoon to herself, she rarely took it. Rather she would help children like seven-year-old Kathy Squires. Kathy was a street beggar who had never attended school until she arrived at the orphanage. And

Johnny Dean, who at eleven, had been boxed round the ears so many times by his drunken mother, that he was a bit deaf. At six years old, Megan and Amy were twins and had spent most of their young lives thieving. They refused to be parted and even slept head to toe in their bed.

Then there was Michael Wilson, the most unruly and disobedient orphan of them all. A year older than Ettie, he was a rebel. All his young life he had lived off his wits. At first, he refused to even look at a book or hold a pencil. And, as for a bible or a catechism, he would declare them poisonous.

But Ettie had patiently appealed to his better nature. She found this in his love for adventure stories; of Daniel who was thrown into a den of lions. Or, Noah who defied a flood and David who had conquered a giant.

'Can't be true,' Michael had at first argued. 'A lion would eat you in one gulp. You'd never get all those animals on a boat. It would sink. And a giant would crush you under his foot.'

'Believe what you like,' replied Ettie, unoffended. 'God gave these men special strength. There are women, too. Like Joan of Arc who fought in battle, as brave as any man. Look, here's a picture of her wearing armour and sitting astride a horse.' She showed him the pages of the old and musty book, like all the books that had stood on the convent's library shelves for many years.

Michael had studied the image with interest. Ettie knew that she had gained his approval. From that moment on, she read him stories of heroic action and adventure. One thing led to another and Michael decided to learn to read in order to investigate for himself.

Ettie came back to the present as Sister Patrick examined the caps and wimples.

'Not a crease among them,' she congratulated. 'What would I do without you?'

Ettie habitually answered, 'You won't ever have to, Sister Patrick. I'll always be here.'

Mostly Sister Patrick's response was the same, too. 'I pray to Our Blessed Lady that you will.' But today, the nun's face clouded. She fiddled with her spectacles and played nervously with the wooden rosary looped at her waist. 'Ettie, come away to the dining room. It's time we talked.'

CHAPTER TWO

'Have I done something wrong?' Ettie enquired.

'No, child. But the sooner you learn the truth the better.'

Ettie hurried after the small, squat figure striding over the convent's stone floors. Finally, they reached the dining room. All the long wooden tables and benches were permanently set with cutlery, mugs and pitchers of water for the nuns' simple meals.

Ettie kept this room as clean as a new pin. Sweeping the stone flags, polishing the table and lighting the fire on cold winter mornings was another labour of love. Once breakfast was over, Ettie and two young women employed from the local village would clean the children's dormitories and tend to the sick.

Sister Patrick sat down on one of the benches. Ettie felt anxious. The vast room echoed with an eerie silence. The strong smell of wax polish wafted up into the air. A smoky haze from the fire curled around the roof's lofty ceilings.

It was late on a winter's afternoon and Ettie moved restlessly. The boys and girls would be waiting for her. She loved her little friends and they loved her. For they all knew from life's experience what it was like to be unloved.

But Sister Patrick was in no hurry to let her go. 'Ettie, nothing in life is permanent, so?'

A little shiver went down Ettie's spine. 'No, Sister Patrick. Nothing lasts forever. Except heaven.'

'Heaven is our eternal home,' Sister Patrick agreed. 'But in this life, we are in the hands of the Good Lord.' The nun's tongue slipped nervously over her dry lips. 'We must accept our fate. The bishop has given us a directive.'

Ettie sat up. This new bishop who had replaced the old one, was very important. When he visited, he arrived in a shiny cab pulled by a fine black horse. A special rug was produced for him to stand on; even Mother Superior knelt down and kissed the ring on his finger.

'Rome can no longer support us,' explained Sister Patrick. 'And there are many repairs to be done. The windows are all broken. There are leaks in the roof of the school house.'

Ettie wondered why this was important. 'We catch the drips in pails,' she reminded the nun.

'Those drips are becoming waterfalls,' Sister Patrick objected. 'The chapel needs attention as well. Sure, the big bell is so rickety it's about to fall from its tower.'

'Can't it be tied with rope?' asked Ettie innocently.

The nun smiled sadly. 'Ah, if only the sisters had your youth! We should do a great deal more than we do now.'

Ettie rarely thought about the age of the nuns. They all looked, well, just like nuns. There was perhaps, Sister Francis who walked with the aid of a stick and Sister Bernadette who sat in a chair most of the day muttering her prayers in French. But now, Ettie realized, there were very few younger faces.

'Already Sister Catherine has left for the motherhouse in Belgium,' Sister Patrick added. 'Soon Sister Enuncia will follow.'

Ettie swallowed. 'Then who will teach the children?'

The nun heaved a sigh. 'Sad it is, Ettie, but they too must go.'

Ettie felt a lump grow large in her throat. 'But where?'

A tender smile touched the nun's lips. 'We must pray for guidance.'

'But . . .'

Sister Patrick put a finger to her lips. 'Quiet, now, Ettie. The problem is that we, the Sisters of Clemency, have lost our patrons over the years. The old bishop took no interest in money. He was a good man but only wanted to save souls. He loved his orphans and thought God would provide. But unfortunately, we are lost without patronage.'

Ettie remembered the wealthy gentry arriving in their fine carriages who once attended Mass in the chapel. But as the East End of London grew poorer, their visits declined. Yet she had been taught that God was loving and merciful. Surely, He would save the orphanage?

'God helps those who help themselves, doesn't He?' Ettie boldly protested. 'We could grow vegetables and fruit for Sister Ukunda to sell at the market. Keep hens for eggs and a goat for milk. Perhaps even a cow. With Arthur's help we could build a stable to keep them in.'

'Arthur is just our gardener, child. He's not a farmer, just as *we* are not builders.'

But Ettie would not give up. 'We could learn to be,' she insisted.

Sister Patrick shook her head sadly. 'Shh, darlin' girl. Rome's decision is final.'

Ettie hung her head. It was hard to keep her tongue silent.

'Life changes,' Sister Patrick tried to soothe. 'We must accept God's will.'

'But Sister Patrick,' Ettie burst out, 'I can't live without you.'

The nun looked lovingly into her eyes. 'My child, you have all your life to live without me.'

Suddenly Ettie realized that something or someone far greater than either herself or Sister Patrick was now governing their lives. It was a frightening discovery. Ettie's heart, which usually overflowed with love and gratitude, felt heavy and lost. At last the dam broke. Her sobs echoed in the big room like loud claps of thunder.

'Hush, my dear one,' comforted a loving voice. A voice that she had trusted all her life. A voice as close to a mother's voice as she had ever heard. 'We have spent many happy years together. God only loaned you to me. Now I must give you back.'

Ettie heard someone wailing. The cries were lifting right up to the rafters. They bounced on the sharp glass of the broken windows and against the faded holy pictures on the walls.

These noises couldn't be from *her*, of course they couldn't! But they weren't from Sister Patrick who was trying to console Ettie.

'I'll never leave you,' Ettie heard herself insist. 'Never!'

'Wherever you go,' Sister Patrick murmured calmly, 'I'll always be in your heart.'

Ettie felt the pain so violently, it felt like an earthquake inside her. Yet nothing could alter the look of defeat on Sister Patrick's face.

Whether or not the nuns approved of Rome's directive, it had to be obeyed. But it was such a dreadful, unkind and heartless directive! It tore people apart and caused such loss, that Ettie, for the first time, questioned the faith on which she had built her life.

CHAPTER THREE

The convent's schoolroom was very old, with brown-painted walls and ink stains smudging the desks and floor. A grey and depressing light seeped in from the broken windows. In the very same manner as Ettie had held tightly to Sister Patrick, the little girls held fast to Ettie.

'We don't want to go,' they wailed, cuffing the snot from their noses.

Ettie had just delivered the news. She wanted to tell the children herself. They had to prepare themselves.

'I want to stay here with you,' Kathy insisted.

Ettie lifted the little girl's chin. 'Say your prayers. Jesus will look after you.'

'We're being got rid of!' accused Johnny Dean, scratching nervously at one of his disfigured ears.

'The nuns don't give a farthing about us,' agreed Michael Wilson, who looked very angry as he clenched his fists. Ettie always smiled when he bragged that he was older and wiser than her. Though tall and skinny as a rake, he was very strong. 'We'll be turfed out on the street,' he declared. 'Or sent to the workhouse.'

Ettie looked into his rebellious grey eyes. 'Where is your faith, Michael?'

'The only faith I've got,' he shouted dramatically, 'is in myself!' His face darkened as he poked a finger at her. 'Can the nuns stop the rozzers from nabbing me the moment I step out of this place?'

Ettie felt her tummy turn over. He could be right; for it was only the nuns' intervention with the law that had prevented Michael's arrest.

'God will provide,' she promised. 'He'll answer your prayers.'

'He's never answered them before,' he retorted. 'Why should he answer them now?'

Ettie wanted to remind him that it was only because of the nuns' request to the police that he wasn't now incarcerated in the boys' reformatory. But she knew this would upset him even more.

From the smaller children there were sobs and gulps as they listened to this harsh exchange. How could she reassure them?

'Let's say our prayers,' she said and obediently they kneeled on the floor. All, except Michael.

'May God surround us with His light,' she prayed fervently. 'May He enfold us with His love. May He protect us and guide us, so that forever we will remain safe in the palm of His hand.'

'I'm clearing out,' interrupted Michael, kicking his boot against a desk. 'While I've got the chance.' He grabbed his grubby cloth cap from the chair. 'Good luck to all of you. You'll need it.'

The younger ones began to cry and Ettie went to comfort them.

'Michael, don't go,' she pleaded.

'Why should I stay?' demanded the angry boy, his cheeks burning as he stood at the door.

'I don't know exactly, but please think again.'

He pulled on his cap over his unruly dark hair. 'I'm off while no one's looking.'

The door banged behind him and the orphans wept even more.

Ettie followed Michael into the cold passage. 'Michael, you can't leave,' she called after him.

'Who says I can't?'

'But where will you go?'

He gave a careless shrug. 'I'll manage.'

'But how?'

'Listen Ettie, you don't understand the world. You've lived in the convent too long. You don't know what life's like on the outside.'

Ettie agreed she had led a sheltered life, but how bad could the world be? Hadn't Michael learned to trust the nuns even a little? Tears bulged in the corners of her eyes.

'Crikey, Ettie don't cry.' Michael looked confused. He put his arm around her.

'You're making me sad.'

'I don't mean to,' he said, squeezing her shoulder. 'You and the other kids, well, I like you all.' He added in a gruff tone, 'You, mostly.'

Ettie stared up at him. Suddenly he seemed much taller and older than she was, though only one and a half years separated them.

'I've never said that to a girl before.'

'Really?' Ettie sniffed.

'It means something special when you tell a girl you like her.'

Ettie smiled, forgetting her tears. 'Thank you.'

'But listen!' He pushed her away. 'Don't get no ideas. I'm not staying, not even for you.'

Ettie felt sad. She would miss this boy with the beautiful grey eyes, but who spoke words that could be so hurtful.

'Friends are supposed to look after each other,' Ettie said softly.

'I'd be no good to you if I stayed.'

'Why not?'

Michael stared at her solemnly. 'Do you really think the bishop couldn't help the nuns if he wanted?'

This was a question that took her by surprise.

'Listen, the Roman candles are rich, Ettie,' he continued passionately. 'They've got more money stacked away than the Queen of England. If the bishop wanted, he could flog that ring on his finger and buy a whole new orphanage! But he won't. 'Cos this is the East End and out of favour with the toffs who fill his coffers. Mark my words, the sisters are done for.'

'Michael,' she gasped, 'please stop.'

'It's the truth. I'm older than you — and wiser.'

Ettie wanted to say that he must be wrong, but the words seemed to stick in her throat. 'Stay for the children,' she begged one last time.

Michael took hold of her shoulders. 'Sorry, kid.'

'You're really set on going?'

He nodded.

She flung her arms around him. 'Oh, Michael, I've grown so fond of you.'

He held her gently as though she was china. 'Tell you what,' he mumbled and made a show of straightening his jacket. 'We'll meet up somewhere like Victoria Park.'

'Victoria Park? Is it close by?'

'Just down Old Ford Road.'

Ettie nodded uncertainly, her brown hair falling across her eyes. 'When?'

'First Sunday in December. Three o'clock sharp at the water fountain.'

'I'll try.'

Michael laughed cruelly. 'You see, you're scared to come, ain't you? You won't even go out on your own.'

Ettie didn't understand Michael when he lost his temper. He'd say things he really didn't mean. She'd always prayed that God would change him. But now she feared that Michael was a lost soul. A tear trickled down her cheek.

'Cheer up,' he said with bravado. 'You're my girl, remember.' He bent and kissed her cheek.

She blushed, trying to ignore the unfamiliar pain in her chest.

'You watch out for yourself, Ettie O'Reilly. This world's a rotten place. The sooner you get used to the idea the better.' He waved jauntily. 'See you soon. That is, if you've got the guts.'

Ettie shivered as she watched him hurry down the passage. She felt so cold without him. As if something was dying inside her. She wanted to go with him. But there were the orphans to consider. She had to look after them until they left the orphanage.

Slowly she returned to the schoolroom, trying to forget the awful things that Michael had said. As much as they hurt, there were tender new feelings growing inside her. And she knew Michael was the cause of them.

CHAPTER FOUR

It was a sombre grey day at the end of November and the temperature in the laundry was almost freezing. Ettie's fingers were numb and red raw. All the children's clothes had to be washed in cold water since there was no soap left to clean them with. This made the scrubbing twice as hard.

Sister Patrick was pushing the wet clothes through the wringer with laboured movements and sighed to herself.

'Sister Patrick?'

'What is it child?'

'Has Mother Superior had news of Michael?'

'Why should she? The boy ran off.'

Ettie was surprised that the nuns hadn't been more concerned at his disappearance. 'Shouldn't we try to look for him?'

'He left of his own accord; there's nothing we can do.' Sister Patrick looked up from the ancient wringer with its huge rollers. She swept the beads of sweat from her cheeks. 'A boy like Michael will always find trouble.'

'He was beginning to change,' Ettie insisted.

The nun shook her head wearily. 'Then God will look after him,' she said and walked slowly to the big basin. 'Ettie, I have some news for you. Dry your hands and sit on the stool.'

Ettie obeyed. Sister Patrick's face was solemn and that could only mean one thing. This news wouldn't be welcome. Ettie's heart lurched.

Sister Patrick said heavily, 'Mother Superior has found you a position.'

Ettie looked blankly into the misted spectacles.

'You are to be placed with a shopkeeper and his wife near the city. Your duties will be much the same as they are here. Your board and lodging will cost nothing.'

'Sister Patrick, I've never been to the city before.'

'London is full of splendour and majesty. You're very fortunate. Mother Superior has provided your new employers with a good Character. She has written the reference herself.'

'Thank you,' Ettie replied. 'When am I to leave?'

'In the new year. After your fourteenth birthday.'

Ettie screwed her hands into fists, her nails biting painfully into her palms; a needed distraction to hide how desperate she felt.

'Ah, my dear girl, I know it's hard.'

Ettie nodded. The news had come as a dreadful shock.

'Your new position is an enviable one.'

'What will happen to the orphans?' Ettie blurted out.

'They will be found homes soon.'

'But where?'

A grim expression crossed the nun's face. 'That's not your business, Ettie.' A cold finger touched her cheek. 'Say your prayers now.'

Ettie hung her head. She shut her eyes tight and asked Jesus, Mary and Joseph to make her request come true. For she knew there was no one else to keep up the children's spirits.

When she opened her eyes, she was alone. Once more she returned to her bargaining with God. This time she offered the only thing she had left. 'I don't care for myself, dear Lord, but help the orphans,' she begged, though after some thought, she added hopefully, 'Or best of all, send a miracle to change the bishop's mind.'

* * *

On the first Sunday of December the terrible news was broken.

The chapel was so cold that Jack Frost had scratched his long nails on all the windows.

'We cannot afford to light the fires,' explained Mother Superior as she stood, hands clenched, before the orphans. 'I am sorry to say there will be no celebrations.'

All the children looked bewildered.

'Nor will there be any gifts.'

At this, a soft murmur went round.

'Instead, the bishop will give us his special blessing. Remember, Jesus gave his life for us and died on the cross. Now he asks you to do something for him. If you make this sacrifice willingly, then He will always take care of you.'

Ettie stared around her, at the sad, grubby faces of the orphans. She knew every one of these children loved Christmas. The nuns always made a fruit cake that was divided into thin slices, one slice for every child. The orphans would receive a tiny parcel carefully wrapped in newspaper. A pencil or chalk for the boys, a ribbon for the girls or even a book. This was the happiest time of the year, especially for Ettie whose birthday it was on the twenty-fifth. But now there was to be only a blessing.

After Mother Superior's announcement they were told to put on their coats before going to the schoolroom. Usually they were eager to play and ran around the yard excitedly. But today there were no smiles.

'We don't want to play,' they complained as they stood, shivering in the cold.

Ettie tried her best. 'Let's have a pretend party.'

'Without presents or cake?'

'We have each other. Come here.' They all gathered together. She began to sing. She was so cold that her voice was shaking. '*Silent night, holy night, all is calm, all is bright . . .*'

The orphans slowly joined in as they pressed their bodies together for warmth. Gradually their voices grew stronger. Smiles touched their lips and roses bloomed in their cheeks.

There in the bleak backyard of the orphanage, they sang the carols they loved best and had always sung at Christmas.

* * *

That afternoon, even though the weather was cold and miserable, Ettie followed Michael's directions to Victoria Park. The convent gates were open for one day only in order to welcome visitors. But it was rare that anyone came now. Donations were expected for the big wooden box, yet people were poor and very few had money to spare. And if they did, it went to their families.

The roads were busy as Ettie made her way through the streets. There were many carts drawn by panting horses and a few pedestrians, though today was quieter than when she walked to the market with Sister Ukunda, where she would wait to carry the nun's weekly purchases. This was a day she always enjoyed. But now she was on her own.

She felt sorry for the beggars huddled in their rags on the corners of the street. Their filthy hands were held out for alms but she had nothing to give them except a smile. In her ill-fitting and threadbare coat, she felt very fortunate to be dressed as she was. Even though her boots were two sizes too large, they still had good wear in them. Her undergarments and smock had been washed so many times they were paper thin but Sister Patrick had knitted a shawl for her. Though it was only made with cheap wool, it kept her warm.

'Can you tell me the way to Victoria Park, please?' Ettie asked a passer-by.

'Wotcha want the park for?' demanded the woman who pulled two small children along with her. They looked up at Ettie with wide, hopeful eyes just like the children of the orphanage.

'I'm meeting a friend.'

'Then watch yerself, ducks. There's layabouts that wait for an easy touch.'

Ettie didn't know what an easy touch was so she just nodded.

'Keep going down this road till you come to Old Ford. You can't miss the park gates.'

Ettie smiled. 'Thank you.'

'Shouldn't let no one hear yer posh accent. They'll 'ave yer for sure. And keep to the path, don't wander.'

Ettie wanted to ask more about this path, but the woman hurried away. The two tiny children stumbled after her, their little ankles blue with cold and bare feet black with grime.

The further she walked on, the worse the poverty became. Every now and then, a beggar would bar her way, pleading for help. Although she was sorry for them, what could she do? A smile wasn't enough. Without Sister Ukunda's company she felt alone and vulnerable.

The road seemed never-ending. Its cobbles were covered in horse dung left to go mouldy and fouling the gutters. The street traders didn't seem to care. Instead they pushed their barrows and carts through the mess, so that the wheels got stuck in the grime. The Lord's Day didn't stop them from trying to sell their wares whenever they spotted an opportunity.

Ettie was beginning to feel very lost as she ventured alone through the thoroughfares of London's East End. The overhanging roofs of the ancient buildings were all leaking from the overnight rain. She thought of the orphanage and how the big puddles would form on the floors of the schoolroom. It seemed to Ettie that the whole world needed to be repaired, yet people managed somehow.

'Where yer off to?' A voice suddenly boomed in her ear. She looked up into the very tall man's unfriendly face. His black bushy eyebrows were so close together they seemed to meet over his long nose. His whiskers were matted and he wore a filthy waistcoat under his torn jacket. A gnarled hand held fast to a stick made of wood. The other hand grabbed her arm.

'To the park,' Ettie said and regretted her words immediately.

'I'm goin' there too. I'll show you the way.'

Ettie tried to free herself. But he held her tight.

'Please let me go,' she stammered.

'I'm offerin' yer my assistance,' he growled. 'A young gel like you shouldn't be on yer own.'

Ettie froze. She looked into his dark, sly gaze. She could smell the drink on him and something much worse.

He pulled her along. There was nothing she could do, except be dragged, falling over her own feet as he marched her along the road. She wanted to call out for help, but the people all looked too busy. Her cries wouldn't carry above the horse-drawn traffic that trundled noisily by.

Every now and then she wriggled to see if his grip had loosened. But each time she did, he pulled her harder, ramming his stick on the cobbles. This frightened her even more.

Now she was completely lost. The road had narrowed to a lane. This didn't look like the Old Ford Road that Michael had told her about. Ettie was terrified that her knees would not support her. She dropped to the ground. 'Please let me go,' she begged.

'Get up,' he ordered.

Summoning her courage, Ettie tried to think of an escape. If she pretended to obey him, perhaps she could grasp the moment and run away. She whispered, 'Just let me catch my breath.'

'You're a nice little type, ain't you?' he spat. 'Got any money?'

Ettie hadn't brought money with her. She didn't have any to bring. But then she thought if she said she had, the moment he let her go to reach in her pocket, she would dart away.

'Well, where is it?' he demanded, shaking her roughly.

Ettie's teeth rattled.

'Turn out your pockets, kid.'

Ettie slid her free hand into her pocket pretending to search for pennies. She saw the look of greed in his eyes. In that second, she pulled herself away. Her heart raced so heavily that she scrambled awkwardly, falling, then rising until in a frenzy of panic she found herself able to move.

But which direction? She didn't know. Onwards she ran, as fast as her shaking legs would carry her. She bolted through the people who were walking along the path and briefly glanced over her shoulder. The man, despite his walking stick, was running too; she tried to run faster.

What would he do if he caught up with her?

CHAPTER FIVE

Ettie could hardly draw a breath as she arrived at the park gates. Her lungs were sore, her legs were trembling. Glancing over her shoulder, she saw the man had disappeared! Several fine carriages pulled up and the drivers assisted the well-dressed men and women to the ground. Soon the children were playing on the green grass as the adults clustered together in groups.

Ettie noticed how they spoke in subdued, discreet accents; even the children were well-behaved. Most of the men wore tall hats and button-down jackets. The women looked fashionable in their silk bonnets, furry muffs and warm cloaks. The park seemed to be a world away from the streets through which she had just run. Perhaps that was why the man hadn't followed her, since here she could see no sign of beggars or traders.

Ettie breathed a sigh of relief. Though she knew she looked less than presentable, she had at least, found the park where Michael would meet her.

Walking slowly under the arch, she saw a long stretch of leafless trees, below which the children played. They rolled hoops and threw balls and there were any number of perambulators being pushed along the path by their nannies. Was this the path the woman had told her about? She would most certainly keep to it.

Perhaps she had just been unlucky in meeting that dreadful man. Now the tranquil atmosphere was broken only by the children's laughter. A little way beyond the trees, she sat on a wooden seat and although it was very cold, a ray or two of sunshine broke through the wintry clouds. Ettie wondered where the water fountain was.

'Excuse me,' Ettie called to a lady dressed smartly in a cloak and fur bonnet. 'Can you tell me where the water fountain is?'

The lady looked her up and down and hurried off.

Tears of humiliation stung Ettie's eyes. She guessed the lady wanted nothing to do with her because of her bedraggled appearance. Her gaze fell upon the boys and girls playing nearby; some had velvet collars and brass buttons on their jackets. The boys' caps were made of fine cloth and their boots shone. Most of the girls wore their hair in ringlets. From under their smart coats she could see a hint of white petticoat.

How could it be, Ettie wondered, that God gave so much to the rich and so little to the poor?

She wrapped her shawl tightly around her head so that no one would see her straggly, unkempt hair. But the contempt in the lady's eyes and the seed Michael had put in her mind had taken root.

She was beginning to see just how unfairly life treated some people and rewarded others.

Living safely behind the convent's walls appearances hadn't mattered.

But today, here in the wide world, she realized how it felt to be poor. The nuns had taught her that everyone was equal. But today she'd discovered this was untrue.

* * *

As she walked to find the fountain, Ettie was so deep in thought, she lost her way. The bushes were thick and the thin branches of the trees looked menacing. It was darker too and the trail was hidden by undergrowth. No longer could she hear the children or the sweet song of the birds. She stopped, her heart hammering.

Which way to go? Was this still the park, or had she strayed out of it? If only she had concentrated on her direction. Remembering the warning she'd been given about straying from the path, Ettie shuddered. This gloomy place was frightening.

Suddenly there was a rustling behind her. She turned, but could see nothing more than brown prickly thorns entangled with the trees. She spun around. Nothing but the wood. She stumbled on faster now, panic pushing her forward.

On and on she rambled, but the rustling seemed to follow her. She stopped, gasping a breath.

'Where am I?' she breathed, hearing the fear in her own voice.

A few more paces and she stepped into a clearing. Just when she was about to give up hope, she saw a tall stone building. It was not very large, and was like the ruined folly that stood in the convent gardens.

She moved towards it and her heart leapt. The pillars that supported it were arranged around a small fountain. Could this be the place that Michael had spoken of? The grass around it was smooth and green and beyond this she could see a winding path. Had she at last found her way back?

Ettie was about to hurry forward when the noise came again. Before she could turn, two great hands landed on her shoulders and sent her flying. She lay stunned on the grass.

'No one gets the better of old Jim,' hissed the man she'd been running from. He loomed over her, his breath coming in short, sharp jerks. 'Where's your money? Give it over and I might let you go.'

Ettie blinked, trying to scramble away. But he was soon upon her, grabbing her roughly and pulling her into the bushes.

'Help!' she screamed wildly.

'No one's gonna hear you,' he snarled. 'So, you'd better cough up or else!'

Ettie was so frightened she couldn't speak. Her body seemed frozen. The smell of the man made her feel sick. What was he going to do to her?

She soon found out.

'You asked for it!' he roared and tore off her coat, pushing his fingers into its empty pockets. When he found they were empty, he let out an angry roar.

'Don't, please!' she cried, as he raised a hand to strike her.

But the slap burned painfully across her dirty cheek. Ettie was stunned. She had never been struck before. This action was something very new to her. The life she had lived with the sisters was one of peace and prayer. The nuns would never condone violence. If any of the orphans were naughty or disobeyed, they were sent to Mother Superior who gave them a passage to learn from the catechism.

As Ettie gazed up at her attacker, she knew that this would not be the last of the blows, when he discovered she had no money . . .

All she could do was to raise her hands to defend herself. The man dug roughly into her smock and Ettie screamed.

Suddenly he stood still. His sweating face had a strange look, a startled expression. Just above his eyes a small round mark appeared on his forehead.

The thud of his falling body made Ettie jump. He lay silent on the ground, his beard entwined with the dry leaves and dirt. A bright red swelling was beginning to appear around the tiny mark.

Ettie scrambled away, afraid he would stir and grab her. But he just lay there, a trickle of saliva oozing from his open mouth.

She stood up and pulled on her torn coat and shawl. To her surprise, a soft voice whispered, 'Don't worry, he's out for the count.'

Ettie swung round. 'Michael!'

She almost didn't recognise him. He was dressed much smarter than she had ever seen him dressed at the orphanage. His coat and trousers were not patched or darned. His dark hair was brushed neatly and cut shorter. Even his boots looked shined and respectable.

'Welcome to the wide world,' he chuckled, his grey eyes twinkling. 'You found yourself some trouble at last. But Old Jim won't bother you again. I took care of that.'

'It was you?' Ettie stared at the still figure.

'I did what David did to Goliath,' he replied and slid a small catapult from inside his jacket pocket. 'Remember the stories you read to us?'

'Yes, but they were only stories.'

'What's the point of the Bible then?'

Before Ettie could answer the man stirred.

'Better get moving, Old Jim's only stunned,' Michael said taking her arm. 'Let's get out of this place.'

'Old Jim? You know him?'

'Everyone does. But I didn't know he came in the park. Sorry. We should have met somewhere else.'

They stood at the fountain and Michael pointed to the trickle of water. 'Take a drink and we'll be on our way.'

Ettie was grateful for the cool, reviving water. But she kept glancing around, imagining Old Jim hiding in the wood. If it hadn't been for Michael, what would have happened to her?

She wiped her mouth on her torn sleeve. 'Thank you for saving me.'

'You're my girl. I'll always look after you.'

Ettie smiled as the warm feeling spread inside her chest. She knew a bond was forming between them.

CHAPTER SIX

Seated with Michael on a grassy bank of the lake, Ettie's legs finally stopped shaking. Michael had assured her that Old Jim would not follow. All around the lake there was a neat path. The well-dressed children were playing in the weak rays of the afternoon sun. Couples were strolling by the water and feeding the ducks.

'He wouldn't dare show himself here,' Michael explained. 'The toffs would call a rozzer.'

'Why did he come after me?'

'The way you speak. It's posh. You looked like you might have some money. If not, he'd have nabbed you.'

Ettie gasped. 'Nabbed me?'

'They say he uses kids to work for him.'

'How do you know all this?'

Michael shrugged. 'I've lived on the streets most of me life.'

'Don't you have any family?' She had never asked him before.

'Hah!' Michael scoffed. 'So far as I know I've got none. And what would I want with them anyway? Someone who chucks their kid in the workhouse is no better than Old Jim.'

'Your parents put you in the workhouse?'

Michael stared at her disbelievingly. 'Where do you think a kid like me comes from?'

'I thought . . . well, I . . .'

'Forget it,' he cut in moodily. Ettie could see the hurt in his eyes. 'I don't care what you thought. Or anyone thinks. I'll prove you all wrong and get rich one day. And, I won't care how I do it or who I tread on to get to the top.'

'Oh, Michael, don't speak like that.' Ettie shivered as she always did when he sounded so bitter.

'Have you been given your marching orders?' he asked sullenly.

She tried to push back the tears and nodded.

'There you are, you see. I told you so.'

'It's what Rome wants,' Ettie argued.

'Rome is where they hoard the loot,' Michael muttered coldly. 'The Sisters of Clemency are skint. The East End is on its uppers and Rome knows it.'

Ettie jumped to her feet. 'I don't like to hear talk like that.'

Slowly, Michael stood up. 'My poor little Ettie. You're so easily fooled.'

Ettie felt humiliated. 'I believe in the good in people.'

'Even the Ripper?' he said mockingly.

'Who is the Ripper?' Ettie frowned.

'You mean you've never heard about the madman who cut up women to get their insides?'

Ettie shuddered. 'No.'

'You must be the only one in the world who hasn't. It was only a few years back and he ain't never been caught.'

'Michael, please stop.'

He laughed. 'That's your trouble, you don't want to know about anything.'

'Not like that I don't.'

'More fool you,' he scoffed. 'I can tell you a lot about people's natures. Take the toffs for instance. They dress up to make you think they're better than you. So, I've done what they do. I've stolen clothes so I can mix with people and pick their pockets. Easy as pie. I can fool anyone.'

Ettie gulped. 'Stealing is a sin.'

'It's better than the jug or the workhouse.'

'What if you get caught?'

'I won't.'

'Michael, I'm scared for you.'

He smiled brashly. 'Don't be. But thanks anyway.' He added passionately, 'You are the one person in this whole rotten world that I give a damn about. Now, it's time to make your mind up, Ettie O'Reilly. Is it the parting of the ways? Or do you want to be my girl? Come with me now and I'll teach you the ropes.'

'Michael, I can't.'

'Why not?'

'I have to look after the children.'

'So, it's them before me?' When she didn't reply he shrugged as if he didn't care. 'You'd only slow me down anyway.'

Ettie looked into his eyes so full of hurt and bravado. As much as she searched, she could not see the bad in him; only the orphaned boy who had a grudge that was eating away inside him.

If she went with him now, perhaps she could save him? But leaving the children was out of the question. She wouldn't desert them, not even for Michael.

She said in a hushed voice, 'Sister Patrick has found me a position.'

His face fell. 'Where?'

'With a shopkeeper and his wife near the city.'

'One of them snooty nosed toffs,' he sneered. 'You'll end up as their skivvy.'

At this, Ettie burst into tears.

Michael drew her to him. 'I'm sorry. I'll keep my trap shut.'

'Oh, Michael, when will I see you again?'

He wiped a tear from her cheek with his finger. 'I'll get a message to you.'

'How?'

His grey eyes grew heavy with sadness. 'Dunno. But I'll find you.' His arm went around her waist as they walked back through the streets.

Whatever this feeling was that she had for him, it was very strong. And, however much he boasted how bad he was, she was certain he had a good heart. Her affection for her dear friend could never fade. She hoped he felt the same.

'Take care of yourself,' Michael told her at the convent gates and she watched him walk away with a careless swagger. How long must she wait before they met again?

* * *

'Where have you been, Ettie?' Sister Patrick was waiting by the chapel when she returned.

'I went for a walk.' Ettie hoped that she wouldn't be questioned but Sister Patrick frowned in a suspicious way.

'Where did you go?'

'To Victoria Park.'

'You've never done that alone before, child.'

Ettie felt her skin flush guiltily. Should she reveal her meeting with Michael? But somehow, she just couldn't.

'I won't have Sister Ukunda with me in the city,' she improvised knowing this explanation would satisfy Sister Patrick.

'Ah, child, thank God you understand,' sighed the nun in relief. 'I feared you'd gone after that naughty boy, Michael Wilson. I know you think highly of him, but sometimes we see only what we want to see. Hear what we want to hear. You are an innocent, Ettie. Remember, put your faith in God not man, as you have been taught.'

Ettie remained silent. Should she admit to the truth? Never before had she told such a lie and the guilt was overwhelming.

'Your new family is a good one,' Sister Patrick insisted. 'You will be happy.'

Ettie wanted to believe her but Michael's warning was fresh in her mind.

'Sure, Ettie, the bishop will visit at Christmas to hear the orphans' confessions. Let's pray together and ask Our Lord to help us all in the coming days.'

Ettie knelt beside Sister Patrick in the chapel. The smell of incense hung in the air from the benediction that had been performed earlier. A pale mist swirled in the shadows and the candles glowed.

But she felt no magical sense of mystery, or stirring of love for her faith. The gold-framed pictures on the walls and the statue of the Blessed Virgin no longer filled her with enchantment.

What will become of the orphans? Ettie worried silently. The bishop will come to sit inside his confessional box. He will draw aside the curtain to hear each orphan's confession. But how could the children have sinned? As God's little ones, they were innocents. They had done no harm. Yet the bishop would bid them say five Hail Marys as penance for the sins they had committed. Was this punishment justified?

Ettie felt as if her head was exploding. Never having questioned her faith before, she now questioned everything.

CHAPTER SEVEN

The new year began cold and frosty; every day Ettie waited at the convent gates. Had Michael forgotten her? Only the deliveries arrived and they were few and far between. She often thought of that day in Victoria Park. Did she regret not going with him? But the orphans came first.

'We want to stay together,' they repeated every day.

'Have faith,' Sister Patrick told them. 'God works in wondrous ways.'

But Johnny Dean wasn't saved. He was the first to disappear. Early one morning he was taken from the boys' dormitory. The next day, three of the younger girls went. When Ettie asked what had happened to them, Sister Patrick repeated her mantra. 'Don't fret. They will be well looked after.'

On a windswept afternoon in early March, a donkey cart pulled up in the drive.

Mother Superior called a meeting. She sent six of the children to wash their faces and comb their hair. They were provided with a fresh change of clothes before being told to wait at the convent doors.

There had been no words of comfort from the bishop. Mother Superior stood with a severe expression, but Ettie saw that her eyes were filled with deep regret.

'Children, you must obey your new employer. The farmer will look after you if you work hard.'

Sister Patrick's face was pale; she couldn't hide her suffering as she whispered, 'Ettie, bid farewell to the children.'

The parting was heartbreaking. Kathy clung to Ettie who did not know how to comfort her. The farmer pulled her away and pushed them all roughly into his cart like animals. Without a word of reassurance for his tiny passengers he jumped up to his seat and whipped the donkey's backside.

Ettie watched until the cart moved away. Kathy's little face was wet with terrified tears.

Ettie could not look at Sister Patrick or Mother Superior. They would see her anger. This heartless employer showed no signs of interest in the children. She knew they would not be happy.

Ettie was unaccustomed to being angry. She ran to the dormitory and sat looking at Kathy's empty bed. The nuns had already removed the blankets and pillows. Only two bed were left made up, hers and Megan and Amy's. She knew this was the end of their time at the orphanage. They, too, would soon be disposed of like cattle.

The next day, Sister Patrick woke Ettie at dawn. 'Child, prepare yourself.'

'Am I to leave now?'

Sister Patrick nodded. 'Come to the dining room.'

Ettie obeyed. A desperation filled her as she dressed. When she was ready, she looked one last time around the room she knew she would never see again. Then she went to Megan and Amy whose little faces poked up from the blanket. Bending down, she kissed each forehead tenderly. There was nothing she could do to save them now.

* * *

There were only ashes in the hearth and the snow was slipping through the broken windows of the dining room and dotting the stone flags beneath. Sister Patrick looked very old, her shoulders slumped under the folds of her habit which hung from her as if there were no bones left to cover.

'Sure, this is goodbye my darlin' girl,' she said in a broken voice. 'Remember I love you. Your mother Colleen O'Reilly loves you, and Jesus loves you.'

Ettie choked back her tears.

'Don't be going all teary on me, child,' admonished the nun. 'We must do as the Good Lord tells us.'

Even if it hurts people? wondered Ettie sadly. Even if it breaks people's hearts? But these were useless questions for she knew the answer. '*God asks us for sacrifice and it must be given willingly.*'

'Work hard, be diligent and pray,' echoed Sister Patrick. 'Himself will reward you.'

Ettie knew the nun was letting her down gently. For she understood, as the nun also understood, that this was the end of their time together.

Mother Superior and Sister Ukunda came to join them. Ettie saw Mother Superior's true emotions for the first time. Her tall, upright body was bent. She did not reach out, but kept her hands inside the folds of her sleeves to hide their trembling.

'God go with you, my child.' Mother Superior's eyes were bright with a shine.

'May He bless you and keep you safe,' murmured Sister Ukunda, pulling out her hanky and blowing her bulbous red nose.

'Your ride is waiting, darlin' girl,' murmured Sister Patrick as she embraced Ettie. 'Sure, it's just the gardener's rickety old cart, but Arthur knows his way to the city.'

Ettie looked one last time at the nuns. They were all the family she had ever had. Now she was losing them as she'd lost the children; all innocent victims of the bishop's cruel directive.

* * *

'Up you go lass,' said Arthur as he unlatched the back of his dog cart with gnarled fingers. His silver hair gleamed in the pale sunshine as he pulled his cap on his head. 'I'm glad to see you dressed warmly. The air is still bitter.'

Ettie sat clutching her cloth bag on the worn wooden seat. Her only possessions were her well-worn bible and rosary beads. After fourteen years of life at the convent she was saying goodbye to her family.

What would she do without the nuns and the orphans?

With a muffled groan, Arthur climbed slowly to the dicky seat and clucked his tongue. 'Giddy-up gal!'

Ettie hugged her shawl to her as the old nag pulled them through the convent gates. The big wooden wheels of the dog cart ground squeakily along. Ettie was lost in her worries. Her life would seem empty without the children to care for. Would she be a welcome addition to this new household?

The prospect was daunting. Tears were still very close. Yet she knew that she was more fortunate than the other children and should be grateful. She couldn't stop thinking about the farmer who had come for his labourers. The heart-rending sobbing of the orphans still rang in her ears.

Ettie tried to pray. But the hurt was too raw inside her. After a while, her thoughts began to settle. For what was the use of all this worrying? She could do no more for the orphans.

When she looked up, they were passing through a bustling market. Tradesmen and shoppers stood bargaining over their purchases. Flower sellers waited on corners and barrow boys pushed carts piled high with fruit and vegetables. It reminded her of the market she went to with Sister Ukunda. Her eyes searched the crowds in hope. But of course, there was no tiny plump figure wearing a black habit. Those days were over, she reminded herself painfully.

A few minutes later the cart turned into a long street. Tall buildings rose either side of the Commercial Road and men in bowler hats and caps rushed in and out of the establishments. Ettie found herself reading the names above the doors; 'Taylor and Sons, Accountants. Brenner, Howarth and Brenner, Solicitors. Millers Wholesale, Importers and

Exporters. Peak and Dulwich, Surveyors.' A large black carriage and a pair of fine horses emerged from an alley. On the side of the carriage, was written, 'Smythe and Enderby, Funeral Directors of the Highest Repute.' After this came another imposing horse-drawn vehicle. 'Coaches and Charabancs for Hire.'

Sister Patrick had told her that London boasted a commercial empire. Ettie decided it must certainly be true.

Soon a majestic sight rose in the distance. Its grey walls and turrets loomed powerfully on the horizon. With a rush of heartbeats, Ettie recognized this sight immediately.

They had arrived at the Tower of London! This was the fortress-like prison that she had read about so often in the convent library books. It was here that traitors and prisoners of the realm were incarcerated, waiting for trial, or even executed without one. Names such as Sir Thomas Moore sprang to mind; a brave Catholic martyr, tried and put to death for treason. Anne Boleyn, the second wife of Henry Vlll, was beheaded after being found guilty of adultery and witchcraft. And, Guido Fawkes; an adventurous young man who left Britain to fight for Spain. On his return he had hatched a plot to blow up the Houses of Parliament. His plan failed and he was executed for his crime. Ettie shivered, wondering what it could have been like to end your life here?

She had barely caught her breath when London's cathedral of politics, the Palace of Westminster appeared. Sitting squarely on the banks of the River Thames on the far side of the River Thames, its spires gleamed in the sunshine. Big Ben's clock face seemed to smile out over the city and welcome all visitors.

The cart clattered along the Embankment, passing a slender obelisk. This monument was, she remembered, a replica of Cleopatra's Needle, created at the behest of an Egyptian pharaoh and transported all the way from Alexandria to London. It was said that a hidden time capsule had been locked in its pedestal. Sister Patrick had taught the orphans that among other precious relics, Queen Victoria had provided a portrait of herself to be included in the container.

Following the queues of horse-drawn vehicles, they passed the gaily painted steamers docked at the river's curve. Tourists flocked around them, eager to board. Ettie wondered if she would ever have the opportunity to travel on water. For the first time in her life, she felt part of something very large and important. No longer hidden away in the safe haven of the convent, she was now in the real world where there was energy, life and colour. It was also, she reflected cautiously, the world that Michael had warned her about.

The old man drove them away from the river as the sun burst through the clouds. Its rays melted away the last traces of snow. The streets became polished, as though swept by a giant duster. Windows gleamed. Roofs shone. Ettie marvelled at this historic city. London was full of splendour and majesty; Sister Patrick's words had come true.

Soon they were passing down a busy main street, where open-top trams and buses mingled with sedate, shiny carriages drawn by teams of powerful but obedient horses. Uniformed men opened the doors for fashionably dressed ladies and gentlemen.

Ettie stared into the array of glass windows of Oxford Street; dozens of select, modern shops displaying their goods. Then they arrived at a line of trees stretching as far as she could see. This, she reflected from her studies, must be Hyde Park and the famous monument of Marble Arch. She had read that it was here that wealthy Londoners exercised their dogs and horses. She had read of Rotten Row, of Speakers' Corner and the rippling waters of the Serpentine. She had imagined them all in her mind. Now she was viewing them in reality.

A few minutes later they drew level to the most magnificent sight of them all. Buckingham Palace lay sparkling in the sunshine, guarded by red-coated sentries wearing tall black hats. Beyond the ornate iron railings stood buildings with graceful balconies, surrounded by wide courtyards. Sleek, groomed horses pranced elegantly along with their uniformed riders. The public queued to peer through the railings; and a kind of hush came over the scene.

Ettie stared, enthralled. Sister Patrick had told the children that by September, Queen Victoria would be the longest-reigning monarch in Britain's history. Her palace was a sight that Ettie knew she would never forget.

CHAPTER EIGHT

Soon the grand spectacle was far behind them. Ettie held fast to the sides of the cart as Arthur urged the horse on. Now they were entering the wide streets of London's stately Georgian houses. What wealth these people must have to live in such luxury; row upon row of luxurious mansions with white stucco exteriors, shallow roofs and sash windows. Front doors boasting fans of coloured glass and below them, black-painted railings standing proudly along the pavements.

Hansom cabs pulled tight to the kerbs, allowing their passengers to exit. Dressed in their silk bonnets and full skirts, the women looked very refined. The men wore top hats and smart overcoats buttoned down to the waist. Some carried gloves and canes. Ettie was transfixed by these wealthy residents of the city. She had never witnessed such opulence before.

After a while the beautiful city faded behind them. The district became shabbier and the pavements filled with traders hawking their wares. The street cleaners and lamplighters trudged wearily along, shouting above the noise of the carts and horse-drawn vehicles. Heavy loaded wagons trundled through the remnants of slush and rubbish that grew into great stinking piles.

Ettie searched for the sunshine that had welcomed her to the city. Now all she could see were shadows masking rows of neglected buildings.

It was not long before she glimpsed the name of Broad Street. Here the lanes were bordered by crumbling terraces and gloomy alleys. Women with painted faces, leaned against the dirty walls, like broken, painted rag dolls.

Ettie recalled reading of the cholera epidemic which had started in Broad Street, Soho. The disease had killed a multitude less than fifty years previously.

The cart swayed and bumped on past the slums, each row so dingy and dilapidated that Ettie couldn't tell them apart. Over the cobbles and side roads the nag plodded until they entered a narrow lane called Silver Street. Here there were more shabby shops and drinking houses. Ettie shivered again remembering the East End taverns she had passed in the company of Sister Ukunda on the way to the market. The nun always instructed her to avoid the eyes of the drunken men loitering outside. She had done as she was told and thought nothing of it, then. But Sister Ukunda was no longer her companion. Why would they have come to Soho, if it wasn't to be their destination?

Her suspicions were confirmed as the cart pulled up outside a shop with a weather-board frontage and two large windows beneath, over which a smoke-stained awning hung. The shop's exterior was faded and scuffed, but a sign announced in bold green and gold letters, '*Benjamin & Son. Salon of Quality Tobaccos.*'

But Ettie thought the premises did not look quality at all, but drab and dreary in comparison to the splendid sights she had witnessed today. 'Benjamin & Son. Salon of Quality Tobaccos' came as a bitter disappointment.

* * *

'Good afternoon,' said a man as Ettie climbed down from the cart. 'You must be Miss Henrietta O'Reilly.'

'Yes, sir, I am.'

'I trust your journey was comfortable?'

'Yes, sir, thank you.'

'You have no valise, Miss O'Reilly?'

Having turned fourteen at Christmas, Ettie had never been addressed as "Miss" before.

'No sir. And the nuns called me Ettie.'

'Then I shall too, Ettie.'

Her cheeks reddened as she looked up at the young man with wiry sandy-coloured hair and very blue eyes. He wore a stiff wing collar and silk cravat with silver pin. Though the shop he had stepped from looked dark and uninviting, his smile was warm and friendly. From under his jacket he took out a silver fob watch attached to a chain on his waistcoat.

'The cab made good time from Poplar, I see.'

Ettie had no idea of the hour, but she returned his smile.

'I am Lucas Benjamin and am very pleased to meet you. Welcome to my salon, Ettie; a rather pompous title for a tobacconist, but it was conceived by my father and goes some way to explaining its use. Like the salons of Paris, both tobacco and trivia are enjoyed by our customers during their visit here.'

He indicated the way in and Ettie turned to thank Arthur. But he was already urging the pony onwards as the clink of hooves chimed over the cobbles.

Ettie entered the gaslit salon, finding it far larger than it looked from outside. Ornate lamps shone down upon the many shelves overflowing with jars of tobacco, pipes and miniatures of snuff. Under the glass cabinets were displays of cigars, cheroots and cigarettes in all shapes and sizes. A heavy, musty aroma hung in the air, but not, Ettie decided, unpleasantly.

'I am a merchant in every conceivable kind of tobacco,' Lucas Benjamin explained proudly. 'The salon provides a private space for smoking and intellectual discourse as our customers select their purchase.'

He walked over the highly polished parquet flooring and drew aside a deep blue velvet curtain. To Ettie's surprise this revealed yet another room. It was furnished with sumptuous looking button-backed leather chairs placed around a low table set with three crystal decanters and matching tumblers. To the rear was a mahogany sideboard. Its polished surface was arranged with yet more tobaccos, pipes and cigarettes. Ettie had only ever seen a person smoking when at the market, though the old gardener had sometimes enjoyed a broken half of a thin cigarette as he worked. She had never imagined such intimacy existed for the sole purpose of talking and smoking.

'You look somewhat surprised. Is this not to your liking?'

'Oh no, Sir, I think your salon is very . . .' she panicked for the right word, 'interesting.'

'Most certainly, yes,' Lucas Benjamin agreed. 'The salon was Papa's inheritance from my grandfather. But sadly . . .' he paused, giving an indecisive shrug, 'Papa was taken early by illness and Mama decided that I should come home from my studies at boarding school and help her to continue the business.'

Ettie saw a wistful look come over his face, as though he was considering what might have been had he not followed in his father's footsteps.

He let the curtain fall back into place and smiled benignly. 'Many gentlemen find it a chore to source their preferences. The salon relieves them of that duty and caters for every taste.' He coughed politely. 'Sitting at leisure in the salon a gentleman may smoke to his heart's content.'

'Lucas, why didn't you call me?' A pretty, but delicate-looking young woman appeared from a door set in the shadows.

'This is my wife, Clara,' said the tobacconist, swiftly taking her arm. 'My love, this is Miss O'Reilly, but we shall call her Ettie.'

'Good day, Ettie.'

'I am very pleased to meet you,' Ettie answered nervously.

'And I, you.'

Ettie found herself staring at this tiny, diminutive figure whose pale countenance was extremely striking. The crimson dress she wore was extremely beautiful but did not flatter her complexion. Her eyes would have been beautiful if they had not been somewhat faded. Her fair hair was parted in the centre and drawn back into a bun behind her head.

'My wife does not enjoy the best of health at present,' the tobacconist said hesitantly.

'I am much better today, Lucas,' declared Clara Benjamin in a breathless voice. 'What would Ettie think of me if I did not welcome her on her arrival?' She lay a small hand on her chest. Encased in it was a lace handkerchief that she gripped very tightly. 'Let us take Ettie into the drawing room, Lucas. I shall sit by the fire while you show her the house.'

'Of course, my dear.' The concerned young man turned to exit through the inner door.

As Ettie followed, another, much stranger smell caused Ettie to frown in dismay. It caused her to think of the orphanage sick room and the strong disinfectant the nuns used to mask the unpleasant odours.

CHAPTER NINE

They left Clara seated by the fire in the small but comfortable drawing room and paused in the room adjacent. Above the mantle hung a gold-framed portrait of a handsome young woman. Her sandy-coloured hair was dressed with modest ringlets and she wore a high-necked gown that covered her throat. Her confident eyes were like Lucas's, a startling sky-blue.

'Rose Benjamin,' announced Lucas in a proud voice, 'my Mama as a young girl — a stunner, wouldn't you say?'

Ettie thought of her own mother, Colleen, and wished not for the first time that she had some keepsake to remember her by. A small fragment of handkerchief, or even a book she might have read. But all she possessed was the story Sister Patrick had told her.

'You will join us for meals,' Lucas said suddenly. 'This room is far too large for two. At last it will fulfil a purpose.'

Ettie gazed admiringly at the gleaming polished dining table and its six upholstered chairs. How grand it was in comparison to the nuns' simple refectory table and benches. She felt more at home in the kitchen where there were many pots and pans hanging on hooks from the shelves. The dirty black-leaded stove needed cleaning, as did the battered copper kettle on the range. The sink was piled high with unwashed dishes. Ettie felt the urge to put things right immediately.

'A small scullery and washroom leads to the privy,' Lucas explained as he pointed through a small window. 'We have running water in the tap and a pump in the yard.'

Ettie followed her new employer into a short passage and negotiated two flights of stairs, which were cluttered with boxes similar to those she had seen in the salon. When they came to the top, he pushed open a door.

'I do hope this room is suitable,' he mumbled. 'The outlook is not very impressive I am afraid. It can be quite noisy sometimes. The tavern spills out the drunkards and the women cat-call after them. But we have tried to make the space as pleasant as possible.'

Ettie gazed around the bedroom. Compared to the rest of the untidy and disordered house, it was immaculate! She could hardly believe her eyes. Daylight spilled in from a sash window decorated with lined flowery curtains and lace. Beneath was a single bed with a matching coverlet, two plump pillows and an extra fluffy white blanket folded at the foot. A tall chest stood next to a marble-topped washstand. Placed upon the stand was a pretty blue and white patterned china bowl and ewer. In the far corner stood a vast wardrobe with two tall doors and drawer beneath, its light oak wood embellished in an ebony trim.

'This room is . . .' Ettie hesitated, for she was surprised at the effort that it must have taken to prepare her quarters. 'Very lovely indeed.'

Lucas breathed out on a relieved sigh. 'Thank goodness for that. My wife is very particular — at least she *was* before her small health hiccup.' He went a bright pink. 'Clara gave me her orders and I carried them out. I hope I have done both her and you, justice.'

'Indeed, Sir. I couldn't want for more.'

'Delighted my dear — that's what I am, delighted,' whistled Lucas through his two prominent front teeth. 'This was Maggie Rowe's room, our previous maid. You'll find her uniform in the wardrobe. She was about your size. My wife has had it laundered.'

'Thank you,' Ettie said again.

'Is there anything you need?'

Ettie looked around the room once more. The strange smell was chased away by the breeze flowing in from the half open window. The pretty flowered curtains fluttered gently over a comfortable easy chair. The thick rug on which she stood felt warm beneath her feet. There was even a bar of soap on the washstand and a soft towel folded neatly beside it. Her eyes lingered admiringly on the pretty floral coverlet of the bed. In comparison to the girls' dormitory at the orphanage, this room was a delight!

'No. I am most grateful, Sir.'

'Good!' He rubbed his hands together and beamed a relieved smile. 'In that case, I shall leave you to rest.'

But Ettie recalled Sister Patrick's words of advice; she was to be diligent and hard working at all times. 'I should like to begin my duties, Sir.'

Lucas nodded approvingly. 'And so you shall. But all in good time. Please enjoy an hour to refresh. At six o'clock we shall eat supper. You will hear the gong. Please join us.' And with that, he turned and quietly left the room.

Ettie felt a faint sense of relief replacing her earlier dread on leaving the convent. Sister Patrick had assured her she would be found a good home and it seemed that this was true. Lucas and Clara Benjamin had welcomed her warmly, going to a great deal of trouble to prepare her room. Clara Benjamin had even got up from her sick bed to greet her. Ettie wondered again what was wrong with the pretty young woman.

Taking off her coat and shawl, she opened the wardrobe. It was so spacious she felt as though she could climb inside and sleep there! Hanging from a rail was a grey, formal looking dress and white apron. She wondered if it would fit her. Taking it down she smelled the cloth. There was a mixture of tobacco and soap ingrained in the weave. Not unpleasant at all. The waist would fit her and the hem came down to her boots. But oh dear, her boots! As much as she had cleaned them, it was evident they were old and worn-out.

Ettie replaced the dress and went to the bed. She sat on its soft surface and sighed. Could a bed possibly be so comfortable? A smile came to her lips, but soon disappeared as she thought of the children. What pitiful conditions were they suffering, while she was enjoying this luxury?

Quickly she jumped up, full of guilt. Her heart began to ache again as it had when leaving the orphanage for the last time. Then suddenly voices drifted in from the street outside. She wandered to the window. Two men were quarrelling in the middle of the street. Both seemed unsteady as they shouted and pushed each other.

Ettie lifted the window an inch. She listened, but had no clue as to what they were yelling. In no time at all they had collapsed to their knees, punching each other's dirty face. A crowd gathered, cheering them on. Ettie had never seen men fighting before. A man's nose splashed blood all over the other and two women stepped forward. They were dressed in long, dirty skirts and blouses that Ettie thought were so skimpy they were about to drop off. One of them raised her booted foot and kicked the man's bottom. He went sprawling, rolling into a pile of dung.

Everyone began laughing.

Ettie couldn't resist a chuckle. If this was to be a daily pantomime, as Lucas had suggested, then she would have no complaint at all.

* * *

Ettie heard the faint peal of the gong and hurried downstairs.

'Good evening,' Lucas said as he met Ettie in the passage. He balanced a fat brown cigar between his fingers. Stubbing it gently into a glass dish on a shelf, he sighed.

'Unlike Mama, Clara does not like me to smoke in the house. But I am allowed to enjoy a few minutes of excellence before a meal. I am sorry if the smell offends you.'

Ettie inhaled the distinctive smell of the extinguished cigar. 'Not at all, Sir. I find it quite pleasant.'

'Very good, very good!' Lucas held out his hand. 'Come this way.'

Ettie followed Lucas into the dining room and past the magnificent portrait of Mrs Benjamin.

Ettie noted there were many books and papers scattered around. A small table bore a variety of unwashed glasses, cups and saucers. A half-eaten sandwich remained on the top of the cupboard. Clearly the Benjamins needed a maid!

Clara was already seated. 'Do join us,' she said, pointing to the chair opposite.

Ettie sat down. Clara had changed into a beautiful deep blue gown with dainty ruffles around the neckline. In her hair she had clipped a sparkling slide. Ettie studied with embarrassment her dowdy shift. What would the Benjamins think of her appearance?

Nothing was said however and Lucas uncorked a bottle. He poured three generous glasses of wine.

'I'm sorry to say that since our maid left us, we have become slovenly.'

'Do you cook, Ettie?' Clara asked as Lucas left for the kitchen.

'Yes,' replied Ettie. 'The nuns taught me.'

'Oh, how wonderful!' Clara exclaimed. 'Perhaps we could impose on you one day?'

'I shall start immediately,' Ettie replied. 'I helped in the convent kitchens from when I was small.'

'My dear, was it a happy life?'

Ettie smiled. 'Yes, indeed it was.'

'There is a church at the far end of Silver Street,' Clara continued. 'Please feel free to worship there on Sundays.'

Ettie knew then she would be very happy with this couple.

'Rightie-ho, my dears,' said a voice behind them. Lucas strode in, a napkin over his arm. 'Are you ready?'

Ettie found herself waiting expectantly as a tray was brought from the kitchen. Although the tureens were made of good quality, she saw it had been many months since they were polished.

Lucas removed a cover. Three lean slices of colourless fish appeared. The next tureen contained diced carrots and mashed potatoes.

'Smells delicious,' said Clara with rather a forced smile.

Lucas produced three slightly chipped dinner plates and a pair of tongs. Very soon a toast was proposed.

'To our new family member,' cried Lucas, raising his glass of wine. 'Welcome again Ettie!'

She blushed. How wonderful it was to be part of a family again!

Lucas nodded to her glass. 'I hope the wine is to your liking?'

Ettie took a sip. Somehow she managed not to wrinkle her nose. 'It's very nice,' she managed, wondering which knife and fork she should use. Quickly she copied her hosts.

Hunger overcame the bitter, sour tang of the fish and the insipid flavour of the mash. She was so ravenous she ate every scrap. While Clara left most of hers!

CHAPTER TEN

Ettie had cleared all the dirty dishes and washed them, returning them to the cupboards when Lucas strode into the kitchen.

'I shall roll up my sleeves and help you this very moment,' he told her.

'No, Sir,' Ettie replied. 'But thank you all the same.'

'I fear you may work your fingers to the bone.'

Ettie smiled. 'No, Sir. My bones are quite strong.'

Lucas chuckled. 'Very well then, but come sit with us for a few minutes before we retire to bed.'

Ettie took off her apron and followed Lucas to the drawing room.

She sat in a comfortable chair by Clara.

'Tell us a little about yourself,' Clara said, curious.

Ettie tried to answer honestly. She described the nuns and the convent she had grown up in and all the orphans who had joined her there over the years. Her life seemed to be of great interest to the couple and Clara had expressed her dismay when she heard of the careless farmer.

'Those poor babies!' she exclaimed. 'If only we were rich, Lucas. We could look after them.'

'Now, now my dear,' consoled Lucas, patting her hand. 'You have a very soft heart. But we can't help the whole world.'

Clara smiled sadly. 'I am overjoyed that we found you, Ettie. Before you were sent off to the wilds. We saw the advertisement for the employ of a maid in the newspaper and Lucas applied immediately.'

This came as a shock to Ettie. She had been advertised on the pages of a newspaper? Sister Patrick had not told her of this. But then, Sister Patrick had not told her very much at all. Not even the names of this couple or where — exactly — they lived.

Ettie glanced up at the large clock on the mantle. It was past ten. She stood up not wanting to wear out her welcome. 'Goodnight,' she bid them, making a small curtsey.

'Goodnight Ettie. Don't work too late,' Clara told her.

The house was very quiet as Ettie continued her chores. The kitchen was warm and functional but needed a good clean. The cupboards had to be rearranged from their higgledy-piggledy untidiness. The mangle and boiler in the outhouse reminded her painfully of the laundry, but this time, she shed no tears. For God had given her a new family and she would work hard to reward them for their generosity. Lucas and Clara had welcomed her so warmly.

As Ettie climbed the stairs to the first floor, she heard Clara's soft tones behind the bedroom door. Then came Lucas's deeper voice. Although Ettie deeply missed the orphans, she was grateful for God's goodness.

Tomorrow she would rise early, light the fires, tidy the drawing room, fetch water from the pump in the yard and cook breakfast. The black-leaded range would smell fresh and look sparkling before Lucas set eyes on it. The house would be swept, dusted and polished before Clara sat in her chair.

And if she had time, she would trace the origin of the odd smell. Ettie was too tired to peep out of the window. Instead she lay under the pretty coverlet of her bed, enjoying its luxury.

Silver Street was noisy indeed — just as Lucas had predicted. Drunkards shouted and women cat-called. But Ettie welcomed the sounds that made up her new world. The world that Michael had warned her about.

The world that Michael himself was part of. If only she knew where!

* * *

Ettie rose at the crack of dawn to say her morning prayers. She included her new family as well as her old one. Neither did she forget Michael who was never far from her thoughts.

She washed with the water from the china pitcher and dressed in the previous maid's uniform. Looping the white apron tightly around her waist, the grey dress was almost her size. She found a round white cap and coiled her dark hair beneath it. Her boots were her only regret. But she soon forgot about these as she sped around the house — cleaning, dusting and emptying the high piles of ash in the glass dish.

Once the books and papers were returned to the cupboards and a fire lit in the drawing room, she washed the dirty china and cutlery that seemed to have gathered around the house. The source of the perplexing smell came from a small pedestal desk in the hall. The drawer was full of small bottles. The smell equalled no other that she could think of, except perhaps the orphanage sick room, where Sister Patrick had the medicines kept under lock and key. Ettie washed each bottle, removing any sticky substance that had dribbled down the sides.

Having done her best to eliminate the smell, she was blacking the stove when Lucas whistled his way into the kitchen. A strong smell of cigar tobacco wafted from him as he looked around.

'My word! My word!' he exclaimed as he rocked on his heels with his thumbs in his waistcoat pockets. 'Is this the abode of the tobacconist Lucas Benjamin and his good wife, Clara? Or have I mistaken my direction? Is this not a palace I see before me? I must be at the wrong address!'

Ettie realized he was teasing her. She smiled shyly.

'Ettie, you have worked wonders.'

'I am only a quarter way through my chores, Sir.'

'Then a quarter is as good as one whole in my opinion.' Lucas beamed.

'Will Mrs Benjamin be eating breakfast, Sir?'

'Indeed she will. I would say in fact, there's no doubt on that score.'

'I'm afraid we only have eggs. But they will cook very well if poached lightly with a little cheese I found.'

Lucas had clapped his hands in delight. 'Manna from heaven!'

'I'll have breakfast cooked in ten minutes, Sir. The table is laid.' She added hesitantly, 'I have toasted all the bread in the larder.'

Lucas thrust his hand through his red hair. 'Please forgive its meagre contents. I cannot leave my customers, you see. Berwick Street market is just down the road.'

'I shall go there today, Sir. Mrs Lucas will have the very best pie to eat tonight.'

'Oh, joy!' Lucas patted his pockets. 'Before we open, I shall give you a whole two and six pence. Is that enough do you think?'

'I am sure it will be, Sir.'

'Then I shall make haste and call Clara.'

Ettie found no difficulty in preparing the meal, even with the few items she found in the larder, for the nuns had taught her how to make a great show of very little.

'I can't recall when we ate eggs cooked so deliciously,' Clara exclaimed as she sat at the breakfast table.

Ettie served the poached eggs on slices of thin toast lavished with butter. Added to the hot coffee, and presented on the very best china that she had discovered hidden at the bottom of the chiffonier, the first meal she had cooked for the couple was a success.

'Do please sit down and eat with us,' offered Clara. 'The house is sparkling. You must have risen early.'

'I have eaten, thank you, Mrs Benjamin,' Ettie replied, although she had been too nervous to eat breakfast.

'A perfect start to the day,' said Clara dabbing her napkin at the corner of her mouth. 'I feel so much better this morning. I am sure I could not eat a fig more.'

'Ettie, you have worked wonders,' said Lucas gratefully. 'If only we had known you before . . .' He stopped and glanced at his wife. 'It is so wonderful to see Clara with roses in her cheeks.'

As Ettie cleared the table, she wondered what Lucas had been about to say.

CHAPTER ELEVEN

Ettie had left for the market, making her way through the crowded lanes of Soho, when she came across a small theatre where a tall man dressed all in black stepped in her path. He wore a floppy velvet hat complete with red feather that danced in time with the music he played on his violin. A performance of *Kiss Me, Miss Carter* was advertised as being shown that night. The poster on the wall showed a woman dressed in her underwear peering from behind a screen. The top-hatted man in front of it had a leer on his face that brought Ettie up short. She had never seen such a thing before.

'Enchanting girl,' invited the violinist, 'are you interested?'

Ettie clutched her basket tightly. 'No sir, thank you.'

'Tell me your wish, then,' came the answer. 'And I shall grant it.'

Ettie shook her head and tried to dodge him. But he blocked her path.

'Or perhaps you would like a serenade?' he persisted, drawing the bow across the strings of the violin. 'Music is the food of love, is it not?'

Ettie felt a wave of panic. The people going by glanced at her with curiosity. Her cheeks went scarlet. She wished she hadn't stopped to gawk at the poster. She was just deciding which way to run when a voice called out, 'Allez nous en, Gino!'

A young woman put an arm around her shoulders. She was dressed in an embroidered shawl and a low-cut blouse over her skirt that showed her brightly coloured petticoats. 'Forgive my friend. He means no harm. I'm Gwendoline. But everyone in Soho calls me Gwen.'

Ettie was grateful for being steered safely away from Gino. 'I'm Ettie O'Reilly.'

'Well, Ettie O'Reilly, pay no attention to Gino. He's not used to nice girls like you.' She paused, frowning. 'And you are a nice girl, aren't you?'

Ettie had no idea how to answer. She said meekly, 'I hope so.'

Gwen gave her a curious smile. 'How old are you?'

'I shall be fifteen at Christmas.'

'I would not have put you past twelve. Those innocent brown eyes had me fooled.' She heaved in a breath, causing her breasts to rise almost to their extreme out of her blouse. 'A word of warning, Ettie. If you have never been to Soho before, be careful. The men will try to relieve you either of your money or your knickers.'

Embarrassed, Ettie gazed down at her boots.

'Ah, don't be shy, little one. Gwen will look after you. Where are you from?'

'Poplar,' Ettie explained hesitantly. 'I'm an orphan and lived with the Sisters of Clemency.'

'A convent?' Gwen asked in surprise.

Ettie nodded. 'But now I work for the tobacconist of Silver Street.'

'Mon dieu!' Gwen exclaimed. 'A baby like you in Soho. Those nuns are mad!'

Ettie shook her head firmly. 'My new family is a good one.'

'Perhaps,' Gwen shrugged. 'But Soho can be a dangerous place. Where are you off to?'

'My employer has an empty larder and I hope to fill it.'

'Have you any money?'

Ettie was reluctant to open her purse. After all, she didn't really know this stranger.

'Don't worry, I'm not going to rob you,' laughed Gwen, 'Keep your money hidden. But you need an honest trader to deal with. Fortunately, I know one. A butcher. I'll take you to him and see he doesn't cheat you.'

Ettie was warming to this young woman. Something about her felt safe.

Soon they arrived at a shop where rows of dead rabbits and assorted fowl hung upside down from the blind. The smell of blood-soaked sawdust greeted Ettie's nose. A stout, red-cheeked man in a greasy apron and flat cloth cap put down the cleaver in his hand.

'What can I do you for, this morning, my lovely?' he boomed.

'Terence, this is my friend Ettie O'Reilly,' said Gwen. 'Give her the best and cheapest cuts you have.'

'Oh!' said the butcher, frowning at Ettie. 'And why should I do that?'

'You know very well,' snapped Gwen. 'If you want tea with me on Friday then you'll see she is satisfied.'

'Tea is it now?' guffawed Terence, patting his fat belly. 'Two sugars will I get?'

'Two or three if you so wish,' answered Gwen flirtatiously.

'All the trimmings?'

'Every one,' agreed Gwen.

'What can I serve you, young lady?' Terence addressed Ettie. She was so fascinated by this exchange that she almost forgot what she wanted to buy.

By the time they left the shop Ettie had bought four large brown hens' eggs, two ounces of lard and six lean rashers of bacon.

'Terence is trustworthy,' Gwen advised on the way to Berwick Street. 'But beware of the traders who give you the biggest smiles.'

Ettie kept close to Gwen as they mingled with the crowds. The market seemed to be much like the one she visited with Sister Ukunda. But Ettie was careful to compare the prices before she purchased the rosy apples and shiny pears, adding a selection of vegetables to the meat in her basket.

The stalls sheltered beneath roofs of canvas stretching across the narrow lane. Marketeers yelled out, offering to knock a penny off here, a halfpenny off there. But Ettie was careful. She recalled how Sister Ukunda had bargained with the traders. Eventually she paid a farthing for a sprig of lavender.

'So you will smell nice for your sweetheart?' Gwen asked curiously.

Ettie smiled shyly. 'I don't have a sweetheart, but Michael is my best friend. We grew up together at the orphanage.'

Gwen seemed eager to know more but Ettie didn't want to talk about Michael. She pointed to the clothes stall.

'I wonder if there are any boots for sale?' There was such a crowd that she couldn't quite see.

'Aggie will sell you the services of her husband for a price.'

'Does he work at the market, too?' Ettie asked innocently.

Gwen laughed. 'Didn't the nuns teach you about the birds and bees?'

'Sister Patrick taught us about nature,' Ettie said eagerly. 'How to tend a garden. And how to scare the crows away.'

'Crows?' Gwen said bewilderedly. 'Non! Les garcons et filles!'

Ettie knew what this meant. 'Boys and girls?'

'What happens when a boy is amorous?'

'The boys at the orphanage only larked around and told silly jokes.'

Gwen took hold of Ettie's shoulders. 'One day you will learn about the world. If you like, I'll teach you.'

Ettie was eager to end the tricky conversation that appeared to be taking place in the middle of the street. 'I had better finish my shopping.'

Gwen slipped her arm through Ettie's as they continued on through the market. 'I live with my friend Lily in rooms behind the theatre,' she explained, swinging her hips. 'We enjoy men's company, you understand?'

'Like Terence?' Ettie guessed, recalling the tea he'd spoken of.

'Yes, like Terence,' Gwen agreed. 'Would you like to visit us?'

'Yes. Very much.'

'Visit any time,' Gwen decided. 'I might be at home. I might not be. You can wait. Lily will entertain you.'

'Thank you.'

'You are a shining light in Beelzebub's fiery pit, Ettie O'Reilly.'

Ettie knew that Beelzebub was the Hebrew word for devil. Her face must have shown her dismay for Gwen nudged her arm. 'A tease, cheri.'

Ettie replied politely. 'I had better hurry.'

Gwen waved her merrily goodbye.

Ettie's steps were light as she walked down Silver Street. As soon as she had some free time, she would certainly visit her new friend.

CHAPTER TWELVE

In the weeks that followed, Ettie attended Sunday Mass at the small church that Clara had told her about. She prayed for the nuns and the children including Michael, and for her new family. Clara had provided her with money to buy a new cape and bonnet from the market and a sound pair of working boots. Ettie felt very fortunate to have such a considerate mistress.

In return, she did her very best to please her employers. Every day there was the cooking, shopping and washing to do; years of neglect blighted every stick of furniture. Clothes were rarely hung in wardrobes, instead left aside to gather the moths. Footwear was discarded in unexpected places. Personal items were scattered far and wide. Newspapers and books accumulated overnight. The cleaning and sweeping were never-ending; making the beds came second only to disposing of the contents of the chamber pots. Although Lucas admitted he only ever smoked in the passage, she found more little glass dishes all hidden away.

Most of all, Ettie enjoyed being with her mistress. Sometimes Clara was full of chatter. At other times, she was withdrawn; a state of affairs that Clara said was due to her delicate health. As time went by, in the absence of her hard-working husband, Clara insisted on Ettie's company.

They played games of cards when Clara was feeling happier. When she was not, Ettie would read aloud to her from a favourite book. If Clara had no interest in either, Ettie sat with her needlework as Clara dozed by the fire.

'I suppose you would like to go to the market this morning?' Clara said despondently one bright May day. Ettie knew her mistress did not want to be left alone; on the days Ettie went to the market, Clara's spirits sank low.

'We might take a stroll,' Ettie suggested. 'Enjoy some fresh air.'

'Not today.' Clara swayed a little. 'I feel quite exhausted.'

'Then rest in your chair.'

'You are so kind, my dear,' Clara said as she sank down.

'Shall I make some chicken broth, your favourite?' Ettie pushed the foot stool beneath Clara's tiny feet.

But Clara seemed not to hear. 'Lucas adored his mama, you know,' she said vaguely. 'Rose was his idol. We were married a year before she died, whereupon my husband was plunged into grief.' Clara stopped and gazed at Ettie. 'I couldn't hope to fill her shoes. She was remarkable.'

'As *you* are, Mrs Benjamin.' Ettie felt sad for Clara.

'Seven years of marriage have left me childless.'

'A baby may yet arrive,' Ettie replied, as she tucked a blanket over Clara's knees.

'I doubt that.'

'Jesus tells us to always have hope, Mrs Benjamin.'

Clara tilted her head curiously. 'Do you miss the orphanage, my dear?'

Ettie had not been asked this question before. She shook her head, not wanting to upset her mistress. For she was kept so busy that she didn't have time to miss the nuns or the children. It was late at night when she tried to sleep that the heartache crept in. She saw Michael in her dreams; his beautiful grey eyes and rebellious expression. He was always laughing and jesting, promising to get a message to her, as he had that day in the park. But when the dream ended, the pain of reality set in. Had he abandoned her? Would he find out where she lived? It was then she was lonely and the missing of her old life returned.

'You are the only one I talk to,' Clara moped. 'My husband is busy. My parents are passed. Sadly, I have no brothers or sisters. Hence, you see, I feel a little neglected.'

'Would you like to read today's newspaper?' Ettie hoped to distract her mistress.

But Clara shook her head. 'I need my remedy.'

Ettie went to the pedestal desk in the hall. She had cleaned its drawer thoroughly to eliminate the strange smell that pervaded the house and was now seeping into Clara herself. But even with vigilant cleaning and the sprig of lavender, the battle seemed lost.

Clara took her medicine and collapsed in the chair. 'I am quite tired, yet I am sure your broth will revive me.'

But as Ettie feared, by the time it was cooked, Clara had fallen asleep. Ettie was certain the remedy caused her drowsiness. In Lucas's absence, the little blue bottle was very much in demand. Nothing would rouse her from her slumber now, so returning the broth to the pan on the range, Ettie began her chores.

Upstairs in Clara's bedroom, her jaw dropped open. It was as though a storm had gusted through the room scattering Clara's lovely gowns and undergarments all over the place.

One by one, Ettie hung them back in the wardrobe. At the bottom of the wardrobe there lay a small bottle like the one in the downstairs cupboard.

Ettie removed the dropper and sniffed the contents. She turned up her nose. The same odour exactly! Was this what Clara was looking for? Did she take this preparation in addition to the contents of the bottle downstairs?

Ettie placed it on top of the dressing table. Then, on second thoughts, pushed it out of sight, into a recess of the ornate wood. Was Clara's dependence on the remedy the cause of her poor health and erratic moods?

* * *

It was at the end of the month when Ettie was given her first taste of freedom.

'Off you go,' Lucas instructed Ettie one morning. 'Put on your new cape and bonnet. It's high time you got out and about.'

'But Mrs Benjamin isn't well today, Sir.' Ettie was worried, for Clara had taken yet another dose of her remedy.

'Titch! Titch!' Lucas dismissed. 'We have visitors arriving. I mean it to be a surprise for Clara. Florence and Thomas are good friends. But they are often abroad and are only home for a month.'

Ettie wanted to say that Clara was too distressed to greet visitors, but her master was eager to have his own way.

'Shall I leave some refreshment?' she asked.

'Yes — yes! A good idea. Cold meat if we have any. And pickles. I do remember that Thomas is partial to pickles. I'll open a bottle of wine to celebrate.'

Ettie added her own suggestions; cheese and biscuits that she had bought from the market only yesterday and a punnet of strawberries and fresh cream. Preparing the light lunch, she left the table set in the dining room.

'Wonderful!' exclaimed Lucas. 'Now put on your bonnet and cape and enjoy the fresh air. Here is a shilling to buy any items we may need.'

'Thank you, Sir. What time shall I return?'

'Oh — seven I think,' Lucas answered distractedly.

'Will your friends be dining with you?'

Lucas drew his hand uncertainly through his mop of red hair. 'I suppose they might.'

'I'll be back in time to prepare supper.' Ettie didn't want to leave Clara but Lucas gave her little choice.

A short while later, she stepped into Silver Street. Lucas had still not roused his wife. What mood would Clara be in when Florence and Thomas arrived?

Ettie tried to push this from her mind and tucked her purse deep in the folds of her cape. She had witnessed the light fingers of the Soho pickpockets — not that she condemned them. For the children had mostly been guilty of such misdeeds before entering the orphanage. Instead she simply said a prayer to Saint Jude, the saint of impossible cases, asking him to convert all thieves.

As she made her way through the thronging Soho lanes she thought about Michael. What was he doing now? Did he miss her? When she thought of Michael, the pain deepened. Would she ever see him again?

Feeling a need for company, Ettie recalled Gwen's invitation. So, she hurried on, past the shops and the shadowy doorway where Gino usually stood. He was not there today. Although she no longer feared him, she felt a little relieved he wasn't there to stop her. Sometimes she smiled politely when she passed him. At other times, he was playing his violin and didn't even notice her.

Entering the narrow alley beside the theatre she felt the coldness of its shadows. Ettie pulled her cloak close and hurried her pace. Thank goodness she passed no one. For she doubted that two people could squeeze in such a small space. When she stepped into the light, she met a familiar figure.

'Well, if it isn't Gwen's little beauty!' exclaimed Terence the butcher. He stood in the courtyard that led from the alley, swaying slightly. Though he was dressed in a long coat and top hat, both had seen better days.

Ettie had grown to like Terence. For whenever she bought meat from his shop, he knocked a penny or two off. He always addressed her as 'Gwen's little beauty' and added a friendly wink. 'So where are you off to?' he asked congenially.

'I'm looking for Gwen's rooms,' Ettie replied, assuming Terence had just enjoyed his tea with her.

The butcher waved a pudgy finger at one of the terraced houses in the courtyard. 'Just there m'dear. But — well, perhaps she's a little busy right now.'

'Oh, Gwen said I could wait,' Ettie declared confidently.

Terence puffed out his red cheeks and blew through his lips. 'In that case, who am I to detain you?' He gave Ettie a little bow and doffed his hat. 'I'll have some nice scrag end on Friday if you pop by, m'dear!' he called as he entered the alley. 'Enjoy your tea!'

Ettie watched as he battled his way through the narrow space. Once or twice he got stuck. With a great deal of snorting and pushing, he found his way through.

Ettie walked up to the small, shabby front door the butcher had indicated. The lace curtains in the window were not particularly clean. And the step needed a good whitening. But the door was open a few inches.

Voices drifted from inside. She gave a rap on the brass knocker. The door squeaked open wide. And there stood Gwen. Or rather, there lay Gwen, on a battered looking brown settee, her bare legs dangling over the side. In the middle of them sprawled Gino. Naked as a baby, except for his hat with the red feather, that was dancing in time with his jerky movements.

CHAPTER THIRTEEN

Ettie stared at the vision of male nakedness. She had seen the orphanage boys running around in their pants, but never naked. And Gino was certainly not a boy. His lean body and round buttocks rolled from side to side until he sat upright on the rug. Ettie gawped at the inked drawings on his chest; a pair of cherubs riding the back of an elephant whose long trunk curled downwards to his navel.

'Cover yourself,' Gwen commanded, drawing on a thin robe that moulded softly to her curves. 'You will embarrass the poor girl.'

'We were only jesting,' Gino laughed as he drew on his trousers. 'Just a little reverie to while away the hours. Laughter is good for the soul, non?' He flexed his bare arms and the muscles of his abdomen where the elephant's trunk was etched, jerked up and down.

Gwen took Ettie's cape and bonnet, drawing her gently across the room to a couch beneath the window. 'The elephant is a reminder from our days with the cirque.'

'The circus?' Ettie translated.

'We travelled all the world. Gino with his trained animals. And Lily and I were dancers. Have you ever been to a circus?'

'No,' replied Ettie sadly.

'Mon Dieu, did those nuns never let you out?'

'On Sunday afternoons I could do as I pleased,' she replied modestly. 'But mostly I spent them with the orphans. Or teaching Michael his letters.'

Gwen sat beside her, reaching out to a small table on which there were glasses and a bottle of green liquid. 'Let's drink to Michael.'

'But I don't . . .' protested Ettie as Gwen filled a glass and pushed it to Ettie's lips.

'Just a sip, a tiny, tiny, sip. The green fairy will restore you from the shock of Gino's penis.'

Ettie swallowed. She gasped as the aniseed flowed fire-like into her chest.

Gwen patted her back. 'Just a little more.'

The effect was to cause Ettie's cheeks to burn red and her head to whirl.

Gwen took hold of her hands and squeezed them. 'Welcome to the real Soho, little beauty. Now you can relax and tell us all your secrets.'

Ettie couldn't reply. Her voice was trapped somewhere between her throat and her mouth. She felt a kind of floating sensation that wasn't at all unpleasant.

Gwen bent forward and rhythmically stroked the back of her neck. 'There, there, child. You will soon get your breath back. Now, what about this sweetheart of yours?'

Ettie giggled. Her head was spinning. The green fairy had washed all her worries away.

Gwen waved her hand, calling out, 'Gino, time you were gone.'

When Ettie looked round Gino was dressed in a crumpled white shirt tucked into his tight black trousers. The crimson feather in his hat bobbed as he fell to his knees beside her and took hold of her hand. Kissing it, he recited in a lilting voice, 'I met a lady in the meads, full beautiful, a faery's child. Her hair was long, her foot was light, and her eyes were wild . . .' He arched his fine black eyebrows. Then springing to his feet, he bowed.

Ettie giggled. Despite his former nakedness, she didn't feel embarrassed. He looked so amusing with his shivering red feather.

'Ah, were you in my arms dear love,' he breathed fixing her with a solemn gaze, 'the happiness would take my breath away. No wish could match such ecstasy!' He pressed a kiss to Ettie's cheek. 'Au revoir,' he murmured and was gone.

A young woman dressed only in her bloomers and stays appeared from another room. She was joined by a tall man wearing a bright red jacket and striped trousers. The heels of the soldier's highly polished boots clipped the wooden boards as he crossed the floor.

Stretching out her hand, Gwen smiled playfully. Into her palm the departing guest dropped a handful of coins. Ettie noted how swiftly they disappeared into the folds of her robe.

'Lily,' called Gwen after the man had gone, 'sit here.'

Ettie's head felt light and her legs even lighter. The furniture went in and out of focus. Lily curled beside her. A soft scent filled the air. Ettie thought how beautiful she was, raven-haired and olive-skinned. She whispered, 'You are much prettier than I expected.'

'Thank you,' Ettie replied politely.

'In the cirque I was known as Delilah. But now I'm just Lily.'

Ettie felt Lily's soft breath on her cheek. Her full lips opened as she peered into Ettie's face. 'Do you know what Delilah did to Sampson?'

Ettie nodded eagerly. 'She cut off his hair and he lost his strength.'

'What a mean thing to do!' Lily exclaimed dramatically. 'When the poor boy was fast asleep.' She snuggled close. 'Can you imagine the shock Gino would have if we cut off his beautiful locks?'

'Better than his couilles,' chuckled Gwen.

The two women burst into laughter. Ettie found herself laughing too, though at what she couldn't say. Her whole body felt as though it was floating on a cloud of happiness.

‘More green fairy!’ cried Lily pointing to the bottle on the table. Ettie refused but Gwen and Lily filled their glasses.

Lily pranced around the room so fiercely that her bosoms escaped from her stays.

‘Tell us about your sweetheart,’ Gwen insisted. ‘Tell us about Michael.’

Her new friends danced around her, whisking her here and there until they fell exhausted on the couch.

‘Michael’s an orphan too, and . . .’ Ettie tried to think of Michael but everything was very vague. ‘He shot Old Jim with his catapult and . . .’ she giggled. ‘I can’t remember any more!’

‘Old Jim!’ screeched Lily.

‘Shot with a catapult!’ exclaimed Gwen.

Once more they were all laughing.

Much to Ettie’s delight her friends began to sing. She was entranced by their beautiful voices and the movements they made which explained the words of the songs. Later they performed mimes from their former days in the cirque. Ettie thought how talented they were, though she doubted Sister Patrick would approve.

When the sun dipped behind the tall chimney pots of the houses in the courtyard, they sat on the rug and ate slices of salt beef from Terence’s shop and soft brown dates from the market. The meal seemed to Ettie to be the most delicious she had ever tasted. No wonder Terence was so happy. And Gino so reluctant to leave.

When a tall wooden clock standing in the corner of the room chimed six, Ettie knew she must leave too.

‘We’ll walk with you to Silver Street,’ Lily and Gwen insisted, dressing in their skirts and blouses.

In a haze of happiness, Ettie walked arm in arm with her new friends. Her mind was full of the wonderful events of the afternoon.

The evening air was soft and balmy. Market traders dismantled their stalls. Late customers jostled for bargains, turning to smile as they passed. Sunbeams danced from the dirty shop windows and played on the cobbles. To Ettie, everything looked perfect.

'Visit again soon,' Gwen said as they reached Silver Street.

Ettie smiled. 'I will.'

'We love you,' whispered Lily, kissing her cheek. 'Goodbye, sister.'

Ettie beamed. *Sister*!

CHAPTER FOURTEEN

Lucas was pacing in the passage, smoking a cigar amidst plumes of smoke when Ettie arrived home. His curly red hair stood on end and two scarlet patches coloured his cheeks.

He put out his cigar in the dish. 'Where have you been?' he asked anxiously.

'I visited a friend,' she replied, 'and have come home well in time to cook supper.'

Lucas nervously fiddled with his watch chain. 'Yes, yes, thank you. But supper won't be necessary. As you can see, our friends have gone.'

'Was lunch not to their liking?' Ettie asked worriedly.

Lucas just sighed. 'Come and see.'

Though the bottle of wine on the dining room table was empty, the food that Ettie had left was only half-eaten. There were newspapers strewn untidily and the fire in the hearth had burned out.

'Oh, Ettie, I am quite put out!' he continued pointing a trembling finger to the stairs. 'Clara is in the bedroom. She has been quite unlike herself today. Beset by a disorder that I can't even describe. At first, she welcomed Florence and Thomas with heartfelt greetings. But her mood swiftly changed. She hardly ate. Would not drink. I am sad to say she barely addressed our friends. Florence and Thomas took their leave, politely of course. But what a dismal failure the afternoon was!'

Ettie quickly took off her bonnet and cape. 'I'm very sorry to hear that, Sir.'

'Please go to Clara and calm her. She will not listen to me.'

'I'll try, Sir.'

'Go quickly!' He waved her up the stairs.

Ettie left her cape and bonnet in her bedroom then returned to the landing beneath. She heard a stifled sobbing coming from Clara's bedroom.

'Mrs Benjamin, it's me, Ettie.'

Almost before Ettie had finished speaking, the door flew open. Clara stood there in her pretty blue silk gown, her face smudged by tears.

'Oh, so you chose to come home after deserting me!'

Ettie took in a sharp breath. She knew her mistress was in one of her black moods. 'Mr Benjamin said I may be of help?'

'Have you stolen my remedy?' Clara demanded.

'No, Mrs Benjamin. It is in the pedestal desk.'

'I have looked — and looked,' sobbed Clara. 'I'm at my wits' end. If only Maggie were here. She would bring it.'

Ettie had heard Maggie's name repeated many times from Clara. The young maid had left unexpectedly without giving notice, so Lucas had said.

Suddenly Clara gave a shriek. 'I must have it! I must have it!' Her face was so pale and gaunt that Ettie thought she might faint.

'Please sit down.' Ettie gently urged Clara to the chair. Sobbing, Clara swayed from side to side, her arms locked tight around her.

'Please don't cry,' Ettie soothed. 'I'll find your remedy.'

At this Clara fell silent. 'Thank you, Maggie.'

Ettie nodded. She knew Clara was sick. But when she arrived downstairs, Lucas had disappeared. Had he taken his evening stroll? Did he not care about his wife's condition? A physician must be called at once.

Ettie went to the pedestal desk and opened it. She lifted the blue bottle. She was not surprised to find it empty. Heart pounding, she returned to the bedroom.

'Maggie!' Clara cried. 'Did you find it?' Her eyes were glassy, her voice low and husky. This was the darkest mood that Ettie had ever witnessed. If only Lucas was here!

Suddenly Clara threw herself forward. Spittle flew from her lips, her hair came loose from its pins and hung in tangles. Her nails dug painfully into Ettie's arms.

'Help me, help me! You know I can't live without my medicine. I will die, I promise you.'

Ettie was frightened. Would Clara die without her remedy? She could feel her mistress's eyes following her as she went to the dressing table. When Clara saw the bottle, she snatched it from Ettie's grasp and put it to her lips. Shivering and shaking, she fell to the floor.

* * *

Lucas and Ettie waited downstairs as the physician from Soho Square attended Clara.

'I shouldn't have gone for my stroll,' Lucas berated himself, pacing the floor again.

'You came back in time, Sir,' she reassured him, though the physician had been with Clara for a very long time.

'What causes my wife to act in this way? To be friendly to Thomas and Florence, then ignore them?' Lucas's blue eyes were filled with confusion. 'She has not been herself for some time. Not since we hired that wretched maid, Maggie.'

He marched to Clara's chair by the fire and sat down with a thump. 'I shall give you my honest opinion about Maggie. She was a thief and a liar. At first it was a china curio or silver candlestick, a brooch or a necklace that disappeared. Then I caught her red-handed one day, stuffing my finest tobacco into her pockets. I dismissed her immediately of course.'

Ettie gazed down at the floor. 'I'm sorry, Sir.'

'It's not your fault dear girl.' He jumped up and went over to Ettie, taking hold of her hands. 'I cannot tell you how relieved I was to find you. I knew at once I could trust you.'

'I tried to persuade Mrs Benjamin not to take her remedy,' Ettie burst out. 'But that only made things worse.'

'I have tried, too,' confessed the tobacconist. He pushed his hands through his hair and sighed. 'I cannot bear to see her upset. And so I give in.'

There were footsteps on the stairs and Lucas went to the door. 'How is she?'

The old doctor, carrying his large black bag entered the room. He looked sternly at Lucas.

'Your wife will sleep for a while now, but it's not good news.'

Lucas rocked on his heels. 'Tell me!'

The physician handed over a small package. 'Administer two drops of this mixture four times a day in water.'

'But what is wrong?' demanded Lucas, staring at the parcel.

'Your wife is dependent on opium.'

'Opium?' repeated Lucas, aghast. 'There must be some mistake.'

'You must have observed the decline in her health? And that rather strange smell in the house?'

'I have been so busy,' Lucas babbled. 'But forgive me. I have no excuse. What can I do to help Clara?'

'This substitute will help, but I cannot guarantee an outcome. Mrs Benjamin must not be left alone. Or be allowed to go out in order to purchase more of the tincture.'

'But Clara will be made a prisoner,' Lucas objected.

'She is one already,' observed the physician dourly, 'of this odious drug.'

Lucas could not hide his desperation. 'My wife has not enjoyed good health it's true. But opium, you say? How did she come upon it?'

'That I cannot tell you, although . . .'

'What is it?'

The elderly man turned to Ettie. 'Are you Maggie?'

'No, Sir, I am her replacement.'

'I see.' He looked sternly at Lucas. 'In her delirium, Mrs Benjamin asked for Maggie. From what I heard, I suspect your former maid had a hand in this.'

'Maggie!' gasped Lucas. 'Of course. My wife relied on her so much. Now I know why. She must have been the one to introduce that wretched drug to Clara.'

The physician closed his bag. 'I shall call next week, but should you want me before . . .' His grey eyebrows lowered in a frown as if to warn of an impending catastrophe.

When he had gone, Lucas pushed his hands over his face.

'How could I have been so blind?' he questioned. 'I should have noticed Clara's decline. But I chose to bury myself in work. Unforgivable!'

Ettie had never seen him so forlorn. 'Sir, shall I make you some tea?'

'What? Oh yes. I suppose so.'

She went to the kitchen and filled the kettle. Her hands were shaking as she put it on the range to boil. Opium! And Maggie had been sent by Clara to buy it.

Ettie thought of the orphanage library books and the lurid drawings of opium dens and their degraded, destitute victims, snared in the drug's thrall. But surely her beautiful, kind and considerate mistress could not be one of these poor souls?

CHAPTER FIFTEEN

Caring for Clara meant Ettie could rarely leave her side. She knew Lucas tried his best to console his wife, but he still had a business to run. His face grew pinched with tiredness and his blue eyes wore a permanent expression of defeat.

Ettie tried to keep Clara presentable, but her mistress had no interest in her appearance. Sometimes she refused to bathe or change her clothes and she developed a nervous, troublesome cough.

Ettie often sat at her bedside, as a strange sickness engulfed her. The malady raged through her tiny body and left her weak. Her recovery was slow and she would sit in her chair by the fire, often falling asleep. Many nights Ettie lay awake, listening to the voices from the bedroom below as Lucas tried to console his wife.

Several more physicians were called. She was prescribed more medicines, all of which had little effect.

One day, on a rare escape from the house, as Ettie walked to the market, two figures stepped out from the alley.

'Ettie O'Reilly, where have you been all this time?' Gwen enfolded Ettie in a warm embrace. A scented cloud of aniseed wafted around her as she tossed back her mop of golden hair. Her pale skin and blonde hair made a startling contrast to Lily's Latin looks. They both wore their colourful dresses with shawls tucked loosely around their shoulders.

'I've been meaning to call but I've been busy,' Ettie explained.

'How boring!' Gwen studied her closely. 'Are you a slave to this mistress of yours?'

Ettie didn't think it was right to talk about her employer's private affairs. 'Mrs Benjamin has delicate health,' she said after some hesitation.

Lily's pretty nose wrinkled. 'That job wouldn't suit me. I'd faint at the sight of blood!'

Ettie smiled. 'There's no blood, Lily. I'm more of a . . . a companion.'

'So, when are you coming to see us again?' Gwen demanded.

'Oh, that might not be for some time, I'm afraid.'

'And we thought you liked us,' wailed Lily slinking her arm around Ettie's waist. 'Our little sister.'

'Oh, I do like you,' Ettie insisted. 'I've never forgotten our afternoon together.'

'Then don't leave it too long to visit us again.'

'I won't.'

'You've missed a kiss from Gino,' Gwen giggled. 'He's gone to Europe again to flex those muscles in the cirque.'

Ettie said quietly, 'He must be very famous.'

Gwen and Lily broke into laughter, hugging her and kissing her cheeks. 'How sweet and innocent you are, little beauty.'

'Now, remember, come soon. A girl's got to have some fun,' Lily whispered. 'Or else you'll be an old maid. You wouldn't want that would you?'

Ettie shook her head firmly.

'My little beauty,' Gwen purred. 'We'll drink the green fairy and dance away the hours!'

'Goodbye little sister,' said Lily.

Ettie knew that it might be some while before she saw her friends again. Clara relied on her so much. Ettie felt like the mother and Clara her child.

* * *

It was early in June when Lucas closed the blinds of the salon and called Ettie from the kitchen.

'I have arrived at a decision,' he informed her. 'The decision of a desperate man.'

Ettie's heart lurched. What could Lucas have in mind?

'I am taking Clara to Europe,' he explained. 'I have heard from some of my gentlemen that miraculous cures have resulted from such a trip.'

Ettie felt a wave of fear. 'Sir, do you think she is well enough to travel?'

'Indeed not, my dear Ettie,' he agreed. 'But I can no longer bear to see her sitting day after day, gazing into the fire. I must give her food for thought, breathe vigour into her bright and clever brain which has fallen into the deepest of slumber. I must wake her up!'

Ettie clasped her hands together anxiously. 'When will you go, Sir?'

'By the time I have arranged our trip it will be September. Leaving a cold and damp England behind can only be of value to my darling wife.'

Perhaps Lucas was right, Ettie thought hopefully. The damp and foggy weather of London would not help at all.

'Unfortunately, our tour will require all our savings. A considerable fortune. But the hardest news,' he mumbled, glancing at Ettie from the corner of his eye, 'is that the salon must close. We shall be away until spring and there is no one to replace me.'

Ettie looked sadly at her employer. How could she help him?

'Sir, could you teach me to sell tobacco?' she asked innocently.

'What?' Lucas jumped, his mouth twitching. 'You — a female? And a child at that!'

'I shall be fifteen at Christmas,' Ettie replied boldly. 'And it was your mother who continued the business after your father's death.'

'That is true,' Lucas agreed. 'But Mama understood the trade from years of experience.'

'I could learn, Sir. I am sure I could,' Ettie insisted.

As was his custom, he pushed his hand through his wiry hair and sighed. 'My gentlemen are sometimes difficult, even arrogant. They are rambunctious even with me. What humiliation they might put you through.' He paused, blushing. 'Forgive my forthrightness, but you are hardly equipped to bargain with men of the world.' Nervously, he gasped in a breath. His two large front teeth showed under a tight grimace. 'I could not ask it of you; too much to learn, to absorb, even for a mature student.'

'Then put me to the test, Sir,' Ettie suggested. 'If I cannot learn to your liking, then nothing is lost, save your time.'

'And Clara? We cannot abandon her,' Lucas remonstrated. 'She needs our attention.'

'I could assist you while Mrs Benjamin rests,' Ettie offered. 'In the evenings we might join her by the fire while you instruct me on my studies.'

Lucas stared; his blue eyes thoughtful. 'I don't know what to say. Your plan is so ambitious that I am hardly able to answer.'

'I'm sorry. I shouldn't have spoken. It's time I cooked supper.' Ettie turned to leave, but Lucas grasped her arm.

'Please, stay.' His eyes filled with tears. 'I am so low, Ettie. Any word of kindness only reduces me to a wreck — a snivelling fool.'

'You are not a fool, Sir. You are a good and generous man.'

He mopped his cheeks with a crumpled handkerchief.

'Oh, Ettie, what have I done to deserve your kindness?'

'Let's join Mrs Benjamin and discuss matters.'

'Yes, yes, let us do that.'

Ettie followed Lucas to the drawing room where they took their seats by Clara and the fire.

'My dear,' said Lucas gently, patting his wife's hand, 'we have had an excellent idea. And that is, you and I shall take a holiday. Our dear Ettie has offered to take care of the salon. A great challenge for one so young, but with a little tuition . . .' He stopped, as Clara began to cough.

When the fit was over, Clara managed a strange smile. 'If you say so, Lucas.'

Ettie knew her mistress was lost in a depression and no one could reach her, not even Lucas.

'Good, good, my dear. A change of scenery will be beneficial for us both.'

After supper that evening, Lucas brought his papers from the salon. He arranged them on the dining room table. As Clara rested drowsily in her chair, he showed Ettie the colourful illustrations of the many tobaccos imported from around the world.

'Sir, it seems I know very little,' Ettie confessed. 'Only that Christopher Columbus discovered it.'

'Columbus? Why, yes!' Lucas exclaimed. His face suddenly came alight. 'What a conqueror he was! Do you know that his intention was to discover all the sea routes to the Far East?'

'No, Sir, I did not.'

'Imagine his excitement when he found the leaves being smoked by the Indians of the Americas. How wonderful that day must have been!' He threw up his hands enthusiastically. 'Gradually the word spread to the rest of the world. Trade was embarked upon. The merchants of old knew that money could be made from its special properties. From Egypt and Turkey came even more succulent and satisfying flavours.'

'And the salon has them all?' Ettie enquired.

'Oh, yes, yes, my dear. We do indeed. Great quantities are shipped in by our suppliers at Tobacco Dock. Grandfather built up the connection and business flourished under Papa. Our customers come from far and wide to sample our stock. Hence the convenience of our smoking room. It is considered a luxury to recline in our chairs and inhale the flavours, roll them on the tongue and taste history in one breath!'

Ettie had never heard him talk this way. It was as if he was possessed by his passion. She listened, enraptured.

'What hurts the most,' he confided, glancing at his wife, 'is that if someone took this pleasure away from me, I would be in anguish! And that is what I have done to Clara.'

'But Sir,' Ettie protested, 'the drug was harmful.'

'Yes, I am fully aware of that.' His head drooped and he sighed, reaching out to hold Clara's hand in his.

Ettie felt her heart squeeze with pity for this kind man who so loved his wife.

CHAPTER SIXTEEN

As each day passed, Lucas taught Ettie more about his beloved tobacco, introducing her to the customers as his assistant. To Ettie's relief, this did not cause much alarm. He showed her how to weigh and display the stock under the glass on the midnight blue velvet cloths. He explained how, during the Crimean War, British soldiers acquired the taste for Turkish tobacco from their allies and how the first English cigarette factory was opened by one of these venerated war veterans. His face took on a glow when he explained how Bond Street, so famous for its select stores, threw open its doors to customers in search of brand new varieties of tobacco. And how in 1876 the salon had won trade with the most notable manufacturer of all, Benson & Hedges. After a handful of years, a certificate of excellence had followed, endorsed by dukes and archdukes of the kingdom, clerics and lords, politicians and celebrities alike.

'That certificate is preserved on the back of Mama's portrait,' he explained as he read from his precious diary. 'Hence the painting now hangs in the dining room, and reminds me each day it was Mama who put food on the table, Mama who had courage enough to prosper the business. But I hold out no expectations for Clara in the business for she is in such a delicate condition.' He paused, his voice containing a soft sigh as he added regretfully, 'and with no heir to take over the business, I cannot predict the future after I am gone.'

'Sir, that is a very long time off.'

He looked at her and suddenly laughed. 'Yes, of course it is Ettie. I'm a chap who enjoys rude health and expect to continue for many years yet.'

It was clear to Ettie that Lucas had been very fond of his Mama and that poor Clara seemed to have paled in her shadow when it came to business matters. But in every other way, Ettie could see that her employer worshipped the ground his wife walked on.

'I have a suggestion,' Lucas said suddenly, returning the diary to the shelf. 'Let us run through a few figures of an evening. I'll try you on your numbers and see what you come up with.'

'Sir, I would like that.'

And therefore, in the evenings they would sit with Clara in the cool of the house. Lucas would test Ettie in sums of addition, multiplication, division and subtraction. Her answers were swift and mostly accurate.

'Heaven's above!' Lucas would gasp. 'Unbelievable.'

Very soon Ettie could list all the income and outgoings of the business. While her head was bent over the ledgers, Lucas walked Clara to the green close by. The short outing seemed to revive Clara's spirits and Ettie began to enjoy her new role as Lucas's assistant.

After just one month, Ettie had memorized the many varieties of snuff, pipes, cigars, cigarillos and cigarettes. Each day as Clara rested, she stood behind Lucas, attentively listening to the top-hatted gentlemen who arrived from their clubs.

'Now, I shall show you a secret,' Lucas said one morning before business opened. He reached up to pull a tiny lever set below a shelf. A wooden panel in the wall creaked open to reveal a large black, cast-iron chest. He took a heavy key from under a loose floorboard and inserted it into the lock. The lid creaked open. Inside were leather-bound money bags, each stacked neatly in line. 'Our safe,' he explained. 'Feel the weight.' He dropped a bag into Ettie's palm.

'It is heavy, Sir,' Ettie agreed.

'Should be. It's full of silver.'

Ettie quickly returned it.

'Don't worry, I trust you, Ettie.' He closed the chest, locked it and returned the key to its hiding place.

'The panel won't open unless it's operated by the lever.'

'Yes, Sir.'

'Each week you will pay yourself wages from here.'

'But, Sir . . .'

He held up his hand to silence her. 'It's true you receive board and keep, Ettie. But now we must make a commercial arrangement. You, as my capable salon assistant — who has passed her test of numbers with flying colours — shall be paid five shillings each month. Are you agreeable?'

Ettie's mouth fell open.

'Good. We are agreed.'

Ettie attempted to protest that she would gladly become his assistant for no profit at all. But Lucas ignored this and the contract was made, giving her the responsibility of the salon in his absence and of keeping the chest and its contents safe, in return for the wage she would earn in her new capacity as his assistant.

From that moment on, Ettie took her new role very seriously. She paid attention to every word that Lucas spoke. Before the working day began, he would select a cigar, remove its wrapper and draw it slowly under his nose.

'Cuban, of superior quality. Strong. Untamed. A hot, sun-bleached landscape. A trek through equatorial hills. Now, you try, Ettie.'

Since she had never visited any equatorial hills, Ettie put her imagination to work. She closed her eyes and breathed in the pungent aroma. 'The smell reminds me of the market. How on a damp day the rain soaks the vegetables and the earth falls away from their roots.'

Lucas threw back his head and chuckled.

'Excellent, Ettie. Excellent! But perhaps "market" might be turned to "jungle" where our gentlemen adventurers might bag a lion or elephant, reminding them of their great achievements. Inflate their egos and they'll grab the cigar right out of your hand!'

Ettie made a mental note to follow Lucas's instructions although she wasn't certain what an inflated ego might be.

'You are a quick learner,' he encouraged her. 'But tell me honestly, what is your true opinion of our tobaccos?'

'I find their aromas quite pleasant,' Ettie declared.

'Hah!' he exclaimed in delight. 'My gentlemen will wish their wives offered such an opinion! Did you know that some men are exiled to the smoking rooms of their houses? They are looked on as a nuisance and not the great heroes and globetrotters they imagine themselves to be. And so, they smoke at their clubs in the company of friends, who reinforce their confidence. Mind Ettie, our courageous champions must also partake of the finest brandy to keep up the glow of success! Therefore, I shall fill the decanters in our smoking room to the brim!' He gave her a hearty pat on the shoulder.

'Yes, Sir. And I shall make certain the decanters are always full.'

'Well done, Ettie, well done! You so remind me of Mama. She was the only woman I have ever met who shares your appreciation of tobacco. Did I tell you of the day when a royal courtier came into the shop?'

Though Ettie had heard this story before, she always shook her head for Lucas loved to tell it.

'The courtier smoked at least four of our best cigars,' he would say proudly. 'The man created a smog so thick that even a veteran smoker might find it challenging. But Mama just smiled in her calm way and was rewarded with a substantial order, not to mention a certificate of excellence from the esteemed manufacturers, Benson & Hedges. What do you say to that?'

'I am astonished, Sir.'

'And so you might be. Remember, select your words carefully. Butter up the good gentlemen. As for the monthly reordering of stock and alcohol, I shall speak to the Tobacco Dock Company and the wine merchant. Instruct them to send their invoices to the Bank of England's accountant for payment while the money you lock in the chest will safely accrue.'

'Yes, Sir, I shall see to it.'

'Then we are settled on all details!' exclaimed Lucas delightedly. 'I am very relieved to know that you have accepted my offer as paid member of staff of the establishment of Lucas Benjamin, tobacconist of Silver Street.'

CHAPTER SEVENTEEN

'Clara must have new clothes,' Lucas declared one hot day in early August. He had just returned from the agents with tickets for the ferry crossing. Mopping his brow with his handkerchief, he collapsed onto a chair. 'We may be buffeted by wind or a strong sea as we sail from Dover. A warm cape will be essential. As for dresses — I must leave the choices to you. Spare no expense.' He gave a little grin and tucked the tickets in the bureau. 'We depart on Sunday 15th September, taking a carriage from London to Dover. After a night's rest we board ship for Calais.'

Thus, the problem of Clara's new clothes was left in Ettie's hands. Since she had no idea where to start, she visited a dressmaker she had seen on her way to the market. It took her only a few minutes to walk to Broad Street and, after discussions with a portly woman called Mrs Buckle, a winter braided jacket, cape and warm coat and undergarments with combinations were ordered. The dressmaker also advised at least two to three day and evening dresses and at least one walking dress.

'How long will your employer and his wife be away?' Mrs Buckle asked.

'Until next year,' Ettie explained as she sat in the sewing room studying the pretty silks, wools and cottons from which Clara's clothes might be cut.

'In that case, you must make a trip to the city for bonnets, muffs, gloves and other things a lady might need. I shall give you a letter to give to a milliner. The shop sells the accessories your mistress requires. Except of course, footwear. The boot mender's shop is in the same row. Take a shoe with you so that he can measure up.' Ettie was relieved to have found someone like Mrs Buckle to advise her.

After informing Lucas of Mrs Buckle's suggestions, Ettie was sent by carriage to the city. They passed the stately houses and green parks she remembered on her ride through the city after she had left the orphanage. A lump lodged in her throat. Six long months had elapsed since she had said goodbye to the orphans and nuns. Longer even, since she had seen Michael. Her heart gave a little twist. Where was he now? Did he still think of her? She had prayed to Saint Jude every Sunday, begging him to look after Michael and keep him out of trouble. For if ever there was an impossible case, it was Michael. But for all that, he still held a place in her heart that would never be filled by anyone else.

Ettie's cab arrived at the milliners of Oxford Street. She had no idea how much all the things would cost but Lucas had provided her with ample money.

'Spend every penny if needs be,' he had instructed her. 'For Clara, nothing is too expensive.'

Ettie was shown bonnets decorated with frills and flowers, fruit and ribbons, muffs of the finest fur, gloves of delicate leather. But none of them appealed to her, for Clara wore understated clothes of very good quality. Instead she selected other items she knew Clara would prefer.

'You have made an excellent choice,' praised the female milliner, who fixed Ettie with a shrewd eye after attempting to persuade her into unsuitable designs.

'Thank you. My mistress has an unblemished complexion and hair the colour of wheat. I am sure this bonnet and gloves will suit her very well.'

The woman gave a rueful smile. 'I can see you are a young lady with an eye for fashion.'

Ettie blushed at this. 'If I have, then the opportunity to develop it has not come my way.'

The milliner looked surprised. 'I am in need of an assistant. Would you consider an apprenticeship?'

This offer came as such a surprise that Ettie wanted to giggle.

'I don't think my appearance would be suitable,' she replied modestly, suddenly feeling self-conscious.

'You have beautiful hair,' said the woman. 'With a little attention to facial powdering, you would model my hats perfectly. Added to your grasp of prices and demure character, you have all the qualities I require.'

Once again Ettie's cheeks turned scarlet. 'Thank you. But I am committed to the service of the tobacconist of Silver Street and his wife.'

'A pity,' said the milliner as she packed away Ettie's purchases. 'You would have done me very nicely.'

Ettie left the shop with light steps and a smile. The milliner, though out for herself and the filling of a position, had given Ettie great encouragement. Did she really have the qualities the woman had listed?'

It was with that same smile on her lips that she entered the boot makers not two doors along. Dressed in a brown leather apron over his working clothes, the surly-faced boot maker greeted her very differently. His gaze went to her boots which were not of high quality, unlike the many rows of expensive-looking footwear that lined his shelves.

'Good morning,' Ettie greeted and received a disgruntled mutter in reply.

But as he examined Clara's pretty shoe that Ettie had brought with her, his manner improved. 'These have silk uppers and foxing on the heel. A very nice job indeed,' he decided.

'I would like two pairs made in the same size and style, but in pale yellow and olive green. Also, a pair of button boots and walking boots of your highest quality,' Ettie requested.

He gave her a suspicious frown. 'I don't come cheap, you know. Each pair of shoes will cost eight shillings and sixpence. Twelve and sixpence for boots. I use the finest leather from Cordorba in Spain; my materials and workmanship are unique. My regular customers, none of 'em short of a pound or two, can vouch for that.'

'Will my order be ready by the first week of September?'

The boot maker looked her up and down. 'You must settle the account up front.'

Now it was Ettie's turn to hesitate. For Sister Ukunda had shown her how to barter and this man seemed not unlike the market traders. 'I shall pay you for the shoes now,' she decided. 'And the remainder in September when the order is complete.'

'You drive a hard bargain,' the boot maker complained, but nevertheless, eyed her plump purse. 'Wouldn't have thought it when you walked in this shop. A child, I imagined, wanting patches on soles for next to nothing.'

'We are agreed then?' Ettie ignored his rudeness. 'Four sets of footwear in total?'

'As soon as I see the colour of your money.'

Ettie opened her purse and took out the note.

The boot maker looked startled. 'Well, well! I should have asked for more,' was all he could say.

Ettie smiled. She had struck a fine deal and been offered a position of some interest, all in one day!

CHAPTER EIGHTEEN

'Good gracious, you would think we were leaving England for good,' complained Lucas later that month, when business was over for the day. He inspected the three cabin trunks that Ettie had labelled, and secured each with locks.

'One is for footwear,' Ettie explained. 'Mrs Benjamin's favourites in addition to her new shoes.' The boot maker had proven trustworthy and had produced the highest quality footwear. Both pairs of shoes and boots fitted Clara perfectly. 'The other is for dresses, coats, underwear and night clothes. The third trunk is yours, Sir, which you packed yourself.'

'And what a tiring job that was!' exclaimed Lucas, heaving a sigh. 'How is my wife today?'

'A little better, Sir,' Ettie said hopefully. 'We took a walk to the green. She seems to be in good spirits.'

'Perhaps the prospect of the holiday has helped?' Lucas suggested.

'Yes, Sir.' Ettie hoped that was the case.

'Wintering abroad is the very best thing, so the Soho Square physician tells me.' And as the days passed by Ettie saw that Lucas could barely contain his enthusiasm.

On the morning of 15th September, he mopped his brow anxiously. 'We must be on time for the cab at nine o'clock,' he muttered as he stood in his best suit, checking his fob watch repeatedly. 'Is everything ready?'

'Yes, Sir. Here are your papers and Mrs Benjamin's medicine should you need it on the journey.' She gave Lucas the small leather satchel and watched him loop the strap across his shoulder. 'I have given Mrs Benjamin a separate purse containing a mirror, a compact of face powder, some rouge en crepe and a phial of eau-de-cologne.'

'Ettie, you are a marvel!'

'There are crackers and sandwiches in the carpet bag, should you be delayed on the road.'

'You have thought of everything. After breakfast, we shall adjourn to the salon; a last-minute refresher will do no harm.'

'I shall write to you with every detail,' Ettie promised.

'Oh, Ettie, my dear!' He threw his arms around her. 'Thank you.'

He was whistling through his two big front teeth as he walked away. It was the first time in many months that Ettie had seen him so happy.

* * *

The cab arrived on the dot of nine. While Lucas helped the driver to stow the trunks, Ettie assisted her mistress inside. She tucked a stray wisp of Clara's hair under her new silk bonnet. The pale rose tint of its ribbons looked tasteful against the dark plum of her cape. Ettie had dusted Clara's cheeks with rouge and fastened her button boots securely about her slender ankles.

'You look most charming, Mrs Benjamin.'

Clara grasped her hand. 'Where am I going, Ettie?' she whispered.

'To Dover,' Ettie replied, a little disturbed at the lapse in Clara's memory. 'And afterwards to France.'

'I shall miss you.' Clara's pale eyes blinked tears.

'And I, you.' Ettie took her mistress's hand. 'Mr Benjamin will hire a maid when you arrive in Paris.'

Clara gave a little choke. 'Goodbye.'

Ettie embraced her. 'Next time we meet you will be your old self.'

'Perhaps,' Clara replied sadly.

'We are all set,' shouted a voice, making Clara and Ettie jump. Lucas stood waiting impatiently.

'May the Good Lord be with you, Mrs Benjamin,' Ettie murmured. 'I shall pray for you each day.'

'Hurry along, Ettie,' ordered Lucas as he waited at the cab's door. 'We must keep to schedule.'

Ettie climbed down the carriage steps. 'Goodbye, Sir.' She watched Lucas settle himself next to Clara.

'I leave all I own in your hands. Don't fail me,' he called.

Ettie stood on the cobbles, watching the cab disappear in the early morning mist. She was worried. Would Clara endure the long journey?

'*I leave all I own in your hands. Don't fail me.*' Lucas's words ran through her mind uncomfortably. She had always been confident when he was with her. But now she was quite alone.

CHAPTER NINETEEN

On Monday morning, Ettie put on her new salon uniform, made for her by Mrs Buckle. A delicate white frill lay at her throat. Two small pearls decorated her fitted bodice. The colour of the wool was not quite the deep brown of her eyes.

With her hair drawn to the back of her head and coiled at the nape of her neck, she hoped she looked older than her years.

'I wish to speak to the proprietor,' said the first customer, a silver-haired gentleman who fixed her with a disdainful frown.

'Mr and Mrs Benjamin are holidaying in Europe.' Ettie repeated the mantra that Lucas had taught her. 'How may I help?'

'I doubt you can,' snapped the man, irritably tapping his cane on the floor. 'Most inconvenient. I have travelled some way to make a purchase.'

'I am sure I can advise you,' Ettie insisted.

'A chit of a girl — advising me!' The man exclaimed angrily. 'I take that as an insult!' He marched to the door and yanked it open. 'Tell your employer he has lost a customer,' he called over his shoulder. 'And will never see me again.'

Before Ettie could reply, the door slammed loudly.

Tears of humiliation squeezed in her eyes. She remembered the day in Victoria Park when she had realized how it felt to be poor. It was a lesson she would never forget. The gentleman today had reminded her of her lowly station.

Ettie tried not to think of the failure. She set about cleaning the shelves and unpacking the crates from Tobacco Dock. Diligently, she examined each box and package as Lucas had shown her. The strong aromas of fresh tobacco filled the salon. After rearranging the pipes, cigars and cigarettes, she turned her attention to the glass cabinets. Just as she was brushing the blue velvet cloths, the door opened. A young gentleman entered.

'Top of the morning,' he said from under his small black moustache. Removing his tall hat, he placed it on the cabinet. His sleek black hair, loud necktie and cheap-looking coat gave him a sharp look. He twitched an eyebrow. 'My, my. Who have we here?'

Ettie shyly lowered her eyes. 'Good morning, Sir.'

He removed his gloves. She noted the slight brown stain on his forefinger and middle finger. This was a sign, so Lucas had indicated, of a dedicated cigarette smoker.

'I would like to speak to the proprietor of this establishment,' he said with a roguish grin.

Ettie replied as she had replied before. 'Mr and Mrs Benjamin are holidaying in Europe.'

'And left you on your own?'

Ettie nodded. 'How may I help, Sir?' If fifty or even a hundred gentlemen scorned her, she would still politely offer to serve them.

'Lucky devils,' said the man, surprising her. 'What I would give to sally off like that. Leave London Town behind me and venture abroad.' He gave a cheeky grin. 'But some of us must work diligently, I suppose. Like you, my dear. Left to hold the fort, were you?'

Ettie was not certain of this man. He was not the salon's usual type of customer.

'What is your choice of tobacco?' Ettie asked politely.

'I prefer something smooth, as soft as a woman's skin.' He gave her a flirtatious wink.

Ettie drew herself upright. 'What brand, Sir?'

'Come close and whisper a recommendation.' He tried to reach for her hand but she snapped it away.

'A cool little madam, I see,' he sneered.

Ettie felt humiliated. While Lucas had been present his customers had all been mannerly. But now she was unchaperoned, she knew she had to be careful. The cheap cigarette tobacco that clung to his coat wafted into her face.

'Is it cigarettes you prefer?' she asked, reaching out to the shelf where the inexpensive makes were discreetly stored.

'Cigarettes?' he questioned.

'Perhaps Sweet Threes?'

'Sharp little miss, ain't you?' He narrowed his eyes, clearly disturbed. 'How do you know I'm after fags?'

Ettie shrank away as he leaned across the counter. 'Every tobacco has a unique bouquet, Sir.'

'Bloody cheek!' He roared, his face flushed. 'You mean I . . . smell?'

Ettie cowered as he almost leapt over the cabinet. She was certain he would have grabbed her had not another customer arrived.

'Don't bother trading here, chum!' bawled the young man to the new arrival. 'She'll tell you that you stink!' He swiped up his gloves and hat, glared at Ettie, then stormed out.

Tears of defeat glistened in Ettie's eyes. Would she ever be able to say the right thing? It seemed so easy when Lucas had been there and now it felt impossible. How could she ever have thought she would be able to manage the salon? It was all she could do to breathe. What a fool she had been!

'What are those tears for, Gwen's little beauty?' enquired the new customer.

Ettie looked up. 'Oh, Terence, it's you!' She had last seen the butcher a week ago when she had purchased a special leg of pork for Lucas and Clara's last dinner.

'It's me all right. Thought I'd pay you a visit as you'd be on your own, unable to get out for shopping.'

Ettie tried to smile.

'Did that dandy upset you?'

'I could smell Sweet Threes on his person and mistakenly told him so.'

With an enormous guffaw, the butcher fiercely patted his stomach. 'Bravo, bravo! You've done yourself a favour. That cheeky pup was on the make, my dear.'

'On the make, Terence?'

'Could tell in an instant. Nasty piece of work. Did he ask for your boss? If you were alone?'

Ettie nodded.

Terence rubbed his whiskers. 'Probably been watchin' the premises. While your back was turned he'd be filching, pocketing, that sort of thing. Fingers as nimble as magpies' beaks. Eyes as sharp as needles. Don't truck with the rascals. Send 'em off with a flea in their ear.'

Was Terence trying to make her feel better, she wondered?

'Look what I brought you.' From his cloth bag he produced a slightly blood-stained muslin. 'Trotters m'dear, fresh today. Boil 'em up with an onion. Do you the world of good.'

Ettie stared at the two, sweating fat pink pigs' feet oozing grease as they lay on the counter. Hiding the queasy roll of her stomach she smiled.

'How much do I owe you?'

'Not a halfpenny, m'dear. A little titbit from old Terence for all the custom you've brought my way. Now, I'll be off. Any problems, you know where to find me.'

But as each day passed, the customers refused to use the smoking room. Instead, they conducted a swift purchase and went on their way without having spent much money. She knew they were not comfortable in her presence. How could she hope to gain their trust?

One November evening, she was sitting alone at the dining table after a quiet day in the salon. The nights were closing in and heavy with city fogs. It was ice-cold in the house but she had not lit the fire. Mindful of the drop in takings, she tried to be thrifty. The succulent stew of pigs' trotters was now a distant memory. Tonight she was feasting on dry bread and cheese, her staple diet.

But she wasn't hungry. What if the business failed? The prospect haunted her.

Ettie turned away from her untouched meal. She closed her hands together and prayed. 'Jesus, Mary and Joseph, I'm desperate. Almost a month and the customers are dwindling. Help me not to disappoint Lucas. Bless Clara and make her well. And wherever Michael is, keep him on the straight and narrow. Amen.'

When Ettie opened her eyes, she was staring into the gaze of the portrait hanging over the mantle. Rose Benjamin seemed to be smiling.

Ettie blinked. After a moment she got up and walked to the hearth. Stretching out her hand she touched the elaborate gold frame.

'*Buck up Ettie! Show the world your mettle.*'

Ettie jumped back. Her heart jumped. Had the portrait spoken? Surely not. The frame was just painted wood, the image inside a replica of Lucas's mother. Yet Ettie had heard the words clearly. Had they come from her mind?

Silence again.

Ettie stared around her, fully expecting to see an apparition. But the room was empty. She had been taught by the nuns never to fear God's spiritual messengers. But there was no sweet voice that Ettie imagined might be her mother, Colleen O'Reilly. The words had come from the portrait. Ettie was at a loss to understand.

She sat down on the chair again. 'Did you speak, Mrs Benjamin?' She asked, while her voice was a shaky whisper.

Only silence filled the room. Her imagination had taken over. Yet, if she was to consider those words, did they have meaning? '*Buck up Ettie! Show the world your mettle.*'

An idea came to her. It was something Lucas had said as he read from his diaries. With nervous fingers she unbolted the door to the salon. Lighting each gas mantle, the dark shadows transformed into golden, glowing shelves of tobaccos. One space remained, where a sturdy brass hook poked out from the wall. Ettie had often studied the faded illustration that hung upon it. A muscled arm sprouting three male hands. The first hand grasped snuff, the next a pipe, the third a pound of tobacco. Ettie smiled to herself. The hook was the answer! And finding herself a stool, she began her night's work.

CHAPTER TWENTY

'God rest ye merry gentlemen,' the carollers sang.

Ettie gazed out of the salon window, her heart lifting at the sight of the raggedy beggars huddled in front of the dirty, cockeyed houses and shops of Silver Street. The scene was transformed into beauty by showers of tiny, pearl-white snowflakes. December had begun with a freezing wind. Now it whistled beneath a threatening sky swollen by purple-grey clouds. She could see the building drifts of snow settling over the smoke-pitted terraces.

Seasonal weather, she thought happily. Cold, gritty weather. Best of all, tobacco weather!

Drawing on her cape, she took two pennies from her purse and went outside. The cold air grazed her face but the weak, hopeful voices of the frozen singers raised her spirits. Raggle-taggle men and women and two small children shivering under worn-out shawls and holed overcoats, but singing all the same.

'Merry Christmas,' she wished them.

The boy and girl, scarlet-cheeked and skinny as reeds held out their frozen hands.

The coins fell into eager palms. 'Thanks, missus. Gawd bless yer.'

Ettie watched them hurry off — a band of brothers and sisters, reminding her of life before Silver Street. A year ago, she had awaited her fate at the orphanage. The bishop's directive had separated her forever from the orphans of the Sisters of Clemency; little innocents, bundled off to an unknown fate in a farmer's cart. She had prayed every night and each Sunday at church for Kathy Squires, Johnny Dean, the twins Megan and Amy and her dear lost friend, Michael Wilson.

Snowflakes melted on her nose as she watched people trudging along. For her, a safe shelter awaited in the salon. For many, there was only hardship and poverty this Christmas.

On her return, she shook off her cape and took her place behind the counter.

Every shelf was now replenished by this morning's delivery from the Tobacco Dock wholesalers. Paying their account from her profits had seemed like a dream come true.

'No,' Ettie said aloud as she hung a sprig of holly from the frame of the portrait. 'Not a dream, but the answer to a prayer.' Her eyes lifted to Rose Benjamin, now the occupier of the space where the three-hand illustration had once hung. 'Thank you,' Ettie murmured, her eyes locking with the blue gaze of the young woman who resembled so distinctly the countenance of her only son.

Rose was now her daily companion and mentor. With Rose's image dominating the salon, Ettie greeted her customers in a confident manner. She had memorized a new speech and was determined to deliver it before the customer could turn tail and run.

'Good morning,' she would welcome, positioning herself directly below the imposing portrait. 'On behalf of Mrs Rose Benjamin and her son, Lucas, the salon welcomes you. I am honoured to act as representative for the family.' Proudly she would indicate the certificate she had mounted and framed on the glass cabinet.

This was a startling event, even for regular customers. There had been many occasions when a jaw or two had fallen open and refused to close. But Ettie was relentless. For it was sink or swim, a decisive profit or a humiliating loss.

'On closer inspection,' she would continue, 'you will see the document is signed by dukes and archdukes of the kingdom, clerics and lords, politicians and celebrities. Our ranges of tobaccos are unparalleled. And of course, we are proud to stock this silver, engraved fob watch cutter.' She would then take out a small box that stored the newly arrived appliance. The metal gleamed under the light of the lamps as she held it up for inspection. 'With this new device, a side of your cigar is removed and on closure, the tab acts as security for finger and thumb. A small loop on the chain can be attached to the waistcoat and used to impress a gentleman's friends and colleagues.' She would coil the cutter invitingly into the box. 'Mr Benjamin has left a small, select, supply of cigars, cigarillos and cheroots and recommends that the cutter be tested out in the comfort of our smoking room.'

This suggestion had even the coolest customer rocking on his heels in order to claim a demonstration.

CHAPTER TWENTY-ONE

The letter arrived a week before Christmas. Ettie recognized Lucas's handwriting at once.

With trembling hands, she lifted the lightly tinted paper sealed by wax. Trying to calm her emotions, she carried it to the counter and sat on the stool beneath the portrait.

'From your son,' Ettie told Rose. 'I shall read it to you.'

Her habit each day now was to address Lucas's mother, for the shop's increase in trade had come — whether by fate or heavenly intervention — since that evening when she had hung the portrait. Ettie wasn't usually given to superstition. However, it felt comforting to imagine Rose's guiding presence. Just as she imagined her mother's. And now there was a letter from abroad!

She drew her fingers across the envelope; *Miss Henrietta O'Reilly, Benjamin & Son. Salon of Quality Tobaccos. Silver Street. Soho. London. England.*

Henrietta! She hadn't been called by that name for many years. Taking a slim knife from the drawer, she slipped its sharp tip beneath the seal. A single sheet of notepaper slid out.

Lucas's flowing, looped handwriting caused her heart to swerve. Was it good news or bad?

'*Clinic les Montagnes, St Moritz, Switzerland*,' she read.

'*My dear Ettie, I hope this letter finds you well and does, with all haste, arrive before December 25th. I shall not enquire about the salon. I trust you will tell me all in your returning letter.*

From Paris we rented a coach and hired a maid, after which we set out for Switzerland. Good fortune was with us. Clara's spirits held up. Had I been aware of the challenges of this arduous adventure, I may never have left London. But finally, in Davos, we settled in a hotel, where we heard of great healing successes, comparable to the climatic resorts of the Mediterranean. Our sojourn here was brief. We ventured on to this famed sanatoria of St Moritz. The physicians have prescribed mineral waters from the spa and a milk diet for Clara (often used upon consumptives). I was sceptical at first. Feared I had made a foul decision by not continuing on our journey through Europe. But by all that is merciful in this world, Clara begins to improve. I shall say no more, for I am as yet unconvinced, though we are totally swept away by the beauty and effervescence of the mountains. I will write again after a test is completed. I pray you remain well and not overburdened with work.

From your ever-grateful friend, Lucas Benjamin. (Who at this very moment is watching his wife as she rests contentedly on her chaise longue on the balcony in the winter sunshine.)'

Ettie read the letter again. And again. Clara was improving! Yet Lucas dare not say more until after this 'test'. Ettie knew that she must pray even harder for Clara.

She gazed up at the portrait. 'I hope you are proud of your son and daughter-in-law, Rose.'

There was no answer of course, but Ettie was content. She would write a reply this evening, telling Lucas of her own successes. The salon was in profit. The customers had not been poached by the well-to-do stores of the West End. Every account was paid.

The rest of the day passed busily. Ettie had prepared tobacco jars decorated with red ribbons. Cigars and cheroots bore sprigs of holly. A selection of snuff miniatures, each with discreet labelling for the discerning male, were placed invitingly on the small table in the smoking room.

That evening was spent with her nose almost touching the salon notepaper. She had so much to tell Lucas. As she dipped her nib pen into the inkwell, she recalled the smeared, wooden desks of the orphanage. How the children who could not read or write would fashion their own markings. She remembered the many hours she had spent with Michael teaching him to read and write. Had he put any of his learning to use?

Ettie returned her thoughts to composing her letter. She poured out her news; the favourable results of the salon, no debts to record, modest profits. How delighted she was to hear of Clara's improvement. Lastly, she wished her dear employer and his wife a happy and holy holiday.

* * *

It was finally Christmas Eve and very cold. Ettie listened to the conversation in the smoking room. The holiday had not come too soon, it seemed, even for the wealthy gentlemen. 1895, so she learned, had been a year of mixed fortunes.

The politicians among the smokers breathed a loud sigh of relief. 'Good grief, what would the country have come to with Rosebery at the helm?' one elderly smoker muttered.

'Rosebery talked himself out of the job,' agreed another. 'After the vote of no confidence, there was nowhere to hide.'

Ettie listened carefully to the opinions on the General Election held back in the summer. The Liberals had been pronounced a failure. The Conservatives, led by Lord Salisbury, had won the day.

'Damn fine majority,' agreed a pipe smoker. 'But down to the Unionists.'

'What's your take on the Panhard four-wheeler?' a young motorist enquired who had boasted he'd successfully truanted from his office.

'Top notch, old boy but a bit rich for the wallet.'

'A Daimler for me!' A cigar smoker added.

'Carl Benz has completed the "Victoria",' mooted an older man as he filled his tumbler.

'I'd strike for the Lancaster,' overruled another.

'Pour me a dram,' requested a new arrival.

One after another, her gentlemen came and went, enjoying the final hours of freedom from their families. 'Gave those Yankees a run for their money,' jested a keen golfer. 'Rawlins left 'em standing at the Open.'

'Damn the golf,' cursed a military man. 'Sending our lads out to Ashanti — bah!'

'Where's Ashanti?'

'Africa, old chap. West a fraction.'

'Too old for that lark now. Did my bit in the Transvaal.'

'Really? Have a snifter.'

And so the day passed, with Ettie amused by the stories she heard as she worked. Her customers regarded her as they might a maid or servant in their own homes, to which — after enjoying the tobaccos and decanters — they now seemed reluctant to return to.

When the day was over, Ettie swept the ash-laden floors and cleared the overflowing glass bowls. She rinsed the tumblers, shined the glass and returned the button-back chairs to their former polished glory.

Finally, she sat on the stool and gazed out on the darkened street. She had extinguished the lamps and sat by a single candle. Peace settled around her like a soft, comfort blanket.

The till brimmed coppers, silver and notes. Orders were taken for January. The accounts were complete. Terence had cooked her a ham and egg pie for Christmas.

Ettie sighed with pleasure. In just a few hours she would attend Midnight Mass to thank God for all He had given her. But most of all she would pray for Clara and Lucas. For the orphanage and the children. And for Michael.

CHAPTER TWENTY-TWO

Christmas Day arrived clear and bright. Ettie woke to an unusual silence. She missed the rowdy voices and cries of Soho's unconventional residents. It appeared that even the drunks and the desperadoes of Silver Street observed 25th December.

After washing and dressing rapidly — since the cold was turning her fingers blue — she peered out of the window to the furrows of browned snow on the cobbles beneath. She shivered, disappointed to discover not one soul in sight.

Downstairs was equally silent, until she coaxed a fire in the drawing room, adding a few paper twists and a shovelful of coals. The crackling and spitting gave a little energy and she sat by it as she ate her breakfast. Last night at Mass she had listened to the carols and remembered the orphans. How they loved Christmas; the thin slices of fruit cake and tiny parcels wrapped in paper, chalks or pencils for the boys, and ribbons for the girls. What would the farmer give them? Ettie felt very guilty as she toasted her bread on a long fork over the fire and drank hot tea from a mug as the tiny scarlet flames danced between the coals.

Today would be a very long day with no customers to serve. What could she do to fill the hours? Perhaps take a walk out? But as morning turned into afternoon, she was still sitting by the fire; a fire that had extinguished to grey ashes. Why can't I think of something to do? She wondered. A little voice in her head replied simply, 'because it's your birthday'.

Ettie's lashes moistened. She was now fifteen years of age, and nothing could change that.

Slowly she rose to her feet, returned the dirty dishes to the kitchen, then washed and dried them. She then set about cleaning, dusting and polishing rooms that already were spotless. Work was her only solace. When she could find nothing more to do, she unlocked the door to the salon. It was here she felt most useful, with Rose and the echo of her customers' conversations.

She swept the floor, dusted the shelves and rearranged the velvet blue cloths. Opening a pack of freshly arrived tobaccos, she arranged a selection of Lucas's most expensive cigars. Now all that was left was to store the week's takings in the cast-iron chest.

Yet Ettie was reluctant to end the day and return to the silent house. There was no one there to share her birthday, as she had done each year with the orphans. How she wished to be back again with the Sisters of Clemency! She wanted to hug Kathy Squires close and tell the twins Meg and Amy a bedtime story. She yearned for the companionship and the laughter that Michael had brought into her life.

Tears stung on her eyelids. Like tiny, poisoned darts of self-pity they reminded her it was Christmas and she was alone.

Her sad eyes met Rose's. How Lucas's mother must have suffered, she thought resolutely. A beloved husband's early and unexpected death. A young son to raise. The business to run. Rose's loneliness would have been even more desperate than her own.

'I'm young still,' Ettie encouraged herself. 'And have my good health. Why should I be unhappy?'

As if in response, a sudden noise made her jump. It came from the salon window. 'Tap, tap,' the noise went. Ettie listened again.

'Tap tap.'

Darkness had descended now. The salon didn't feel quite so friendly. Ettie crept to the door. The blinds were closed. Should she draw them and take a look?

Another 'tap, tap'. This time louder. Then a cry of impatience.

'Ettie O'Reilly, where are you?'

At once she recognized the voice. Drawing the lock, Ettie was almost bowled over as Gwen and Lily rushed in. A freezing draught followed as they drowned her in hugs and kisses and the faint, unmissable scent of aniseed.

'Joyeux Noel,' cried Lily. 'Terence told us you are alone.'

'In this dark and gloomy place,' Gwen said as the two girls made their way in, squinting into the flickering shadows.

Ettie closed the salon door, startled but happy to see her two friends. 'Mr and Mrs Benjamin are holidaying in Europe.'

'Fine for some,' snorted Lily. 'But for you, Ettie, have you not a minute to spare for your friends?'

Ettie blushed, knowing she should have found time to visit Gwen and Lily.

'No excuses, little beauty,' laughed Gwen, throwing off her coat and bundling it into Ettie's arms. 'We are here and that's all that matters. See, we've brought supper with us.'

Lily placed a wooden basket on the cabinet. 'Cold meats, pickles, plums baked in syrup, tarts and biscuits. And of course, a little green fairy.'

Without further ado, the two girls linked their arms through Ettie's. 'Show us the way to a nice fire, won't you?'

A little uncertainly Ettie led them down the passage to the drawing room. She would never have taken such a liberty if Lucas and Clara were here. But since they weren't and Gwen and Lily were being so generous and kind as to call on her, Ettie felt obliged to respond.

'This is a very nice room,' Gwen said, looking round. 'But so cold! Where is the fire?'

'I lit one,' Ettie apologized, 'but it went out.'

'Let's make another.'

'There isn't much coal . . .'

'We'll burn something else then,' Lily said, untroubled. 'Have you any wood?'

Ettie shook her head, then remembered the broken crates that were to be returned to the Tobacco Dock company. She led the way through the kitchen, a room which drew cries of approval from her friends.

By the light of an oil lantern, they searched the yard. Soon there was laughter and giggling as Gwen and Lily made short work of the crates. Ettie laughed too as they lifted their skirts, kicked and showed off their bloomers, as the scent of aniseed curled in the air.

With arms full of broken pieces, they returned to the house. Gathered by the drawing room hearth, they piled the wood in the grate. Taking a newspaper package from the wooden basket, Gwen unwrapped a green bottle.

'Say bonsoir to the fairy, Ettie!' She waved the bottle in the air. 'It's your birthday after all.'

Ettie gasped. 'How do you know?'

'You told me when we met,' Gwen chuckled. 'Remember?'

Ettie thought back to that first day when she had gone to the market. 'Yes, I remember.'

'I have a good memory. Now find us some tumblers — à votre santé.'

Ettie went to the kitchen. She felt a curl of happiness inside her. Gwen had remembered her birthday after all this time. Together with the lit candle, she placed three glass tumblers and Terence's egg and ham pie on a tray. Slicing the pie thinly, she added a half loaf of bread and the very last thimbleful of butter.

When she returned, Gwen and Lily were making balls of the newspaper. They pushed them into the wood and Lily lowered the candle's flame. Wax dropped in melting pearls on the grate. The taper sent scarlet flames leaping upward. Heat flooded the room.

'Qu'est-ce que vous voulez boire?' teased Lily into Ettie's ear.

Ettie tried to remember her French. 'Non, merci, Lily,' she refused politely.

'Just one sip,' persuaded Gwen, putting her arm around Ettie's shoulders.

Ettie began to smile at the funny faces her friends were making. She didn't see what harm could come of taking one small sip. After all, this was her birthday.

The aniseed rolled over her tongue like cream. It soared into her belly like fire. It brought back the happy memories of Gwen's house and the afternoon she had spent there.

'You see, that wasn't so bad,' urged Gwen.

'Happy birthday, sister,' sang Lily.

'Thank you,' said Ettie elatedly. She felt light and floaty. Her legs were tingling and her insides were warm with pleasure.

'If Gino was here, he would recite to you,' Gwen said, a coy smile in her eyes. 'He thought you were enchanting, Ettie.'

'Did he?'

'A princess,' added Lily. 'He was smitten.'

Ettie blushed deeply.

'Another toast,' said Gwen, as she filled the tumblers.

'To Gwen's little beauty and Gino's princess,' Lily cried.

Ettie drank again and Lily snuggled beside her.

Gwen leaned her blonde head on a cushion and kicked off her boots. She swirled the green fairy in her glass. 'We love you, Ettie O'Reilly.'

Lily put her tumbler to Ettie's lips. 'Drink from mine and I'll drink from yours. Then we'll truly be sisters.'

Ettie looked into Lily's dark eyes. They were round, deep and very mysterious. In Gwen and Lily's company she felt truly alive.

'Our little beauty,' whispered Lily, licking her lips.

CHAPTER TWENTY-THREE

'The people of France adore the cirque,' Gwen reminisced hours later as they lay outstretched beside the fire. 'They come to watch us! Every night after our dancing we drank champagne.'

Ettie listened in wonder. To her, the life that Lily, Gino and Gwen had led was a fantasy. Once again, she had that floating, dreamy feeling. All her loneliness had disappeared.

'Look, we shall show you!' Gwen stood up and pulled Lily to her feet. They pushed back the chairs while Ettie curled up on the couch. Gwen clapped her hands and sung a little melody. Lily snatched the ends of her skirt. Twirling round and round, she bounced up and down kicking her legs high. The higher her legs went, the higher the skirt lifted.

'Bravo,' cried Gwen turning to Ettie. 'Sing for us, Ettie.'

'But I don't know any songs.'

'Let the music come from your heart.' Gwen grasped a tumbler from the mantle and pushed it into Ettie's hands. 'The green fairy will help you.'

Ettie could only remember the hymns and the carols that had once been so much a part of her life at the orphanage. But she knew they wouldn't do at all, even if she tried to sing them faster. No, they wouldn't do at all for Gwen and Lily. She took a small drink and with a deep breath she sang a few notes.

'Keep in time with us,' cried Lily as she waved her skirts in the air.

Ettie sipped again and this time a song began to flow. It was wordless and formless, but the joy burst tunefully out of her throat. Lily and Gwen threw themselves around the room. Ettie could see the tops of their stockings. Legs were stretched and raised, half-crossed, then uncrossed. Feet kicked and petticoats flounced. In a flurry of cartwheels, Gwen and Lily sank to the floor, their legs stretched wide.

'Our finale,' cried Lily triumphantly, 'le grand écart.'

Ettie was astonished at their suppleness. She applauded fiercely.

Some more green fairy was poured. More songs were sung and dances danced. The last of the ham and egg pie was enjoyed.

'Let's play charades,' said Gwen when the bottle of absinthe was drained. 'Ettie, you and Lily go first.'

But Ettie could barely stand. Her head seemed to be going 'round on her shoulders. Lily rushed to her side and held her.

'Come into the salon,' whispered Lily. 'Where Gwen won't hear us.'

Ettie shook her head. 'Mr Benjamin wouldn't approve . . .'

'Come,' insisted Lily, tickling her ribs and gently pushing her down the passage. 'No one's here. Stand behind the counter. You shall be Mr Benjamin. I shall be your customer.'

Ettie tried to steady herself. She felt as though the floor was moving.

'Now, I should like to buy a cigar,' boomed Lily, in a deep, masculine voice.

Ettie shook her head. 'No, Lily, we mustn't. Not here, in Lucas's salon . . .'

'This one will do,' interrupted Lily disdainfully. 'Don't worry, we are just pretending!'

Ettie watched as Lily's deft fingers wiggled under the glass cabinet. Out came a cigar and she slipped it between her lips.

'Disgusting!' declared Lily, turning up her nose. She threw the cigar on the floor.

'Lily, don't!' Ettie cried.

But Lily reached into the cabinet again. She pulled out the blue velvet and with it, Ettie's careful display of tobaccos.

Ettie felt a frightened sob stick in her throat. What was happening?

'That boss of yours is a swindler!' shouted Lily, stamping on the cloth and crushing the cigars. 'His tobacco is inferior. I'll wager he sits all day long and counts his money. And you are his slave Ettie, his willing slave!'

Ettie tried to tell Lily that she was wrong. How kind and generous Lucas was, how he would never cheat anyone. But the words that came from her mouth were all muddled.

Lily banged her fist on the counter. 'Tell the truth, Ettie! You're free to say what you like now. Admit to being the puppet of a greedy old miser!' Lily's face was changing, spite and bitterness darting out of her eyes.

Ettie's stomach lurched. She didn't feel like playing charades any more. Or hearing lies about Lucas. She just wanted Lily and Gwen to leave. Then she could sit down, or even better, lie down. But Lily was behind her, pushing her forcefully towards the big brass till.

'That's it, that's it,' Lily growled. 'Now open it!'

Ettie tried to turn away. 'Lily, no!' she cried again.

But Lily wasn't listening. The till sprang open. Ettie was surprised to see it so full of money. Why hadn't she remembered to lock it away?

Suddenly the room spun violently. Ettie's legs buckled and she fell.

'Foolish little soeur,' she heard Lily laugh.

* * *

There was someone in the street making a terrible banging, Ettie thought as she woke. A terrible, terrible banging. The pale light at the window told her it was not yet dawn. She tried to get up but the moment she moved, her stomach heaved. Not only did she feel the impulse to vomit, but a vile pain shot through her head. It was an agony so severe she fell back on the pillow. She was afraid to breathe, lest even the passage of air into her lungs should make it worse.

The banging, she realized, did not come from Silver Street. The pounding was in her brain, as though some part of it had come loose, tumbling from one side to the other. Coupled with the waves of nausea, Ettie knew there was something very wrong. But what was it?

She tried to remember as she lay there. Why hadn't she taken off her clothes? Why did she feel so ill? Had she eaten something rotten? Or had she caught a disease?

Retching violently, she toppled to the floor. Her trembling fingers grabbed the chamber pot. She began arching and gagging above it. A foul liquid spewed up from her throat. The noises she made were like an animal's. She choked, breathlessly waiting for the next eruption. A hammer attacked her skull. Yet more revolting fluid cascaded up, a fearful green liquid that soiled the white chamber pot.

Her body trembled. Her nails dug into the rug. Her forehead dripped sweat. Even her toes curled inside her boots.

Ettie lay on the floor. Her body felt drained of energy. She climbed on the bed again and pulled the cover over her. It didn't matter that she still had her clothes on. Or that she couldn't remember what day it was or barely who she was.

She fell back again into a dark, disturbed sleep.

When Ettie woke again it was daylight. A delicate sun's rays spilled across the floor, encircling the shocking sight of the chamber pot. She must still be dreaming!

She shook her head, trying to clear it. But as she did so, the hammer returned; a persistent drumming in her brain.

She lay there, impassive, waiting for relief. But it was only after some while that she felt able to move. Stumbling to the window, she lifted the sash. Soho air was not fresh at the best of times with the rotting vegetables, horse and cattle dung, and blocked drains. But today, any air was welcome.

Beneath her window, a ragged boy and girl played. They jumped lines made from sticks and pulled each other's hair. Their shouts joined the hammering in Ettie's head.

She put on her apron to hide her dirty smock and carried the chamber pot downstairs. Disposing of its contents in the outside privy, she recalled Gwen's words.

'The green fairy will help you . . .'

But the green fairy had not helped, Ettie reflected miserably. The absinthe had poisoned her.

Carefully she picked her way across the splinters of Tobacco Dock crates and held her head under the pump. Ice-cold water soaked her hair, ran into her eyes and trickled down her throat. She tried to wash away the terrible feeling.

After forcing down a bowl of porridge, she sat by the drawing room hearth. Memories tumbled back, clearer now. Gwen and Lily's tap tap at the window. 'Joyeux Noel,' Gwen had cried, after which the merrymaking had followed. The dancing and acrobatics as tumblers of green fairy passed from one to another.

Then the swirling of skirts and petticoats, laughter and gaiety. Ettie saw it all again, as motes of coal dust spun over the untidy, dishevelled room where the ashes were now spilled across the floorboards and Clara's lovely cushions thrown carelessly on the rug.

A wave of emotion shuddered through her. She saw the dirty tumblers on the mantel. And yes, the empty bottle of green fairy.

How could she have allowed this chaos to happen?

She rested her head back on the chair trying to remember. A few vague images appeared; Lily's rough hands pushing her along the passage, greedy fingers snatching the cigars from inside the glass cabinet. Lily's voice becoming cold and harsh. Her taunting laughter at Lucas's expense.

Ettie sat bolt upright. 'The velvet blue cloths!' she cried in horror. 'Our most expensive cigars!'

In a wave of cold fear, Ettie recalled Lily's parting words, 'Foolish little soeur'.

Hurrying to the salon, Ettie pulled the blinds. As she had feared, daylight revealed the crumpled blue velvet cloths spread over the floor and the trampled remains of Lucas's cigars.

Ettie held in a sob. What had happened to make Lily so angry? As if Ettie herself was the cause of Lily's unhappiness.

'What did I do to make it so?' Ettie asked Rose, bending down to scoop up the broken fragments. 'I thought Lily and Gwen were my friends.'

There was no response, of course. She collapsed on the stool, looking sadly at the empty glass cabinet; Lucas's pride and joy. Why had Lily behaved so badly? It was as if she had changed into someone else before Ettie's eyes.

It was then that another memory came back. And this, the worst of all. She jumped to her feet and ran over to the big brass till. Faintness overcame her as she saw the empty drawer.

Yesterday the till had been full of coins and notes folded carefully into the till's compartments. Not a half-penny of the thirty-five shillings remained.

Another, more terrible thought struck her. The chest behind the wooden panel! Had they discovered it? She hurried across to the shelf and pulling the lever, bent down and took the key from under the floorboard. Inside the cast-iron chest, she found all the bags of money she had stored since Lucas had gone away.

Ettie couldn't cry with relief although she dearly wanted to. What if, in her altered state of mind, she had given away her secret to Gwen and Lily? The consequences were too terrible to think about. Lily and Gwen had not come to celebrate her birthday. Or to bring her good things to eat, or to dance and sing with her as though they were true friends.

They had used the green fairy against her.

A painful sob lodged in her chest. Not only had Gwen and Lily betrayed her trust, but thieved from Lucas, too.

PART TWO: REUNITED

CHAPTER TWENTY-FOUR

March 1896
Davos, 19 February

'*My dear Ettie, thank you for your letter of the 27th January. To hear that all is well at the salon is a great relief. I congratulate and applaud you. Though perhaps you could have told me a little more, a few details to relish? However, this is just a minor point. Especially in the light of what has transpired in Switzerland. Wonderful news! The medical test has been passed! Clara's blood is now healthy, rid of the opium and running through her veins without hinder. The substitute medicine has ceased. The kind nurses have ministered to Clara in every good way possible. Hence, she has put on a little weight and the milk diet has achieved a good, clear pallor. But before today, I could not have told you she had wholly improved in mind. I feared that despite the positive physical result she might remain depressed. The sanatoria physician, Professor Ruegg, assured me he would do his utmost to resolve her condition. But I saw that he, too, was a little dismayed. Clara's moods had settled, but in a low way. Her counselling was tricky, to say the least. I have spent many hours with my dear wife under the shadow of the truly magnificent mountains. We have watched the sporting types in their gay attire and the climbing types, full of bravado. The rich and famous who arrive incognito, only to tire of not being recognized and adored and so reveal themselves on the slopes, with champagne and strawberries aplenty.*

Davos has truly been an eye-opener. But my thoughts are mainly on my darling wife. I have come to investigate every sigh, every little nuance as I study her, hoping for improvement. So dear Ettie, can you imagine this scene just a few days ago? I was reading the English column of the Swiss paper, in particular, an article detailing our sovereign Queen's Diamond Jubilee next year, when lo and behold, Professor Ruegg, a moustachioed man in his late fifties, and of a sombre bearing, appeared at Clara's bedside after breakfast. "Good day to you, sir," he says to me in his impeccable English! To Clara, he is almost exuberant! The man paces a few steps, then lets off the firework. And, the expression on Clara's face is so totally unfamiliar that I hardly recognize her! For the rest of the day, Clara and I are dumfounded, overjoyed, elated, ecstatic, there's no words to describe! For Ettie, my dear, dear Ettie, we are to have a child! After our years of disappointment, your benevolent God, the God you have such faith in, has blessed us. Dr Ruegg has agreed that Clara's confinement will be conducted, as an exception, here at the sanatoria. An arduous journey back to England would not be advisable. Naturally, we shall extend our stay. Ettie, my pen trembles as I write . . . in the hopes that you will see your way to remaining my salon assistant until then? As faithfully and hopefully as ever, Lucas Benjamin.'

Ettie gulped a deep breath. She glanced up from the letter — which she knew almost by heart since it had arrived two days ago — and into the cheerful, bewhiskered face of Terence the butcher. What would she have done without his presence in her life since Christmas, Ettie wondered?

Terence sat in the kitchen in his usual chair by the stove. Here, during a half hour's break from his butchery, he enjoyed Ettie's freshly baked fruit cake and warmed his hands by the stove. She filled their cups with a rich, dark brew and added a little milk.

This was the highlight of her week, when Terence brought her a small, lean chop or leg of fowl or even a little stewing beef. It was Terence who had called at the salon two days after Christmas and discovered Ettie in a severely distressed state. It was Terence who had promised her that life would eventually return to normal.

'Good news indeed, m'dear, wouldn't you say?' the butcher observed.

Although Ettie was cheered by Lucas's announcement, the shadow of Christmas still hung heavily over her.

'You brought the couple good luck, m'dear.'

'And lost them almost a fortune,' declared Ettie woefully. 'I was ashamed to write to Mr Benjamin. I couldn't say what happened in a letter. I've decided to wait until the family comes home. I might even be dismissed.'

'Come now, dear girl,' objected Terence, 'the world's not at an end. You won't be the first to be twisted, nor will you be the last. Just imagine if they'd pinched something you couldn't replace? Like a personal treasure. Or maybe a silver hairbrush or box of jewellery.'

'I packed Mrs Benjamin's personal belongings in her trunk. There was nothing left here of value.' Ettie didn't mention the heavy chest behind the wood panel. Though Terence was a kind and considerate man, she now realized it was dangerous to trust anyone.

'Good, good,' nodded Terence approvingly. 'Grateful for small mercies, eh what?'

'If only I hadn't drunk the green fairy.'

'I'd agree your first testing lesson has come early in life. But it's one you won't easily repeat.'

'I'll never drink again, Terence.'

'Aye, aye, nor will you.'

'And I'll repay every penny of the debt.' Ettie was determined to forego her wage in order to replace what had been stolen.

'Good going m'dear. Though the crime should have been reported to the coppers.'

Ettie had considered this course of action. But Gwen and Lily had disappeared into thin air. She had no evidence at all of the crime. And suppose the police called Lucas back from Switzerland? What would happen then?

She had been done over good and proper — in Terence's words. For he too, had been done over.

'They ran up a chit as long as me arm,' he confessed. 'Only the best meats, the freshest dairy, the tenderest of cuts. All on the slate. Wolves in sheep's clothing, young Ettie,' he said, eyeing her closely. 'We was fooled. They took advantage, the buggers. Like that young fella who tried it on, sniffing around the salon and making up to you.'

'I should have known,' Ettie fretted. 'Why would strangers be so nice to me?'

'Cos *you* are nice,' Terence answered heartily. 'Genuinely, honest. You deserve good friends, course you do. But those two, well they had me fooled. And, a lot of others, I'm betting.'

'Do you really think they danced in a circus?'

'Shouldn't be surprised.'

'Gino wore a tattoo of his circus elephant. I thought it very — interesting.' She blushed as Terence raised an eyebrow.

'Well now, you know those ladies did more than dancing?' Terence looked abashed.

Ettie nodded. 'Gwen told me they enjoyed men's company.'

'Mine included,' the butcher admitted. 'I paid for Gwen's services. Wasn't a hot cup of tea I was after. No, oh no! Truth is, I miss my old Gladys. She passed away five years back. Was a good 'un too. Helped me in the shop. Had a good eye for the cleaver. Strong as an ox, till the flu got her. Matter of days it was. Nothing I could do about it, neither.' His eyes grew moist and his voice was husky. 'Gwen filled a gap. Made me feel like I was special, see, like Glad did. Clever that. Clever. Kept me dangling, so's my hand was always in my wallet. So ducks, you wasn't the only one. Fact is, I'm four decades older than you and should have known better.'

'I'm sorry your wife died.' Ettie felt a great sympathy for this lonely, hard-looking man who had such a soft inside.

'You don't think the less of me?'

'Why should I?' Ettie replied softly. 'We've both lost people we love.'

'You miss them kids from the orphanage, don't you?'

Ettie nodded. 'The nuns and the children were my family.'

'Well, here's an idea for you. Listen to old Terence. A baby is to come your way. I'll wager a year's profits you'll be nurse and nanny to the tobacconist's child afore long.'

Ettie had been so deep in her misery that what Terence proposed came as a shock.

'Do you really think so?'

'There's a nursery to be got ready, ain't there? Toys and such like. Babies' whatnots. Mittens for its fingers and shoe-sies for its little toe-sies.'

Ettie laughed. Terence always brought a smile to her face.

He frowned. 'Your good mistress won't keep it in a drawer, will she?'

'A baby sleeps in a crib.'

'A crib, yes, that's good! We'll find one.'

'And he or she will want a shawl.'

'Them things you wrap 'em in?'

Ettie laughed again. 'I can knit one.'

'Perfect m'dear. Perfect!'

'But where shall I find the wool?'

Terence patted her hand. 'As your good employer writes, m'dear, God is benevolent,' Terence said gently. 'Now I must get back to my business. Them dead rabbits won't jump in my customers' baskets.' He stood up and patted his round belly under his mucky apron. 'Thank you kindly for the tea and cake. There's a nice bit of liver in the newspaper, there. Fry it up with a potato or two. Last you a few days, m'dear.'

'Thank you, Terence.'

'Don't mention it,' he chuckled. 'Now chin up, girl. And think of the baby!'

CHAPTER TWENTY-FIVE

It was April and even the few sparse trees in Silver Street had begun to bud. But Ettie rarely strolled under them. Her priority was to make up for the lost week and invest in new stock. Therefore, she opened for business at seven each morning except on Sunday and closed at seven in the evenings. The gentlemen from the city approved, for now they didn't have to rush from their clubs and could dally a little longer with their friends. The young working men would call on their way to their offices and sometimes afterwards, too.

By the end of the month, Ettie had repaid four pounds of the outstanding debt. With the help of Mrs Buckle, all the blue cloths had been replaced at minimal cost. Fortunately, trade was so brisk that she was able to meet the next order from Tobacco Dock on time. But this didn't ease the guilt that still remained with her daily. She was filled with foreboding at the prospect of making a confession to Lucas. Might he forgive her when the full story was told? Would Clara think she was to be trusted enough to help with the baby?

These were the worries that Ettie tried to put to one side. At Sunday Mass she would pray to her mother for assistance. To Saint Jude that he might restore Lucas's good favour and understanding. To the Blessed Virgin, to safeguard Clara and her child. And to the crucified Christ to forgive her for the sin she had committed in drinking the green fairy.

At night, she would dream once again of the great catastrophe of December. She would hear Lily's harsh voice, and see the torn velvet cloths and empty till drawer. Sometimes Lucas would appear. His kind face and gentle eyes would be full of rebuke. His silence hurt far deeper than any spoken word. And Clara — Clara! She was absent from Ettie's dreams. Ettie would wake, sweating and disturbed, feeling as though Clara had shunned her, refusing to allow her even one small glimpse of her newly born child.

It was on an early May morning, when an elegant horse-drawn brougham arrived outside. The damson-red carriage was decorated with shiny gold trimmings. The driver, clad in uniform, flat peaked cap and highly polished leather boots, jumped down and assisted his passenger out.

To Ettie's surprise, the young woman made her way into the salon, leaving the driver to stand outside.

'Good day,' she said, smiling at Ettie. For all Ettie's endeavours to increase the business, she had not expected the arrival of a female customer. And, one so young and lovely at that!

Lucas had told her the stores of the West End were sometimes favoured by wealthy women, in search of tobaccos for their fathers, brothers or husbands. But for a lady on her own to visit a Soho establishment was not generally advised. Though Lucas, somewhat biased, had insisted the day would come when *Benjamin & Son. Salon of Quality Tobaccos* would be a lady's preferred tobacconist.

The young woman was pretty with bouncy fair curls that peeped out of her bonnet. Her large green eyes were spaced widely in her oval face and a silk bow was tied discreetly beneath her chin. The pale grey gown she wore flattered her slender curves. She carefully removed each finger of her gloves and leaned forward to inspect the contents of the glass cabinet.

'I'm looking for a gift,' she explained, 'for my twin brother who is seventeen next week.' She looked under her long lashes and whispered coyly, 'I caught him smoking against Mama's wishes. And thought I might tease him a little.'

Ettie roused herself sharply. 'I think I can help you,' she said at once and turned to the shelves behind her. She drew out three boxes and set them on the counter removing the lid of the first. 'These fine cigarettes are made by the Carreras factory of Mornington Crescent — an established and trusted manufacturer.'

'They look rather plain,' decided her customer.

Ettie lifted the lid of the second box. 'These are the purest of Cuban cigars found in stores like Robert Lewis of St James's Street.' A powerful odour drifted from the box and the young woman wrinkled her nose.

'Quite interesting.'

Ettie moved to the third box. Slowly she revealed its contents. Two miniature snuff boxes with mother-of-pearl inlay and six pristine pipes lay on a bed of smooth raffia, their highly ornate bowls overshadowing their slim stems. Set in the centre, were a pair of miniature pipes, toy-like in their appearance.

'The snuffs are popular,' Ettie explained. 'But so are the pipes. Being small, they can be discreetly hidden in a lady's bag or man's pocket.'

The young woman gasped. 'Ingenious! Mama would definitely disapprove.'

Ettie lifted a dainty pipe, its bowl embellished with a briar rose and thorns. 'And only seven shillings and sixpence halfpenny.'

'Why, the cost of a parasol!'

'The pipe is unrepeatable,' Ettie replied quietly. 'A parasol may be bought in dozens.'

The girl laughed. 'Well said. Here, let's see if the pipe will fit in my purse.' She opened her dainty bag. Ettie placed it inside.

'Perfect,' said the girl, but then glanced at the snuffs. 'But I am undecided.'

Ettie smiled. 'Both are excellent choices.'

'I've decided on the pipe,' said the girl with a flourish of her hand. 'And some of those rather boring cigarettes for my brother. Please wrap them separately. He shall have his silly smokes and I shall have my clay pipe and boast to my friends.'

Ettie thought how spirited this young woman was. Not at all afraid of breaking convention or offending a parent. But then, she reflected, to have so much wealth when young, must give a kind of confidence.

When she had her two parcels the customer paid and left with a gracious, 'Goodbye. Perhaps, on another jaunt to Soho, I may look you up for a miniature snuff.'

Ettie followed her to the door and peeped out. To her surprise her customer paused on the cobbles and handed her driver the packages, gazing up at him with an expression of mischief. Words must have been exchanged and they seemed very close.

Ettie was fascinated. It was almost as if he was about to take her in his arms but stopped at the last moment. Instead, she raised her gloved hand to his shoulder, her eyes interlocked with his, in silent message. Playfully, she tilted his flat cap and knocked it to the ground, giggling as she skipped to the carriage.

The driver brushed back his thick, ruffled dark hair and bent to retrieve his cap. Then checked to ensure his mistress was safe inside the carriage.

For the first time, Ettie was given full view of his face.

The world seemed to thunder in her ears. Everything stood still. She felt her throat tighten and wondered if she could breathe again. A rush of heat swamped her. She blinked hard — and harder still. Her eyelids seemed to be the only part of her body able to move.

Unaware of her gaze, he leapt up to the high seat and snatched the reins.

Ettie's fingertips pressed against the glass. A cry left her lips. Was there time to attract his attention?

But the carriage moved forward, its two large rear wheels spinning up the Soho dust in a gritty cloud. Ettie was left with a fleeting memory of a damson-red brougham that might have belonged to aristocracy. But most memorable of all, its beautiful passenger whose departing presence made Silver Street seem more desolate than it ever had before.

She stood still, her heart racing. Could she be mistaken? But no, her eyes had not deceived her. The driver was still the same Michael as she remembered him. Taller perhaps and broader. But he was still her handsome Michael who had once made a vow in Victoria Park that she was his girl.

CHAPTER TWENTY-SIX

That evening, Ettie sat alone in the big, empty house. She hadn't stopped thinking about the young woman who had visited the salon. Or her driver who had waited outside as she purchased her tobacco and pipe. Michael had only been a few feet away . . .

There had been an intimacy between the two young people, an understanding that belied their stations of mistress and servant. They had stood close enough to almost touch one another; their gaze connected. The playful movement of her fingers had made him smile as she knocked his cap to the ground.

Had I known it was Michael, would I have had the courage to go outside and greet him? Ettie wondered.

But the more Ettie thought about this, the clearer the answer became. There was an affection between the girl and Michael. One so obvious that it hurt Ettie deeply to see. She knew the feeling inside her must be jealousy. A fierce emotion that pushed everything else from her mind; the wrench at leaving the orphanage, Gwen and Lily's deception, the theft of Lucas's money and even the admission of her neglect when Lucas and Clara came home.

All of her woes seemed insignificant now. Around and around in her head went the image of Michael and the girl. He had looked so handsome in his uniform. A life of crime had certainly not entrapped him. What were his feelings for his wealthy young mistress who had teased him so playfully?

Her feelings for Michael, Ettie realized, were more than friendship. Jealousy hurt so much. Was it love? She had prayed that one day she would see him again. Then today she had. But now he was a new Michael; someone she didn't know.

Ettie went to the salon and lit a candle. She took it to the counter and sat on the stool beside Rose. Here in the flickering glow, she poured out her heart.

'What would he have said to me if we'd spoken?' she asked, peering up at the portrait. 'Would he even have remembered me? I thought we'd be together in the end. He told me I was his girl. But now I know I'm not.'

Ettie tried not to be miserable. The good Lord had answered all her prayers. Michael had prospered and left his wild ways behind him. Lucas's business was all in good order; his recent letter had expressed his delight at Ettie's own news. Clara's good health and happiness had returned since Dr Ruegg had told her the baby would be born at the sanatoria in August. The result — a long-awaited child that would unite Lucas and Clara forever. And for herself, Ettie thought selfishly — if she was forgiven for December's mistake — a chance to help Clara look after the baby.

It wouldn't do to mope like this. It certainly would not do!

'*Buck up Ettie! Show the world your mettle.*'

The words came out of nowhere.

Ettie smiled through her held-back tears. 'I will try, Rose,' she promised, blowing out the candle. 'Thank you and goodnight.'

But for all her good intentions, she lay awake, unable to sleep. Michael was all she could think about; Michael and the beautiful young woman who had captured his heart.

* * *

'Ettie, Ettie, are you there?' It was just after she had closed the salon door when there was a loud bang on the kitchen door. 'It's me, Terence.'

She hurried to open it. 'Terence, what's wrong?'

'Not a single thing. Didn't want to trouble you during business hours. Come and see this.' He tugged her out into the warm May evening. 'What do you think?'

Ettie stared curiously at the scruffy wicker cradle perched lopsidedly on a four-wheeled iron frame. 'It's one of these new-fangled perambulators,' Terence said proudly. He lifted the cradle and set it down again on the chassis straps. 'Nothing wrong with it, m'dear. Bit rough round the edges. But all in all, a bargain.'

'Where did you get it?' Ettie stepped forward to inspect the odd-looking contraption.

'Aggie,' he told her excitedly. 'The old girl had it priced at a couple of bob. I said it was for you. She says, so the tobacconist's girl has a baby? I says, not her own personal baby, oh no. A little one, coming soon from elsewhere. So, Aggie says, Terence my boy, she can have it. And she can have these thingies, too. Dress it all cosy. And so forth.' He picked up a bundle of clothes tied in string. 'No cost to Aggie. They arrived by the back door, if you see what I mean.' He gave a sly wink.

Ettie smiled up at her old friend. 'Aggie's very kind.'

'When she knew it was for the poor innocent victim of them circus charlatans — she coughed up.'

Ettie was embarrassed. 'Does everyone know about what happened at Christmas?'

'Didn't need to tell 'em. Look at this.' He pulled a rolled newspaper from his apron pocket. Stretching it out over the cradle, he jabbed a finger. 'See here. *The London Daily*. Told you we wasn't the only ones to be rooked.'

'Two women and a man were apprehended in Winchester yesterday, formerly of Soho, London. Suspected to be members of a band of dangerous vagrants and thieves touring the

country, they were found in possession of jewels and silverware stolen from the country seat of Lord Grosvenor. The opportunists were caught in the act. Thought to have duped their victims by portraying themselves as French artistes, these Whitechapel born and bred criminals resisted arrest to their cost. The male was shot in the foot. Unfortunately, a policeman was severely injured during the fracas. Charged with resisting arrest, burglary and grievous bodily harm to an officer of the law, this vicious gang will stand trial for its crimes at the Old Bailey.'

Ettie took in a sharp breath. She felt slightly faint. 'Do you think this could be Gwen, Lily and Gino?'

'Certainly m'dear.'

'A vicious gang?'

'Dangerous thieves, vagrants, the newspaper says. Lived in Soho. Not French at all. Jewels and silverware. Just think yourself lucky m'dear. They could have done you in.'

'I'm sure they wouldn't.' Yet Ettie couldn't help thinking of Lily and her menacing change in character.

'I can hardly believe it meself,' sighed Terence, shaking his head. 'Wouldn't have thought butter'd melt in Gwen's mouth.'

'So they didn't belong to the circus?'

'Doubt it, m'dear.'

Ettie held fast to the perambulator. Her knees felt weak. She had taken a gang of thieves to be her true friends.

'And there was me,' muttered Terence, interrupting her thoughts, 'cutting up my best meat for free, serving it to — well, they wasn't ladies, no no! And there was you, an innocent. Could've been so much worse, far worse.' He raised his hairy eyebrows. 'The law has 'em now. They'll not be out thieving and deceiving again. Strikes me you could bring a charge, m'dear. The coppers might get your takings back.'

'But what could I hope to gain in accusing them?' Ettie replied. 'Lucas's money will surely be spent.'

'True. But you would have reprisal.'

Ettie shook her head. 'I should never have drunk the green fairy.'

'They fixed you, child.'

'I learned a lesson.'

Terence gave her a sound pat on the back. 'That's it. That's it. Look to the future, that's right. Now, what say we take this vehicle out for a walkies? Up to the green and back. 'See what needs oiling and repairing.'

Ettie smiled. She now had a perambulator to wheel the baby in and some clothes to wash and darn. And on Sunday after Mass, she would set about clearing the small spare room next to hers. It was full of tobacco boxes and other unwanted salon items. The room was small, but large enough to accommodate a baby, with curtains put up at the window, a set of drawers and a pretty picture for Clara's little girl or boy. For Ettie, there would be a tiny person to love and take care of for Clara.

Ettie felt a flicker of her old happy self; the Ettie before Gwen, Lily and Gino. The Ettie before losing Michael.

CHAPTER TWENTY-SEVEN

A soft June breeze lifted Ettie's newly hung curtains in the nursery. It was here in this small room that Ettie had spent many hours preparing for the baby's homecoming.

Whenever the salon doors closed, it was in the nursery she could be found; cleaning, polishing and dreaming of the family's return.

Her greatest achievement so far, was her trade with the rag and bone man. He had, with some persuasion, exchanged a crib and nursing chair for the collection of battered Tobacco Dock crates that had accumulated since Christmas in the salon's backyard. Ettie was delighted. For though the crib was old, it swung to and fro on a squeaky iron mechanism. She had made a liner for its interior and a frill of white cotton for its sides. As for the nursing chair, it had needed a good wax but was perfect for Clara's petite form.

A tobacco box, covered in brown paper now stood in the corner on the thick rug that Ettie had carried in from the floor of her own room. This box would contain all the toys that would doubtless appear. Perhaps there would be a pretty porcelain or wax doll if the baby was a Charlotte or Emily or even a Clara. Or a tiny wooden dog with a real horsehair tail for a John, James or Lucas.

Then there were the silks that Clara would buy for her daughter as she grew and learned to embroider. Or the wooden frame and its many coloured beads a little lad might enjoy to learn his numbers.

Ettie had all this planned, and though the room looked a little sparse with only the crib and chair, it was clean as a new pin. The next time Terence called she would ask him to help her remove an elderly chest from the attic. Though threaded with cobwebs and needing a good dust, it was free of worm and would fit snugly under the window.

Into its deep drawers she would lay the baby's clothes. Aggie's bundle had been washed, ironed and darned. Ettie loved to hold close the long white dress, somewhat faded but still entirely practical. The fragrant smell of the newly laundered article reminded her of the convent laundry. Of those freezing days, when her fingers turned blue with cold as she wrung out the nuns' wimples and folded them over the rack. And, the summer afternoons, when a flood of sweat oozed from her every pore.

Ettie often allowed herself a reverie as she worked in the nursery. Sometimes she sat on her heels and rocked an imaginary baby. Sometimes she whispered words of love or sang hymns. And at night, should the future child wake, she would rush to comfort and soothe. Just as she had done for Kathy, Megan and Amy.

If only she had a small crucifix to hang on the wall! Jesus would watch over His dear child and keep Clara and her baby safe on the long journey back to England.

Ettie knew there was only one place she could find this gift.

* * *

The mid-day Angelus was ringing out over Soho as the pony and trap arrived outside the salon. Ettie climbed aboard, dressed in her Sunday best. She wore a soft blue wool summer coat purchased from Aggie and a straw Panama hat with an upturned brim. Ettie had covered an unsightly hole in the base of the crown with a pale blue ribbon. To keep it steady on her head she had folded her long, thick hair into a neat coppery bun, pinning it accordingly. Before she left home, she had taken her rosary from the crib and tucked it in her pocket. Perhaps the nuns would allow her a half hour's prayer in the chapel.

Ettie leaned forward to pay her fare in advance. She had hired the driver's services yesterday as he'd passed by the salon. He wore a cap over his eyes and was not very talkative as he sat up on the dicky seat but he agreed to take her all across London and back to the East End for a fair rate.

It was now over a month since she'd seen Michael. The ache inside her heart had not healed but time had brought acceptance. And with it, came a desire to make peace with the past. A flicker of excitement went through her as she began the journey back to her old home.

Out the pony trotted from the dingy, dishevelled terraces and shops of Soho and into the wide streets of London city. They passed grand mansions with their gleaming white stucco exteriors and pretty front doors, black-painted railings and top-hatted gentlemen, stately hansom cabs, landaus and carriages, shady greens and flowery borders. London was a city resting from its busy week.

Ettie recalled her last journey to Oxford Street to buy Clara's new clothes. Perhaps her next visit would be made with Clara and the baby?

When Buckingham Palace appeared in all its shining glory, Ettie took a breath. One day she intended to push the perambulator past the red-coated sentries who stood to attention in their tall black hats and tell her tiny charge about how the young Victoria had inherited the throne at just eighteen. How she had fallen in love and married her first cousin, Prince Albert. And best of all, how the couple had won the people's hearts and minds.

As the pony trotted towards the great River Thames, Ettie began to think of the news she would give to the nuns.

How she had learned to keep accounts and open the salon in Lucas's absence. Sister Patrick would raise an eyebrow at the gentlemen's conversations on politics and the military. But then there was the problem of mentioning the decanters and their regular filling to keep the patrons happy. This perhaps, could be no better or worse than the incident of the green fairy.

Ettie's pale cheeks flushed in confusion as the warm breeze rushed past blowing whips of coppery hair around her face. Might she spoil all her positive news with an event so bad?

After some thought, as the green trees of the parks passed by, Ettie came to a decision. She would instead, describe the magnificent mountains of Switzerland and the good Dr Ruegg who had cured Clara of her malady. For if anyone appeared to be a saint it was this clever man. Only praise could be heaped on his head, a far more wholesome topic of conversation. And one that shed a far better light on Ettie's new life. A life that Mother Superior herself had arranged. A life that had been approved by Sister Patrick.

CHAPTER TWENTY-EIGHT

All the sights that Ettie had witnessed on the day she travelled to Soho, returned again. The magnificent Houses of Parliament reflected in the water of the great river, Cleopatra's Needle pointing upward to the heavens, the steamers and river traffic, an Embankment enjoyed by the Sunday strollers and the Tower of London and its looming shadow that gave Ettie a chill on the back of her neck.

This time they went by way of Ludgate Hill and Ettie glimpsed the spectacular dome of Saint Paul's Cathedral. She held her breath as the clouds parted and a ladder of sunshine reached down to its summit. It was a sign, Ettie decided, that her plans for the day had received God's blessing.

It was at the bottom of the hill that the pony tired a little and the trap bounced slowly over the rough cobbles of the East End. Ettie recognized the sights and sounds of the Commercial Road and her heart beat even quicker. For just a little further on was Poplar and her destination.

By the time they arrived in the East India Dock Road, the old nag refused to continue.

'You'd better get off here, Miss. I'll water and feed her in the tavern stables,' the driver told her. 'You know where you are?'

Ettie nodded as he helped her dismount. 'The convent isn't far from here.'

'Hope you find it,' he replied, taking the reins and beginning to lead the pony towards the drinking house. 'Can't say as I've heard of it but then I'm not from round this way.'

'Where shall I meet you?'

'I'll be here when you want your ride back.'

Ettie felt nervous as she walked down the street. Just a short distance away was the market which she had visited so often with Sister Ukunda. A short walk on and she would arrive at the high walls of the convent. What would it be like to see the nuns again?

As if her blessing was continuing, the late May sunshine spilled down on the narrow streets, tracing a golden pathway for her to follow. There was no market held today, but the traders' stalls were collapsed and leaned against the dirty walls of the terraced houses. Stray dogs and mice scurried here and there. Street urchins in their tatty caps and torn breeches sat on the upturned sides of barrows. A rank smell of rotting vegetables rose up with the briny odours of the docks.

Making her way through the rubbish-strewn lanes and smoke-tarred terraces, Ettie came to a long road that she knew so well. At the end of it was the convent of the Sisters of Clemency and the orphanage where she had lived for the most part of her life.

And where she was returning today.

CHAPTER TWENTY-NINE

The old gate was tied with a length of rope, its frayed ends tucked into a plank of wood that substituted for the broken lock. The squeak that the gate emitted was loud enough to send a wild tabby cat shooting out from the bushes.

Ettie now not only felt nervous, but apprehensive, for the long path leading up to the convent and orphanage was completely overgrown with weeds and briars. She lifted her skirt to avoid them catching on her hem and studied the way forward as best she could. One trip and she'd end up in the undergrowth or a prickly bush.

Breath held, she advanced slowly, noting that it was impossible to see very far ahead or either side of her. The tall, slender trees that had once provided an elegant entry to the grounds were now a dense wilderness. Mother Superior had always insisted that the gardener's priority was the entrance to the convent. For it was here that the bishop arrived, driven on the sandy path in his elegant coach right up to the doorstep, where a carpet or rug was placed down for him to walk on.

But this might be another world altogether, Ettie thought, as she negotiated the clumps of dandelions and tall grasses that had invaded the driveway.

When at last the convent came into view, she stopped abruptly, her eyes opened wide at the unrecognizable scene. For the beautiful pale brick building and belfry had changed beyond recognition. Every window had been boarded or was partially covered, though not in a very secure way. Some of the glass was exposed, with needle-like fragments that revealed a bare interior.

The belfry itself had collapsed, and lay at a twisted angle above the broken slates, as if any moment it might fall in on itself. The roof was a puzzle of exposed timbers, that had attracted a community of pigeons.

Taking a hesitant step towards the entrance that was now entirely covered in ivy, the smell of dampness and decay emitted from a broken window. Carefully she picked her way towards it, recoiling at the obnoxious rotting smell.

Keeping her distance, she tried to peer inside. Where was the heavy, ornate door that led to the chapel? Her eyes adjusted slowly and to her horror she saw there was nothing there. The chapel or what was once the chapel was now just a space in which vegetation grew over what remained of the altar. Stepping a little closer, Ettie stared at the ravaged interior. The rows of pews had vanished, the beautiful glass windows and holy pictures were now just crumbling walls. A stranger would never know that this was once a place of worship.

With her heart drumming under her ribs, she retraced her steps over the weeds and took a side path to the schoolroom and dormitory at the rear. But as she came upon the place that she knew so well, tears filled her eyes.

Burned timbers pointed upwards where once the desks had stood in their neat rows. Blackened rafters lay crisscrossed on the earth between piles of ashes. Over all the chaos had crept a bright green lattice of ivy, clinging to even the smallest fragments of debris.

'How could this have happened?' Ettie questioned as she carefully negotiated the derelict site, her eyes scouring the charred remains of what had once been her beloved classroom. Had she not known that it had been a schoolroom once, where children had occupied the wooden desks and learned their lessons from the books the nuns so lovingly preserved, then she would not have recognized it at all.

With a sense of foreboding she picked her way over the thistles and briars towards the dormitories. Even before she reached the annexe that housed the boys' and girls' sleeping quarters, she guessed that she would find very little of the home she remembered.

But to discover the skeletons of a dozen broken and rusted metal bedsteads piled one upon the other in an overgrown thicket was almost more than she could bear. There was nothing that remained of the dormitories but a scrapheap reclaimed by nature. Ettie could no longer hold back the tears. Her heart felt again as though it was breaking. Where was the home she so loved and fondly remembered?

It was some while before she thought of the laundry. Drying her tears on her handkerchief she made her way slowly down the incline to the outhouse where she had worked summer and winter alike with Sister Ukunda and Sister Patrick. Afraid to discover another ruin, she could barely bring herself to look for the ancient building that had accommodated the nuns' ancient wash house.

So, it was with some surprise that she discovered a clearing where the laundry still stood. It was a little more ramshackle than it had been almost two years previously, but otherwise appeared in good repair; with a roof that had not collapsed, though it sagged dangerously in the middle. Small windows still retained their glass. A battered wooden door swung open as if to greet her and from inside, a faint movement.

'Hello? Who's there?' she called.

The sound of shuffling footsteps and the door creaking wide caused Ettie to hold her breath.

An old man stood there; silver-haired, bent and bearded, but with a stumble he came forward and squinted into her face.

A shaky smile went over Arthur the gardener's lips as he said in a gruff whisper, 'Well bless my cotton socks, if it ain't the O'Reilly girl! She said you'd be back one day, and she was right.'

CHAPTER THIRTY

Ettie looked fondly around the laundry's interior, which had never been in the best of order but had always felt homely as if the many years of washing and scrubbing had become part of its character. The ancient washtub and dolly — now unused — lay on its side, fallen from the bricks it was once steadied on. The glass windows that had run with steam were now crudely half-boarded to preserve the glass and the ceiling rack on which the nuns' wimples had dried, was missing. But Arthur had made a home for himself here, she could plainly see. There was a chair that was holed and missing its stuffing, a few pots and pans piled on the wormy dresser and a stove of sorts that somehow heated his food.

'The fire from hell broke out not long after the nuns left,' Arthur told her as they sat together by an old table. 'As if the devil had been waiting to make his mark.'

Ettie felt the hairs on her neck stand up as he described the event that had ended the convent's days. The gardener's lined face was barely visible under his silver cap of hair that straggled over his ears to join his unkempt beard.

'Sister Ukunda took ill, see,' he continued as he gestured with his arthritic hands. 'She lay on her bed and never got up again. They found her one morning, cold as ice. We buried her ourselves, the two nuns and me, down the hill by the convent wall, just as she said she wanted.'

Ettie's eyes were moist with tears. 'What happened then?'

'The bishop sent 'em packing, the poor cows.'

Ettie wiped her eyes again. 'If only I'd come before.'

'Wouldn't have made no difference. The land was sold from under the nuns' feet. Just as if it wasn't a sacred, holy place that had stood for years doing good and giving kids a start in life. But the new owners got their comeuppance and went to the wall. Some say they was cursed for what they did. Some say the bishop was cursed an' all. 'Cos he died an 'orrible death in the fire.'

'The bishop died in the fire?' Ettie gasped.

'No one knows why he come back here that day. But rumour has it that the greedy old fox came sniffin' around to see if there was anything left valuable like. When they found him after the fire, there wasn't much left, just his shoes. Always wore the best polished leather. Don't matter about the starving kids on street corners with nothing but bare skin on their feet. Oh, no, don't matter about them!'

Ettie shuddered. It was hard to believe the bishop had died in such a gruesome way. Had he really been cursed?

'I lost me old nag this year,' Arthur continued. 'So I retired and made meself at home here. Rozzers don't mind. I keep an eye on the place for 'em.'

'What will happen to the land now?' Ettie asked.

'Who knows?' Arthur shrugged. 'They say it's been nabbed from Rome's coffers by the revenue men.' He poured her tea from an ancient tin pot and handed her the chipped mug. 'No milk, but it's hot.' He leaned back in his chair and pleating his silver eyebrows, he told her again, 'She knew you'd come back.'

'Sister Patrick?'

'Said you was like her own kin.'

Ettie felt weak with a deep sense of loss. 'Did she leave a message for me?'

Arthur nodded vigorously. 'Said you was to go to the chapel and there you'd find her letter on the pew.'

'But that was before the fire?'

'I wish I could tell you otherwise.'

Ettie bit her lip hard so that she wouldn't cry. When she thought of that precious letter going up in flames, it was almost a physical pain.

'I miss her,' she whispered hoarsely. 'I miss them all. The sisters and the children and the convent.'

'Was a terrible deed that bishop did to the nuns, not to mention them poor kids. If you want my honest opinion, I reckon it wasn't just the earthly flames that got him, but another kind, that don't ever burn out.'

Once again Ettie shivered at the bitterness in the old man's voice. What good would bitterness or anger do now? The Sisters of Clemency had given service to God for many years before the new bishop arrived and made his fatal directive. Whatever God's intentions were for the nuns, they had avoided the dreadful fire that had claimed their beloved convent.

'There was an orphan boy called Michael Wilson,' she said suddenly. 'Do you remember him?'

'The one who'd been in trouble with the law?'

Ettie nodded. 'Has he ever come back?'

'Not that I know of. But doubt I'd recognize him. The old mince pies are not what they were. I'll have to get meself one of them spyglasses.'

This made her smile as it brought back her childhood and the happy days she had spent in the care of the nuns. 'Sister Patrick wore little round spectacles on the tip of her nose that misted up as she worked over the washtub.'

Arthur sat forward and narrowed his gaze. 'If my memory serves me right — which it don't much these days — you was always around them nuns, trailing after 'em and working like stink in this very laundry. I used to think it weren't much of a life for a kid.'

'I owe my life to Sister Patrick,' Ettie insisted. 'She found me in my dying mother's arms just outside this laundry on

Christmas Day. Her name was Colleen O'Reilly and she was born in Dublin, a place named Henrietta Street, after which I'm named.'

''Enrietta, Street, eh? You ever been there?'

'No, but one day perhaps.'

The old man rose to his feet with a rheumatic groan. 'Got something for you, gel.'

Ettie watched him hobble to the washtub. He beckoned her over. 'Can't get down on my knees these days. Reach inside and you'll find something there.'

Ettie knelt and put her hand in the dark space filled with cobwebs.

'Right at the back it's hidden.'

At last she felt a package and drew it out. Brushing off the dirt and dust she handed it to Arthur.

'It's yours,' he told her.

Ettie slowly unwrapped the faded newspaper covering. Piece by thin piece the layers dropped away until she held in her hand a shining silver crucifix.

'Belonged to that bloody so-called bishop,' Arthur wheezed. 'Found it 'afore the coppers came, buried in all the — well, what remained of the blighter. Reckon it's got to do someone some good. Might as well be you.'

Ettie had forgotten that her purpose in coming here today was to ask the nuns for a crucifix. It was as if Heaven itself was answering her prayer.

'I'll give it to someone who needs it,' Ettie said as she thought of Clara and the baby and the space on the nursery wall.

'You do that. Hope it brings better luck to them.'

Ettie tucked it in her purse. 'Arthur, would you take me to the place where you buried Sister Ukunda?'

'Give me a minute to put on my coat and boots.'

When Arthur was dressed in his long overcoat and hobnail boots, he led the way from the laundry and down the incline to the bottom of the slope. There in the shade of the trees was a small hump of grass, bearing a hand-hewn wooden cross.

'I carved it meself. Don't read or write see. By the time I got 'round to puttin' it in the ground, the nuns had gone orf. But she knows it's for her as I keep the grass short. Nice little spot, like she wanted.'

'Thank you, Arthur.'

He gave a throaty cough and Ettie listened to him walk away, his heavy, laboured footsteps the only sound to join the song of the birds.

Ettie closed her eyes tight as she stood there and thought of her life with the Sisters of Clemency and the children of the orphanage. The tears that squeezed through her eyelids were ones of gratitude and love for the nuns who had taught her to put her trust in the Lord and to believe that there was always hope, no matter how hard the obstacles in life were. And though her faith had been tested, it was only dented a little.

Just a little.

'Rest in peace, dear Sister Ukunda,' she whispered. 'I miss you. I miss you all. Amen.'

* * *

It was growing dark as Ettie made her way to the tavern and found the driver sitting outside the stables with a group of cartmen and their horses.

'Did you find what you was looking for?' he asked when he saw her.

'Yes, but the convent and orphanage burned down.'

'Waste of your money coming all this way, then,' he observed but Ettie thought differently. For the crucifix was tucked in her purse and she believed, had come to her by miraculous means. The fact that it had previously belonged to the bishop was a little disconcerting. But, she intended to hang it on the wall in the nursery, where it would do far more good than it had ever done in his possession.

Her driver stood up and bid farewell to his acquaintances, then led Ettie round to the stables. The little pony was munching on the last of its chaff and gave a snort of recognition when it saw them.

Ettie climbed up into the trap and settled herself for the long journey back to Soho. By the time they reached the Commercial Road and then Aldgate, the sky had become stormy with clouds hanging in swollen grey pouches. The Tower looked even more menacing. The River Thames had turned to gunmetal, whipped into white crests as the tide bore in from the estuary.

But Ettie's thoughts were no longer on the scenery. They were with Sister Patrick and Mother Superior who were now far away in another land. She saw in her mind's eye the charred embers and rusting bed frames that were the only remains of the convent and orphanage; a place where homeless children had found sanctuary, just as her mother had on that Christmas Day in 1880. It had been a refuge full of love and hope even though the life there was hard. The orphans had known that the nuns cared for them in a very special way. Ettie considered herself the most fortunate of all in having the affection of Sister Patrick. What had been written in her letter? Ettie wondered. What personal sentiments had it expressed?

She would never know. But Sister Patrick had considered it important enough to leave word for her and that in itself was enough to comfort Ettie.

As the cab turned into the city and followed along the shadowy banks of the river, her thoughts travelled to a small green mound at the bottom of the hill where Sister Ukunda was buried. It was as if, no matter what happened in the years to come, there would always be a guardian angel to watch over the holy space that the convent and orphanage had once occupied.

CHAPTER THIRTY-ONE

A letter of a far different kind arrived later that month. Though the handwriting was Lucas's and there was no mistake it was from abroad, Ettie felt there was something disquieting about its presence on the mat.

She held it in her hands for a few moments, before sitting on the stool as was her custom before drawing the blinds and checking the accounts and orders were correct. She kept a very close watch on the salon's performance. It was important to vary the tobaccos, pipes and the boxes of snuff in the smoking room, so there was always fresh interest for the gentlemen. As a matter of routine, she completed the accounts each month with her own addition of five shillings, though last month she had kept aside a small sum for groceries.

But this morning her attention was riveted on the personal letter placed on the counter before her. What was so different about this envelope, she asked herself? The paper quality was the same as was the franking, yet her heart was racing with apprehension.

It was the way Lucas had written her name and the address; a little too wild, loops entangling and punctuation erratic. As if the joy and excitement that always comprised Lucas's letters lately had been exchanged for speed.

Ettie took the knife from the drawer and slipped its tip beneath the fold.

Just one sheet fell out. The address. The date. A paragraph. A scrawled signature.

> *'Dearest Ettie, I cannot write more than a few words. I am here, seated in the shadow of the towering mountains on the chaise longue, but Clara is not here today. She has been taken to the hospital wing of the sanatoria. Since June she has been a little unwell. Dr Ruegg has called in the very best specialists. I felt confident in their judgements and was positive of mind until yesterday when Clara had a painful spasm. In the night, another pain took her. Early this morning, Dr Ruegg and the specialists attended. I write in order to ask for your prayers, to the God in whom you have such faith and who has answered you before. I am not a brave man. I am weak with fear. Pray for our dear Clara, Ettie, and for our little one. Your miserable friend, Lucas Benjamin.'*

Ettie did not read the words again for they were too heart-wrenching. Instead she returned the letter to its envelope and for a few minutes more sat on the stool, her hands clasped together in prayer as Lucas had requested. But soon the first customer arrived, a young gentleman from a city office requiring swift attention.

When Terence called the next day with half a dozen freshly laid hen's eggs still warm on the straw, for the first time Ettie showed little enthusiasm.

'You've not been right since your visit to Poplar,' he complained as she brewed the tea. 'Are you still grieving?'

'No, Terence. After all, what's to grieve about? Buildings are nothing, really. It's people that count.'

'It was your home an' all. Burned to cinders.'

'I have a good home here.' Ever since receiving Lucas's letter, Ettie had not thought about the convent, or Sister Patrick and Sister Ukunda or even the crucifix that was now hanging on the wall above the baby's crib. Her head had been full of Lucas, Clara and the baby and what was happening all those many miles away in Switzerland.

She showed the letter to Terence. He read it and looked up at her, a frown on his forehead. 'So the mistress is ailing?'

Ettie nodded. 'The thought that she might be ill again and with Lucas so miserable, well, it upsets me.'

'Now, now, lass, chin up.'

'Do you think the baby is suffering?'

'Dear me, no. Mother and child are in the best of hands. Specialists an' all. The tobacconist said so, didn't he?'

'Yes, but Clara isn't strong. And the baby . . .'

'The best you can do for 'em,' Terence interrupted, 'is say them prayers of yours. Over and over, say them. Just like you was asked.'

Ettie attempted to smile. 'I'll try, Terence.'

'If I could say prayers, I'd join you. But me mind wanders like. Goes off at a tangent. Best thing I can do is ask my Gladys. She's nearer to the Gov'nor than I am.'

They drank their tea together as usual, but this time Ettie found little to say and Terence even less.

That night Ettie said her prayers for the family as she knelt in the nursery under the crucifix. They were very intense, just as her prayers for the orphans had been. And the thought crossed her mind as she climbed into bed — a thought she felt guilty for even thinking — that despite all her praying, life had brought a catastrophe along one day and eased it briefly the next, only to repeat the cycle again.

* * *

Lucas's next letter arrived only a week later and it sent her into a complete panic. Without putting on her bonnet, she ran down Silver Street, all the way to the butcher's, where Terence was hanging out his rows of dead fowl. The late July sunshine was beginning to fry the cobbled streets, already stinking and fly-ridden.

'Lord love us, what's up?' Terence asked when he saw her, an expression of alarm on his face.

'Terence, I've had another letter from Mr Benjamin.'

'It's not his missus, is it?' He pushed his grubby fingers over his dirty apron, then took a rag and wiped each one. 'Or the baby?'

'No, it's not about my mistress or the baby,' Ettie faltered. 'Well, not directly, although it concerns the money . . .'

Terence held up his hand. 'Stop there a minute, lass. What money?'

Ettie felt her stomach drop. In order to ask for Terence's help, which was the only way to carry out Lucas's wishes, she would have to reveal her secret. But her mind still replayed the scenes of terrible mischief that had been done to her by Gwen and Lily. What if Terence had befriended her in order to wait until the day when he would learn something to his advantage?

'Ah, don't answer, my dear,' said Terence before she could reply. 'If it's got to do with shekels or politics my advice is to keep schtum. Steer clear of two subjects that always get people's heckles up.'

'But Terence, I'm in a dreadful fix.'

'I want to help you,' Terence said calmly, 'but I can see it's tricky. You know I'm your friend?'

Ettie felt herself blush to the roots of her hair. 'I know, yes I do, but . . .'

'But some friends are not what they seem, like them circus rotters?'

Ettie hung her head. She was ashamed of the distrust and caution inside her, as though it was a poison left behind by the green fairy.

The buzzing of flies around the open mouths of the dead animals and the shouts of the marketeers erecting their stalls, caused Terence to grasp her arm and wheel her into the cool of the shop. Ettie saw that the slabs of meat had not yet been laid out for his customers' inspection. She guessed that even Terence's patience might be tested if she dithered.

'Now Ettie,' he said firmly as they stood on the sawdust floor, as yet unsullied by trade. 'You can trust me, yes, course you can. I'm just an old fella who's been grateful for the friendship you've given me — a young lady who didn't bat an eyelid when I told her of my indiscretions with them lying, deceiving women. But I'm too old to do a moonlight flit. Too fond of you to tell a tall story. Too respectful of your Christian nature to deceive you, my dear. No, no. I wouldn't. But you must make up your own mind. Weigh up what you know about Terence the butcher. Put the good and bad on the scales and judge for yourself.'

Ettie smiled hesitantly. 'I do trust you, Terence.'

'I'm glad to hear it.'

'I've been given a duty to perform and can't do it alone.'

'And it concerns this — money?'

Ettie nodded.

'Can the problem wait until after business? There will customers appearing soon and there won't be a sausage out for them to inspect.'

Ettie knew that Lucas's request was of the utmost urgency. He had written in large letters 'I BESEECH YOU ETTIE, DO THIS WITHOUT HESITATION'.

'Will you visit me this evening?'

'Indeed I will.'

'I'll wait for you.'

'Good, m'dear, good. I'll not let you down. And don't go worrying yourself. We'll get a result, so we will, whatever it is.'

But all day, Ettie was on tenterhooks. Between the customers coming into the salon, she read the short letter over and over again. Every minute that passed by seemed to be wasted. Every customer a distraction to the plea that Lucas had written with such urgency.

CHAPTER THIRTY-TWO

The butcher arrived at a few minutes past seven o'clock. Ettie drew the blinds securely and beckoned him into the salon where, in the light of a single candle, she passed him Lucas's letter.

'My dear,' said Terence with a puzzled frown after reading it, 'I see it quite clearly now. The tobacconist writes with some urgency I agree, and I can only assume it's of some financial importance. Says here he has written ahead to advise them of your visit to deposit a sum of money. In view of the request, I recommend a sturdy purse or portmanteau and the hire of a reputable cab.'

'Terence, I can't call a cab. And neither a purse or portmanteau would be of use.'

'Why ever not?'

'Because . . .' Ettie had little doubt now that she must reveal the hiding place. For she could not transport the cast-iron chest herself, or even transfer it to a large bag as Terence had suggested. 'Because Terence, well — I'll show you.'

Checking again that the blinds were securely drawn, Ettie went to the shelf and the lever. Operating the mechanism took only a few seconds and when the wooden panel was released, Terence gave a muffled gasp.

'My dear, what's this?'

Ettie lifted the floorboard. She took out the key and unlocked the chest. When the lid was fully open, Terence let out an astonished gasp. 'Good grief, good grief! By all the saints!' Terence stared at her and back to the chest brimming with leather moneybags. 'Are my eyes deceiving me?'

'No, Terence. Every bag is full.'

'By gad, business must have been good?'

'Yes, very good indeed.'

'And you've stored it all here in the wall?'

'Just as Mr Benjamin told me to.'

'But you could be raided!' suggested the butcher fiercely. 'Them circus harlots might have fleeced you. Might even have done you in. Your tobacconist needs his brains tested. Leaving a little 'un like you to guard his fortune!'

Ettie shook her head. 'Mr Benjamin's brains are full of his wife's condition. He has no one else to help him.'

'Even so, this is a liberty,' blustered Terence. 'The man should engage an accountant or solicitor to oversee his profits! Why there must be a hundred pounds or more in that box!'

'Three hundred and thirty pounds, ten shillings and six-pence to be precise,' Ettie said quietly. She had counted every coin to make sure.

Terence made a choking noise. 'Three hundred and . . .' he coughed and spluttered, flapping his hand wildly.

'Including the return of my wages to settle my debt.'

'Your debt?' he repeated aghast. 'My dear, you have no debt to settle! It's the tobacconist who is in debt to you!' He brought out his handkerchief, a little cleaner than usual and tipping back his hat, pushed it over his sweating face. 'Ettie, you are but a child and he a grown man! And though I know you think the world of your employer, he has saddled you with a dangerous duty. Transporting this chest — well, how would you do it? Every eye in Silver Street would be on you. Any cab driver, a rogue. Perish the thought, but you might be held up and robbed!'

'But I have to try, Terence,' Ettie wailed. 'This letter is different — it's desperate!'

'There, there, don't upset yourself.' The butcher's gaze softened as he studied her with care and concern. He raised his hands in defeat and slapped them on his knees.

'You are like a daughter to me and I can't refuse you. No, I would not do that even though I'm inflamed with indignation at this man's expectations. I would like him to know that I protest at the situation he puts you in.' He puffed out his red cheeks in annoyance. 'Nevertheless, I suppose we must do something.'

Ettie flung her arms around him. 'Thank you, Terence, oh, thank you. When will we go?'

'I suppose it must be soon,' he muttered.

'It's of the utmost urgency, as you can read.'

He rolled his eyes and scratched his chin. 'Then let me think of a plan.'

Ettie waited anxiously, listening to his protesting mumbles and sniffs as he frowned in concentration.

'Most important we don't let on about our errand,' he decided at last. 'Or we'd be lambs to the slaughter.'

'Then how do we transport it?'

The butcher heaved in a breath and lowered his voice. 'Here's what we'll do. I shall hire a cart and horse from a smithy I know this very evening. Not a comfy ride to the City, no, but workmanlike and won't arouse no suspicion. At six sharp in the morning, I'll arrive in your backyard. We shall load that monster between us before Silver Street is awake. With luck and a fair wind, we'll be back before nine.'

'I'll be waiting, Terence,' she assured him.

'Now you'd better lock the chest away or the scent of all that loot will seep under the door and alert the whole neighbourhood.'

When the wooden panel was reinstated and Terence had left to hire the horse and cart, Ettie went to her bedroom. She took out her Sunday best coat and bonnet for she wanted to look presentable tomorrow when she turned over Lucas's chest to London's Bank of England.

CHAPTER THIRTY-THREE

Ettie was ready long before Terence arrived, a little knot of anxiety in her chest. The morning was overcast and Terence sweated as he took the greater weight of the chest and they dragged, pushed and hoisted it aboard the waiting cart. It was a few moments before he restored his breathing but once their burden was hidden by sackcloth, Ettie felt much relieved their struggle was over.

A fresh breeze struck up as they passed down Silver Street, keeping Ettie alert for unwanted attention. But it was only the marketeers who, bleary eyed, were rigging up their stalls. Once Soho was behind them, Terence began to whistle, resuming his usual calm demeanour.

The lamplighters were out with their long poles, working amidst the early morning smells from the coffee stalls and bakeries. The roads were not yet congested and recognizing very few landmarks, Ettie suspected that Terence was taking a short cut to the city by way of back lanes.

'You all right, young beauty?' he asked as he tickled the horse's rump with the whip and adjusted the tilt of his battered hat, a tri-corner style suited to a man of his generation.

Ettie smiled, thinking how they had both made an effort to look presentable for the clerks of the Bank of England.

She had read in the convent's history books that the bank was named The Old Lady of Threadneedle Street, which had amused her until she thought of all those precious books now lost in the fire. It had taken a few minutes to remind herself how lucky she was; if it wasn't for Terence, she would never have been able to make this journey.

'How long now?' she enquired.

'Just a half hour up the road there's Princes Street and we'll turn down Bartholomew Lane. There's a place we can leave the cart and horse tethered.'

'Have you been there before?' Ettie asked in surprise.

'Once or twice maybe. Came up to town with Gladys to enjoy the occasional show at a decent music hall that wasn't an excuse for a doss house.'

'What's a doss house?' Ettie enquired innocently.

The butcher laughed as he urged the horse on. 'Sorry, lass. I keep forgetting myself. A doss house is a glorified lodging like the one near Silver Street where our friend Gino sold his wares. The place was supposed to be a theatre of sorts, but what they got up to inside ain't for a young girl's attention.'

At the mention of Gino, Ettie shivered, but she soon rallied and said with a smile, 'My attention has been brought to a lot of new things while living in Silver Street, Terence. My vocabulary is expanding faster than ever it did with the Sisters of Clemency.'

At this, Terence threw back his head and roared with laughter once more. Ettie joined in too and suddenly the day seemed more like a pleasurable outing than one of intense concern.

She had never known anything of her father and barely much more of her mother, but she liked to believe that her parentage might involve someone like Terence, whose second name she didn't even know and didn't care that she didn't know, for his intrinsic goodness shone like a lighthouse across a stormy sea. He had revealed that he thought of her as a daughter. She was beginning to believe that even if not related by blood, there was a connection between them.

Gradually the city came to life with its monuments and pillared buildings, tall grey spires, and historic places that she had only ever seen replicated on paper. Ettie marvelled at the many classes of vehicles beginning to congest the roads. Bicycles, trams, carts, wagons, cabs and buses all merged on the City, as the bowler-hatted gentlemen scurried to their offices. Once more she felt excited, as she had done on the very first day of seeing the capital.

Then with a slow trot, the pony was guided towards a small row of cut trees that grew like a fringed skirt around the most formidable building of all.

'Here we are,' said Terence, pulling on the reins so that Ettie could get a clear view, 'The Old Lady of Threadneedle Street herself.'

Ettie was taken aback at the sight of the forbidding building; a fortress of dark, carved stones reaching high above the ground to a summit of sentinels perched on the top of the roofs. The austere and dominating facade overshadowed all the other buildings of the street, reminding passers-by of its world-renowned importance. Whatever she had previously imagined, she was filled with a kind of awe even greater than the first sight of the Queen's residence, Buckingham Palace.

'Impressive, eh?' Terence said as he slapped the reins and the horse trotted on slowly behind the traffic. 'Your tobacconist certainly knew where to put his money.'

Ettie couldn't take her eyes from the vision of great national importance. Yes, she was sure Terence was right. The money in the cast-iron chest that she had so carefully saved on behalf of her employer now seemed a drop in a very big puddle. All the same, he had been in no rush in the first instance to bank the salon's takings in his absence. Yet now, his letter had stated great urgency.

'This looks like the turning,' said Terence, drawing the pony into an opening where a guard stood behind a pair of strong iron gates.

'Open up, will you?' called Terence.

'What's your business?' came the reply.

'We have a delivery to make,' called Terence.

'You want the tradesmen's entrance,' barked the man. 'Turn your horse round and be on your way.'

Terence grumbled in annoyance. 'Not that kind of delivery. We are on financial business. I'll show you.'

Ettie noticed how impatiently the guard moved to meet Terence who had jumped down and was waiting at the back of the cart. A smile touched her lips as she saw the guard's expression when the sacking over the chest was removed.

'One in the eye for him,' muttered Terence rejoining her and urging the pony through the slowly opening gates. 'Thought we was common tradesmen. Soon wiped the smile off his face.'

Ettie could see that Terence was a little anxious under all his bluster. But then, she supposed, anyone might be, who came to make a transaction with The Old Lady.

Her instincts were proved right as they entered the courtyard. Here she could view many lantern windows, some with tiny domes and others that seemed so small even a head might not be able to poke out of them.

Terence drove towards a large bay where other vehicles were parked.

'Wait here. I'll find an attendant to help us.' He jumped down and tethered the animal with others that drank from long troughs. But it was more than half an hour before Terence returned, as Ettie kept watch on a clock set high above on one of the building's towers. He was accompanied by an official with a scowl on his thin face and dressed in a black frock coat, stiff collar and necktie. Ettie supposed this must be one of the stuffed shirts that Terence had spoken of.

'This is Miss O'Reilly,' introduced Terence in a gruff tone as they stood looking up at her. 'You'll take instructions from this lady who is expected by your bank on a duty of some importance and urgency.'

Ettie felt herself go bright red under her bonnet. Her stomach clenched as the man scrutinized her appearance with suspicion.

CHAPTER THIRTY-FOUR

'Don't worry, this won't take long,' Terence assured her as they followed two burly porters hailed by the attendant, who carried the chest between them, along a winding corridor to a well-paved hall. 'Once we have a receipt we'll be on our way.'

Spread along one wall there were many kinds of wheels and cylinders creating a loud noise and warming the air intensely. Terence whispered to her that this must be the powerhouse of the bank where the gigantic engine serviced the complete works.

The stairs they climbed next were steep. Finally, the porters turned a sharp left and one of them unlocked a pair of plain but very strong-looking doors. A quietness fell about them as they entered a large room with many divisions. There was no natural light — as Ettie had noticed from the road outside — not even a small lantern window. Spaced in these divisions were mahogany desks and bowed heads sitting behind them, the bank clerks writing or attending to the general public as they entered by another door.

Above them in a circular fashion was a high-vaulted saloon, with a cupola and lanterns and too many library shelves to count.

The two porters delivered the chest to one of the clerks and set it on the floor beside his desk. They said nothing, but left without a word as the clerk continued to write.

Ettie waited, noticing the restless shuffling of Terence's booted feet. All around them were cautious whispered movements and the rattling of silver and gold pieces that were shovelled onto scales with miniature brass shovels.

It seemed an age before the clerk looked up and addressed them. 'Yes?' was all he said.

Ettie stepped forward. This man with a pair of spectacles like Sister Patrick's, balanced on the end of his nose, had not even glanced at the chest.

'Good morning, I am expected,' she said in a quiet manner. 'I've come to give the bank some of my employer's money. It's locked in this chest.'

'You mean make a deposit?' said the man curtly with a brief glance down.

'Yes, that's it.'

'On whose authority?'

'Mr Lucas Benjamin, who owns the tobacconist's of Silver Street, Soho and who is away in Switzerland for a short while. This is my friend Terence who helped me transport it here.'

'Pass Book,' said the clerk, ignoring Terence.

'What's that?' asked Ettie.

The clerk glared at her. 'Every account is linked to a Pass Book and is used when making transactions.'

'I haven't got one, as it's not my account,' Ettie mumbled, her confidence fading. 'I expect Mr Benjamin has it.'

'Then Mr Benjamin must present it.'

'I told you, he's in Switzerland.'

'Without account identification, I cannot help.' The clerk looked back to his writing. 'Take your — chest — and please make way for the other customers.'

Ettie felt the humiliation burn in her cheeks. She was certain she wouldn't be treated with such disdain if she was one of their wealthy customers. It wasn't even as if she was trying to get money out. She was attempting to put it in. Suddenly a pair of hands gripped her shoulders.

'Ettie love,' said Terence, as he moved her to one side, 'go and take a seat over there. See, where them people are sitting, waiting. I'll have a word with this young whippersnapper.'

Ettie glanced back at the clerk. He was scribbling furiously and rudely ignored them, as though they were nothing but time-wasters.

Terence gave her a little push towards what appeared to be the waiting area. 'Leave it to Terence.'

Ettie reluctantly obeyed, crossing the room to settle herself on a chair that looked very uncomfortable with a hard seat and back, but she supposed the bank did not want people to stay for very long. At least, that was what the clerk had inferred by his rude manner. And what could Terence do that she couldn't? Although he meant well, he had no connection with Lucas.

Sighing to herself, Ettie decided to take off her bonnet. The big room was stuffy; hot air she guessed, was generated from the discreet conversations held between the clerks and their wealthy looking customers. Placing her bonnet in her lap, she lifted her fingers to nervously touch the coppery coil of hair at the back of her hot neck. Her large brown eyes, so close to tears a moment ago, were now filled by a flicker of anger. On behalf of Lucas they had brought a great deal of money to be stored at the bank. This famous bank did not deserve its noble reputation if it treated the public in such a dismissive way.

What would she do if they refused to take Lucas's money? She could not possibly write back to Lucas and tell him she had failed to do such a simple thing. And yet, without this Pass Book, her mission seemed impossible.

Just then, Ettie saw Terence making a sign with his hands as if to argue with the clerk. Her heart raced and thudded. What if Terence got them thrown out? The clerk who was now very red-faced, had removed his spectacles and stood up.

Terence made the gesture again. The clerk hurried from his desk and almost ran over to another clerk. The second clerk looked just as agitated, and jumped to his feet.

In the confusion another man strode over. He was tall, slightly stooped and lean as a rake, wearing trousers with a faint grey pin-stripe and a sombre black jacket. After a lengthy discussion with Terence he sped across the floor and disappeared out of sight.

Ettie feared that her suspicions about being ejected from The Old Lady might prove true. Had the man gone to call the porters?

She looked anxiously back at Terence, who was giving the evil eye to the two clerks. It was rarely that he became annoyed but, on this occasion, there was no doubt of his intention to engage in a fight as he squared his shoulders and glowered in anger.

CHAPTER THIRTY-FIVE

'Good day, Miss O'Reilly, I am the under-manager,' said the man with the striped trousers, who approached after rejoining Terence. The under-manager seemed of middle age with sucked-in cheeks and a severe side parting to his hair that Ettie thought made him definitely in the category of a stuffed shirt. 'Please accept my apologies,' he began. 'The clerk did not realize . . .'

'Your clerk needs a lesson in civility,' interrupted Terence, sharply. 'Now, forget giving us all the frills and fancies! Can we please get on with the job, so me and Miss Reilly can return to our businesses where we make the money to keep your great institution going?'

'Yes, yes, of course,' the under-manager agreed in a humbled tone. 'I shall have the credit made immediately. Would you care to wait in my private office?'

'No thank you,' said Terence, sniffing haughtily. 'We'll sit right here and watch all your goings-on.'

'As you wish,' said the man and turning to Ettie, he made a little bow. 'My apologies again, Miss O'Reilly. Er, the chest I presume is locked?'

Ettie searched in her purse and drew out the key.

'Thank you. We shall not keep you waiting.'

Ettie was open-mouthed as Terence sat beside her, puffing out his breath causing curious glances to be cast, both at the departing figure and the cross-looking butcher.

'Terence, what happened?' Ettie whispered.

'Told 'em a few home truths about their service, that's what,' growled Terence. 'Said they was missing out on well over three hundred pounds and if they checked their records, they would find a letter from Lucas Benjamin, a client of their bank and British citizen abroad in Switzerland, who had notified them by letter well in advance of our visit. And, I says, that if that letter wasn't turned up, I would take my complaint to the under-manager's manager and then his manager.' Terence took a moment to catch his breath. 'So, the under-manager scuttled off to the manager's office and returned shame-faced. I ask you, what a palaver!'

'But the missing Pass Book!'

'They are making out a temporary one. You will be asked to sign it as your employer's courier.'

'What does that mean?'

'The Pass Book is just a glorified diary of today's transaction. Your tobacconist will have to produce the original on his return.'

'Perhaps it's at home in a drawer.'

'Perhaps it is, young beauty.'

'Terence you saved the day!'

The butcher at last, gave a rueful smile. 'Very nearly did that miserable clerk a serious injury.'

'Terence, you wouldn't!'

He chuckled. 'At my age?'

Ettie put her hand on his sleeve. 'I don't know what I would have done without you.'

He gave a shy shrug. 'Not at all dear girl. Done me good to tell 'em what for. Made me feel like a young man again.'

Ettie gave a little giggle. 'You certainly set the cat among the pigeons.' She nodded to the two clerks who were working rapidly to count and weigh the contents of the chest.

Just as the under-manager had promised, the business was concluded promptly, a temporary Pass Book appeared and Ettie gave her signature. With more apologies they were escorted out by the two porters who carried the empty chest through the beating heart of the great building to the square outside.

As Ettie climbed up on the dicky seat beside Terence she heard the clock strike nine. Soho would be up and bustling, and doubtlessly, a few customers would have turned up at the salon only to be disappointed.

But this didn't bother her at all; she was happy to have accomplished the mission that Lucas had set her and a smile played on her lips all the way home.

Her amusement deepened as she thought of the two clerks and the under-manager and the way they had almost bumped into one another to rectify the mistake the first clerk had made.

Ettie decided their change in attitude must have come from Terence informing them in the strongest terms of the business they were about to lose.

The Old Lady of Threadneedle Street with all her airs and graces had been given a severe lecture by an unassuming Soho butcher.

CHAPTER THIRTY-SIX

Summer came into full bloom and the streets of Soho filled with tradesmen and opportunists eager to make a quick penny or two. In the heat of the day, the dust rolled over the cobbles and crept in the salon door, so that Ettie spent hours dusting and cleaning, welcoming her customers with the offer of a shady retreat in the smoking room.

On the occasional evening, she strolled down to the green that Clara loved so much. Here, sitting on the bench, she would imagine how she'd rock the baby in the perambulator, listening to the child's soft mewing.

Whether boy or girl, it didn't matter. She would love it with all her heart and take care of it when Clara was resting or needing her quiet.

Ettie knew that her affection for little children was born in the orphanage. Often as she sat in the setting sunlight, her mind went back to those days. But she refused to be maudlin for her own happiness would be complete when the family returned to England.

There would be a larder full of fine food waiting. Every surface would be dusted, every floor swept clean. The house would sparkle for Clara. Already in the nursery stood the perambulator; every spoke of its wheels cleaned and oiled and a little frilly cover laid under its hood.

Over the weeks Ettie had added small personal items to the nursery; a child's hair brush made of bone and painted with fairy figures, a decent soft flannel that Aggie had sold her on the cheap, and a pair of shoes, each hardly larger than a matchbox, made of soft cloth and little bows. She had knitted bonnets and mittens in some white wool that Mrs Buckle had no use for, and sewn pretty cot blankets from floral material discovered in a cupboard in the kitchen. This, she suspected was a remnant from the curtains hanging in her own room. And the crucifix, all shined and silvery, would protect the baby as it grew into a healthy and happy toddler.

The nursery looked so pretty she knew Clara would approve in every respect.

Ettie's one disappointment was that no letter of reply had arrived from Lucas. She had written to tell him of her adventure to The Old Lady and of Terence's help in the matter and the successful conclusion to his request. But the days passed and the end of the month drew near.

'My guess is,' said Terence one day as he drank his tea, 'they'll turn up on the doorstep. Surprise you. All three of them.'

Ettie hadn't considered this. 'But the house might not be ready!' she exclaimed in panic.

Terence laughed his hearty laugh. 'Young beauty, there's not a mote of dust on the shelves or a dull corner. The stove don't look as if it's been cooked on. See this table here?' He gestured to the spotless scrubbed wood. 'Why, I'm afraid to lean my elbow on it!'

Ettie studied the kitchen. Terence was right. She had cleaned it so many times, there was nothing left to clean. The bedrooms were stocked with fresh linen. She never ate in the dining room, but polished the surfaces weekly. The drawing room was the only space she liked and since the nights were so warm, there had not been a fire in the hearth for months.

'But the larder, Terence, it's empty.'

'Don't fret, I'll give you the very best cuts the moment they return. Eggs and butter too.'

'The journey will be long and arduous,' Ettie persisted. 'Perhaps two days, even three or four! Will they bring a maid? Or a nanny for the child?' This, too, was a new thought. Would Lucas have engaged a person to look after the baby?

'Now, now,' said Terence, returning his mug to the table and standing up creakily, 'all those questions will be answered in good time.' He slapped on his cap and chuckled. 'Your employer and his wife will approve of every preparation and the infant will turn everyone's heads and hearts and poor old Terence will be neglected!'

Ettie jumped to her feet. 'Terence, I'll never neglect you.'

'Nor I you, dear girl.' Whistling a merry tune, he went off through the backyard.

Ettie watched him go, promising herself that the very first ride she gave to the baby in the perambulator, would be to Terence's shop, the very best butcher in all of Soho.

* * *

The next day, just after she had opened the salon, a carriage arrived outside. Ettie was standing behind the counter when she saw it and reached out to steady herself. For there was Michael, sitting proud on the seat of the damson-red brougham, a crop in one hand and the reins in the other. From the carriage window, the young girl gazed out, prettier than ever, her sweet face framed by pale honey curls and a bonnet of crimson satin.

Michael jumped down and lowered the set of small steps, his smiling, confident face turned towards his passenger.

Here was *her* Michael, and her heart throbbed at the thought!

What will I do if he comes in? She considered. Do I smile and greet him? Or do I pretend not to know him? No, I can never do that, she answered herself, not even if he is ashamed to acknowledge me. But why should he be ashamed? another voice demanded. Only the years separate you, not the affection that surely must still be in his heart.

The young girl, all dressed in silks of lilac and deeper purples that swirled in full skirts around her dainty feet, held out her hand to be assisted into the salon.

Her hand was taken — and firmly. Arms brushed, a coy smile here, another there and mischievous eyes yet again held her driver's gaze in an intimate connection.

Ettie forced her attention away, turning to the shelves and pretended to be busy rearranging the tobaccos. Would he come inside this time? If so, should she acknowledge him and how would she do it? Her, a mere shop assistant, brazenly announcing herself as a friend?

'Good day,' interrupted the sweet, articulated voice that Ettie recalled so well. 'I've come to buy your silver snuff miniature with the mother-of-pearl inlay. I hope you have it still?'

Ettie turned, her heart jumping into her throat, or at least, it felt that way as her gaze fell on the young woman whose soft greeting had felt as forceful as the tide of the river rushing in to break over its banks.

'Yes . . . yes,' Ettie heard herself reply, though her voice seemed faint. 'The snuff miniatures are still for sale.'

'May I inspect them? Be as quick as you can. I have just a few minutes to spare.'

This new piece of information collided with the movement of the tall figure standing outside on the cobbles. Michael was positioned where he had waited before, his broad shoulders towards her, a perfect line of dark hair just visible under his flat cap. A leather belt was wrapped around his slim waist and the jacket smoothed over his hips to meet his trousers in such a way that he might have pressed his own clothes with a hot iron not two minutes before! But it was his figure beneath, she realized with sudden shock, that caused the uniform to appear so grand, for he had grown in both height and stature it seemed, even from when she had last seen him.

'I say, did you hear me?' The girl's voice, harder now, with a touch of irritation, broke into Ettie's thoughts and she reached quickly for the box that contained the snuffs.

'Let me see them open,' the girl said as Ettie, with trembling fingers, placed them on the counter, slipped the little catches and allowed the lids of each miniature to spring up.

'Delightful,' said the girl, removing her gloves and taking one. Ettie thought for a moment she might dip her finger into the perfect oval of powder. But instead she nodded and handed the box to Ettie. 'Is it the same price as the pipe?'

Ettie nodded.

'Wrap it as you did before. My brother was pleasantly surprised with his smokes and Mama completely distressed when she discovered my pipe. I argued of course that it couldn't be smoked and was merely a decoration. But I could see I had aroused her suspicions, which gave me a great fillip.'

Ettie carried the box to a corner of the shop, hardly aware of what she was doing. Out of sight of her customer, she took a sheet of brown paper and ball of string. But her movements were clumsy and she almost cut herself with the scissors.

'Hurry please,' called the girl and Ettie glanced back to see a dainty bare knuckle rapping on the window. The sound alerted the driver who turned on his booted heel and gazed in.

'Michael,' Ettie whispered as though her lips spoke of their own will. 'Michael?'

But his attention was fully on the girl as she pressed her face, smiling, close to the glass. The moment seemed to linger and grow like an invisible thread between them and it took all of Ettie's willpower not to cry aloud from the pain that seared into her chest. It clamped around her breastbone like a vice and penetrated to the core of her being.

'Michael . . .' she half called, unable to restrain herself. 'It's me, Ettie . . .'

The girl turned in alarm as though she herself had been summoned. 'What was that?'

'Nothing. I . . . I am just coming,' Ettie blurted, fumbling to tie the ends of the string.

'I can wait no longer,' decided the girl, plainly annoyed, and she sped across the floor to where Ettie stood. 'Here is your money.' She pushed the coins into Ettie's hand, snatching the box with the other.

Before Ettie could reply, her customer had whisked away, opening the door of the salon and departing under the protective gaze of her driver.

By the time Ettie reached the window, Michael was swinging himself high onto the seat of the damson-red brougham and settled there, lifting the reins.

The carriage was already moving away when Ettie's palm reached the same inch on the window that the girl's knuckle had touched. Her cry, though, was more pitiful than her own ears could possibly bear for it was of anguish, and desperation, and regret she had not been quicker, all mixed.

'Michael! Michael, it's me, Ettie!'

But even when she called again, this time from the street outside, the carriage was almost out of sight. Only the tip of the crop was visible as Michael drove away.

CHAPTER THIRTY-SEVEN

It was the last day of August and much to her dismay, Ettie still found herself thinking of Michael. It was clear he had done well for himself, although his beginnings were as humble as her own. Yet the young woman in whose service he now found himself, must come from an aristocratic family, most likely owners of vast estates. Did they approve of their daughter's friendship with a commoner?

Instantly Ettie berated herself for this unjust thought. The nuns had taught her to believe that love and affection knew no bounds. But whenever she found herself thinking of Michael and the girl, a pain snaked around her ribs and left her breathless.

Jealousy was a sin. She remembered the Song of Solomon; '*love is as strong as death and jealousy as fierce as the grave*'. Ettie had never understood this before.

But now she did.

Recalling Michael's strong spirit, she suspected that nothing would stand in his way if he wanted this beautiful girl. And, Ettie knew the girl wanted *him*. This was what hurt the most. The gestures and little touches. Unspoken words conveyed with the eyes.

Ettie understood it all now. She wished she could call Michael back and say precious words of her own. If only she had decided to approach him, but her pride had stopped her. She had been ashamed of her own lowly status in comparison to the girl's!

She had other worries, too, for the wholesalers of Tobacco Dock had made no deliveries since June and her supplies were almost exhausted. Ettie had written to them and also to the wine merchant, but neither consignment had appeared.

It was late on a Saturday evening when Ettie was considering ordering a cab to make a visit to both suppliers when a bedraggled figure appeared in the twilight of Silver Street.

It was not unusual, Ettie supposed, to see such a character for Soho was home to beggars and the down-and-outs of all kinds. But there was something about this man who walked with a slight limp, leaning on a staff to support himself. His collar was turned up to his felt hat, and his shoulders hunched under the weight of a dirty knapsack.

Ettie gazed through the window, her eyes narrowed in order to see through the gloom. A vague unease filled her. She was certain she knew this man. Though it was impossible to tell who he was, a familiarity was there.

Quite suddenly he turned towards the salon, striking the staff in the ground. With some visible effort he placed his booted feet apart as if to steady himself. His free hand went up to his face, half covered by his collar and his eyes met Ettie's.

A cry left her lips. She felt as if her insides had paralysed with shock.

The young man she had once known, was now an old and haggard shadow of his former self.

She ran to the door and thrust it open. 'Mr Benjamin, is that you?'

There was barely a nod in answer.

* * *

Ettie took his arm for it was now quite plain that her employer was in need of assistance. He was so light that Ettie still had doubts this was the happy, boisterous man who had left Silver Street a year ago. A stranger had replaced him; unkempt, unwashed, neglected, with a straggly beard and eyes robbed of their vibrant blue.

But to Ettie the deepest shock was that he was alone. Yet she feared to ask him more as she helped him inside. Glancing up at the portrait of his mother, he heaved a great gasp. Tears filled the unhappy eyes and a cough trembled on his lips.

'I hung the portrait there to keep me company. I hope you don't mind?' Ettie said although she knew he wasn't listening. The tobacconist of Silver Street was not his old self and instinct told Ettie to say no more. Instead she guided him along the passage to the drawing room where he looked around him as though viewing a long-lost life.

'Please sit down,' Ettie urged as she steered him towards the fireside. 'Here, let me take your bag and staff.'

He offered no resistance and after putting them to one side, Ettie helped him to the chair. He sank down, his head falling forward.

After some minutes, Ettie lifted away his hat and placed it with the staff and bag. How dull and lifeless his once vibrant wiry hair had become! A few thin streaks of the handsome sandy-gold remained, barely disguising the little round pennies of bare scalp.

What was she to do for the best, she wondered? How dearly she wanted to know about Clara and the baby! And to be reassured they were well. But all her questions must wait.

Leaving the exhausted man, she went to the kitchen to steady her nerves. Putting the kettle on to boil, she prepared a bowl and flannel, with a little lavender oil to refresh the skin. But Lucas was fast asleep when she returned and she hadn't the heart to wake him.

Carefully she lifted his feet to the stool. Removing his holed boots, she disposed of his socks and replaced them with his slippers. Unbuttoning his coat, a sweet and putrid smell came off his skin. Perhaps he hadn't washed in days?

The next hour she spent in preparing a broth, boiling lean scraps from the rashers of bacon that Terence had served her last week. Several times she returned to the drawing room. On each visit, she found the slumbering man breathing noisily. She propped his head back but it only fell forward again.

By ten o'clock Ettie decided that nothing would wake him, not even the wholesome aromas of the cooked broth. She brought covers from the bedrooms and curled on the other chair, watching the rise and fall of his chest under the blanket.

Midnight arrived and he had turned restlessly, kicking over the stool. Ettie's thoughts went to Clara. Why had her husband travelled home without her? Perhaps the journey was too difficult for the baby? Yes, that must be it. Yet why should he arrive in such a state? Had there been an accident? Had the carriage overturned somewhere along the route?

Yes, this must be the reason, Ettie decided as her lids closed. It was an explanation that almost satisfied her as she fell asleep.

CHAPTER THIRTY-EIGHT

She woke as daylight broke through the curtains and lit the room.

Throwing off her cover, she hurried to her employer who was struggling to ease himself from the chair.

'Mr Benjamin, let me help you.'

'Am I home, Ettie?'

'You are home, Sir, though I can see you are weary from your long travels.'

'I am, I am,' he confirmed. 'Give me my staff and I shall visit the washroom. After which, I shall answer all your enquiries.'

She placed the staff in his hand as he stumbled away, his figure that of an aged man. She felt the impulse to go after him, but instead put two hens' eggs on to boil and sliced a loaf, adding a little salt and pepper to the breakfast tray. By the time he returned she had set the dining room table and their meal was ready.

He made no murmur as he sank to his seat and ate without enthusiasm. A sad fondness crept over her as she recalled the younger, happier Lucas Benjamin who always enjoyed his meals with such gusto.

'Thank you,' he said at last. 'I haven't eaten so well in many days.'

'Sir, that is distressing to hear.' She waited for a further explanation but once more he drifted into his own thoughts and sat mute.

Ettie cleared the dirty crockery and busied herself in the kitchen, repressing the urge to beg him to tell her what had happened. When she returned, she found him in the salon, staring up at the portrait.

'I hope you don't mind that I removed it and hung it there,' she apologized once again.

'Secrets,' he rasped. 'We all have secrets.'

Ettie thought this was rather a peculiar answer, but she nodded and replied, 'I never knew your mother. But I imagine she was very beautiful.'

'Love must be blind,' he whispered. 'For that is the only explanation.'

Ettie moved a little closer. 'I am sorry, Sir, I don't understand.'

'Lies, Ettie, all lies. A nest of them.'

'Sir, you are confused from your journey,' she insisted, 'come and rest. I shall call the physician.'

'A physician cannot cure what ails me.' His lips quivered and she thought he might collapse. 'I shall tell you from the beginning,' he choked on a rattled breath as he sank to the stool. 'You see, I have been travelling for nearly a month. A coach here. A carriage there. But in the end, all were beyond my means. Instead I ventured on foot, until at last I reached the French coast. Enough, saved, yes, enough to cross the Channel by boat. But after that . . . I have returned here destitute!'

'But Sir,' Ettie replied in bewilderment, 'after your letter, I did as you asked. With a friend's help I took the chest to the Bank of England.'

He gave a low groan. 'Don't ask me about them!'

'But why, Sir?'

'Don't ask! Don't ask!'

Ettie could make no sense of what he was saying. 'Your wife, Sir, and the baby, what of them?' she burst out. 'Please tell me.'

Desperate eyes looked up at her. 'Clara and my darling child, my family, they are gone, Ettie. Gone!'

Had her employer lost his senses? She wondered in fear. 'Gone, Sir, gone where?'

'Perished, both of them,' he cried desperately. 'In childbirth. Or in death, both are the same for me — and for them!'

She swallowed, trying to absorb this madness. Was Lucas delirious? Had hysteria overtaken him? 'Sir, I shall call the physician,' she repeated.

'A priest would be better, for it was I who killed them. I who failed them. I still hear her cries and see her dead face that was once so alive and beautiful. And my son, deformed and no larger than my hand, his poor, twisted body dragged from her, not a breath in his lungs, or cry from his mouth.' He bent forward, arching his chest with howls so dreadful that Ettie could not bear to hear them.

'Hush now, Sir.' She knelt beside him and took him in her arms. His sobs travelled through her like punches, each one more violent than the next.

CHAPTER THIRTY-NINE

'I cannot live without Clara,' he sobbed as he raised his head from her shoulder. 'I have no desire to exist.'

'But how can this have happened? Are you sure, Sir? Is there not some mistake?' She knew this was a foolish remark, but hope remained inside her for just a few seconds. Perhaps Lucas might be wrong, his senses scattered from hunger and exhaustion?

But her hopes were soon dashed.

'I held her dear body in my arms. I beseeched her to wake from her sleep. I kissed her cold skin, as frozen as the grave. I took my son, as lifeless as she, and offered my own life if only theirs be spared. But death refused me and I was left with corpses the sight of which I will never forget. There's no mistake, Ettie! We shall never see them again.'

Tears overwhelmed him until he fell back in such distress, that all she could hear was the prolonged and heartbreaking agony of an abandoned man.

Ettie did not know how long it was that she stayed beside her employer as he tried to release his anguish; one minute babbling incoherently, the next too consumed by his woe to speak.

All the while, she tried to reserve some small part of herself. For if she let herself go, sorrow would devour them both. The loving, hopeful couple who had departed the shores of England a year ago, were now reduced to one. Perhaps less than one, Ettie feared, for this man was broken.

It was no easy task to assist him to the bedroom, for he was unsteady and dithered on every stair. But eventually he sank to the bed and allowed her to remove his clothes.

This intimacy would once have caused them both great embarrassment. Now he seemed not to care and obeyed her gentle commands. Filling the pitcher and soaking the flannel in the bowl, she bathed him tenderly, as if he was a child. The sight of his emaciated body distressed her beyond words. But after a while she composed herself and continued with her nursing, drawing on his nightshirt and bringing him broth to eat.

For a while he slept, but was so restless that Ettie stayed all night in the chair, listening for his every movement. By morning, a fever had set in. His ramblings grew worse and Ettie hurried down to the salon, where she took a sixpence from the till.

'Run to the physician of Soho Square and tell him he is needed at the tobacconist's of Silver Street,' she instructed the dirty urchin who had taken to occupying the step outside the salon on Sundays. 'If you bring him, there's another sixpence waiting for you.'

The tousled-haired boy scampered off and Ettie returned to the bedroom.

Her patient tossed in distress, the delirium she had feared, now overcoming him. She bathed his forehead with a rag and washed his sweating limbs with cold water. And all the while he talked in riddles. His Mama's name was constantly on his dry, swelling lips. But his soft and gentle pleading soon changed to anger and accusation when he spoke of his Papa.

'Lay still,' Ettie begged him as he writhed about, refusing to be covered. The sweat poured from him and his forehead burned red hot.

By the time the physician arrived and Ettie had paid the boy, Lucas was in a deep delirium.

'How long has he been sick?' he enquired.

'I don't know, sir. Mr Benjamin returned from Switzerland only yesterday. He was most distressed. I am grieved to say his wife has passed away.'

'The same lady I came here to treat some while ago for her addiction?'

Ettie nodded sadly. 'She died in childbirth, so he told me. But I am not certain why. His only description was that the baby . . .' here Ettie had to forcibly command herself to continue, 'the baby boy was deformed, only the size of his hand and . . . and twisted.' She could barely bring herself to say the word.

But the physician nodded slowly. 'I am not surprised.'

'What does it mean, sir?'

'Since I was not her consultant, I cannot say for sure. But I have seen others . . .' he paused, bowing his grey head. 'The interference of that poisonous drug in a body's system may be responsible for such a tragedy.'

Ettie swallowed, feeling her head swim. Had Clara not escaped the opium's effects after all? But such a price to pay! It was unthinkable. Yet, Ettie sensed this misfortune might very well be true.

'Your employer has a dangerous fever. He must be tended day and night. Give him a teaspoon of this linctus for his cough. If the fever breaks, he will survive.' He took a small brown bottle from his Gladstone bag. 'Bathe him frequently and though he might not eat, fluid is essential. I shall call tomorrow.'

* * *

The Sunday bells were pealing across Soho for evening prayer as Ettie brought coddled eggs and warm milk to the bedroom. Setting it down on the bedside table, she drew away the bed sheet and pushed up the damp pillows behind Lucas's head. He clutched her arm.

'The Pass Book — have you got it?' he babbled.

'No, Sir. What Pass Book?'

'I must have it. I must!'

'Eat first and I will find the Pass Book,' Ettie replied, trying to turn, but he pulled her close.

'Mama will give it to you, but beware, if he tries for an advance, warn her to refuse.'

Suddenly afraid, Ettie stared into his eyes that were wide with fear. 'Who, Sir, who will try for an advance?'

'Papa,' he gasped. 'There will be nothing left to pay our debts. Mama will bear the burden.'

'But Sir, I . . .'

'I shall stop him, I must, for Mama's sake. May he rot in hell if he tries!' The curse was uttered with ferocity.

She stood, quaking, for the man in the bed was not Lucas Benjamin, nor the weak and disabled stranger who had returned from Switzerland. This was a soul possessed, burning not just with fever but a savage anger.

'Devil!' he shouted so passionately that Ettie jumped back against the wall. She saw his attention was riveted on something other than her. He pointed a shaking finger, half rising from the bed like a wild animal about to spring. What would she do if he leapt up? Could she prevent him from doing himself damage? For he would surely fall without her help. And yet there was an energy in him that radiated. Those burning eyes, the loathsome expression, were all directed towards this unseen figure.

Ettie trembled from head to toe. She believed in the power of angels, but there was no good spirit in this room that felt protective or holy.

Edging her way to the door, she left him with his eyes fixed upon this supernatural force as the moisture ran down his face and into his beard. Taking the stairs two at a time, she burst into the nursery and snatched the bishop's crucifix from the wall. Without pause for breath, she returned to the bedroom.

'Mr Benjamin,' she cried, 'I have this to comfort you.'

A sudden moan came from his parched lips.

Ettie shuddered as his eyes, previously so fixed and furious, rolled upward into their sockets. Then, as if all the violence inside him drained out, he crumpled to the bed.

Ettie's heart was thundering, her senses alert for any sudden movement. But there was nothing, not even a gasped breath.

'Mr Benjamin, Sir?' Ettie bent to touch his hand. Though damp with sweat, she felt the tremor of life. Gently pulling him back to the pillows, she slipped the crucifix beneath.

'Jesus, Mary and Joseph, protect this kind and distressed soul and bring him peace,' she prayed.

Wiping a tear from her eye, she loosened the buttons of his nightshirt as the fever consumed him.

CHAPTER FORTY

That evening, Ettie drew every blind in the salon and by the light of a single candle took the quill pen and began to write. '*We are closed temporarily for business. With many apologies, Lucas Benjamin, Proprietor.*'

Fixing string through holes she made on either side of the notice, she hung it directly from the door.

Casting her eyes briefly around the shelves that were now almost bare despite her attempts to fill the vacant spaces, a heavy truth descended. Should her employer recover from his fever, his grief would not allow a swift recovery. For his life without Clara and his son would indeed be empty. His suffering would continue, as would hers as she nursed him. The prospect of this huge eruption in their lives, did not bring tears to Ettie's eyes. For she must keep her senses about her. Even if it was possible to restock the shop and invite the gentlemen again, she could not care for an invalid and conduct a business single-handedly.

There was no doubt in her mind as to her priority and she looked up at Rose whispering a sincere request. 'Won't you help your son in his distress?' she begged of the silent image. 'He loves you dearly and regrets the terrible injustice you might have encountered in this earthly life. But cruelty has visited him too and I fear for his sanity.'

A few seconds passed and Ettie gathered herself, returning to the bedroom with supper. She tried a few spoonfuls of oatmeal, but his lips compressed as though, even in his derangement, he had no need for nourishment.

She took her position in the chair and kept watch all night, reassuring him when he shouted out and in the early hours of the morning, when the fever intensified.

When the physician called in the afternoon, he had no answer for her questions. The fever was unstoppable, the fires of grief and distress burning through every inch of skin.

* * *

The days slipped by and were only relieved by the visits of the physician, who could add little to his diagnosis of 'brain fever'. This condition, he said, was caused by the shock of his recent bereavements.

In rare moments Ettie found Lucas calmer, but then an explosion of emotion would drive him to sit bolt upright. His stare would fix on the invisible creature that haunted him. 'Waster! Scoundrel! Gambler!' This was repeated time and time again.

Ettie pressed him back with as much force as she could but her consoling murmurs offered no solace. He seemed possessed and she feared a calamity. Either he would leap out of bed and injure himself. Or, she would fail to dodge the unnatural strength of his arms.

The bouts of delirium persisted against his father, whom he accused of the most heinous deeds. Lucas's skin grew flushed and swollen with agitation. By night, he slept in a trembling stupor from which one morning, he did not rouse. Ettie leaned close to listen for his breath, but it came only shallowly. This turn of events frightened her the most and she could barely wait for the physician's visit.

'The crisis is coming,' he warned. 'I can do no more. Have you a neighbour to call on?'

'No, sir.'

'My dear, you cannot stay alone.'

She felt a coldness seep into her. 'I'll manage.'

'How long is it since you've slept?'

She gave a disinterested shrug. 'I can't remember, sir.'

The physician grasped her shoulder. 'Does the tobacconist have family or friends?'

She thought of Florence and Thomas, who had not appeared since Clara's peculiar behaviour. But she neither knew where the couple lived or if they would come, if summoned. She thought, too, of Clara's admission that she had no brothers or sisters. Ettie knew for certain Lucas had no one. Her employer and his wife had been each other's only friends and soulmates. 'No, sir. Just his gentlemen customers.'

'You must call on someone,' the physician insisted.

As she sat there, it came to her. 'The butcher, Terence,' she answered. 'He takes tea with me each week.'

'Then I shall leave the rear door unlocked and alert him of your circumstances,' said the physician kindly.

After he had gone, Ettie pulled the chair close to the bed, for she had no strength in her legs. Reaching for her employer's hand, she held it tenderly. He was calm now. So calm and quiet that Ettie believed the physician's diagnosis was wrong.

'Can you hear me, Sir?' she whispered, watching intently for a sign. But the swollen lids of his closed eyes did not move. Nor did his lips, so cracked and puffed that she took the wet flannel and bathed them repeatedly.

'I am here, Sir, beside you,' she said as she slipped her small fingers around his again. 'I will not leave you. But I beg you to wake. For life is worth living. Your wife and son are in God's hands. They are safe and happy at last and would only want the best for you, a dear husband and father, who cared for them with all of his heart . . .'

Ettie could speak no more for the sadness welling up inside her was too much. With every word she felt bereft as she reached out to comfort her dear friend.

CHAPTER FORTY-ONE

At half past six that evening, Ettie said her last goodbyes. In the company of Terence, who had not left her side since he had arrived an hour after the physician had called, Ettie regained the use of her legs in order to kiss the fevered cheek that in death, was finally chilled.

'God rest the poor man and his family,' Terence said softly, as he slipped the sheet lightly over the tobacconist and took his little friend gently to one side. 'He'll meet his maker with dignity,' he assured Ettie. 'Imagine his joy when he sees his darlings.'

But even the kind ministrations of the butcher did not help as she tried to picture the little family reunited. She tried very hard. And she knew, that it should be she, not Terence, who possessed the strongest faith. But her feelings were instead an unpleasant anger, just as she had felt at the bishop's cruel directive. This germ had not gone away after all. Instead, it had festered; the injustice of tragedy! The unreasonable twist of fate! The taking of people she loved. An innocent child she had imagined so often, cooing and smiling in her arms. A family's future denied. How could this be?

'Come and sit downstairs,' Terence urged her, guiding her to the door. 'And you can tell me all that happened.'

Ettie felt the shaking of the bonds that bound her to this room and hesitated. But Terence refused to let her remain and took her to the drawing room where he made her rest.

'Tea, that's what we'll have. And a talk, before I do — well, what's necessary for our departed friend.'

Ettie listened to Terence's movements in the kitchen. They were comforting and for a little while she regained some normality. But then the full impact of what had transpired overshadowed her.

Her employer was gone and so, too, was his beloved wife. She would never cook for them and serve them breakfast or dinner again. She would never shop at the market in order to buy the best vegetables and fruit. She would never clean and dust the household and hear Clara's grateful thanks, spoken in her soft and gentle voice.

And the nursery! What of that room filled with the trappings of welcome? The perambulator and crib, the pretty curtains and nursing chair. Now Clara would never rest there and Ettie would never watch mother and baby with immeasurable happiness. No, the chair would remain vacant in that silent, unoccupied room. The happiness and laughter that was expected — *that* happiness would never, ever be.

'Now, drink this all the way down.' Terence pressed her cold fingers around the warm shape of a mug. 'Don't expect you've looked after yourself, have you?'

Without seeming to expect an answer, he sat in Clara's chair, his face full of concern. 'Now, dear, tell me what happened?'

Ettie drank a little, but felt no refreshment. The thought of the desolate nursery was lodged in her mind; the empty crib, the stationary perambulator, the crucifix meant to protect and was now an emblem of death beneath her employer's pillow.

'Ettie, rally yourself, girl,' Terence implored her. 'Let loose on Terence whose shoulders are broad and waiting.'

She gazed into his kind face, all round and full with good health — unlike the face she had left upstairs, with eyes closed that would never open again and lips sealed, never to take a breath.

Suddenly the outpouring came; a flood of tears followed by great, gasping sobs that prevented any speech. In the same way she had comforted her employer, Terence comforted *her* and every now and then, offered a consoling pat.

He pulled a crumpled rag from his apron pocket and pushed it into her hands. 'Dry them cheeks now, little beauty. Mop 'em up, but don't stop weeping till you're as empty as that fire grate. I didn't stop for my Gladys, no. Must've been a whole week I bawled. Maybe more. And to think of vittles, even a nice pork chop, well, my stomach revolted at the prospect. It's the weeping comes first, see? Then the hole. This great big, rotten black hole that gulps you up, mixes you round till you don't know what time of day or night it is, not that you blooming well care about time.' He sat back with his hands on his knees and sighed. 'So Terence understands and is listening. The physician told me the tobacconist's sad story, but there's more to it I'm sure. Now, I know your departed employer was grieving the loss of his family. But the appearance of him, well, it shocked me!'

Ettie mopped her eyes, smelling on the rag the wood sawdust that covered Terence's shop floor and a whiff of the dripping he sold on his counter.

'He couldn't have eaten in days.'

'How did he travel to England?'

'He said a coach here, a carriage there. Then he went on foot to the Channel.' A sob rocked her as she caught her breath. 'And arrived back here, penniless.'

'Penniless?' repeated Terence with a frown. 'Why this very business, his family's fortune — a security that would enable him to travel like a king! Did you tell him about The Old Lady deposit?'

Ettie nodded. 'I did, but he grew angry at the mention.'

'Why, that is very strange!'

'In his confusion, he asked for the Pass Book.'

'The temporary one?'

'His thoughts were so entangled, I could make nothing of them. He spoke kindly of his mother, but grew furious at his papa. It was as if he . . .' Ettie trembled at the memory of those blazing eyes fixed into nothingness, 'as if he could see him in the room and hated him.'

Terence leaned forward to mutter, 'Now, now, dear girl, the poor man was off his mind.'

'Yes,' agreed Ettie and dabbed her wet cheeks. She looked anxiously at the butcher. 'What will happen now?'

Terence drew in a deep breath. 'The physician will certify him. The undertaker will bury him. And the living will mourn him.'

Ettie remembered when the old bishop had died during Lent. The tabernacle and the altar, the holy pictures and statues were draped with deep purple cloths. The coffin stood overnight before the altar and in the morning all the orphans had crowded in, their eyes fixed on the ornate wooden box with gleaming brass handles. The nuns had sung hymns of great solemnity and the new bishop had conducted the Requiem Mass.

None of them had known then it was the end of an era.

But it was.

CHAPTER FORTY-TWO

The undertaker suggested the open casket should remain in the drawing room for seven days, which to Ettie, seemed an unnatural length of time.

The old bishop had lain in his wooden box for just two days in the convent chapel. To Ettie, the recollection of this, though some years ago, seemed natural and in accordance with her beliefs. During Requiem Mass the nuns and congregation had filed past the coffin, solemnly bowing their heads and making the sign of the cross.

The orphans were too small to view the marble-white features of the old man and had been ordered to remain seated on their pews. But Ettie had attended the benediction the previous day. Being taller in height she had paused at the coffin. She had never seen a corpse before but, in the company of the nuns, the old bishop had only looked a little pale and asleep.

Not so Lucas. His bloated features revealed the full ravages of his suffering. Each time Ettie gazed on him, her heart broke again.

It was with Terence's help that she had dressed him in his best suit before he was removed to the drawing room, where it was said that mourners could visit. Another notice had been hung on the door:

'Mr Lucas Benjamin has passed away and respects are welcomed. The funeral service is to be at Highgate Chapel, 14th September, at 11 o'clock precisely.'

But there were few visitors. Just Mrs Buckle who dabbed her nose and kissed Ettie's cheek reverently and Terence, who offered to keep Ettie company throughout. But she had politely refused. Discussing the loss only upset her more.

Her prayers felt repetitive. The habit which had once seemed so essential to her life, now seemed redundant. The God she had begged to spare her family had turned a deaf ear. Even Rose, Lucas's own mother, had remained aloof.

The great hole that Terence warned her about, had opened up. She fell deep inside and prayers had no power in this endless pit.

The only relief she found was in the nursery. Here she sat in Clara's chair and recalled the joy that was lost. She saw Clara and the baby boy, his bright blue eyes like his father's as he snuggled against Clara's full breasts. She even at times — a little guiltily — imagined holding him in her own arms and soothing him.

Each day she fell into dreaming; this angelic infant became as real to her as the children outside in Silver Street. His features were handsome; a small nose like Clara's, and Lucas's toothy smile, an abundance of golden curls and skin as soft and tender as a puppy's.

She rocked him in her arms, this child of her imagination. Perfectly formed and healthy, with no lesions or scars or deformity, he was perfect in every way.

Perfect . . .

It was here, the day before the burial service at the Highgate chapel, that Terence discovered her. Having given him a key, he let himself in and out, delivering the choicest cuts and little treats in order to sustain her.

'My, my, what's this?' he asked in surprise as he entered the nursery.

Ettie looked up, disappointed to be disturbed from her reverie. Her hands fell to her lap but she managed a small smile. 'I didn't hear you call.'

'Many times I did,' he said frowning. 'Come, young beauty, you shouldn't be in here all alone.'

'I like it,' she replied.

'You may, but it ain't healthy. Close this place up now, Ettie.'

'But the baby . . .'

'The baby and its mother and father are not present, my love. This room is as empty as your larder downstairs. Come with Terence now. And let's fill its shelves.'

Ettie didn't want to leave. She felt safe, comforted. And that wooden box was downstairs, where a man lay; a man she could not bear to look at, to witness his suffering again.

'Come now,' Terence took her arm and hoisted her from the chair. 'This lamenting will do you no good. Come with old Terence.'

And so Ettie went, though reluctantly.

'Promise me, that's the end of that,' Terence said unusually harshly as he sat her down at the kitchen table. 'Promise me?'

Ettie bowed her head. She was afraid of the pain that would surely flow into the pit and drown her if she could not sit in the nursery. All the same, she dutifully nodded.

'We have a matter to discuss,' said Terence who drew up a chair beside her. 'I've an offer to make you. Though it will take some thinking on from your point of view.'

Ettie did not feel like being made an offer of any sort; her head and heart were still attached to the nursery.

'You are still very young and have a future ahead of you.'

Ettie looked into the butcher's steady gaze. 'I have. Though where it is, I don't know.'

'These premises may stay open. They may not. Who do they belong to, I wonder?'

'I can't think,' replied Ettie.

'I advise you to go through the house, my dear, for there must be papers to alert you as to what might be the outcome.'

'The outcome of what?'

'Dare I say it — death. If the business is sold and even if not, you can't put no reliance on staying here. You do understand my meaning, young beauty?'

Ettie was silent for her mind was clouded.

'A new home will have to be found; a worthy one that fits your skills, for now, after all this time in business, you have learned many.'

'As an assistant you mean?'

'As a livelihood that deserves your attention.'

'But where will I go, Terence, to find such a home?'

In his usual calm manner, he smiled and raised a finger.

'Terence has thought it all out. I have a spare room, nothing fancy, nothing frilly. But it's yours while you decide. There may be a position in the paper. Or a shop in Soho that needs an assistant. You are educated, oh yes! And honest and trustworthy. Why there will be many opportunities I am sure.'

Ettie felt her world slide, as though it was about to topple her yet deeper into the pit. This was where she belonged, the tobacconist's house on Silver Street.

'You understand me?' Terence coaxed gently. 'A change is in order. And I'll help you in every way — yes, yes, no need to worry at all.'

But Ettie didn't feel worried; above all, she felt resentment raise its ugly head and bare its teeth.

'Good girl,' Terence praised with fatherly affection. He patted her shoulder as he always did, as if to say there was no problem he couldn't solve. But Ettie knew deep inside that Terence was part of this new misery. Whenever she looked at him, whenever she thought of the butcher and remembered his kindness, she also thought of her loss.

'Now,' he said with a happy finality, 'I've brought some bangers; good juicy ones an' all. We'll mash up the spuds and you'll feel better, you'll see, once they're eaten.'

But Ettie did not care about the bangers and spuds. She did not care about anything.

CHAPTER FORTY-THREE

Since Ettie had no money of her own to pay the burial costs, she used what she had stored away since their visit to The Old Lady. To keep things straight, she wrote the expenses in the accounts, just as Lucas had taught her.

He had left no instructions on the matter, though Ettie had searched the house from top to bottom, as Terence suggested. Lucas had neither spoken of death in any respect nor where his parents might be buried. No legal representative was ever named, or parson or vicar, or church or chapel. She knew the finer details of his life and the tobacco that was his passion. But with regard to death and dying, Lucas it seemed, had denied its existence.

Three pounds and ten shillings were dispersed to the beneficiaries. Ettie made two requests of the officials; the first that Lucas Benjamin's last resting place might be amongst trees and pleasant greenery. The second, that if ever transported to England, the remains of his wife and son might join him.

Ettie's hopes were realized as the morning dawned with a soft breeze that blew bonfire smoke and crumpled brown leaves through the pretty wilderness spilling with wild flowers under the autumn trees. At least, Ettie thought, this miniature garden would be approved of by Lucas. He had written so beautifully of the mountains. He would surely approve of this sweet little dell?

An unknown vicar conducted the service, remembering, at the graveside, to include the family names and brief history of the tobacconist of Silver Street. This stilted information, Ettie reflected, had been prepared from the notes that she had provided, in the absence of any other.

The event attracted few mourners, though notices had been posted in the newspaper. The gentlemen whom Lucas had so loyally served, the acquaintances he had made and even Florence and Thomas — none of them attended.

The coffin arrived, supported by four strong shoulders, one pair belonging to Terence, bareheaded, and dressed entirely in black to befit the occasion.

The butcher played his part with elegance and helped to lower the coffin into the ground. When freed from its tethers, Ettie stepped forward to cast in a handful of earth from the gravedigger's mound. The rich, moist soil lay fresh on the polished wood surface.

Tears slipped gently from her eyes onto her Sunday best coat; the same coat she had last worn to visit The Old Lady. It was an innocent, happy time when she had believed the tobacconist of Silver Street, his wife Clara and their child, were soon to return from the towering mountains of Switzerland, to England.

* * *

The day after the funeral, Ettie coaxed herself into the salon, intending to remove the notices that still hung from the door. But her fingers stilled as she drew the blinds.

Her heart was not in it. To destroy the evidence of the tobacconist's life and death was beyond her.

Instead she took up the duster and began to clean the neglected room. Who would take care of these same shelves, polish the glass counter and keep Lucas's secret safe behind the wooden panel, she wondered, when as Terence had warned her, the business was sold and she was dismissed from her duties? Who would care for the salon then?

Her thoughts were suddenly interrupted by a tap on the door, where an elderly man stood, peering in. He was dressed formally in a long, dark coat and black necktie and carried a portmanteau.

Was this some distant relative, she wondered? Or a business colleague who had just discovered the tragedy?

Quickly she left her dusting and unlocked the salon door.

'Good day to you,' he said and removed his tall hat. Casting a beady eye over her shoulder he enquired, 'Am I addressing one Miss Henrietta O'Reilly?'

'Yes, sir, that is me.' Ettie could not put an age on him, but thought that his salt and pepper dark hair, silvering at his whiskers might put him in Terence's category. He was not very tall and quite stout and somewhat out of breath as he paused there.

'I am Mr Pike, a representative of the attorneys at law, Shingle and Dover.' His plump cheeks quivered a little but his small, dark button eyes were keen and fixed on Ettie. 'I have some business to conduct in regard to the late Mr Lucas Benjamin.'

Ettie stood back, alarmed. 'But Mr Pike, I am just an assistant. I mean, I was . . .'

'Indeed, I am acquainted with your circumstances, Miss O'Reilly, through correspondence with your late employer. May I come in? Better to be seated,' said Mr Pike, increasing Ettie's concern.

'As you wish, sir,' agreed Ettie hesitantly.

She locked the door and led him along the passage to the kitchen. After the funeral she had closed off the other rooms, draping sheets across the furniture and drawing the drapes.

'Please take a seat,' she offered as Mr Pike opened his case. He placed a number of papers on the table, seeming a little uncomfortable amongst all the cooking paraphernalia.

Ettie chose a chair at one end, Mr Pike the other. An offer of refreshment was not made, nor did the attorney request any.

'First,' he began, locking together his fingers, 'my condolences on what must have been an unexpected outcome to your employment here. The steps you took on your employer's behalf, post-mortem, are commendable.'

'Thank you,' replied Ettie curiously. 'But how did you know Mr Benjamin has passed away?'

'Once the death certificate is signed and funeral notices posted, the bank is impelled to act in a case like this.'

Ettie looked blankly at the little man. 'In a case like this?' she repeated.

'I am aggrieved to say a demand for repayment of the substantial debt incurred before the late person's death, has been issued.'

Ettie swallowed, unable to understand this statement. 'Sir, there cannot be a debt. With the assistance of a friend, I delivered three hundred and thirty pounds, ten shillings and sixpence to the Bank of England. I have a temporary Pass Book to prove it.'

The old man opened his portmanteau again and took out a small black book just like the one she been given by the under-manager.

'This is the genuine Pass Book sent from abroad to my firm by the late Mr Benjamin. For the sake of clarity, I will allow you to examine it for yourself. Can you read?'

'Yes, sir, I can.'

'Please note, the debt was incurred initially by Mr Lucas Benjamin's father. In short, it doubled and trebled until, before his death he took out another loan, this time against his home and business in order to offset the extraordinary costs of his wife's foreign treatments.'

Ettie took the Pass Book and opened it at the first browned page. There were many lines and columns of figures, all arranged neatly and accompanied by signatures. At the end of each page was a total, just as, in the same way, she had completed the salon's accounts. The clear difference was, that as the months and years had passed, the figures ran into many hundreds of pounds.

'You will see that for a while, the cash-flow problem was resolved somewhat, when Mrs Rose Benjamin took over the running of the business. However, this state of affairs did not reduce the overwhelming historical debt.'

Ettie turned to the last page of the Pass Book and was shocked to see the many entries made of Lucas's withdrawals, paid to the physicians in Switzerland.

'You understand now, I hope, Miss O'Reilly?' Mr Pike said with raised eyebrows. 'With no hope of repayment, I am here to take possession of the properties that in law, are now owned by the Bank of England.' He reached forward and lifted the book from her hands, sliding it carefully back into his portmanteau.

'I must warn you that our receivers will be here at mid-day tomorrow to oversee the bank's claim.' He looked at her a little more kindly and said, 'my advice would be to collect your belongings together and leave before their arrival. Have you a key?'

Ettie sat dumfounded. This had all happened too soon. She had known the end had to come, but in such a manner?

'Yes, I have a key.'

'And cash? Is there any?'

Ettie nodded.

'Then I must have it.' The older man stood up. 'Shall we go?'

With legs that barely had the strength to walk, Ettie led the way to the salon where she showed Mr Pike the wooden panel and the key to unlock it. He was swiftly on his knees and removed every coin and note to his portmanteau.

Ettie watched in stunned silence. When he had finished his business, he asked, 'And books? Accounts? I shall take those too.'

Ettie gave him the accounts book and scraps of paper she had collected together with the temporary Pass Book.

'Please remove the remaining stock to the safe,' he ordered and watched as she went to the shelves and cleared them, laying all the tobaccos that remained in the cast-iron chest. After which, Mr Pike locked it and closed the wooden panel with the lever.

'By law you must return any property either loaned or given, by the late proprietor, to the bank,' he reminded her.

Ettie could not think of a single thing and shook her head. 'Just my uniform.'

'Please leave it before you go.'

Ettie looked into this man's small, piercing eyes and felt the final indignity. Even the clothes she wore now belonged to The Old Lady.

Mr Pike put on his hat and bid her good afternoon. A carriage had arrived outside and he climbed into it, without a glance back.

She could not help but gaze around the bare and empty salon and her tears fell again as she gazed up at Rose in a new light. Her enigmatic smile hid so much anguish. Lucas's father had created the downfall of their lives, just as Lucas had insisted in his delirium. The debts incurred through his papa's squandering were unbreakable chains binding the family's ankles. Chains from which neither Rose nor Lucas had ever been able to escape.

CHAPTER FORTY-FOUR

It was now late afternoon and Ettie had recovered a little from Mr Pike's visit. There were many things on her mind; the keenest of them all, to visit Terence, the friend to whom she was indebted. Without his presence in her life, her world would have been a far lonelier place.

'Just look at the ray of sunshine that spills in my door!' Terence exclaimed when she stepped inside his shop. 'I'll wrap you a nice bit of mutton for stewing. No fat, just tender meat to fall off the bone.'

Ettie smiled, but in as few words as she could think of, she began to describe the attorney's visit.

'What an intrusion! What a liberty!' Terence exclaimed, swinging down the meat cleaver so hard that its sharp blade stuck firmly into the wooden slab. 'You should have run down to me. I would have put the cheeky fellow in his place.'

'Mr Pike was only doing his job.'

'Mr Pike lorded it over a young girl! Then besmirched a dead man's name.'

'Not exactly, Terence. The bank is owed the property and will take it.' Ettie did not want to elaborate too much, for she knew that Terence would make a great fuss. A fuss out of the kindness of his heart and one that she appreciated, but he could do nothing to change the salon's fate.

'I shall shut up shop,' Terence decided, casting the cleaver into a pail of water. He wiped his hands on a soiled cloth and drew them down his apron. 'And come with you to pack your things. By nightfall you'll be settled in my spare room. Tomorrow we can set about a fresh start. Soho is kind to its own. We shall tour its streets and discover a position befitting the late tobacconist's clever young assistant.'

'I would prefer to stay a last night in the house,' she murmured, hoping she gave no offence. 'To make certain it's left in a presentable state.'

'Why my dear!' he objected, throwing up his arms, 'that blessed bank don't deserve a presentable state. It deserves a kick up its backside!'

'If only Mr Benjamin had been able to repay the debt,' Ettie murmured sadly, 'the salon might have been saved.'

The butcher nodded slowly. 'You may be right, but that don't mean a stuffed shirt might put you under the cosh.'

Inhaling the familiar and beloved smell of sawdust on Terence's clothes, Ettie kissed his cheek.

'What's that for, dear girl?' he said in embarrassment.

'You've been a dear friend.'

'Truly *my* gain,' he replied with a choke.

Ettie's heart ached. She knew, though Terence did not, that her mind was made up for the future.

She could not walk the streets of Soho to find a position. Or live in Terence's spare room and each day, see again, the sights of Soho that had brought her such happiness or remind her of whom she had lost. The family's ghosts would always be there, shadowing her footsteps; Lucas and Clara and their boy, half in another world now, but trapped in this earthly limbo by Ettie's own painful longing.

She would not wish to extend their suffering, but free them to go their way, as she must hers. Though it would cost her every ounce of willpower, her life in Soho had come to an end.

‘I’ll allow your request,’ said Terence stoutly, clearing his throat with manly fortitude. ‘But tomorrow, my beauty, at nine o’clock sharp, I shall call for you. Carry your bags I will and we’ll parade down Silver Street with our heads held up high.’

Ettie smiled, forcing back the tears so that Terence would not guess that this was a parting.

Their final goodbye.

CHAPTER FORTY-FIVE

Ettie sat for the last time in Clara's nursing chair. She felt the gentle breeze blow through the window, as if Clara was answering her thoughts and bidding her goodbye with nature's own sweet breath. The candlelight flickered and Ettie smiled as if they were together in a pact.

The perambulator and crib stood with their pretty covers and the little table with its trinkets and brushes that Ettie had arranged.

Rose's portrait now hung where the bishop's silver crucifix had hung; its nail secured by use of the kitchen rolling pin, to support the frame's weight. Rose looked benignly down on her grandson's room. Ettie knew that whatever might befall this building, she had done her very best to send it off, like the Vikings of old sent their barges to Valhalla, and the people of the Ganges, might send their funeral pyres. She had read of these commemorations in the convent's history books and now it seemed, they had guided her to this moment, when her life had returned full circle to its beginning.

Memories of Sister Patrick and Sister Ukunda, and the orphans surrounded her. Michael appeared, undiminished in her mind from the young rebel of her early years at the orphanage. And together with Lucas, Clara and the baby, was her mother, Colleen O'Reilly of Henrietta Street in Dublin, Ireland.

That night, she went to Lucas's bedroom. Gone was the agony her employer had suffered. 'Goodbye, Mr Benjamin,' she whispered as she took the crucifix from under his pillow. 'We'll meet again one day, I am sure. You are free from the chains that bind you here. Take care of your little family.'

Dawn broke and Ettie left the letter she had written for Terence on the glass counter. She had promised to write to him, though when she could not say. Slipping on her coat and taking her cloth bag, she slipped quietly down Silver Street and away from the place she had once called home.

CHAPTER FORTY-SIX

Ettie reached Oxford Street just as the city began another busy shopping day. She had banked all her hopes on the milliner's offer of an apprenticeship and she opened the door cautiously, hoping to see a friendly face.

'Is the milliner here?' Ettie asked as a haughty looking woman appeared. Her expression showed that she clearly disapproved of Ettie's appearance.

'I am the new owner,' she replied.

'Oh dear . . .' Ettie had not expected this turn of events.

'How may I help you?' the new owner enquired, not sounding as though she wanted to help Ettie at all.

'The lady who was here before, offered me an apprenticeship . . .'

'What are your skills?' interrupted the woman before Ettie could finish her sentence.

'I was employed as an assistant to the tobacconist of Silver Street in Soho.'

'Soho?' the new owner repeated, stepping back a little as if she might catch a disease. 'I'm afraid there are no vacancies here.'

'But I was . . .'

'I bid you good day,' came the reply, leaving Ettie in no doubt that their conversation had ended.

With shoulders drooping Ettie left, wondering why she had not considered the possibility there may have been a change in the shop's circumstances. Disappointed that her one realistic hope of employment had vanished, she walked the length of Oxford Street, gazing in the shiny windows, ashamed of her dowdy reflection.

It was not surprising that the new owner of the milliner's had refused her request. Nevertheless, she continued her search, enquiring in the busy shops that were now filling with customers.

'All positions are taken,' said the owner of a restaurant, as he kept her standing at the entrance, unwilling to let her in.

'Clear off, we don't want your sort round here bringing down the tone of the area,' scolded a red-faced woman behind the counter of a prosperous-looking bakery.

'I suppose you're on the cadge from the parson,' demanded a policeman when she asked the way to the nearest church.

'I should like to pray,' Ettie replied unwittingly.

'Go back to the East End,' he ordered, 'and don't let me see you round here again.'

Ettie felt her cheeks burn with humiliation. Did her appearance condemn her so badly? If only she had cared for herself a little more, but she had lost interest since Lucas's return from Switzerland. Her thick chestnut locks had seemed nothing but an inconvenience and she had scooped them back into a plain bun. The last time she had looked in the mirror a pale and gaunt stranger had gazed back at her. Before she had left Soho, she had folded the brown uniform she loved so much into a neat pile for The Old Lady's men to find.

Darkness began to fall and the shops of the city turned off their lights. Front doors were locked and the West End lost its glow of life. Only the gentlemen's carriages passed, transporting their wealthy occupants to their clubs. And so Ettie was forced to seek shelter in the park, where at least, she was able to rest her weary legs.

There on a bench, she huddled up, staring into the unknown shadows which reminded her uncomfortably of Old Jim. She thought of Michael and wondered where he was. And how sad a sight she would make if he set eyes on her now. Perhaps he wouldn't even recognize her!

She slept just a few hours, dreaming of Michael who, wearing a handsome new suit and top hat, walked past her, his well-to-do lady friend on his arm.

The next day, as the sun rose over the city, she hauled her aching bones from the bench and began her tour of the city once more. This time she visited the hospitals and hotels. She was prepared to do any menial work; scrubbing, cleaning, or washing the sick and disabled. But the answer was always the same when they saw her crumpled coat, dishevelled hair and dust-covered boots.

'No vacancies!' they exclaimed. Another door closed in her face.

'We don't employ vagrants,' they cried.

'Go away. The West End doesn't need your type.'

Where once the insults hurt, Ettie grew to expect them. She sensed even before the people spoke to her, she was to be rejected.

The only kindness she found was when she joined a queue for distressed women who stood at a small hut by the river. Here free tea was dispensed to the thirsty and a crust of bread to the starving — followed by a severe lecture on their morals. Ettie didn't listen to what was being said. She was grateful for the refreshment, for without it, she might have faded away.

That evening, she walked by the river to the mud flats where she saw beggars settling against the mossy wharves and under the bridges. These spaces were damp and smelly, but not as frightening as the parks.

One such niche provided her with brief rest. For early in the morning the tide rushed in and chased her away.

The third and fourth nights, she huddled under the railway arches and scavenged from bins, just as she saw the others doing.

As Ettie gazed up to the moon one night, shivering and exhausted, she knew this state of affairs could not continue. She had never felt so hungry in all her life. Her feet were covered in blisters. Her clothes were torn and foul-smelling. On the eighth night a rabble of stray dogs chased her from a café's bins, snapping at her heels and growling so menacingly, she almost fainted with fright.

Somehow, she escaped the vicious pack and eventually found a doorstep to rest on. As the cold bit into her body with teeth as sharp as the wild dogs', she thought of Terence and that safe, warm room above the butcher's shop. Had he found her letter?

Perhaps she should return to Soho? This city held no prospects. If she was not to starve or freeze to death, what alternative was there?

But in her depths of misery, Ettie knew it would be unkind to impose on such a good man's nature. She had taken the decision to leave Silver Street and she must stick by it.

Her stomach churned emptily. The cold wind howled into the doorway like a whirlwind. As dawn broke, she trudged on, leaving the city and all her hopes of employment behind her. The sights she had marvelled at before, she now dismissed for they offered no solace to her fatigued body and despondent mind.

Even the chiming of Big Ben at the tallest height of the Houses of Parliament did not cause her head to turn. The Tower of London and the sight of the busy professional classes that sped from Blackfriars to the shores of the south, no longer held any excitement. The city had rejected her and Ettie trudged on, towards her old home.

By evening she saw the low flying gulls of Docklands and the ships that sailed proudly along the estuary. Tall-masted and majestic as kings and princes, they anchored midstream, awaiting their turns to dock. The salt and tarry air that she remembered so well, was even more potent as a round and confident moon cast ribbons of silver across the river.

Ettie followed its gentle curve beneath the stars, entering the narrow streets of smoke-stained terraces that fringed the horseshoe of land surrounded on three sides by water. The Isle of Dogs, the beating heart of London's East End.

It was not to the burned-down convent she had returned but to the place that Michael had always feared. And which she now feared, too, but was too desperate to ignore.

CHAPTER FORTY-SEVEN

Ettie stumbled through the high gates of the Municipal Workhouse and knocked on the wooden door. A heavy lock was drawn inside; a key rattled in its hole.

A face half-hidden by a frilled white cap, peered out.

'Will you take me in?' Ettie pleaded. 'I've nowhere else to go.'

'What time of night do you call this?'

'I'm sorry. I've walked a long way.'

'Where from?' returned the curious voice.

'I lived in Silver Street, Soho.'

This had a strange effect as slowly, the door opened. 'Soho, you say?'

'I've tried in the city for work. But there is none.'

'Looking like that, I'm not surprised.' The woman, dressed in a sombre brown uniform let the door swing open. 'You'd better come in. You're lucky. The Master is still in his office.'

Ettie was taken through a dark, unpleasant smelling passage and shown into a room at the far end. A man sat at a desk, his stomach protruding from his waistcoat and his bleary, red-veined eyes, unwelcoming. Ettie saw a half-full glass of amber liquid among the many papers.

'What's this, Matron?' he demanded.

'A latecomer. Says she's from Soho.' There was something in the Matron's voice that Ettie didn't care for.

'Does she indeed?' The Master leaned back and wiped his lips with the back of his cuff. 'Name, wench?'

'Henrietta O'Reilly, Sir.'

'Age?'

'Fifteen, Sir.'

His gaze grew interested. 'So you're a working girl, eh?'

'I was an assistant to the tobacconist of Silver Street, until his recent death.'

He quirked an eyebrow under his thick, greasy black hair. 'And what else did you do in Soho? Speak now and be honest!'

'Sir, it's the truth.'

'Have you any money?' he asked with a frown.

'No, none.'

'Friends, relations or enemies wanting you?'

Ettie shook her head. 'I am from the orphanage of the Sisters of Clemency.'

'Hmm.' He narrowed his gaze intimately over her body and Ettie shivered from head to foot. 'They taught you right from wrong I suppose?'

'I was given a Christian education, Sir.'

His expression told her that he was not impressed. 'I care not what you have learned, only that you cause me no trouble. No fighting, no cursing, no meddling. Keep a civil tongue in your head and you'll be fed and given shelter in return.' With a flick of his hand he barked, 'Scrub her up Matron and tomorrow we'll put her down the tunnels. See if she knows the meaning of real work.'

Without a pause the Matron grabbed her shoulder and marched her off. Ettie sensed that even before they entered the washroom in the yard this would be a humiliating experience.

Matron pushed her forward into the rank-smelling room soured by strong disinfectant. A large stained tub stood amidst a puddle of dirty water. Beside it, an assortment of stiff bristle brushes hanging from the peeling wall.

'Strip, O'Reilly! Every article,' ordered the Matron, folding her arms. 'Now we shall see what the cat's dragged in.'

PART THREE: THE WORKHOUSE

CHAPTER FORTY-EIGHT

November 1896

Ettie gazed into the fetid waters of the underground sewer. It was here in this cramped space that she had been put to work as a flusher for the past three months. Leaning heavily against the slimy wall, she closed her tired brown eyes. How much longer could she endure this backbreaking work?

From the day Ettie had arrived, she had fallen foul of the Matron, who had been only too eager to make her life impossible. The very next morning, Matron had marched her into the yard.

'Your work is down there,' she had instructed, pointing to a wooden grate in the cobbles. 'Don't come up until I call you!'

The stench that had issued from the hole as she lifted the heavy covering almost made Ettie faint. After climbing down the rickety ladder into the underground tunnels, Ettie had discovered how treacherous a flusher's work could be. Her job was to break up the piles of London's sewage as it flowed towards the river. Clogging the main arteries were rats, mice, corpses of dogs, cats and even cattle. But it was the remains of tiny babies and children that were the most distressing.

Sometimes it was only a pathetic limb or tiny fingers that made them recognizable.

At first, Ettie had retched and gagged as she pushed the spade to clear the congestion. Her stomach had turned. Her skin had crawled, but over the weeks she resolved to survive all that befell her. She refused to die in this loathsome place.

And therefore, she continued each day, leaving the dormitory in the morning where the women and children slept. She returned at night to eat a paltry supper and join the army of roaches that infested their quarters.

'Keep yer head down,' the women always advised her. 'Make sure you keep out of that bugger's way,' they warned. 'The Master's a devil that escaped hell. And even Satan himself don't want him back.'

And so Ettie had avoided the attention of the Master. But at times like this with the smell of death all around her in the tunnels, she almost wished that death would take her, too.

'You're wanted,' Matron's voice suddenly bellowed from above.

Startled, Ettie gazed up. The small ring of daylight from where the summons had come almost blinded her.

'I'm not finished,' Ettie called back nervously.

'The Master wants you. Them's your orders,' returned the Matron who unhelpfully dropped the drain's cover. The light vanished and gloom returned.

Ettie knew she was left with little choice and hung her spade to the ladder's hook by the Tilley lamp. She grasped the damp rungs, each one more slippery than the last. At the end of the day her fingers were sore and each movement was hazardous. Below her, the giant lumps of fat and excrement floated, grotesque islands of filth bobbing along on a putrid sea. Even a brief dip into the rotting tide would soak her tunic.

Carefully she ascended, leaving behind her prison. What could the Master want? All the women scattered when they saw him and Ettie was no exception.

She paused unsteadily on the top rung. Raising one hand, she pushed on the heavy grate. It refused to give way. Why hadn't Matron left it open? She knew the answer, though. Nowhere in the workhouse rules did it say that inmates must be treated with care and consideration. Instead, they were thought of as vermin; less than the rats that ran freely in their millions in the tunnels below the streets of the East End.

'One more push,' Ettie encouraged herself. Finally, the cover gave way. A world of daylight engulfed her and she gasped in the fresh air. Pulling herself up, she sat on the ledge for a few minutes to recover. She was back in the world of the living.

Across the workhouse yard stood Matron. Her sleeves were rolled up to her nobbly elbows and her fists curled impatiently on her hips. 'Think yourself lucky I filled them pails with water. I only done it as the Master wants you quick. There's a clean shift on the peg and a pair of drawers. Put 'em on as fast as you like.'

This news came as another thunderbolt. For new clothes were never issued to inmates. What could the Master want of her so urgently she wondered again?

'Hurry, don't dawdle!' the Matron ordered and marched off.

Ettie hauled herself to her feet and sucked in as much oxygen as she could.

Padding over to the pails, she hauled them one by one into the wash house. The stink from here was almost as stifling as the sewers. Removing her boots, tunic and underclothes, she scrubbed at her skin but the sewer smell was ingrained in her flesh. With the aid of a threadbare cloth, she dried herself.

The shift was rough and heavy and the new clogs a size too small. At least they were clean. Yet why had she been issued with fresh clothing?

December's nip was icy in the air as she stepped into the yard. Ettie's throat tightened. What was about to happen? She had always done her best to avoid the Master. Many times Ettie had considered running away. Other inmates had done so, only to return, half-starved, broken and more desperate than ever.

Common sense prevailed and Ettie made her way to the Master's office. Only last week she had asked Matron to be transferred to the kitchens. Her request had promptly been denied. But had a vacancy occurred? If only that were so!

Standing outside the Master's office, her nerve almost failed. She tapped lightly on the door. When no answer came, she tried again.

There was a crash and an angry groan. The door flew open and the swaying figure of the Master appeared. 'Get in here,' he slurred.

She stepped warily inside. 'Yes, Sir?' she said in a timid voice.

'You took your time.' He pushed his hands over his drink-stained waistcoat. A drooling smile flickered across his lips. He was not a tall man but was broad-shouldered and weighty. A hard leather belt encircled his ample girth.

'I heard you want to work in the kitchens,' he said in a threatening growl.

Ettie was too frightened to answer. Her mouth opened but the words stuck in her throat.

'Well, girl? Answer me!'

Ettie nodded. 'Y . . . yes, Sir. I do.'

The sweat poured out from under his lank hair and onto his forehead. His thick lips curled as he lifted a fat finger to scratch his stubbled chin.

Ettie was so nervous she could hardly draw breath. Was he going to grant her request?

'I have been very generous to you,' he muttered. 'Do you like your new clothes?'

'Yes . . . yes. Thank you.'

'Our supplies for our inmates are very low.' He looked over her slowly. 'Very low indeed. You have been favoured.'

Ettie knew this was untrue. She had seen the well-stocked shelves in the Matron's cupboards. Still, it would not be wise to disagree.

'I've decided to grant your request, Mistress O'Reilly,' he said, stepping closer so that she could smell his sour breath. 'You'll be a flusher no longer. Instead you will be a workhouse skivvy. You'll be scrubbing the floors and washing the walls, disinfecting the lavatories, and sweeping the dormitories and passages. And, when you've finished that, you'll help with the potato? peeling, skewering, and cutting and stringing up of the meats.'

Ettie could not believe her good fortune. She was to leave the malodorous underground tunnels and tide of excretion that poured ceaselessly into the River Thames. Any work would be better than that!

'I am very grateful—'

'You are, are you?'

Ettie lowered her eyes, for suddenly she suspected what was in this drunken man's mind and it terrified her.

'Did I not put a roof over your head and provide decent employment? Have I not fed and clothed you and given you a comfortable bed to sleep in, where no danger may befall you?'

Ettie forced herself to nod. But how could he imagine that she enjoyed being imprisoned in those stinking tunnels? A decent roof, he said! Had he not witnessed the dormitories in which the inmates lived, running alive with bugs? The rooms were so cold in winter that death came as a relief to the frail and elderly.

'Then show me your gratitude!' he shouted.

Ettie shrank back as he reached out. 'Please, Sir, no!'

'Slut! Whore! Am I not as deserving as your Soho types?'

'I am not a . . .' Ettie stammered in panic. 'I . . . I was raised by nuns who taught me it was a sin to . . .'

'Liar!' the Master exclaimed, giving her a rough push. 'You ungrateful wench! If not for me you would have rotted on the streets. Yet you deny me a little cuddle?'

Ettie wanted to be sick at the thought. All that the other women had told her was true. She tried to move away from his grasp but he barred her path.

'Stay still,' he growled, grabbing hold of her arm. She resisted and with a bellow of annoyance he threw her against the wall. The blow sent her flying. 'Give in to me, slut, or you'll pay!' He pulled at her clothes, ripping the cheap material until her breasts were exposed.

Ettie fought as hard and long as she could. But even in drink, his strength was overpowering. When she continued to resist, he balled his fist and struck her hard in the belly.

Ettie keeled over, the air forced from her body. Again he struck her and again until, dizzy with pain, she fell to her knees.

'I'll teach you a lesson you'll never forget.' He was breathless now from the exertion of the blows he had delivered and collapsed on top of her, straddling her between his knees, fumbling to unbutton his trousers.

CHAPTER FORTY-NINE

'Give way or you'll perish,' he threatened and Ettie's heart froze. This man was a heartless thug. Fight as she may, with teeth and nails and whatever strength was left to her, he'd do as he promised. Of this she was certain.

But even if she succumbed, would he show mercy? Or, might she end up in the sewer tunnels, rotting and stinking, a lifeless corpse?

'I beg you, have mercy,' she croaked.

Another blow silenced her. Recoiling in agony, Ettie stared into the Master's drunken, gloating face. She could barely see his ugly features, for her eye was almost closed.

She recalled the stories she'd been told of the women who had fought him with bravery. Many had perished from their injuries, no match for such a brutal attack.

Is it my turn now? Ettie wondered as she closed her eyes, the one with sight, the other blind in its swollen socket. She had fought all she could. Now it was up to God to save her.

Suddenly the Master's hands were thrusting apart her legs. His curses were vile as he tore away her underclothes.

'Whore, slag,' he growled and her skin became a trembling cloak under his touch. What kind of monster was he?

Ettie was filled with silent loathing. But she could not contain her scream as he arched above her. It was both a sound of horror and yet of defiance.

After that scream followed a strangled gasp that was not hers. It came instead from the Master's throat. His face, so violent and moving, became still. Spittle hung suspended from his lips. His cheeks, half-hidden by glistening whiskers, sucked in a gasp.

He stared at her with startled eyes. His fingers stilled around his now limp appendage sagging against the ale-stained cloth of his trousers. Swaying back and forth he gurgled and groaned. In spasms he seemed to be, as she watched his blackened fingers quiver up to his throat.

Ettie dared to move, fearing he would rouse and drag her back again. But he seemed not to notice as the unknown devil writhed inside him.

Once more he tried to recover, but the spasm held fast. It flushed his face to purple, spat white foam from his mouth, bulged his eye sockets venomously, arched his back and contorted his expression. With jerks and starts, he fell on his side. Thrashing and floundering, he squirmed on the mucky floor.

Ettie huddled against the wall as the spectacle transfixed her. Suddenly, as if waking from a nightmare, she clutched her clothes and drew them on. With her back to the wall, she moved slowly, not daring to take her eyes from the fitting man.

Escape was within reach. Would the Matron be waiting outside? With shaking fingers, she opened the door. The gloomily lit passage was empty. There was no movement, though she could hear Matron's voice drifting from far off.

Standing breathless and trembling, she paused. When all was silent, she ran as fast as her feeble legs would carry her, back to her bed in the dormitory, the only place of safety that was left to her.

CHAPTER FIFTY

Every bone in her body ached. She lay still in the dawn's early light, trying to control her fear. She wanted to pull the worn blanket over her head and return to that safe place in sleep.

Now that she was awake, she must face the day. She had temporarily escaped the attentions of the Master. The hand of fate had intervened. But the memory of his hands intruding over her body still haunted her. His evil face appeared in her mind, sweat laden and contorted. Yet the Matron had not come in the night to punish her.

'Wake up, gel,' a croaky voice whispered. 'Wake up!'

Ettie pushed back the blanket and saw the bent figure of an old woman standing over her. Rheumy eyes stared out from under her tangle of snow-white hair and her workhouse smock bore many stains and tears.

'Time to rouse,' she croaked. 'You've slept late. Everyone else has gone.'

Ettie sat up, her head banging painfully. She gazed round the dormitory. All the female inmates had left for work. 'Has Matron done her rounds?'

'No, but she's likely to any minute. And you'll get a chewing off if she catches you.'

Ettie felt the chill of the morning as she slipped from her bed. She still wore her torn shift, too frightened to remove it last night. Lifting one end of her straw mattress, she pulled out her shawl; it was more holes than wool, but it would cover the bruises.

'Better get a move on,' warned the old woman. Hobbling out of the dormitory, she left Ettie to escape the attentions of Matron.

But was she too late? Ettie froze as she heard heavy footsteps coming along the corridor. They came closer, fast and furious. As though the wearer of the studded boots was determined to issue a punishment.

Instead of the Matron, another figure appeared; a sour-looking woman dressed in severe grey robes.

'O'Reilly!' she bellowed. 'What's this?'

'I . . . I was just leaving,' Ettie stammered. She had never seen this woman before and did not like the look of her.

'We'll have none of this laziness,' snapped the stranger. 'I am here to enforce new rules and see they are kept.' She narrowed her eyes suspiciously. 'How came you by a blackened eye?'

'A speck blinded me, ma'am.' Had she been reported after all? Sweat clung to her spine and her heart raced. Was she about to be carted off?

'Are you unfit for work?'

'No, ma'am. I can see well enough.'

'Then you have no reason to dawdle. Idleness will not be tolerated in the workhouse.'

Ettie decided the less she said the better.

The angry woman poked Ettie painfully in the shoulder. 'Get yourself along to the medical room.'

'Please no!' Ettie pleaded, fearing the doctor, reputed to be as fearsome as the Master.

'Do as I tell you or you will be punished.'

Ettie forced her legs to move. They felt as though they might snap in two with the bruises from last night's attack. Her eyes briefly met the woman's hard, resolute stare.

Though Ettie was terrified at the thought of being sent to the doctor, she knew this hovering bully was waiting to pounce.

The very last thing that she saw as she stumbled away was the smile of satisfaction on the woman's cruel mouth.

CHAPTER FIFTY-ONE

Ettie stood shivering, expecting the worst. But today the doctor was absent, replaced by a young female orderly.

'Who give you them bruises?' the girl demanded.

'I fell in the tunnels.'

'Don't look like a fall to me.'

'I'm fit to work,' Ettie insisted. 'The sewers are slippery and I hit my head on the side.'

The orderly pushed a stray lock of dowdy brown hair under her mob cap. 'I ain't here to listen to your complaints. Get down on yer knees and stick yer head over that pail. I'm using the carbolic to kill those buggers in yer hair.'

Before Ettie could protest, she was pushed down on the wet floor. The strong smell of the lice-killing disinfectant washed into her nostrils. The girl's needle-like fingers probed into her scalp.

'Now finish yerself off,' panted the girl after her exertions. 'My back is breaking.'

Ettie raised her arms painfully, trying not to reveal the agony each movement caused. Her thoughts returned to the salon and the pump in the backyard where she had washed her hair, enjoying its gentle flow. On a fine morning, the sun would dip in between the roofs and dry it. She had never thought then that her life with the Benjamins was to end.

'Hurry!' the orderly commanded. 'I ain't got all day. Dry yerself off and make yerself presentable. There's others to come after you.'

Ettie wondered who the others were? But before she could ask, the girl pushed a coarse towel into her hands.

Ettie drew her hair over her shoulder and plaited it, relieved at least to have a little more sight in her eye. When she had finished, the girl wore an expression of disapproval.

'You're as ready as you'll ever be, s'pose,' she huffed.

'Am I to go before the Master?'

'The Master?' the girl repeated in surprise. 'Ain't you heard? Early this morning they dragged him 'orf on the back of a cart. Him trussed up like a stuck pig ready for the knacker's yard and Matron bawlin' her eyes out beside him. Good riddance to the pair of 'em, I say.'

Ettie stared in disbelief at the orderly. 'You mean he was . . .'

'Dead as a doornail.' She stuck her hands on her hips, eyeing Ettie spitefully. 'But don't get yer hopes up, dearie. A new Master might be twice as bad as the old. And where you're going might be even worse than here.'

CHAPTER FIFTY-TWO

Ettie stood huddled against the wall of the exercise yard. The news of the Master's demise had come as a shock. Had he died as a result of the fit after she left his room?

Standing beside her was a thin man with red, bushy hair. He was so thin that his bones stuck out from under his ragged coat. Next to him a young boy scratched at the pus-filled blisters on his face. A hunched and bedraggled woman stood with two little children; their starved features almost skeletal. Beyond this were the lame and aged who shivered violently in the cold December wind.

Her alarm increased as a stranger strode into the yard. He walked with a slight limp and was aided by a cane. Wearing a large felt hat positioned over his eyes and a heavy greatcoat, he came to a sudden halt. Two burly male orderlies stood with him.

'Be quick, bring the rest,' said the man to one of them. 'I've much to attend to today.'

The orderly hurried off and Ettie was filled with trepidation. Why were the inmates made to stand out in these bitter conditions? The grey walls loomed above them and the stormy sky threatened rain.

Two young women with painted faces swaggered into the yard. They tossed back their tousled hair with defiant expressions. She guessed they must be new to the workhouse as she had never seen them before.

The man with the cane addressed them, though Ettie couldn't hear what he'd said. One stepped forward and crudely adjusted her blouse to display her full breasts. This sight had no effect whatsoever on the man. The woman, apparently enraged that her offer had been rejected, broke into a stream of vile language. Her companion soon joined the fracas.

Ettie's heart thumped wildly. Under the brim of the man's hat, she glimpsed a cold, impenetrable stare. He gave an instruction that soon had the two women removed.

When all was quiet, the man limped slowly up and down. He inspected every one of the inmates. When it came to her turn, Ettie cast her eyes down, as she had learned to do in the workhouse. The seconds dragged as his shadow hovered over her.

By the time he limped away, Ettie was certain that he had decided on some terrible fate to befall her.

'I am the new Governor,' came a harsh voice that roused Ettie from her fearful thoughts. 'I want you to pay attention. I will be assuming the late Master's position. My wife will assist me as Matron.'

Ettie's head came up, as did all the others along the row of inmates. She stared at the new Governor. The woman who had come to the dormitory this morning must be his wife. So, the Master really was dead.

'I have been charged with the duty of reforming the workhouse,' the Governor continued. 'The borough is not a philanthropical society. It does not have bottomless pockets. And it has come to our understanding that this workhouse suffers from a squandering of generosity. This means I shall trim off the excess fat, cut down to the lean, and restore order.'

He took a slow, inward breath. 'The healthy amongst you will be found more *productive* work to do. Your wages will be added to the government's coffers in repayment for your board and lodging.' He straightened his shoulders and leaned both hands on his cane. 'All of you have been inspected and passed the medical examination. Think yourselves fortunate to be among the first to offer your assistance to this noble country in return for the hospitality it has shown you.'

Ettie glanced at the poorly-dressed and starving men, women and children who stood shivering beneath the workhouse walls. Most were sick. Some like her, had received severe beatings. What kind of *productive* work had this Governor planned for them?

'Obey your new employers. Disobey and you will find yourselves punished.'

Ettie choked down a sob. Not for herself, but the unfortunate souls in the workhouse who had done nothing to deserve such injustice.

* * *

Very soon they were sent through the workhouse gates to the street outside. Here a line of horse-drawn vehicles were waiting. Ettie's heart raced with fear — or joy — she did not know which. For she had not been outside the gates since entering the workhouse.

She watched in dismay as the red-headed man and the boy were roughly pushed aboard a brewery cart. The mother and her two children were dealt with as unkindly, sent off in the rear of a horse-drawn vehicle. A young, dark-skinned woman and an aged cripple were loaded like sacks upon the back of a refuse wagon. One by one, the others were dispatched in the same fashion.

Ettie was the last to go. Would the work she was to do prove any better than the tunnels? She stood watching the line of carts trundle off. The look on the faces of their passengers made Ettie sad. Each man, woman and child, had been sold into slavery by the new Governor.

A youth jumped down from the remaining wagon. He was dressed in a black, woollen duffle coat and patched working trousers. He tugged his waterman's cap into place over his thick, dark hair.

'Mistress O'Reilly?' he demanded as he approached.

'Yes?'

'I have orders to collect a full-grown woman, not a child.'

Ettie lifted her chin. 'I assure you sir, I am sixteen years this Christmas Day.'

He jerked his head towards her swollen eye. 'And your injury?'

'I slipped,' Ettie replied shortly. 'But I am fit to work and can see perfectly well.'

'I suppose you will do,' he returned with a shrug, 'though what my employer will say I don't know.'

'Sir, who is your employer?' Ettie asked boldly.

'You haven't been told?' The young man crooked an eyebrow and answered in a pompous voice. 'An agreement has been made on your behalf to work as a trial for Sir Albert and Lady Edwina Marsden, of Chancery House, Poplar.'

'If the work is honest,' Ettie replied with dignity, 'then I am pleased to do it.' It made little difference to her what she did; to be free of the workhouse was a blessing.

Tugging on his cap as if giving himself time to think, he took a deep breath. 'Well, Mistress O'Reilly, before you accompany me, you should know Lord Marsden's artisans labour in all weathers, be it sunshine or frost, or downright damnable. Should you be allocated to domestic service in the house, you will find the same exacting standard. In return you shall have three meals each day, clean water to drink and accommodation. Should you disagree with this contract or are displeased in any way, then please say now and I will return you from whence you came.'

Ettie thought these terms very generous and the offer of three meals a day quite unbelievable! 'How long is this contract for, sir?'

'I was told for one month. With an amendment. If you are found to be satisfactory, an extension may be granted.'

Ettie's hesitation was brief. 'Then I agree to work for your employer.'

'Good enough,' he replied sharply.

Ettie had not considered refusal, for what was her alternative? If she returned to the workhouse, she may face investigation over the late Master's demise. A month of freedom would be preferable to the purgatory of the sewers.

He gestured towards the cart. 'Let us be going, then.'

Ettie walked to the rear in order to climb aboard.

'You will ride more comfortable alongside me.' He pointed to the high seat above the shiny rumps of the two black horses.

'I shall travel quite safely in the back,' she objected.

'You may ride there safely perhaps,' he agreed, 'but not comfortably. I don't wish to add to your injuries.'

Reluctantly she did as she was told, surprised at the gentle hand he put under her arm.

'Take this,' he said as he jumped up beside her and tossed her a blanket. 'Put this about you. A storm is brewing.'

'I'll do quite well without it,' Ettie refused proudly.

'Mistress O'Reilly, I find you quite vexing,' he grumbled. 'Are we always to argue about such small matters?'

'That would depend on the matter.'

A wry smile lifted his lips. 'Do as I say or I shall get a lecture.'

'From whom, sir?'

'Wait until you meet Mrs Powell,' he said, even more amused. 'You'll soon understand my meaning. Now cover yourself or else you will soon be soaked.'

Ettie lay the blanket over her knees. This youth was not entirely displeasing. He was certainly a marked improvement to the staff of the institution from where she had just come.

CHAPTER FIFTY-THREE

Not a word passed between them as they travelled the narrow lanes of Docklands. Sharp darts of rain fell from the sky and blew against her face. Thunder boomed overhead. The wagon splashed through filthy brown puddles and clumps of horse dung. It veered so close to the green, mossy wharf walls of the river that Ettie could've reached out to touch them.

She was full of wonder at the bustling and chaotic world she had not seen for three long months. Even the grime-ridden two-up, two-down dockers' houses bordering the narrow streets looked pleasant. Here, where people lived and walked freely, she breathed the river air, filling her lungs with the salty brine.

She marvelled at the street buskers and the musical language of the shouting costermongers.

'A penny a pound pears!'

'Taters for a tanner, Mrs!'

'Get your Uncle Reg here!'

With dustcart workers and lamplighters, organ grinders and cheeky newsboys, the crowds were lit up starkly by a bolt of lightning. A man with plump, flushed cheeks sold hot chestnuts from his brazier. A fish stall appeared with a pretty young girl crying, 'Cockles and mussels, alive, alive oh!'

Ettie's mouth watered. The streets were full of tempting food.

The driver drove onwards along the dock roads. The horses' pricked ears twitched and their fat bellies shook and steamed. Their thick manes grew damp and tangled over their nodding heads.

The strong smell of the sweating horses brought back so many memories of Soho. She had often watched the brewery drays plod by the salon, delivering their casks of ale to the taverns. Only the wealthy gentlemen could afford the carriages drawn by fine horses and chauffeured by drivers like Michael, unlike these plodders, whose stained fetlocks and roughly shod hooves grazed the cobbles of London's East End.

Ettie swallowed hard at the thought of the young girl who rode in such a carriage and had visited the salon to purchase a frivolous gift for her twin brother. She had been very beautiful. Ettie had thought long and hard about Michael's circumstances. It was no surprise perhaps, that a boy from Michael's background might be impressed by his mistress. Enough to offer her an intimate smile and closeness and perhaps even more as time went by?

Now, as the walls of the docks gave way to the moorings where the boats pulled up from the foreshore, Ettie's thoughts were interrupted by the sight of the great, flowing River Thames, as slithery as an eel. Weaving under the towering wooden cranes it meandered with quiet grace. Tall ships with their rigging heaved in the wind like beasts of the ancient civilizations she had read of in the convent's library books. Many vessels lay at anchor, aloof and haughty. Others spewed muck into the flotsam, worn and weary from their travels. Little steamers puffed up stream and others crept between the great ships' hulls like waterborne ants towards Tower Bridge.

The scene was intoxicating. After her long imprisonment in the tunnels, the wind and the rain seemed to call to her. Up here on dry land, the great river looked magnificent and Ettie yearned to be part of this beautiful world again.

The rain had eased as they entered a long road that turned west and away from the docks. To the east, in a misty haze, stood the ancient dockside cottages of the Isle of Dogs. Ahead she could just see the roofs of the larger, wider-spaced houses belonging to the gentry of Poplar.

Ettie sat quite still, her eyes fixed on the junction in the road that she had last passed when she had taken a carriage from Soho to visit the convent. Now she knew that only charred remains were left. There was something unbelievable about it. All her early life and memories had gone up in smoke.

Ettie shook her head slightly, and was relieved when the young man turned the horse in the other direction. She did not want to be reminded of that barren sight where once the convent and orphanage of the Sisters of Clemency had stood.

CHAPTER FIFTY-FOUR

When the cart pulled up, the young man jumped down and assisted Ettie from her seat.

'Have we arrived?' she asked, glancing up at the tall building and the air of affluence that glittered off every clean windowpane.

'This is Chancery House.' He nodded to a wooden gate. 'Follow me.'

Ettie had imagined they would be entering the drive of a large estate, tucked somewhere deep in the heart of the countryside. But Chancery House was a townhouse and at least five floors in height, with attic gables at the very top. The sight was impressive as though the house may have been transported from another era with its Regency styled windows and soft, pale brick.

Ettie gathered her skirts and followed the young man inside. Here a beautiful garden was filled with neatly tended borders, small trees and plants. The winding path led to an extension off the main building and once through its door, Ettie could see many pairs of boots, riding jackets and hats hanging from pegs.

'All staff use this entrance,' the driver told her. 'The family and their carriages pull up at the front of the house on Poplar Park Row. Leave your footwear on the flags and put on your house shoes.'

Ettie stared at him. 'I haven't got any.'

'Then you'll have to go barefoot.' He marched off, clucking his tongue. His boots, which he did not remove, snapped on the floor.

Ettie tucked her clogs neatly under the shelves and followed him. At the end of the passage, a young girl stood waiting. Ettie guessed she was about the same age as herself. Her pretty face was spoiled by a rather unfriendly expression. Her frizzy brown hair poked out untidily from her mob cap but her large, dark eyes softened when she saw the driver.

'I was wondering when you'd turn up,' she called. 'Mrs Powell wants to see her right away. Where's her trunk?'

'There *is* none,' replied the driver, looking a little awkward. 'See you tonight?'

'P'raps. If Cook doesn't want me.'

This conversation took place as though Ettie wasn't there and the young man hurried off without a word more.

'Me name's Mary. I'm the scullery maid,' announced the girl, ushering Ettie in. 'Don't you have no luggage at all?'

Ettie held up her cloth bag. 'Just this.'

'Who gave you that shiner?'

'I tripped,' Ettie replied, keeping the lie short.

'Looks like someone walloped you.'

Mary beckoned her towards a pitcher that stood on a table by the door. Taking a rag from her apron pocket, she dipped it into the pitcher. 'You'd better get clean. Tidy your hair an' all so you look half decent.'

Ettie pressed the rag against her tender eye as Mary's footsteps faded away. Dipping the rag into the pitcher, Ettie found that, after several applications of the cool water, she could see clearly. Pressing the loose wisps of her hair into the bun at the back of her neck, she waited for the maid.

'S'pose that will do,' said Mary on her return. 'Now follow me and we'll go by the back stairs to Mrs Powell's quarters. She's the housekeeper. But you don't answer to her.

She'll just give you a lecture and tell you all the things you can't do. It's Nanny who's in charge of the nursery staff.'

Ettie thought there must be a mistake. A nursery meant children and babies! But how could this be, when only today she had stepped from the sewers of a workhouse?

Swiftly they made their way from the lower ground floor and up to the next. Finally, they came to a set of doors. Mary pushed them open, beckoning Ettie after her.

'Sorry we're late Mrs Powell,' said Mary curtseying as they entered a large, gloomy office crammed with ledgers. Ettie glimpsed an equally dismal-looking sitting room beyond.

'Get back to your duties,' snapped a woman who sat behind a well-used desk. Her dark hair was severely drawn up under a white lace cap. She wore a plain black dress buttoned up to her chin. Her close-set eyes were dark and piercing.

Ettie heard Mary close the door behind her.

'Henrietta O'Reilly?'

'Yes . . . yes that's me.' Ettie was startled that Mrs Powell knew her full name.

'You will answer, "*Yes, Mrs Powell*".'

Ettie gulped. 'Yes, Mrs Powell.'

'You have arrived at the home of Sir Albert and Lady Edwina Marsden. However, Sir Albert and Lady Edwina are not in residence at the moment but at their country estate. Before they return you will have time to familiarize yourself with the nursery and your duties. I understand from the Governor of the workhouse you were educated at a Christian establishment and can read and write.'

So the new Governor had passed on this information! Had he also told Mrs Powell that she had worked as a flusher?

'You were then sent into service for a Soho *tobacconist*?' Mrs Powell's long nose wrinkled in distaste. 'How, may I ask, did you end your employment there?'

'The proprietor,' Ettie explained simply, 'died from a fever.'

'Was this fever contagious?'

'No, Mrs Powell. It was grief for his dead wife that had struck him.'

'Grief, indeed!' Mrs Powell sniffed, frowning at Ettie's ragged clothes. 'I paid the Governor handsomely for the hire of an educated young woman for employment in our nursery. But I receive a chit of a girl with limited experience of life.'

'Ma'am — I –' Ettie began but was stopped short by the housekeeper.

'You are not to interrupt,' Mrs Powell boomed, her beady eyes narrowing. 'Do you understand, O'Reilly?'

Ettie hung her head. 'Yes, Mrs Powell.'

'The position you will fill is for one month only. Should I find you lacking or disobedient, dismissal is immediate.'

Ettie didn't dare speak.

'Think yourself lucky to have secured a post with this household,' Mrs Powell intoned. 'You will not mix, speak or fraternize with the house staff except Mary and Cook. Your meals will be taken in the nursery. You will avoid contact with the footmen or opposite sex.'

Ettie did not move. She felt that even a brief glance in Mrs Powell's direction might be her undoing.

'No foul language,' continued Mrs Powell. 'No tobacco or alcohol, or visitors without prior permission from me. You must observe the times of your work punctually and will be given nursery rules by Nanny.' Mrs Powell closed the thick ledger on her desk. 'Dismissed!'

Ettie had heard nothing about the children of the house. What were their names? Ages? When she did not move, Mrs Powell clicked her fingers. The fierce gesture made Ettie jump. She turned away quickly.

'Why are you barefoot?' Mrs Powell demanded as she reached the door.

Ettie looked down at her toes turning blue with cold. 'I have no house shoes. Er . . . Mrs Powell.'

The piercing black eyes surveyed her. 'You will be issued with a pair — don't let me catch you barefoot again.'

Ettie scurried out. Her palms were sweating. Her heart was beating so hard she wouldn't have been surprised if it jumped out of her chest.

CHAPTER FIFTY-FIVE

Mary was waiting in the corridor.

'Did she ask about your eye?' the maid asked at once.

Ettie shook her head.

'Good. You don't want to be known as a troublemaker,' Mary huffed with a sneer. 'Come on, follow me.'

Ettie was so relieved to be away from the presence of Mrs Powell, she barely noticed the winding route they were taking through the gaslit passages of the house. She did, however, smell the delicious aroma of bread baking. At the end of a corridor she saw many moving figures. These she guessed were the footmen, valets and housemaids. They carried trays and silver tureens and all passed one another silently with only inches to spare.

'Is that the kitchen?' she asked Mary.

'Yes, and they're rushed off their feet at this time of day. You'd better hurry up or else Cook will be in a bad mood. She's only happy if she's got *me* to boot up the backside.'

They ran up the stairs to the next floor. When they reached a solid-looking door with a shining brass handle, Mary stopped.

'This leads to the entrance hall of the house and lowers like us don't go there. Not unless there's extra cleaning to be done.' Mary sped off again. 'And here are the family bedrooms,' Mary said on the next landing. 'Next floor is the guests' quarters.'

Ettie felt dizzy. The house seemed to go on forever.

'The nursery,' explained Mary as they rushed up another flight of stairs. This door had a long crack in the wood.

But Mary didn't enter the nursery. Instead she flew up a narrow set of uncarpeted stairs. At the top, Ettie paused, trying to catch her breath as they stood under the low ceilings of the attic.

'This is the way to our room,' said the scullery maid, pushing a squeaky door open. 'The housemaids and nursery staff are on the other side of the attic. But as you ain't tried and tested yet, you're put with me. The men are downstairs. Mr Gane, the butler, has his pantry and rooms by the main dining room as he's called on at all times of day and night. As you saw, Mrs Powell's rooms lead off from her office. Jim's the only groom here, along with the stable lad. They live in the carriage room outside in the lane.'

Before Ettie could reply, Mary hurried off along the grubby, cobwebby passage. 'Not exactly the Ritz,' she cackled as Ettie stepped into the interior of a small room with a sloping roof. 'That's where you'll sleep.' She pointed to a truckle bed on the floor. 'Put your clothes on the chair.'

Ettie gazed around the sparsely furnished attic. An extinguished candle stood on a wooden stool with three legs. The bare window above was splattered with pigeons' droppings. Ettie remembered with a pang, her bedroom in Silver Street where the flowered curtains had hung so prettily.

'This is *my* bed,' said Mary threateningly. An iron bedstead with brass fittings was covered with a crocheted quilt. An ancient marble-top washstand with a pitcher and china bowl stood beside it. 'You keep to your side of the room and I'll keep to mine. I hope you ain't a snorer. If you are, I'll chuck cold water over you, just like I did to the other girl who slept here. Not that she lasted long.'

'What happened to her?'

'Mrs Powell didn't like the look of her. Now, I'm off to the kitchen.'

'Where do I find Nanny?' Ettie was sure she would get lost in this huge house full of dark passages.

'The nursery, you dumb cluck!'

Left alone, Ettie stood in the silence of the dirty, damp-smelling room where the green mould was eating into the walls. She went to the window and stood on tiptoe. Between the pigeon droppings and smears, she could see all the rear entrances of the elegant houses in Poplar Park Row. All were neatly spaced, with pretty gardens. Ettie wondered if those beautiful homes had rooms of green mould tucked away in their attics, just like this one.

* * *

Ettie remembered the door with the cracked wood that led to the nursery. She tapped several times, but there was no answer. With her heart in her mouth, she entered a kind of vestibule where interior doors led off to the right and left. The polished wooden floor in front of her gleamed. A table with carved legs stood under an ornate oval mirror. One large window let in a shaft of daylight. Its heavy curtains were tied back with cords and the view was breathtaking. In the far distance she could see spires reaching high above Docklands. She pressed her nose against the glass and saw the house fronts, their black-painted railings and flights of steps up to the impressive front doors. A pavement on the other side of the road bordered a green park. Shady trees, which although leafless now, still shielded the neatly trimmed hedges beneath.

Ettie could see that every house had wide white steps and some even had tall pillars. Just as she managed to locate the shining white steps below, a movement startled her.

She jumped, spinning round. An older woman addressed her, small in stature but stout. Her thin, greying hair was parted in the middle and drawn back into a severe bun. But her round, puppy-like brown eyes and flawless complexion gave her face a youthful appearance. She wore a shawl of cream lace that fell in a waterfall to her voluminous black dress. In her hand she held a dainty white handkerchief with the tips of her tiny fingers.

'Who might you be?' she demanded in a high-pitched voice.

'I'm Ettie O'Reilly,' spluttered Ettie, feeling as though she had been caught doing a mischief.

'Why are you standing there?'

'Mrs Powell sent me.'

'You're the workhouse girl?'

Startled, Ettie gave a nod.

'You are to address me as Nanny at all times.'

'Yes, Nanny.'

'A curtsey would not go amiss.'

Ettie made a curtsey though the only time she had ever done so before was when she genuflected at the chapel altar.

'Ungainly child! You must practice.'

'Yes, Nanny.'

'Another thing. We do not recommend reveries,' Nanny squeaked, patting her chest as her voice rose. 'Windows are to be cleaned, not used to daydream.'

Ettie saw the white handkerchief flick, suggesting she should follow.

CHAPTER FIFTY-SIX

Nanny's quarters, Ettie discovered, were very different to Mrs Powell's. The framed embroideries hanging on the walls beside the photographs of children gave the atmosphere a warm character. The round dining table was covered in a pure white linen cloth with an embroidered edging. Around the table were arranged four cushioned chairs with oval backs. Thick dark rugs covered the wooden floor right up to the hearth.

Nanny seated herself in a comfortable chair by a simmering fire and gave a long sigh, sniffing lightly as if chasing off a bad smell.

'Mrs Powell tells me you can read and write.'

'Yes, Nanny,' Ettie replied. Perhaps her duties would include reading to the children?

'Well, child, it is not reading or writing that I require of you,' Nanny continued. 'It is hard work and punctuality.'

Ettie swallowed. 'Yes, Nanny.'

'You will take one free day every month, and return to the house by seven o'clock at the latest. As the under-maid to the nursemaids, you will wait on the under-nurse, the head nursemaid and her maid and the night nurse who sleeps in the nursery with the children. We do not mix with the lower servants but you will eat supper in the kitchen with the scullery maid. Mrs Powell, I believe, has explained the house rules which correspond with nursery rules.'

'Yes, Nanny.' Ettie was very disappointed that none of her duties included the children.

'The head of nursery staff will give you your uniform. She will explain your duties fully and the hours you must keep.' Once again Nanny sniffed and dabbed her nose. 'My own wishes are to be observed first and foremost. This fire must be lit before I rise at seven o'clock. After I am gone at nine o'clock to the nursery you may clean my quarters. Touch nothing. Dust and sweep with care. My bed requires clean linen every third day.'

'Yes, Nanny.'

'I trust you have no questions?' The elderly matron asked, but Ettie sensed no answer was required.

'Good. Now off you go and find Head.'

Head? Ettie wondered. Who or what was Head? Dare she enquire? But before she could ask, Nanny had risen, bustled her way into the next room — which Ettie supposed was the bedroom — and firmly closed the door.

She waited a few more minutes, then left by the door she had entered. While taking a last look over her shoulder, Ettie almost bumped into a tall figure standing in the vestibule.

'Look where you're going, girl!'

Ettie looked up, for the woman was the height and strong stature of a man. Dressed in a light blue uniform, white frilled apron and a lacy white mob cap that covered her dark hair, she considered Ettie carefully.

'O'Reilly is it, the workhouse girl?'

'Yes, ma'am.' Ettie hung her head.

'I'm the head of Nursery staff known as *Head*.'

'Yes, Head,' Ettie replied quickly.

'This way.'

Once again, Ettie found herself on the march. The tall woman took very long strides, and pushed open door after door, leaving Ettie to dodge them as they swung closed. Finally, they came to a very abrupt halt.

'What are you to call me?' The question came sharply.

Ettie opened her mouth and croaked, 'Head!'

'Good enough. Where are your shoes?'

'I . . . I left my clogs in the boot room, Head.'

Ettie tried not to look down at her dirty feet poking out from under her skirts.

But Head said no more and they were on the move again. Eventually they entered a room filled with children's toys. Two desks and a case of books stood beside a beautiful, dappled grey wooden horse. Daylight flowed in through the huge windows and lit up every sparkling corner. Ettie let out a small gasp of delight. The nursery was the most beautiful room she had ever seen.

Head strode on, leading the way into a passage where she opened a large cupboard. Every shelf was full of crisp, clean clothing and bed linen. She slipped out a pressed uniform of rough grey linen and a white apron. These were followed by a nightgown, pantaloons, girdle and petticoat.

'Thank you, Head,' Ettie gasped, not expecting to be issued with so much.

'Keep yourself and your clothes clean,' Head ordered. 'There is a rota for bathing in the nursery bathroom.'

Bathing in a bathroom? Ettie thought joyously. She couldn't imagine such a luxury.

'You'll need these, too.' A pair of soft leather house shoes was dropped onto the pile. 'How old are you?'

'I shall be sixteen on Christmas Day, Head.'

'Sixteen?' The tall woman pulled her thin shoulders back sharply. 'My advice to you, is to perform your duties to the letter. There has been a long line of hopefuls before you and none of them has survived.'

Ettie trembled. Had they died?

'Be warned, child.'

Ettie clutched her small bundle of new possessions close to her chest. Head looked as though she might have done away with them all.

CHAPTER FIFTY-SEVEN

At last it was the end of the day and Ettie, exhausted and footsore, followed Mary to the kitchen.

'Hurry up, or else Cook won't give us supper.'

Ettie was still trying to remember all the duties that Head had given her. Cupboard upon cupboard to be cleaned and restocked in the nursery. Lines of shelves to be washed and furniture to be polished. The nursery staff's quarters to be tidied, the laundry to be parcelled up and sent to an outside firm. Floors and stairs mopped in preparation for the following day. An endless maze of corridors and stairwells to negotiate. Hearths to be swept. Fires to be laid. On and on her duties went . . .

A bowl of hot broth and a platter of bread awaited them on the long, scrubbed scullery table. Ettie's mouth began to water at the sight and her tummy rumbled.

'You sit there,' Mary ordered and Ettie took her place at the end of the bench.

Mary pushed a bowl towards her. 'That's yours.' She greedily snatched two large chunks of bread, leaving the smaller piece for Ettie. 'What do you think of Head then?' she asked as she stuffed the bread in her mouth.

'I hope I can remember all my duties.'

'If you don't come up to scratch, you'll be let go immediately.'

'Without a chance to speak up for myself?' Ettie enquired unadvisedly.

Mary spluttered, pushing the second crust into her mouth. 'Ain't no use arguing either. Skivvies like us keep their traps shut.'

Ettie shivered, recalling Head's warning about her many predecessors.

'Just do as you're told,' Mary continued letting out a loud burp. 'That's my advice.'

'Can I go to church on Sunday?' Ettie ventured.

Mary stared at her curiously. 'You're one of those Holy Joes, I suppose?'

'Not really.'

'Fact is, the lowers couldn't give a tinker's cuss about saying prayers. They go to church just to get out of the house. God must have a laugh when he sees them sitting all pious-like in the pews.'

'I'm sure God doesn't mind.'

'You are, are you?' Mary sneered, narrowing her eyes. 'Got your ear, has He?'

Ettie felt the sting of tears. Why did everyone in this household behave so badly? She stared down at her bowl of broth. She no longer felt hungry. What was happening in this new life of hers? She had been naive to imagine she would work as a nursemaid to the children. Her head was spinning and her empty stomach groaned, yet she could not bring herself to swallow food.

'Look here,' said Mary, wiping her mouth on the cuff of her sleeve, 'you are the lowest of the low here. Just look at the colour of your uniform. Grey, ain't it?'

Ettie gazed down at the small pile of clothes beside her.

'What colour was Head's?'

'Blue,' Ettie replied.

'My point exactly.' Mary lifted her hands in an impatient gesture. 'Dogsbodies are grey, rest of the staff blue. Until you change the colour of that uniform, you count for nothing.'

Ettie thought of the workhouse. These rules were just the same.

She watched as Mary gulped down her broth. When she'd finished, she licked her lips and burped again.

'Truth is, you are here to wait on the whole bleedin' household, not be one of them.'

'Will I ever see the children?' Ettie asked sadly.

'Never,' Mary snapped. 'Not with your nose to the grindstone every day.'

Suddenly a noise made them jump. A woman entered the scullery, wiping her hands on her apron. She had brown curly hair tucked under a cap, and a great bosom. Ettie gauged she was close to sixty; her cheeks were bright pink and her eyes very blue.

'So, you're the new girl. O'Reilly, is it?' She padded over to where Ettie was seated.

'Yes, er . . . ma'am,' Ettie stammered, rising to her feet.

'Sit down, dearie, we don't stand on ceremony round here. Now, let's have your first name, shall we.'

'I'm known as Ettie, ma'am.'

'Ettie, eh? I'm Cook, ducks. Pleased to meet you.' There was a smile forthcoming; the first that Ettie had witnessed all day.

'I'm pleased to meet you, too, Cook.'

'Now finish your broth,' Cook replied in a firm but affectionate manner. 'Would you like some apple pie after?'

'If you have any to spare. Thank you.'

'After the day you've had, you probably need feeding up.' The smile was still there and Ettie felt as though a ray of sunshine was bursting its way into the dark and depressed corners of her spirit.

'What about me?' Mary cried in alarm. 'I've had a hard day, too.'

‘Oh, stop your caterwauling, miss,’ Cook chuckled good-naturedly. ‘You won’t be left short. You know that very well.’

‘You’ve fallen on your feet there,’ sniped Mary as Cook disappeared. ‘Must be that posh accent of yours.’

Ettie didn’t know what kind of accent she had, or indeed that she had one at all. But it was obviously not to Mary’s liking.

Just then Cook called and Mary grabbed her bowl and hurried out. This time, Ettie was swift to do the same. On entering the warm scullery, the delicious smell of Cook’s apple pie baking in the black-leaded oven reminded her of the convent kitchens.

‘A spoonful of custard won’t go amiss either,’ Cook offered.

Ettie could hardly hide her delight as Cook spooned the piping hot crusty apple pie into her bowl. At least God had sent one welcoming soul along. If the rest of the day had been a bitter disappointment, then Cook was a gift from Heaven.

As if Mary was reading her mind, she nudged Ettie’s arm. ‘Don’t enjoy yourself too much,’ she whispered. ‘We’ve a mountain of washing up to do yet.’

‘That’s all right,’ Ettie told Mary with a shrug. ‘I’ll do it all if you like.’

‘What?’ Mary stopped eating.

‘I worked every day in the orphanage kitchen.’

‘That’s a turn up for the books. I’d have had you down as a posh type fallen on hard times.’

‘Then you’d be very wrong.’

‘Blimey,’ said Mary in surprise. ‘You’ve got no one then, just like me?’

‘Yes,’ agreed Ettie, ‘just like you.’ She knew now why Mary had acted in such an unfriendly manner. She suffered from the often-fatal condition of being unloved, just like the children of the orphanage.

CHAPTER FIFTY-EIGHT

Late that night, after helping Cook to clear the kitchen, Ettie climbed the many stairs with Mary to their attic room. It was pitch black inside until Mary lit the candle.

The shadows cast themselves in the flickering light as Mary flung herself on her bed with a loud yawn. 'I'm tired,' she complained, undressing and letting her clothes drop to the floor. 'We've only got one po, so if you want to wee, do it quietly. In the morning you can empty it. If you don't this gaff will stink like a drain.'

After Ettie had washed, she took her rosary and knelt by her bed.

A few seconds later, Mary sat up in bed. 'What are you doing now?' she bellowed.

'I'm saying my prayers.'

'That again! Well, you can say whatever you like, but not with the candle burning. We only get issued with one every month.'

Ettie quickly extinguished the flame and the smell of wax curled into the darkened room. A half-moon provided a little light through the small window pane. Even so, she managed to stub her toe on the truckle bed.

'Go to sleep,' roared Mary. 'Or else!'

Ettie slipped into bed and reached for her cross tucked under her pillow. She would say her prayers in bed, in future.

Mary's snores were so loud they seemed to vibrate through the walls. Ettie lay awake thinking of Sister Patrick and her gentle Irish accent. Of Sister Ukunda and her clever bartering at the market. Of Soho and the family that would never live at the salon again. Of Gwen and her band of thieves and Terence; all the people who had passed through her life until now.

Lastly, she thought of Michael. It was just a few weeks to Christmas. She wondered if he thought of her, as she thought of him; if he missed their close friendship? Or was he at this very moment, lying in the arms of the beautiful young woman he had accompanied to the tobacconist's of Silver Street?

* * *

The moon was still shining when Ettie rose the next morning. Woken by Mary's snores, she lit the candle and poured a little water to wash with into the china bowl. She bathed her entire body, enjoying the luxury. How good it felt to be clean!

Gently probing around her eye, she was relieved to find the swelling, if not the bruising, had vanished. Tipping the dirty water into the chamber pot, Ettie turned her attention to dressing. Shivering like a jelly, she drew on the pantaloons and fastened her girdle. Unlike the soft brown uniform that Mrs Buckle had made to her exact measurements, the grey dress was several sizes too large. But once held in place by the ties of her white apron, Ettie was satisfied with its fit.

She bent to shake Mary's shoulder. 'Mary, wake up.'

Mary roused sleepily, pushing back her frizzy mop of hair. 'What time do you call this?' she demanded crossly.

'I heard a clock strike four.'

'Go back to bed. We don't start till five.'

'Where do I empty the chamber pot?'

'Down in the slops room of course. Now bugger off.' Mary pulled the blanket over her head.

Carefully folding a cloth over the pot, Ettie took the lit candle in her other hand and made her way carefully to the back stairwell. On each floor she hesitated, trying to remember the route Mary had taken. Finally, she came to the basement and a long, dark passage. Would the slops room be here? The candle flame flickered, caught in a cold breeze from the far door.

'Slops room's along on your right,' said a voice and Ettie jumped, nearly dropping the po. A tall figure loomed over her.

'It's me,' said Jim, dressed in his breeches and vest with his braces looped over his shoulders. A towel hung around his neck and his dark hair was wet. 'There's a pump in the courtyard outside if you need it.'

'Thank you,' said Ettie, suddenly embarrassed.

'Is Mary up?' He glanced over Ettie's shoulder.

'Not yet.'

'You'll have to kick her out of bed. Tell her I said so.'

Ettie was mystified as he hurried off, letting in a shaft of moonlight as he went out to the courtyard. What kind of message was that?

Remembering that she had many duties to perform, Ettie quickly followed his instructions. Two great sinks dominated the slops room. A line of chamber pots stood on the opposite wall and next to these a large wooden contraption. Ettie dispatched the contents of the pot into the hole and used the water from a pail to clean the white china. Returning to the passage, she found her way back upstairs to the attics.

Reluctantly, she shook Mary's shoulder.

'Go away!' came the angry retort from under the bedclothes.

'I saw Jim downstairs, Mary.'

A pale face appeared. 'What?'

'He gave me a message.'

Mary immediately came to life. 'What did he say?'

'Just that I should wake you.'

'Did he indeed?' She gave a humourless smile as she stretched her skinny arms. Blinking in the candlelight, she muttered, 'I hope you ain't going to disturb me again at four o'clock.'

'No, I'm sorry.'

'What time is it now?'

'Close to five I should think.'

'Why are you up so early?'

'I'm going to Nanny's quarters first.'

Mary gave a groan and flopped back on her pillow.

Ettie tiptoed out, the thought occurring to her that Jim might have been waiting to meet Mary. The young man had sounded quite put out when Ettie had said that she was still sleeping. But Mary hadn't seemed to care at all.

CHAPTER FIFTY-NINE

It was almost Christmas and Ettie's routine was the same every day. She attended to Nanny's quarters first, before a housemaid arrived with Nanny's tea and breakfast. She was then free to perform all her duties including the cleaning and polishing of every room on the nursery floor and stairwell.

Her own meals were eaten in the nursery hall, except for supper, when she joined Mary in the house kitchen. In the absence of Lord and Lady Marsden and their two children, Amelia aged three and George four, Mary complained at being at the mercy all day of Mrs Powell and the butler, Mr Gane. 'I'm given all the jobs no one wants. I hate Christmas. I hate everything to do with it.'

'You won't say that when you're sinking your teeth into my roast drumsticks,' Cook reproved. 'Be grateful for small mercies, that's what I say.'

'Why should I be grateful?' was Mary's regular reply. 'I'm working me fingers to the bone.'

Ettie had become used to Mary's moods and her habit of sleeping late. It was as if she did it deliberately, hoping to blame Ettie for not waking her. But Ettie was always up bright and early. Since the house was being scrubbed from top to bottom in the absence of the family, every nook and cranny was to be investigated and cleaned.

Very soon she knew most of the lowers and they knew her. She was always quick to smile and to offer her help when it was needed.

One evening, as Cook served Ettie and Mary their suppers, Jim walked into the kitchen. Mary blushed deeply as Cook pointed a wooden spoon in Jim's direction. 'You've had your supper young man.'

Jim's usually surly face bore a smile as he glanced in Mary's direction.

'So that's the way of it, is it?' Cook said ruefully. 'Come, Ettie, if you're finished, bring your plate to the scullery.'

Ettie joined Cook at the big china sinks; this was the place she liked most in the whole house, surrounded by pots, pans and the pleasant warmth of the cooking ranges reminding her of the convent.

'Give those two a moment, shall we?' said Cook in a low voice as she plunged the plates into the washing water.

'Jim seems very fond of Mary,' Ettie observed as she began to dry the dishes.

'He is that. But Mary — well, you know Mary by now.' Cook gave a sigh and her bosoms heaved under her apron. 'Not an easy child.'

'How long has she worked here?' Ettie asked softly.

'Must be five years now. The mistress, on one of her charity missions, found her on the streets. Couldn't have been more than ten — didn't even know her own age. The kitchens are where she's been ever since. As you've discovered, she don't get on with people. That's why the others left. The girls before you.'

'Because of Mary?'

'Didn't give 'em a moment's peace.'

'I thought it was because Mrs Powell didn't like them?'

'Mrs Powell?' Cook looked surprised. 'On the contrary. The housekeeper came to the end of her tether hiring decent lasses, only to have them leave. She knows it's our Mary who was the thorn in their sides, but sacking Mary wouldn't please Lady Marsden. That's why Mrs Powell went to the workhouse governor . . .' Cook stopped and clapped a wet hand over her mouth.

'And paid for *me*,' Ettie said, without taking offence.

'Me and my quick tongue,' Cook apologized. 'But it's the truth. And you was worth every penny. All the staff have taken to you. All except for our Mary. I hope you don't disappear too.'

'I don't want to go back to the workhouse.'

'Course you don't.' Cook dried her plump hands. 'But Mary will test you to your limit, mind, just like she tests that poor boy. Seems anyone who shows an interest in her, she spurns.'

Ettie thought of Michael when he had first arrived at the orphanage. Even the kindness of the nuns hadn't impressed him.

Cook looked at her curiously. 'You're an orphan, aren't you?'

'Yes, but the orphanage burned down.'

'Oh ducks, who did it?'

'I don't know.'

'Is that how you landed in the workhouse?'

'I was found a position in Soho . . .' Ettie stopped. A lump filled her throat as she thought of Lucas, Clara and the baby. 'But my employer died.'

'Heavens! You've been through the mill,' Cook said gently. 'Let's go and see if Jim has managed to put a smile on our Mary's face.'

But Mary stood alone in the kitchen. Tears brimmed hotly in her eyes.

'Whatever is the matter?' Cook enquired.

'Nothing. I told him to leave me alone.'

'Why?' Cook said in annoyance. 'He's a nice lad. You don't deserve that boy's attention.'

Tears ran down Mary's face. 'I hate you. I hate *her*,' she spat, pointing at Ettie. 'And I hate *him*.' She turned and ran off.

'What did I tell you?' Cook mumbled grumpily. 'You'll have to grow a thick skin, my dear, if you want to work here.'

It was a warning that Ettie was to remember over the coming weeks.

CHAPTER SIXTY

It was Christmas Eve and Mrs Powell had given the lowers permission to attend the midnight service at the local church.

'Are you going?' Ettie asked Mary as they climbed the stairs to the attic.

'No.'

'You might enjoy the service.'

'I don't believe in an old man in the sky with a long grey beard who sits on a cloud all day,' Mary said as she walked into their room and flung herself on her bed.

Ettie smiled. 'Neither do I.' She put on her coat, one that Cook had loaned her for the occasion. 'Christmas is a lovely time. I love singing carols, don't you?'

'No, can't say as I do.' She pointed to the coat. 'You look like an old lady in that.'

'I might, but it's nice and warm.'

Mary jumped up. 'Don't you ever get angry?'

Ettie laughed. 'Why should I?'

'I thought you'd be gone by now. The others all went.'

'Mary, I have nowhere else to go. So, can we be friends?'

This seemed to make Mary even crosser. 'Friends let you down. Like Jim. He's dropped me for someone else.'

'How do you know that?'

'He makes excuses not to see me. I know he's got a roving eye.'

'If he has, I've never seen it.'

Mary frowned at her suspiciously. 'I'll bet it's you he's having it off with!'

'I like Jim,' Ettie said without taking offence. 'But we hardly speak, except when he asks me about you when I go to the slops room in the mornings.'

'I'll bet!' Mary exclaimed. 'I hate him. I hate him. And I hate *you*.' She sank down on her bed again. Holding her hands over her face, she wept fiercely.

Ettie sat beside her. 'You don't really hate people. And they don't hate you.'

'How would you know?' Mary sobbed, her frizzy hair falling out of her mob cap and over her damp face.

'We could be friends if you tried.'

Mary ignored her, her sobs growing even louder.

'Come with me tonight.'

'You'll be with the others,' Mary mumbled.

'I'd prefer to be with you.'

Mary slowly dropped her hands. 'I don't understand. I've told you I don't like you.'

Ettie stood up. 'Well, I like *you*. Merry Christmas, Mary.'

'Go away,' Mary insisted, swiping her wet cheeks with angry fingers.

Ettie left the attic and went down the stairs, glancing up to see if Mary was following. But there were no steps echoing, only her own.

Outside in the courtyard, the staff had gathered. Amongst them was Jim.

'Is Mary coming, too?' he asked Ettie.

'I don't think so.'

'Each year I ask her. Each year she turns me down. I won't bother again.' He walked away under the light of the star-filled sky. It was such a beautiful night. A glistening frost dotted the courtyard walls and the winding path that led to the lane along which Ettie had first arrived. There was not a breath of wind, and the soft murmur of the others' voices was all she could hear.

The group began to move off and Ettie followed. Jim seemed to be striding along in front, his shoulders slumped under his greatcoat. Was he missing Mary she wondered?

As the little band wandered into the gaslit streets of Poplar, she thought of Mary alone in their room. Perhaps she should have stayed to keep her company? But as they neared the brightly lit church and the strains of Christmas carols being sung, Ettie heard another sound. She paused as the footsteps grew closer.

'Thought I might as well come,' said Mary breathlessly, her breath curling up into the frosty air. She pulled up the collar of her old coat. 'Got nothing better to do anyway. And you'd only disturb me when you came in.'

Her voice must have reached Jim's ears, since he glanced over his shoulder. A few minutes later they were walking three abreast behind the main party.

Ettie pushed a wayward lock of her chestnut hair back into its pins, managing to hide her smile as Jim and Mary held hands.

* * *

Since the family were spending the holiday in the country, the entire staff were to enjoy Cook's Christmas dinner served in the servant's hall. It was the first time Ettie had been invited to join the other staff and she eagerly helped with the preparations. Garlands of holly were hung from the walls and a very small tree placed under the window. Below it, Mrs Powell had instructed the footmen to lay out the gifts.

'Everyone gets a present,' Cook explained as Ettie and Mary helped in the kitchen. 'Mrs Powell gives them out. Lord and Lady Marsden are very generous. The valets and footmen are given money or personal items. Last Christmas I received a leather wallet to keep my recipes in. The maids might get clothes like a nice petticoat. And . . .'

'I didn't even get that,' interrupted Mary in a surly tone as she diced the parsley.

'You were given a quality piece of cloth,' Cook argued. 'But what did you do with it? Stuck it under your bed.'

'Everyone else got a dress.' The knife went down with a clatter. 'Why can't we all get money like the footmen?'

'Because you'd only squander it.'

Mary's cheeks went scarlet. Ettie saw the angry tears glint in her eyes.

'Are the family away every Christmas?' Ettie asked Cook quickly.

'No dear, not when Lord Marsden is busy with his politicking. Easier for him to be here in the house *then*. They are visited by some bigwigs, you know.'

'Hoity-toity snobs,' supplied Mary under her breath.

Cook threw her a reproving glance. 'Enough now, Mary!' she exclaimed. 'Lord Marsden is an aristocrat, very well respected in his circles.' She gave no chance for Mary to comment as she bellowed, 'Charles, Arthur, where are you?'

The footmen swiftly appeared, with the housemaids in hot pursuit and the flurry of activity began as Cook oversaw the platters and tureens that were to be moved to the servants' hall.

Ettie had never seen or smelled such delicious food; two huge, roasted turkeys were carved, together with the mouth-watering addition of a side of beef, boiled and roast potatoes dripping in fat, vegetables of every shape and colour laced with butter and herbs and, a plum pudding that was almost the size of the mixing bowl in which it had been prepared.

Mince pies sprinkled with sugar followed and Mr Gane had the distinction of leading the way to the hall, his proud bearing and formal features beneath his neatly combed dark hair softened by an occasional smile.

Mrs Powell, Head and Nanny and all the upper servants who had remained at the house, were seated at the top of the long, decorated table in the high-ceilinged hall. Jim, the stable boy and the gardener sat with the lowers, while Ettie and Mary joined the staff chosen to serve the vegetables, as the footmen poured the punch and beer. Mary and Ettie's task was to follow Hilda Rawlins, an older housemaid, helping her to distribute the sauces. When all was ready for Mrs Powell to say grace, Mary and Ettie took their seats at the far end of the table.

All heads bowed and Mrs Powell's voice intoned a few brief lines of thanksgiving to God and the absent benefactors, the family.

'A very merry Christmas,' said Mr Gane, raising his glass. 'And grateful thanks to Cook for our dinner.'

Cook gave a little choke of appreciation and a cheerful applause was returned from the rest of the company. All except Mary, who whispered, 'And tomorrow we'll have to work twice as bloody hard, see if we don't.'

But as she enjoyed the succulent slices of beef and chicken that filled her plate, together with a generous serving of punch, her gaze slipped to Jim, whom Ettie noted, returned her glance.

'Have you two made up?' Ettie asked curiously.

'Might have.' Her eyes shifted in Jim's direction.

'I'm very glad to hear it.'

'What's it to you then?' Mary snapped.

'Nothing, but you look prettier when you're happy.'

To this, Mary opened her mouth and closed it again as if thinking better of making a smart retort. Ettie noticed how Mary's blush deepened and the corners of her mouth lifted into a trembling smile as her gaze returned to Jim.

CHAPTER SIXTY-ONE

That evening, after Christmas dinner and the giving of gifts was over, Mr Gane returned to his pantry and Mrs Powell to her sitting room, where she invited Cook and the uppers to enjoy a glass of sherry. Meanwhile the other servants dispersed either to their own quarters or to sing carols around the piano in the hall as they enjoyed their gifts.

'I got mittens,' complained Mary as she helped Ettie in the scullery to wash, clean and sweep up after the long day's celebrations. She nodded to their gifts; fingerless woollen gloves and Ettie's warm scarf, deposited on the chair. 'What am I supposed to do with *them*?'

'We can swap, if you like.' Ettie hung the very last pan on its hook above the range. It had been a labour-intensive hour of work in the scullery, but Cook had rewarded them with a bag of her homemade toffee. 'A scarf might look nicer when you go out with Jim.'

'I don't know when that will be.'

'He's probably waiting to see you in the hall. Let's go back there after we're finished.'

Mary grinned. 'I'll just do me hair in Cook's mirror.'

A little later Ettie and Mary walked arm in arm along the passage towards the servants' hall. The sound of voices singing, *God Rest Ye Merry Gentlemen* took Ettie back to the orphanage and the sweet voices of the orphans as they gathered in the schoolroom, eager to open the small gifts the nuns had wrapped for them. The memory caused a warm feeling inside her and she wondered if, at last, she had found somewhere in this big wide world to belong.

Suddenly Mary stopped. 'There's Jim,' she said excitedly pointing to a figure in the doorway.

'He's been waiting for you.'

'Do you think so?'

'Of course, Mary.'

But just as Mary moved forward, a voice called out.

'O'Reilly!'

Both girls turned sharply to see Head.

'Crikey what does she want you for?' whispered Mary in alarm.

'Come this way,' Head called sternly.

Ettie had no time to reply and followed, trying hard to keep up with the long strides. As they went, she wondered what could be the matter? Was Mrs Powell dissatisfied with her work? Had she done something wrong? Ettie felt sure this was so. As they rounded the stairwells, she felt her legs weaken.

By the time they reached Head's room, Ettie could barely contain her fear. Sweeping her long, straight skirt to one side, Head took a seat behind her small desk. The expression on her gaunt face hardened.

Ettie felt about to faint. She stood with clenched hands wondering what was to befall her now?

'O'Reilly, you have been with us over a month.'

'Yes, Head.'

'Did you understand Mrs Powell when she explained your position in this household was to be reviewed?'

Ettie swallowed. 'Yes, Head.' Was she to be sent back to the workhouse? Had they found a decent girl to replace her?

'Mrs Powell finds you satisfactory — for the moment.'

Ettie heart galloped. What did this mean?

'You are to be employed here until further notice.'

Ettie didn't hear what was said next. Her body filled with joy. Her knees went weak with relief.

'Did you hear me?'

'Yes, Head. Thank you, Head.'

'Observe the rules and you won't go far wrong.' Head's voice softened a little. 'One thing more.'

Ettie blinked. 'Yes, Head?'

'You are sixteen years today, are you not?'

Held-back tears felt like grit in Ettie's eyes. Head had remembered her birthday! 'Y . . . yes, Head,' she stammered.

'This is yours. Happy Birthday.' Head placed a small cloth on her desk.

Hesitantly Ettie picked it up.

'You are not singled out from the others. All the lower staff are given a new cap to wear on commencement of a position.'

Ettie held the cap against her chest. 'Thank you — thank you, Head.'

A small smile flickered on the compressed lips. 'You may go.'

Ettie left the room on wings. She could not believe what had just happened. Had she dreamed it? Standing outside the nursery, she felt the tears finally release. Slowly she went up the stairs to the attic room. A Christmas moon sent slats of welcome light across her bed.

She was not to return to the workhouse!

Was this the place she might finally call home?

PART FOUR: A NEW ERA

CHAPTER SIXTY-TWO

June 1897

Ettie stood for the very first time under the vaulted ceilings of Chancery House's drawing room. She had never been inside the main house before and could not believe she was enjoying such a privilege.

All the staff were gathered, lined up beneath the collections of magnificent paintings hung on every wall, studded by smaller gilt-framed artworks. Ettie had never imagined such beauty could be contained in one house. Cook had informed her there were many more rooms where the mahogany woodwork and antique furnishings had been restored to modern-day style by Lord Marsden himself.

The sitting room, she explained, and its inlaid-marble chimney-pieces dated back to the late seventeenth century. But Cook had forgotten to describe the breathtaking hall through which all the servants had just entered. Waxed, stone flags and painted panels gleamed under the light of a chandelier. Great ceramic pots that were taller even than Ettie herself took her breath away.

The wide, red-carpeted regal stairs were embellished with brass fittings. The staircase flowed upwards to the first floor and wound higher. Every wall boasted a work of art or a sculpture. Light beamed from the beautiful recessed windows and a banister of ornate polished wood coiled into the centre of the house.

Ettie had almost missed her footing as she gazed up at the ceilings and their frescos; with figures of plump cherubs and reclining maidens attended by creatures of the forest and little imps. But, with no time to appreciate the marvels and pushed forward by the retinue, she now found herself in the stately drawing room, crammed with cushioned sofas and chairs that gleamed green, gold and ruby in the morning shafts of sunlight from the long windows.

A sudden clap of hands from Mr Gane, who had positioned himself by the great fireplace, brought everyone's attention to the moment.

'You are all to greet Lord and Lady Marsden and the family. So straight backs, please. Hands to your sides and chins up. And, of course, silence as the announcement is made on this auspicious occasion.'

Ettie felt the assembly, including Mary to her left, stand to attention. A few moment's silence reigned until a door opened at the far end of the room. Lord Marsden entered, a tall man, whom Ettie had glimpsed before from the windows of the nursery. In his early fifties, he was dark-haired with no hint of grey and clean shaven. Below his stiff collar and tie he wore a sporty silk waistcoat and a shorter jacket of striped greys.

Lady Marsden followed, her coiffured golden hair and fresh, youthful skin accentuated by the deep blue of her long gown, holding the hand of a small boy with a tangle of blond curls, Ettie recognized as four-year-old George. Nanny brought up the rear, with three-year-old Amelia, and the children's governess, a short, fidgety little woman of middle age. Behind her filed Head and Mrs Powell.

Much to Mary's disapproval, Ettie had become acquainted with George and Amelia. One of the nursemaids had once asked her to hold Amelia as she sat on the rocking horse. With her arms around the cuddly little body, Ettie had laughed and giggled with the child. Brushing the infant's silky corn-coloured hair from her blue eyes, she had returned to the happy days in the orphanage schoolroom. George, she had found quick to learn. The little boy's attention rarely strayed from the stories Ettie offered to read to him in between her duties. These stolen moments with the children were the times Ettie loved best of all.

'Good day,' said Lord Marsden in a deep and official voice. 'Thank you for joining Lady Marsden and I this morning.' He turned to give a polite nod to his wife. 'I am sure you are all aware of the tremendous importance of the impending celebration.'

The room stirred a little but soon returned to silence as Lord Marsden continued.

'You may know that Her Majesty, Queen Victoria, has worn the crown longer than any other sovereign in our history. She has made Great Britain the most powerful country on this earth. The British Empire has dominion over more than a quarter of the world's population.'

Another little ripple went through the room and Ettie strained to hear every word.

'Our Queen's Diamond Jubilee will be celebrated on Sunday June 20th. We shall consider this day the beginning of the Festival of the British Empire!'

To this exclamation, Mr Gane led the applause until the room became a sea of jubilant faces.

'Indeed, indeed,' agreed Lord Marsden, raising his hand for order. 'Our monarch will begin the day with a private thanksgiving service at Windsor Castle. Our Colonial Secretary Joseph Chamberlain has proposed that we celebrate with the representatives of all the countries in our magnificent Empire. The following day at Buckingham Palace, Queen Victoria will entertain heads of state including Archduke Franz Ferdinand, at a state banquet.'

Ettie glanced at Mary who was idly inspecting her nails. That was, until the speaker, in a deeper and more energetic tone, added, 'Therefore, Tuesday June 22nd, has been designated a public holiday.'

The gathering could not contain itself. Even Mary's head came up with a snap. The applause was loud and the footmen and valets cheered. Even Mrs Powell, Ettie saw, made an exception of smiling, though the smile was brief. The two children tugged excitedly at their mother's skirts and were eventually led off by Nanny.

'My wife and I and the children have been invited to celebrate at parliament and will be away for the week. Therefore, you will all be given free time on Tuesday for your own celebrations. May we wish you a happy Diamond Jubilee in honour of our most beloved monarch.' He offered a few private words to the butler, then gestured his wife to lead out the entourage.

The moment the last figure departed, a hubbub of excited chatter began.

'We're to have a holiday,' Ettie said to Mary. 'Isn't that wonderful?'

'Don't know.'

'It's Queen Victoria's Diamond Jubilee. We've been given permission to celebrate. Perhaps we could go up to the city?'

'Then who's gonna cook the dinners? And clean up after that?'

'Cook will let us off for an hour or two, I'm sure.'

Mary frowned and tossed her head as if she didn't care. But Ettie knew that she did. For regularly every morning now, it was Mary who visited the slops room. And Ettie guessed the reason why. Mary's rosy cheeks, bright eyes and defiant expression as she tucked her hair into her cap, left very little to the imagination. Cook had labelled her only yesterday, as looking like the cat who'd got the cream.

And Ettie certainly wouldn't disagree with Cook.

CHAPTER SIXTY-THREE

Tuesday 22nd June arrived and Ettie could barely contain her excitement. She and Mary were to be released for the half day; and Jim had secured the use of the cart as transport for all the lowers. As it was such a special occasion, Ettie had arranged her copper-coloured waves into a neat plait that fell down her spine. She had borrowed a navy-blue skirt and white blouse from one of the nursery maids.

'I wouldn't be surprised if Mrs Powell jumps out of the bushes and stops us from going,' said Mary as she took off her uniform. 'This ain't never happened before.'

'There's never been a Queen's Diamond Jubilee before,' Ettie reminded her friend.

'Do I look all right?' Mary pushed her hands anxiously over her green frock, the only one she possessed. 'What about my hair?'

'Shall I pin it up for you?'

Mary plonked herself down on the bed and Ettie fought a hard battle to tame her wilful mop. But at last it was neatly pleated, with the exception of a few delicate tendrils over her ears.

'If only we had a mirror, you could see how nice you look,' Ettie said with a sigh.

Mary rose to her feet. 'I've got one.' From under her pillow she drew out a small hand mirror. 'A gift from Jim,' said Mary coyly. 'It's real silver.'

Ettie admired the delicate pattern of tulips winding around the handle. 'Jim must think a lot of you.'

'He does. He told me so.' Mary glanced at Ettie. 'I'm glad we've made friends. I wasn't very kind to you when you first came.'

'We're friends now and that's all that matters.'

'Ettie, I've never said this before, but don't let no one walk all over you. Not like they've done to me.' Mary's eyes filled with tears.

Ettie placed the mirror and slide on the washstand. She put her arms around the stiff little figure. 'Hush now, there's nothing to be upset about. Today is very special.'

'I know. And you are, too.' She quickly stood up. 'I'm going soft, that's what I am. Come on, the others will be waiting.'

As Mary had predicted, Jim was downstairs, cap in hand. His hair was neatly combed to one side. He wore a smart grey suit that Ettie had never seen before. When Mary saw him, she looked happier than Ettie had ever seen her look before.

Ettie knew instantly that Jim and Mary had fallen in love. This must be the reason for her friend's unusual behaviour. It seemed a true romance had blossomed, thanks to Jim's persistence.

'Well, then, shall we get going?' Jim invited.

The two girls followed through the house to the boot room and garden beyond. Unlike Christmas Eve, when they had walked to church in the freezing cold, today was warm and overcast. Jim led the way to the cart in the lane, already crammed with the lowers. Ettie climbed into the rear. All heads turned in surprise as Mary took the dickie seat next to Jim.

Ettie's heart lifted, for she understood that this was Mary's way of telling everyone that she and Jim were a couple. What better occasion could there be for Mary to announce her feelings for Jim?

To add to the atmosphere of celebration, there was a bubble of excitement in every street. Ettie watched in wonder as people set out chairs and tables for the parties to be held that day. Streamers of bunting blew overhead in the soft breeze; barrel organs, pianos pulled onto the cobbles, church bands and choirs, stalls of muffins, toffee, bagels, and pies and pastry, abounded. A variety of street traders rushed eagerly to satisfy the hungry citizens.

Ettie decided that if the East End was a riotous mass of celebration, then the city itself was completely transformed. From Ludgate Hill to the parks bordering the palace walls, hundreds of thousands had gathered to watch the royal parade that very morning.

Jim found an empty space for the cart close to London Bridge and all the lowers quickly dismounted.

The stable boy was left in charge of the horses and Jim took Mary's arm.

'I'll walk you both. You won't mind, will you Mary?'

'As it's Ettie, no I shan't mind. But keep your hands to yourself, Jim my boy,' Mary retorted, giving Ettie a shy wink.

The trio walked joyfully through the crowds, laughing and jesting with the vendors of flags, chinaware, books and hats. The picket line of bayonetted soldiers who had formed the Queen's escort earlier, was now dispersing.

'She still wore black,' the lady stall-holder told them as they paused to buy ice cream. 'She loved her Albert, that she did. Refused to set aside her widow's weeds. Came right by here she did. Could see her little face. Like a doll she was. We all sang, "God Save the Queen" as she passed and blow me down, I swear she wiped a tear from her eye.'

After, they went to Trafalgar Square, where under the tall spire of Nelson's Column, people were splashing in the fountains.

'Let's rest awhile,' Jim suggested as they sat on a bench.

'Did the Queen pass by here too?' Ettie asked an elderly lady who sat next to them, feeding the pigeons.

'I waited here to see her,' replied the woman. 'She was beautiful. I saw her close-up as the carriage slowed.'

'You were very lucky.'

'Indeed I was, love. Six miles of the city's streets she travelled. But it upset me when I heard the news she couldn't get out of the coach at the Cathedral.'

'Why not?' asked Mary.

'Like me she's got arthritis. Couldn't get up those big steps. They say she shaded herself with a parasol and didn't move an inch as the Archbishop said his prayers.'

'She's very brave,' remarked Ettie.

'Brave ain't the word, ducks. A saint, I'd say.'

With this they departed, Jim leading them on again, through the city and back past Buckingham Palace for one last look.

CHAPTER SIXTY-FOUR

The royal guards were dressed in their uniforms of tall furry hats and red coats and stood to attention outside the gates. The public pressed their noses against the railings hoping to catch sight of their Queen.

But it was in Hyde Park that the real party was just beginning; water was being dispersed liberally to overheated revellers. Picnics were set out in the shade. Children played on the green grass, delighting in their day of freedom and the prospect of the late night to come.

'Let's go over there,' said Jim, shouldering his way through the crowds. He found a leafy tree to sit under and Ettie watched Mary cuddle up to her beau.

Around them was a mass of smiling faces; some people sang, some danced and others were content to sit on the benches and watch the world go by. Couples strolled hand in hand, oblivious to their surroundings. Intent on each other, like Jim and Mary, they whispered words of endearment.

Ettie remembered how much she had once loved someone, too. And still did. Michael was never far from her mind and she thought of him now. It was over a year since she had last seen him in Silver Street. And even then, he hadn't noticed her.

She heard a sudden movement and looked around to see Jim take Mary's hand and draw her close. Ettie stood up.

'I'm going for a short walk. I won't be long,' she assured them, discreetly leaving the sweethearts alone together.

She was happy for Mary. Jim seemed to be a sensible and loyal young man. He had won Mary over in the end. His love had changed her life and to a degree, her character.

Ettie walked through the park, her thoughts preoccupied. Everywhere she looked, Londoners enjoyed the sunshine. If only the world could always be in love there would be no wars or unhappiness!

Her life at Chancery House had become her world. Had she not been purchased by Mrs Powell, she might still be a workhouse flusher. The memory made her shudder.

Her thoughts returned to happier times; of Soho and the salon. She could see in her mind's eye, the salon's gaslight glow spreading an enchanted light over the shelves of tobaccos. She could smell their aromas as if they were all around her now. She could see Rose looking down at her, with her confident expression. Rose Benjamin, a woman she had admired and in whose footsteps she had tried to follow. Then the most bitter-sweet memory of all; her friend and employer Lucas with his twinkling blue eyes and passionate nature and Clara's fine features, her pale hair a halo around her face. Ettie had grown to love them both and to love the baby she had imagined she would rock in her arms.

Surely, they could not be gone?

'Watch out!' a man yelled and Ettie stopped abruptly. Her feet were only a few inches away from the spinning wheels of a passing carriage. Her heart jumped into her throat. She stood, trembling and shaken. She had been so deep in thought, that she hadn't seen the oncoming vehicle.

'Th . . . thank you,' she stammered to the concerned man.

'Don't thank me,' he replied. 'If it wasn't for that driver pulling sharp on his reins, you'd be celebrating in hospital tonight.'

Ettie felt both foolish and fortunate to have avoided such a calamity. The man walked off and Ettie cast her eyes towards the departing carriage. Was there still time to express her thanks to the driver? Seated on the high seat of the open carriage where two young women reclined in the back, he was hatless and broad-shouldered.

Ettie recognized Michael immediately although she could not quite believe her eyes. She raised her hand and called out his name. But the noise around them swallowed her cry and he continued to drive in the opposite direction.

'Ettie!' a voice said and she turned. 'Who were you calling?' Mary enquired as she stood hand in hand with Jim.

'Oh!' Ettie faltered, 'just someone I thought I knew.'

'Well, we've something important to tell you.' Mary blushed as she looked up at Jim.

Ettie tried to compose herself. Had she really seen Michael or was it a figment of her imagination? Had he only been a few feet away?

'You tell her, Jim,' Mary said breathlessly.

'Well . . .' said Jim hesitantly, 'it's like this . . .'

'Oh, for goodness sake,' Mary burst out, 'I might as well say it meself. Ettie, we're going to elope!'

'Elope?' Ettie repeated. 'What do you mean?'

'We're running away to get married,' Mary confirmed.

'But your jobs,' Ettie blurted. 'You can't leave them.'

'Rubbish,' Mary replied. 'I've had enough of the toffs. And so would you if you'd been slaving away for 'em for nigh on six years.'

'But Lady Marsden took you off the streets, Mary.'

'I didn't ask her to, did I?' Mary snapped.

'Why don't you ask permission to get married to Jim?'

'They'd never allow it,' Mary insisted. 'They'd stop us somehow.'

Jim put his arm around Mary's shoulders. 'Ettie, you've got to understand the way it works. Lady Marsden only took Mary in as a charitable cause. To impress her friends and the society she moves in. But you've seen the way these people live. They all show off to each other and don't give a monkey's uncle for us lowers.'

'But where will you go?' Ettie tried to reason. 'You both have a good home at Chancery House.'

'In reality I'm just a groom and they come ten to a penny,' said Jim sourly. 'Mary will never be more than a downstairs lackey. So we've decided to marry in Scotland.'

'Scotland! But that's so far away,' Ettie gasped.

'Far enough away to start a new life.'

'It's what I want Ettie,' Mary said softly. 'And what this little 'un wants, too.' Blushing, she placed her hands on her belly.

'Mary, you're not . . .'

'I am — and proud to be,' her friend boasted. 'I love Jim and he loves me. And we've made something of our very own.'

Ettie knew by the resolute looks on their faces she could do nothing to stop them. But what could the future hold without money or connections and a little one on the way?

'Are you sure?'

Jim drew Mary close. 'I've saved a little. Enough to get us to Gretna Green where they will marry us, no questions asked. I've heard tell they need men on the fishing fleet. That's a life I wouldn't mind. And, we'd have plenty of fish for supper.' He gave a chuckle. 'Life can't be any worse for us there than it is here. And it might be a good deal better.'

'I'll pray for you and the baby,' Ettie said, close to tears herself. 'I know how much you love each other and I wish you luck.'

'I'm sorry again for being such a cow,' Mary said softly.

'When are you leaving?' Ettie managed to ask.

'We're leaving London by coach in an hour,' replied Jim. 'The stable lad will drive you home.'

'Jim left a letter for Mr Gane,' Mary confirmed. 'Not that I would have bothered. I say good riddance to bloody Mrs Powell forever! But Jim felt it was the decent thing to do.'

'There's bound to be a bit of a ruckus,' Jim warned. 'If we've dared to leave our jobs, they'll be worried the others might, too.'

'Please keep what we've told you a secret,' Mary made Ettie promise. 'I can't write so I won't be able to send you a letter. Mrs Powell would only open it anyway. But somehow I'll get a message to you when we're settled.'

After a final, tearful embrace, Ettie stood amidst the celebrating crowds, watching the couple make their way to the Marble Arch exit. Would she ever see or hear from them again? Somehow, she didn't think so.

It was a lonely walk back to London Bridge for Ettie, despite the excitement that was consuming the city. Today might well be the Queen's Diamond Jubilee but for Ettie it would always be the day in history that would remind her of her two dear friends, Mary and Jim. Emboldened by love, they were determined to seek a better life for themselves and their child.

Might her own life have been very different, Ettie wondered, if she had gone with Michael that day in Victoria Park?

CHAPTER SIXTY-FIVE

It was growing dark as the stable lad drove the cart packed with exhausted but jubilant lowers back to Poplar.

'Where's Mary and Jim?' everyone wanted to know.

Ettie said nothing and tried not to look guilty. She was relieved when it was suggested that no doubt they were still celebrating, both a bit worse for wear.

'They'll get a pasting,' a footman suggested, 'if they don't show up bright and early tomorrow.'

'Doubt they're bothered,' decided a chambermaid. 'All over each other they were.'

Ettie pretended to doze, as the cart rocked along. But interest was soon lost in Jim and Mary as the glow of the bonfires on the hill south of the river took everyone's attention. Ettie's thoughts, however, were no longer on the celebrations that would continue deep into the night. All she could think of was Michael, sitting up high on the open carriage seat with his two young passengers in the rear. Neither of them, it appeared, had noticed the clumsy pedestrian with whom they had nearly collided. Yet the man who had called out to warn her had said it was because of the driver's quick action that disaster was averted. Perhaps Michael *had* recognized her and chosen to ignore her?

Ettie went over that moment many times in her mind. She heard the animated voices around her and the cries of astonishment as fireworks soared high into the night sky. She thought about Jim and Mary and wondered where they were and if they would reach Scotland.

The stable lad drove the cart into the lane behind Chancery House and the voices quietened as the lowers prepared to resume their duties. Ettie joined the hungry queue into the boot room, but she avoided the kitchen where Cook had left a cold buffet for the staff. The thought of eating held no appeal as she climbed the back stairs to the attic.

Tonight she would sleep alone. She couldn't quite believe that Mary had gone. Or that she would not lay awake listening to Mary's snores. Or that, in the morning, she would not watch Mary dress hurriedly in order to meet her sweetheart. For all Mary's black moods, she had become a good friend.

To Ettie's surprise, there was a light under the door of their room. Perhaps it was the reflection of fireworks and bonfires through the window? But as she opened the door, a long shadow fell over Ettie.

Head's face was grim in the light of the candle she held. Ettie guessed immediately that Mr Gane had found Jim's letter.

CHAPTER SIXTY-SIX

'So, you've returned at last,' Head accused. 'You were told to be back by seven o'clock. It's now nearly eight.'

'I'm sorry, Head.'

Ettie knew better than to offer excuses as Head swept past her. 'My room in five minutes,' she barked.

The door closed with a loud thud. Ettie pressed down her blouse and skirt with trembling hands. Had Mr Gane discovered Jim's letter?

When Ettie opened the door to the nursery, she found it deserted. Most of the nursery staff had accompanied the family to the city. An eerie silence filled the air as Ettie stood outside Head's door. What was she to say to the questioning? As much as she considered the problem, Ettie knew she could not disclose Jim and Mary's whereabouts.

'Enter,' summoned the voice after Ettie knocked.

She had only visited Head's room once before, a space no larger than a broom cupboard. She stood stiffly before the small desk where Head was seated. Her thin face and arched eyebrows were drawn into a grim expression.

'Do you recognize these?' The unexpected question came, a bolt from the blue as Head lowered her eyes to the table. On its surface lay Mary's hand mirror and tortoiseshell slide. 'I found them in your room on the washstand,' Head continued. 'Make a full and honest confession and you may not be prosecuted.'

Ettie's stomach dropped. Prosecuted? For what reason? The slide and mirror belonged to Mary. 'I don't understand, Head,' she said bewildered.

'You know very well that these two items belong to the laundry maid. She reported them missing from her cupboard over a week ago. You visit the slops room each morning and have access to the cupboards.'

Ettie swallowed, her throat suddenly thick with bile. It was not her, but Mary who visited the slops room in order to meet Jim. And Mary who had told her the mirror was a gift from Jim.

'Seizing your opportunity, you helped yourself,' accused Head.

'No! No . . . I . . .' Ettie stopped, realizing that if she denied the accusation, she must also implicate Mary.

'Yes, O'Reilly? You were about to say?' Head steepled her long, bony fingers.

Ettie looked down at the hand mirror. Its pretty tulip engraving caught the light of the gas lamp. What could have possessed Mary to steal these things? Mary may have told small lies and exaggerated the truth, but she was no thief. Ettie couldn't believe she was. And yet here was proof to the contrary.

'Have you nothing to say for yourself?' Head demanded.

Ettie could only shake her head as she tried to think of an answer. But whatever she said in her defence, must also shift the blame to Mary.

'The theft and admission of it, will be reported to Mrs Powell and the authorities in the morning. Have your bags packed and the attic tidied.'

Ettie felt her blood run cold as she waited, hoping this was a terrible mistake. But Head's accusing black eyes left no room for doubt.

The blame for the stolen articles was now placed squarely on Ettie's shoulders.

* * *

Early the next morning, she stood before Mrs Powell, Mr Gane and Head, in the butler's pantry. Mr Gane had informed her that a serious infringement of her duties was the reason she had been summoned there to face judgement. Suspected of being a thief, punishable by immediate dismissal, Mrs Powell had also voiced the threat of prosecution.

Ettie had never before seen inside this cavernous room with its long, spotlessly scrubbed dining table and many chairs tucked under its length. Surrounded by cabinets full of the best china, silver and brass, Ettie felt as though she was in a courtroom and three stern judges were assessing her.

In reply to their repeated questioning, she had been unable to give answers. Had she done so, any one of them may have incriminated Mary. Not one question though, had been put to her about their disappearance. It was as if she no longer counted as part and parcel of the lowers. Instead, she had been found guilty and was to be exorcised from their midst.

The early morning light shone bleakly down on the cold stone flags at her feet. Her workshop clogs reminded her of the day she had arrived here. Now she stood once again in the clothes she had worn then; a workhouse shift, her moth-eaten shawl and an expression of hopelessness on her face.

'You have offered no reason or apology for your actions,' Mr Gane decided at last. His chin was raised over his stiff collar and his back ramrod-straight under his black jacket. 'We must assume it was greed and greed only that led you to committing the crime. You have betrayed our trust, O'Reilly, and that of the entire household.'

Ettie felt her head drop with shame. Even though she was innocent, she felt Mary's guilt. To steal from another was also a sin; not hers in this instance, but nevertheless, the butler's words pierced her heart. Tears splintered on her lashes as her world fell around her.

Mrs Powell stepped forward, her hands clenched in front of her.

'You are fortunate. The maid from whom you stole has not initiated proceedings. Therefore, this embarrassment will not go before the police. Nor will your disgrace be revealed to Lord and Lady Marsden.'

Ettie raised her eyes, too full of unshed tears to see clearly the three faces in front of her. But the words Mrs Powell had spoken only deepened the wound in her heart.

'You will leave Chancery House immediately.'

Ettie gasped a breath. Her body trembled under this final blow. She could not even beg for another chance; there was no hope her plea would be heard. For in their eyes and in the whole household's, she was now confirmed a thief.

Silence descended and Ettie realized there was no more to be said. She turned, her shoulders drooping in mortification. Somehow, she walked from the room, clutching her cloth bag.

Her steps were slow and halting as she passed the kitchen passage. At the end of it, stood Cook, dabbing her eyes with the corner of her apron.

Ettie raised her hand hopefully. Cook, whom she considered to be her friend. Cook, who surely would not believe she was guilty?

But Cook turned away, rejecting her gesture, leaving the passage empty. No other member of staff appeared. Ettie knew the whole household had been given orders to ignore her.

With the unbearable weight of this unfair disgrace, Ettie left Chancery House. Her head hung as she stumbled through the boot room; the tradesmen's entrance from which only yesterday afternoon, she had departed in high spirits with Jim and Mary to celebrate the Queen's Diamond Jubilee.

PART FIVE: HOME

CHAPTER SIXTY-SEVEN

November 1897

'Clear 'orf, you perishing nuisance,' yelled the angry man as Ettie rifled inside the stinking bin. There was nothing there but mouldy skins of vegetables, clumped together with fat. But she always held a faint hope she would find something edible.

The café owner lifted a potato sack, twirled it above his head and took aim. Although there were only a few rotted potatoes left inside, the weight winded Ettie and she went sprawling across the alley. Hard wooden pallets broke her fall, their spiky edges digging into her skin. 'You're no better than a bleedin' animal. If I see you round here again, I'll call the coppers.'

Ettie picked herself up and ran away, leaving the mouth-watering smell of the café's open kitchen door behind her. She had been foolish to come here in broad daylight and should have waited until dark. But hunger had driven her to take chances. And today the emptiness of her belly, which had not truly been satisfied in many days, had a particular quality. She could not quite say what it was. Only that it made her so desperate to feed, she would eat anything, no matter what it looked like or where it came from.

For five long months, she had trudged the streets of the East End searching for work and shelter. But who would employ a filthy and homeless girl who wore a workhouse tunic and raggedy shawl? None of the factories would consider her; even the match and rope factories had their standards to keep.

The great River Thames was the only provider for an army of half-starved skeletons who scavenged its shores for items lost in the mud. Ettie divided her days between begging on the busy thoroughfares of the metropolis and the watery banks of the city's fast-flowing river.

Now, as Ettie trudged on, a cold mist descended. A blanket so thick it threatened a river fog. She passed the many shadowy figures of scrawny, sick children who like herself were born from misery, ignorance and vice. She thought often of her mother, who had died in Sister Patrick's arms. Had she, too, suffered such shame? With no one to care or help her? And only a nun to join her in the last moments of life.

A frozen tear slipped down Ettie's cheek. She tried to wipe it away but her fingers were too sore. She caught sight of herself in a shop window; an unrecognizable heap of rags with a head of hair so entangled, wild and knotted that she looked inhuman.

'Am I really me?' she croaked. 'Henrietta O'Reilly, Colleen O'Reilly's daughter?'

Ettie turned away, attempting to step over the ditch into which the drains bubbled and gurgled. She remembered the sound from the tunnels and stepped back again. All around her there was the bobbing, endless tide of human waste passing a few feet away.

Ettie hurried on, desperate to escape the hideous slums and misery of the people squashed inside them; innocent victims of the poverty into which they had been born.

Where was Lady Marsden's charity now? Ettie wondered. Why was she not here, on the streets of the East End, to say a kind word or show a good deed to the impoverished and desperate of London?

Suddenly she found herself by the wooden bridge that crossed to the Isle of Dogs. Here was the greatest poverty and unfairness of all. One road led to the affluent district of Poplar where fine homes like Chancery House stood in its elegant surroundings. The other led to the remains of a convent orphanage whose holy truths had been its undoing.

Sick at heart and in body, Ettie knew she could go no further. Stumbling to the wooden bridge, she crept unsteadily down its bank to the muddy stream that would eventually lead to the river's estuary.

Tonight she would sleep here under the little bridge. Here in this dark space, where she might rest awhile.

The fog thickened and she curled tighter into her corner. The fingers she had used to forage were so painful, she could not move them. Her legs felt as numb as wood. A tight band encircled her ribs. When she coughed, a sticky knot of green glue came into her throat.

Ettie began to feel light-headed. Memories came bursting into her mind like whirling dervishes; children she remembered from her wanderings, half-naked and freezing in the cold. Young women crying out for alms, their tortured bodies no longer saleable. Young men deformed by diseases of the muscle and lung. The aged, too sick or disabled to crawl to the warmth of a brazier fire.

She shook her head a little, yet still the visions attacked her. A fiery heat burned through her and she trembled violently. Closing her eyes, she finally slept. But soon the nightmares returned and there was Clara, claimed by her addiction. And Lucas! She saw as clearly as she had seen him then, his sweat-drenched body and the cavernous pouches beneath his sunken cheeks. She heard their cries for help as clearly as if they were lying beside her.

Ettie cried out, too. She was broken by their agony. She could not help them. For how could she even help herself?

Then, from out of the fog beneath the bridge, walked Rose. Her tall, stately figure so graceful and proud, that even the fog dared not block her path. Ettie tried to tell her about

Lucas and Clara. They were there, in the darkness waiting . . . needing her help.

But Rose raised her finger gently. 'Hush now, Ettie. I know.'

Ettie felt as though she was drenched in love; a peace that flowed through her as Rose bent close.

'*Buck up Ettie! Show the world your mettle.*' Her words were as clear as they had been at the salon.

'I'm tired,' Ettie whispered.

'I'll help you.' Rose held out her hands. 'Come home.'

Ettie began to cough, trying to resist the band that tightened around her heart. 'But where?' she murmured. 'Where is home?'

'I'll show you the way,' Rose beckoned.

But the night grew darker and colder. And suddenly Rose was gone, as though she had never been there. Desperation filled Ettie once more. A fit of coughing seized her. She fell forward, ejecting the poisonous bile from her mouth.

When the choking was over, she looked up to the perfect, velvet blue sky where a sea of stars glittered brightly above the earth. Towards heaven.

Ettie knew then, with a joyful certainty, that at last she was going home.

CHAPTER SIXTY-EIGHT

The old man shifted uneasily, as if something had woken him from his dream. Though what the dream was about he could not say — only that he knew he must rouse and put on his clothes, the same working duffle and trousers that he had used to garden in for many years. They were patched in many places, but serviceable, and would do him until the end. Which, he felt, could not be far off.

He had reached his eightieth year. Passed it in fact. But here he was, still on this earth; a caretaker, a groundsman, a gardener and a grave digger. Just one grave, mind. And he visited her grave daily. He spoke to Sister Ukunda about old times; the orphanage and the Sisters of Clemency and the years he had spent in their service. But although he knew she listened, she never answered him back.

A good woman that.

Arthur hauled himself from the bed and pulled on his pants, grinning toothlessly at the fact that it would only be the Almighty who'd shift him from this spot. The bastard bishop had tried. And look where it got him. The nuns had tried. And look where it got them. The weather had tried. And almost succeeded last winter. And the coppers had tried. Just a little but not too much. Not to such a degree as to move him on.

He served their purpose. And his purpose was to care for this unholy lot of weeds and tangles that were fast becoming his greatest foe. Old bones did not make new ones. And the jingle-jangle of his aches and pains lately, told him that the land would win in the end. Out of them all, nature would be the victor.

But so what? It was here he had spent a lifetime, assisting quietly in the background as the nuns did their very best to save humanity. Another smile lifted his white-whiskered jaw into a semblance of amusement. For hadn't he done the very same of late? To the north of the plot lived Lofty, all five feet five of skin and bone. He'd escaped the debtors' men a year ago and was still leading them a merry dance. His one companion was his horse, who, even older than Lofty himself, grazed down the weeds and brambles, and sometimes was harnessed to Arthur's cart for a trip to the market. Camped by the southern wall, a hundred feet past the burned-down schoolroom, the gypsy was no hinderance.

Then there were the two imps. Well, what was he supposed to do about those? Couldn't be more than six or seven. You could barely see 'em in the day. Blink and you'd miss their shadows. But they were there alright. They could trap a rabbit all by themselves. He'd found the bones of fowl and fish, dead heads with eyeballs glaring up at you. Must've gone down to the wooden bridge and done a bit of fishing.

He'd caught them kipping in the long grass and up a tree and even in the cinders. They painted their faces black with the soot and tried to scare him. But, he'd whistle his way past and raise his hand in salute. They'd giggle like kids did, though whether girls or boys, he couldn't tell. But they were happy to be free and he hoped they'd stay that way.

Arthur gulped down his breakfast, a crust of bread and crackle of bacon. He always put out the rind. And it was gone in a split second. But this morning, he only had mouldy cheese, so he carved off a sliver, grinned at his generosity and chucked it out of the window.

He blinked and might have missed the flash. But he'd seen the little devils. The cheese was gone and they knew he knew it was them.

He knew alright. And he wished them luck.

By the time he stepped out of the old laundry to be greeted by a frost as keen as a carving knife, he was ready to begin his day. Stamping his feet to warm them, he lifted the scythe from his empty cart. Turning unhurriedly, he almost jumped out of his skin. Two small black faces with wide white eyeballs appeared from a bush.

'Strike a light,' he gasped and jumped a step back.

The faces disappeared, only to reappear in a thicket. The shrub did a little dancing and shivering, so that the frost skittered down to lay glistening on the ground. The eyeballs emerged under haystacks of hair, fixing him intently.

'I know you're there,' grumbled Arthur. 'You nearly stopped this old heart of mine with your antics.'

The bare branches rustled. More frost fell. Arthur swished the drip from his nose. 'Come out you little buggers. Show yourselves for once.'

Arthur hadn't a hope they would. But even so, he couldn't be angry. They were wild, untamed; and he'd long ago learned to appreciate nature in its natural state.

'Well, you can both sod off if you ain't answering me. I've work to do.' He marched away, making for the hill that led down to the gentle slope of the grave. But before he'd gone many paces, there they were again; two faces black with cinders, bodies swathed in bug-ridden rags, and no boots at all!

'Gawd blimey!' exclaimed Arthur. 'Boys, ain't you? Twins?'

They stared at him and he stared back. 'What's your names?' he demanded impatiently, not meaning to lift the scythe as they both hopped back.

'I ain't about to hurt you,' he said. Throwing caution to the wind, he rested the tool against the nearest tree. 'So what is it you want of me?' he asked in a kinder tone. 'You kip on my land and you know I lets you. You know I chucks out stuff to fill your bellies. And we all know you do a bunk the moment a copper pokes his nose in.'

The two heads bobbed, enough to let Arthur know they'd understood.

'Ain't you going to say nothin' at all?' he demanded.

Two identical mouths opened.

He gave an irritated frown. 'Listen, if you want more to eat, this time you'll have to ask me for it, right? Don't take much to offer a word of thanks.'

But all that happened was the mouths opened wider. Arthur was about to repeat his request, when something caught his eye. Something he didn't like the look of at all. He took a cautious step closer. When he saw what he saw, his stomach turned.

'Christ Almighty,' he gulped. 'You're mutes?'

Two heads nodded and two mouths closed.

'Somebody done it to you?' he said, clearing his throat.

The nods assured him he had guessed correctly. But it took him a moment or two to compose himself, for the sight of the poor little perishers' tongues with their sliced off tips had given him quite a turn.

'Can't you say nothing at all?' he enquired. But nothing was returned. Only a pointing finger, that hailed him, indicating he was to follow.

To Arthur's own surprise he found himself doing as they'd bid him, going past the old laundry and the cart, to the gate that led to the big wide world outside and the little wooden bridge at the end of the lane.

CHAPTER SIXTY-NINE

There were voices as she stirred, though to whom they belonged she could not tell. The light dazzled her and was so bright, she let her lids close sleepily together. If this was heaven then it was a bumpier ride than she'd expected. Her head bounced a little, not too much as to be uncomfortable; in fact, the motion was soothing. She knew she lay at an angle and wondered if the body she had left behind under the little wooden bridge, resembled the same immortal shape as her spirit.

Sister Patrick had said she was certain that on the Christmas Day she had found Colleen O'Reilly, she had seen a pure soul, lit up by the presence of God and all his angels. And when her mother's earthly remains lay lifeless in the bed of white snow, a beautiful apparition raised out of it that was beyond the nun's words.

Are angels whispering to me now, Ettie wondered? The same angels sent by my mother to escort me to St Peter's gates? Ettie felt a wonder fill her, a bliss so perfect that she almost opened her eyes.

But the sensation drifted and what returned in its place filled her with fear. The fever that had burned in her body as she lay in that dark corner under the bridge, ignited again.

This time, it raged through muscle and skin and into her bones. Would it soon reach her heart and switch it off?

Beset by terror, Ettie felt the drowning phlegm fill her lungs and creep slowly upward. Surely this could not be heaven? Could it be hell? she asked in confusion. Had her earthly sins brought her to this, to face judgement far harsher than Mr Gane and Mrs Powell's? Would Head appear soon, her piercing eyes full of accusation?

'A thief,' Ettie cried out deliriously. 'I am a thief, to be judged and sentenced!'

Her eyes flew open. Her senses reeled. She was lying in a cart and looking up at the grey sky. Two faces bore down on her, with eyes wide and white as saucers and cheeks blackened by limbo's soot!

She choked on the rising tide in her throat. Her gaze clouded. How had she come to this? Never to see her mother again or to know the ecstasy she had been promised by the nuns?

Her questions were answered unexpectedly. For with gentle consideration, came the touch of little fingers around hers. Each of her hands, together with its sores and scabs and scratches, lay in the tender clutch of another's. Comforting. Reassuring. Squeezes of affection from the ghosts of her childhood. Yes, the children had come to guide her!

In her hour of need, God had sent the orphans.

CHAPTER SEVENTY

The day before Christmas Eve

Ettie opened her eyes to a room she had never seen before. She could see a dresser, bearing a blue and white china bowl and a pitcher with a delicate, curled spout. Winter green holly, its spikes and proud red berries curved over a glass vase. A bright, square window was dappled with winter's snow. Curtains . . . pretty flowered curtains much like the ones she remembered . . . but from where? And, a chair; a small wooden chair with a cushioned seat.

She was in a bed, soft and warm, with her body tucked beneath a coverlet. Her hands were at her sides, swathed in bandages. The door . . . ajar, as if someone might be listening outside. And then came a smell, warm and familiar, drifting in. A broth perhaps, wholesome and nourishing.

Ettie rolled her tongue across her dry lips. She watched the flakes of white dance on the window; building a snowy bridge across the sill . . .

A bridge?

A wooden one. Where the water beneath had flowed down to the great river.

A cough tickled at her throat. Her chest was tender, as though she had suffered a blow. She managed to move her legs and watched thankfully, as her toes lifted the coverlet, one bob, then two, then three and four.

The room came at last into proper focus; a clean and delightful room, as though someone had arranged it especially. Was she back at Chancery House? But no, it was impossible. This was not the attic. Memories cascaded back of the night she found Head waiting in her room. Of her accusations of thievery and her disgraced dismissal by Mr Gane and Mrs Powell.

Ettie raised her head to peer at the top of her nightdress; a white, soft linen with lacy frills. Who had dressed her in this? Why was she lying here in this comfortable bed, and not under the bridge, where she had expected to meet her fate?

A movement alerted her. She looked anxiously at the door. A face peered in, eyes wide and expectant. Terence crept forward, as though fearing to disturb her. He was dressed in a clean white apron with his cap stuck deep in the pocket. In his big hand he held a cup and saucer.

'You've woken at last!' he exclaimed, lowering the teacup to the bedside table. 'I can't believe it!'

'Terence?' Ettie muttered sleepily.

'That's me, your old pal.' He inspected her keenly.

'Where am I?'

'In the safe care of yours truly, m'dear.'

Ettie tried to sit up. But her hands were too painful.

'Let me help,' Terence said, assisting her. 'A joy it is to see you awake.'

Ettie smiled drowsily as she rested against the pillow. 'I thought I'd gone to heaven or perhaps to hell.'

'Good grief, no,' Terence assured her as he pulled up the chair. 'The pneumonia gave you those sinister visions.' He lifted the cup to her lips and Ettie sipped. The tea was very welcome.

'Three weeks you have lain here,' the butcher explained. 'It was Arthur who brought you here in his cart.'

'Arthur, the gardener?'

'Curled up under a bridge, you was. Soaked to the skin. Arthur's two little rascals found you. Imps he calls 'em. Waifs and strays. Lets 'em live in the grounds of the convent.'

'Do they have dirty faces?' Ettie enquired, remembering her visions.

'Dirty ain't the word. Stunk to high heaven an' all. But it was them discovered you, all right.'

'They held my hands,' Ettie murmured. 'They comforted me.'

Terence took a great breath. 'My dear, my dear, where have you been all this while?'

Ettie forced her eyes to keep open. 'The workhouse.'

'The workhouse!' Terence exclaimed in horror.

'The governor sent me . . . sent me into service, where I was accused of . . . of thieving . . .'

'How dare they!' Terence demanded before she could summon the breath to explain. 'What an outrage!'

'Terence, don't be upset.'

'Sorry m'dear,' he said contritely. 'Here's you, just back from the brink. And here's me, in danger of sending you back there!'

Ettie smiled.

'I came looking for you, you know,' he said tenderly. 'Me and Mrs Buckle. We travelled up to Oxford Street to the milliner's. I remember you saying you was offered a job. But there's a new owner. So I tried finding that young man of yours. Went up west to look for him and that damson-red carriage he was driving . . .' He paused. 'But I can see you're tired now and I'll save that story for another day.'

Ettie's eyes began to close.

'You are in Terence's care now,' Terence whispered. 'Rest assured that not only will you get well, but you'll be skipping around like a spring lamb very soon.' He gently stroked the hair from her damp forehead. 'Mrs Buckle will pay us a visit tonight. She kitted you out in that pretty nightdress, washed you like her own child. Put up them pretty curtains and tidied your room.'

A tear of gratitude slipped down Ettie's cheeks. How would she ever be able to repay these kind people?

'Close those little peepers now,' urged Terence, tugging up the cover to her chin. 'And sleep well.'

Very soon, as the snow fell in soft white pearls on the window pane she slipped back into a tranquil sleep. This time, no hellish illusions attacked her. Instead, she dreamed of meeting her mother outside the convent laundry. Arms linked, they walked joyfully under the trees and down the gentle slope to meet Sister Ukunda and Sister Patrick.

CHAPTER SEVENTY-ONE

Christmas Day

'That's it, dinner's cooking!' Terence clapped his hands in delight as they sat by the fire in the parlour at the back of the butcher shop. The cosy room was decorated with Christmas jugs of winter blooms and even a small green tree. The dwarf fir stood in a pot by the window, between the heavy brown drapes. Little sparkles glimmered from its thickness and a star was pinned to the top branch. Ettie remembered the opulent Christmas tree at Chancery House. It had looked very impressive with all those gifts beneath, waiting to be unwrapped. She had been excited to receive her cap and to know that her future home was secure in service to Lord and Lady Marsden. Or so she had thought. How wrong she had been. And how swift her downfall!

With a wave of gratitude, she looked at this kind man sitting beside her, a father in all but name.

'We'll eat like royalty today,' he continued and leaned forward to lift the poker into the fire. With a friendly whoosh, the flames spat and sparkled in all directions. 'I'll slice the beef so thin it will fall from our knives. The spuds will roast so crisp and crunchy, we'll be elbowing each other for seconds.'

'Terence you are too good to me,' Ettie said, unable to disguise the hitch in her voice. 'After leaving you as I did . . .'

'Now, now. Don't fret,' Terence dismissed before she could finish. 'Is Glad's shawl to your liking?'

'It's beautiful, Terence. Very warm. I hope Gladys would approve.'

'She'd be tickled pink to see you wearing it.' Ettie looked down at Terence's late wife's fringed shawl that she had borrowed, with its delicate panels of interwoven laces falling over her nightdress. There was even a jewelled pin attached to the scalloped collar.

'My Glad was lovely; I wish you'd known her,' Terence reminisced. 'I've kept that shawl 'cos it was her favourite.'

'Gladys had very good taste.'

'That she did,' Terence said on a sigh. 'But so does Mrs Buckle. She's going to visit in the new year and sew you up some proper clothes. Bit of a dab hand is our Mrs Buckle.'

Ettie smiled, for she had an inkling that Terence and the dressmaker were forming a close friendship.

A little uncertainly, Terence asked if she felt well enough to tell him about her life at Chancery House? Though she didn't want to speak ill of anyone, least of all Mary and Jim, she knew she could confide in Terence.

'They shouldn't have pushed off to Scotland like that,' he muttered when he heard the whole story. 'Leaving you to take the blame.'

'Mary didn't do it deliberately,' Ettie said in her friend's defence.

'Still, m'dear, she was Little Miss Light-fingers, and cleverly escaped her punishment.'

Ettie wondered if Mary could have left Chancery House for reasons other than Jim? A little fib here and there was understandable. But to steal someone's property? Had she done it before?

Terence cocked his head and refrained from asking more. They sat in companionable silence, staring at the flames cascading into the chimney. Ettie remembered the salon's drawing room and how she had spent many happy hours sitting by the fire with Clara. Would she ever have the courage to walk to Silver Street again and look at the salon?

'Did you find the letter I left?' she asked Terence.

'I read it a thousand times,' he said sorrowfully. 'And grieved for you as I would a daughter. You said you had to find a future without the painful memories. But, dear girl, memories will come heedless; good and bad they are part of our lives.'

Tears of guilt filled Ettie's eyes. 'I know that now. Can you forgive me?'

'There's nothing to forgive,' he said mildly. 'Let's not dwell on the past, for today is Christmas Day and you are seventeen years old.' He held out a small parcel. 'Happy Birthday, my beauty.'

Ettie felt the tears slip down her cheeks as she unwrapped the ribbon and pretty paper. Inside she found a notebook with a soft leather cover and a quill pen. Its white feathers were silky and the nib finely pointed.

'Terence, these are lovely!'

'A diary for your new life.'

'But it's Christmas and I've nothing to give you.'

'Your word is all I ask. Tell me you won't go running off again.'

Ettie looked fondly into his dear face. 'No, Terence, I shall never run away again.'

'Then I'm a happy man.'

Ettie watched as he got up and tapped the glass cover of the mantle clock with his knuckle. 'Almost midday. I'm going to prepare the grub. Meanwhile, m'dear, keep your feet up on that stool and rest.'

Ettie knew Terence was doing all he could to help. She rested her head and closed her eyes, dozing in the warmth.

She recalled the Christmas when Gwen and Lily had given her the green fairy. But out of the bad had come the good; her friendship with Terence which now meant the world to her.

* * *

Ettie woke to the sound of carols being sung outside and voices in the passage. The fire had burned low. Terence must have left her to sleep. She could smell the delicious roast cooking, but who did the voices belong to?

'*Silent night, holy night* . . .' the carollers sang. Were they the little band of ragged children who had sung outside the salon that Christmas and to whom she gave the sixpence? But no, it couldn't be, since they would now be older. She blinked her sleepy eyes and wondered if her weak legs would take her to the passage that led to the side door. She was very unsteady, and dare not chance it alone. Though Terence had said the physician from Soho Square had assured him that rest and time would heal all.

'*Round yon virgin, mother and child* . . .' The words drifted in, clearer now, returning her to the orphanage and the Christmases that she had spent with the orphans before the new bishop arrived. She wondered where those children were now; one in particular. Michael. Had he married the wealthy girl who he'd driven in the damson-red brougham?

The whispers grew stronger. Ettie wondered who might call on Christmas Day. Could it be Mrs Buckle perhaps?

She smiled, for more than anything else this Christmas, she wished that Terence might be rewarded for all he had done for her. When she was well, she would try to repay him somehow. Arthur too, and his little imps. And if ever she saw Mary and Jim again, she would hold no bitterness in her heart, but embrace them as old friends.

Ettie gave a deep sigh, for she knew that she must not dwell on the past. She was trying hard, as Terence had advised her, to start afresh. She knew that was why he had given her the diary, a symbol of the future.

The voices came closer.

The air stilled around her.

Ettie's heart began to beat hard under her ribs, though she did not know why. A little tremble began in her bandaged fingers. She sat forward, straining her ears to listen.

The fire seemed to leap into life just as the door opened. Terence stood there, his eyes full of good cheer — and something else. It was as if he had been waiting . . . and at last he could tell her. But what?

A tall figure dressed in a dark overcoat followed. A head taller than Terence, snowflakes had settled on his short dark hair and dotted the length of his broad shoulders. The soft grey pools of his gaze brought a wave of love so intense she could barely breathe. All the pictures of Michael as she had known him, rushed into her head. But she had no need of memories now. For Michael was standing before her, as familiar and handsome in the flesh, as he had been in her dreams.

EPILOGUE

Six days later

It was Ettie's first day of walking out since Christmas and she clung tightly to Michael's arm. Never in her life would she have believed that she might be recovered so fully as to make the short walk to Silver Street. Michael had insisted he bring one of the three carriages he now owned, to make the journey. But she had wanted to use her legs again. With Michael at her side, she had no fear. She glanced up at him now and felt like pinching herself. How had this miracle happened?

A question that would surely have been answered immediately by Sister Patrick, in her rich Irish brogue. Or Mother Superior, or Sister Ukunda, all giving the holy credit to one saint or another, but Ettie knew who she had to thank for Michael's return to her life. It was her mother Colleen, she was certain. And it was her mother whom she had to thank for the heavenly help that was now leading her to the doorstep she had so feared to tread over.

The snow had melted from Soho's pathways and left the cobbles to shine beneath a watery sun as Michael guided her gently towards the salon. The market traders were replenishing their stalls, obviously hoping to make a great success of the very last day of the old year. Beggar children played in the dirty gutters, searching for scraps and leftovers from the Christmas jollity. The door was open to the small theatre where once a tall man had stood dressed in a black floppy hat pierced by a red feather. Now the space was occupied by a pair of working girls who slouched against the worn paint, smoking and eyeing the passing trade. The poster of '*Kiss Me, Miss Carter*' had been replaced by a sign announcing the sale of entertainments to discerning gentlemen.

All this and more reminded Ettie of her life in Soho, but she had never expected to be walking here on Michael's arm. Dressed warmly in a pretty blue silk bonnet and cape that Mrs Buckle had delighted in making her, Ettie could barely gasp a breath as they turned into Silver Street. For as they drew closer, the sign over the salon no longer announced, '*Benjamin & Son. Salon of Quality Tobaccos*' but in wide-spaced letters painted in shiny black, '*Wilson's Fine Carriages For Hire*'.

'Michael — is that you?'

A grin spread across his face. 'Michael Wilson — of Wilson's Fine Carriages — that's me!'

Since Christmas and their first meeting, he had visited her every day, promising such a surprise. Not only had they talked for hours, but discussed every moment they had been apart, until the day Terence and Mrs Butler had hailed his cab in the city.

Ettie stared through the window, where the blinds had been removed to allow daylight to flow into the interior that was painted entirely in white. Four sturdy gas lamps reflected their pristine newness.

'What do you think?' Michael asked. 'This will be the office where we'll take the orders. At the back I've built a lean-to for the carriages. I bought three of 'em second-hand, and did them up. Made a few bob so far. I'm gonna buy another one in spring, a Victoria. Popular they are, open traps — all leather, cloth, and sometimes corduroy. I've got plans for the future, Ettie, and you are part of them.'

‘Do you remember standing there?’ Ettie said, nodding to the very spot outside the salon door. ‘Twice you came to the salon and twice you disappeared. Until I saw you again in Hyde Park when I nearly stepped under your carriage.’

‘My cab had been hired for the celebrations by a couple of ladies. I remember having to swerve, but I didn’t know it was you. You couldn’t have thought I did?’

‘When I saw your pretty passengers . . .’

He tightened his hand around her waist. ‘I told you, *you* were my girl, Ettie. It’s never been any different.’

‘But I waited for you at the orphanage gates that Christmas. You never came.’

‘I’m sorry I never showed up,’ he said, his expression remorseful. ‘I got my collar felt for being too cocky, thinking I could nick from the market and not get caught. But I learned my lesson and spent six months in the jug. When I got out, I came looking for you.’

‘Did you go to the orphanage?’

He gently took her hand. ‘Come inside. There’s something I must tell you.’

Ettie watched him unlock the salon door. She hesitated. Was she ready to confront the ghosts of her past?

Michael held out his hand. ‘It’s all right. I’m with you now.’

Ettie grasped his strong fingers and could hardly breathe as she felt a rush of intense emotion. Would a young man with wiry, sandy-coloured hair and very blue eyes suddenly appear before her? And behind him a woman whose flawless pale skin radiated the gentleness of her nature? Lucas and Clara, were they still here?

She stood, her heart racing as she gazed around the light and airy space that no longer cast shadows in every corner. The glass cabinets and shelves containing Lucas’s precious tobaccos were gone. The smoking room too, had vanished. Now a large map on the wall displayed the city’s many thoroughfares. Beneath it hung a variety of ornamental horse brasses and lanterns, strategically placed to take the client's eye.

No, this was not the salon she remembered. Michael's character was stamped powerfully into every space.

'That girl I brought here,' Michael hesitated. 'I never took a real interest in her, Ettie, though you may believe I did. Her family paid well and that was what I wanted. I was a mercenary sod, but the money went straight in the bank to buy my carriages. Meanwhile I had to swallow my pride and work hard.'

Ettie smiled as a feeling of overwhelming peace flowed through her. Michael had changed his ways, something she had always hoped for him. 'I thought you might marry her,' she said softly.

Michael's serious features gave way to amusement. 'Marry? She was engaged to a lord's son and liked to think she could fool around, making eyes at her lowly driver. I admit I did nothing to discourage her. Why should I? I needed that job to earn a decent crust. As long as my wage packet was regular, she could do what she liked.'

'Even kiss you?' Ettie blushed, her cheeks flushing under her bonnet.

'I'm sorry,' he apologized. 'That must have been rotten to watch.'

'It was. I was jealous.'

He gave a cheeky smile. 'I like that. Means you thought something of me.'

'But jealousy hurts.'

'You won't ever have cause to be jealous in the future, I swear.'

Ettie looked into his beautiful grey eyes. 'Do you mean that?'

'Course I do.' He bent and lifting her chin, kissed her tenderly on her lips. It was then Ettie knew her life was transforming; separately they had grown from children to adults, yet now they were united as one.

Hand in hand, they walked along the empty passage to the drawing room. It was completely bare. There was nothing, not even a chair to sit on. The fireplace was sealed up and Michael gave a shrug. 'The chimney needs sweeping. The floorboards are creaking. The walls need painting. But since I took over this place, most of all, I knew I needed you. Terence told me what happened after your gaffer died here and how he found your letter one morning. You know, don't you, you nearly broke the old boy's heart?'

Ettie felt the tears prick. 'I know, Michael.'

'He's a good man; one of the best,' said Michael fiercely. 'I reckon it was one of those holy angels of yours that caused him and his lady friend to hail my cab one day. He told me he'd been searching the city for the damson-red brougham.'

'You don't believe in angels,' Ettie said and he lifted a lock of chestnut hair from her face, gently tucking it inside her bonnet.

'I do, some of them anyway.'

'Michael Wilson, you've changed.'

'Yeah, you could say that.'

He led her through to the dining room, which was just as bare, but where Rose's portrait now hung over the fireplace.

Ettie gasped. 'Didn't the bank's men take it?'

Michael chuckled. 'Terence nabbed it before they arrived. He knew how much it meant to you.'

Ettie stifled a little choke as she looked into Rose's face. 'I thought I would never see her again.'

'Surprising, eh, what life holds in store?' He lifted her hands in his and stroked them lightly. 'Do your fingers still hurt?'

'No, they're better now.'

'They're not too badly scarred. But maybe scars are a good thing sometimes. They remind us what we shouldn't do. Although, well, I don't regret . . .'

Ettie watched as his face turned pale. 'What, Michael?'

'I did a bad thing.'

Ettie felt a shiver go over her neck. 'What is it?'

He took off his coat and rolled up his shirt sleeve. Over the proud muscle of his right arm, his skin had withered and turned pale pink. Knitted together across his elbow were ugly discolourations and Ettie sucked in a breath. 'You've been burned?'

Without replying he rolled down his sleeve and put on his coat again.

'It must have been a fire, then.' She stopped, the truth suddenly dawning and she trembled at the thought.

'It was me who killed the bishop.'

Ettie stared at him wordlessly.

'I went back to the orphanage one night. I had to see if it was true that the nuns and you and all the kids had gone. When I got there, there was a light in the chapel. I looked through the window and saw someone had lit the altar candles. I couldn't believe my eyes when I saw it was the bishop. He was nicking all the valuables, stuffing 'em in a bag.'

'What did you do?' Ettie couldn't believe that a bishop would do such a thing.

'I went in and confronted him.' He paused, the muscle in his jaw working. 'It was his directive that split us all up. He wasn't no bishop to my mind. And that proved it.'

'Oh, Michael, how could he have done such a thing?'

'He didn't bat an eyelid. Had the nerve to threaten me. Told me to keep my trap shut or else he'd tell Old Bill it was me who snaffled the stuff. And the coppers weren't going to believe otherwise, were they? But I saw red and went for him. He tripped over his bloody bag and fell into the candles. He went up in seconds along with the cloths on the altar. Didn't help himself by running out and the wind whipped up the flames. I tried to bash them off, but they caught me an' all. That's how I got this.' His expression darkened as he whispered, 'It was horrible, Ettie. He just didn't stop burning.'

'Oh, Michael, what an awful thing to happen.'

'I couldn't do nothing more. But I laid low for months 'cos I was scared Old Bill would blame me.'

'It wasn't your fault. He should never have tried to take what wasn't his.'

He shuddered and took in a deep breath. 'Well now you know the truth.'

'Thank you for telling me.'

'It was what happened to the bishop that made me go straight. I knew I had to change before I ended up like he did.'

'I'm very proud of you.'

'You don't blame me?'

'Michael, you must know I love you. You are my other half.'

'I love you, Ettie. I want us to marry and live here and run our business and have a family. Not be afraid of the past, because we'll have each other. Do you want that too?'

'More than anything,' she answered and he kissed her with all the passion that she knew was in his nature.

She clung to him, knowing that they had both suffered and yet through their suffering they had found each other again. God, in his wisdom, had reunited them, most strangely of all, in a place that meant so very much to her.

She gazed over Michael's shoulder and looked at the portrait of Rose, who seemed to be smiling and Ettie, wiping a tear from her cheek, returned her smile. For hadn't she done as Rose had whispered all that time ago?

'*Buck up Ettie! Show the world your mettle.*'

And, in doing so, she had found her true place in life at last.

THE END

ALSO BY CAROL RIVERS

STANDALONE NOVELS
GIRL WITH SECRETS
CHRISTMAS CHILD
CHRISTMAS TO COME

Thank you for reading this book.

If you enjoyed it please leave feedback on Amazon or Goodreads, and if there is anything we missed or you have a question about, then please get in touch. We appreciate you choosing our book.

Founded in 2014 in Shoreditch, London, we at Joffe Books pride ourselves on our history of innovative publishing. We were thrilled to be shortlisted for Independent Publisher of the Year at the British Book Awards.

www.joffebooks.com

We're very grateful to eagle-eyed readers who take the time to contact us. Please send any errors you find to corrections@joffebooks.com. We'll get them fixed ASAP.

Printed in Great Britain
by Amazon

31550261R00187